BURN

A KINGDOMS OF EARTH & AIR NOVEL

KERI ARTHUR

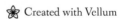

With thanks to:

The Lulus
Indigo Chick Designs
Hot Tree Editing
Robyn E.
Chris W.
Julianne P.
Marjorie A.
The lovely ladies from Central Vic Writers
J Caleb Design for the amazing cover.

FOR INEKE

Who wanted her namesake to be a baddie dying a gloriously gruesome death, but who will have to settle for a drakkon helping to save the day instead.

AUTHOR'S NOTE

While each book in the Kingdoms of Earth & Air series is set in the same world and has the same rules of magic, it is a stand-alone series. Every book is set on a different continent and features a different hero and heroine. Time frames may also differ.

ONE

I woke to the cold restraint of metal cuffs, the gentle chink of chains, and the sway of a slow-moving vehicle.

The scents that rode the air were thick and sharp and spoke of blood, unwashed bodies, fear, and anger. Underneath all that ran the heavy musk of at least two dozen men, but there were women here too—four or five of them, sitting to my left. The fear was strongest from their direction.

Fear *and* pain.

I flared my nostrils, unobtrusively drawing in the wider aromas while keeping my eyes firmly closed and my head down. There was little other information to be found in the stale stirring of air. Wherever this prison might be, it was locked down as tightly as the cuffs on my wrists and ankles.

There was no conversation to be heard. Not inside. Not outside. Nothing other than the occasional stifled sob from the woman seated beside me.

Why were they all here?

Why was *I* here?

I had no memory of this place. No memory of the events that led to being incarcerated.

No memory, even, of *who* I was.

What I *did* remember was a fire so fierce it could destroy entire cities in the sweep of leathery wings. A shout of warning—an order to retreat. And then light. Bright, fierce, *white* light that froze in an instant. Falling, a cry on my lips and agony ringing in my ears and mind. Crashing, not into land but into water.

Drowning. And then not.

Then nothing until these cuffs and chains.

It wasn't amnesia, of that I was sure. Rather, there seemed to be a barrier of ice between more recent memories and me. I rather suspected that until *all* those barriers had dissipated, I'd have to put up with informational gaps.

Aside from that absence of memory, there was a strange void in my soul, a dull ache above my left eye, and vague twinges in back muscles that had taken the brunt of a fall that should have killed me. My clothes and boots were damp —no doubt a result of my plunge—and the weight of my guns and knife was absent. The latter was likely the result of my being captured, but I couldn't be certain. Like my name, it was knowledge that remained locked behind the ice.

In fact, there was only one thing I was absolutely certain of right now—unlike the majority of people in this pod, I hadn't been beaten or otherwise abused.

I took another deep breath and this time tasted little more than the ash and anger emanating from the man sitting to my right. His tension rode the air, and the arm that pressed against mine was taut with the fury I could sense but not yet see. He might be chained but—unlike most in this place—he was not defeated.

And it was rather odd that I was so quickly getting the measure of a man I hadn't yet viewed.

I carefully opened my eyes. We were in a long, silver cylinder that was pointed at one end and flat at the other. There were no windows, no guards, and no visible means in and out of this place. It had old fears stirring, but I ruthlessly pushed them aside; now was not the time for a childhood phobia to rear its head. Besides, there logically *had* to be a way out. Magic was capable of many things, but I doubted they'd yet created a spell able to transport people through metal walls.

The men sitting opposite were chained in pairs and looked to be as mentally broken as they were physically. But beneath all the blood and the bruises were weather-beaten faces that spoke of long hours in the sun and calloused, dirt-stained hands that suggested they were farmers rather than warriors. Earth witches might be responsible for keeping Arleeon's farmlands fertile and productive, but those capable of harnessing the full power of either the earth or the air were a rare commodity and, as such, treated almost as royally as those who'd once ruled. Of course, witches never personally tended the fields or grew the crops; that was a task reserved for the needy or for those accused of minor crimes—it was both a form of repatriation and a means of providing work, food, and shelter for Arleeon's less fortunate.

And given the importance of such farms, they were also very well guarded, even though Arleeon had not seen a hostile incursion by anyone *other* than the Mareritt for centuries. There had to have been a major rebellion for farmers to be this badly beaten.

Of course, there was no guarantee I was actually in Arleeon, even if those in this prison vessel had similar coloring to myself. Given the vague memories of falling, it was always possible we'd somehow been blown far off course and crash-landed on another continent.

But even as that thought rose, an instinctive part within whispered *no*.

I frowned and shifted my gaze to the left. The women were in a similar state of disrepair, though their demeanor and the haunted look in their eyes suggested the attack on them had been of a far more personal nature.

Something sparked inside of me, something that was born of anger and yet held a fiery heat that hungered for retribution. I could understand the use of force to quell a rebellion, but there was no excuse for rape. But it wasn't like I was in a position to either help these women or track down those behind the assaults. Not until I was free, anyway.

I shifted fractionally to get a better look at the man sitting on my other side; the chain that linked his cuff to mine rattled, and a red light flashed in warning. A movement detector was active within the pod.

"Act broken and do not move," the stranger beside me said, his words so soft they were barely audible. "It will, in the end, save you some discomfort."

His voice spoke of deep, dark mountains and soaring ice-covered peaks. Of plunging valleys and aqua blue lakes. Of home, even if I couldn't exactly remember where that was right now.

"Perhaps it would be wise if you followed your own advice, given your anger burns the air." I paused, my gaze sweeping his long length. He wore the same rough woolen pants and sturdy boots as the rest of those in this pod, but I was certain he was no farmer. The callouses on his big hands spoke of a familiarity with weaponry rather than tending and tilling fields. "And if they watch, do they not also listen?"

"They care not about words in this pod, only actions."

"Then they're fools." Words could raise an army, cause it to achieve success against almost impossible odds, make it fly hard and fast toward certain defeat. I'd seen it—experienced it.

Just for an instant, a memory rose. A dark-haired woman standing on a high dais, her blue eyes shining as her words carried easily over the kin and drakkons filling the pass. The roar of approval that had followed her speech, and the deep, deep pride that had welled through me even as my voice joined the others. My commander, my sister...

"Perhaps," the stranger was saying, "but they are fools who currently hold our lives in their hands."

But not for long, if the barely repressed anger rolling in unseen waves from him was anything to go by. There might be no immediate escape from this pod, but once beyond the metal of these walls, all bets were off, chains or no.

I leaned my head back and surreptitiously studied his profile through narrowed eyes. His skin, like mine, was brown, but his nose was strong and almost too sharp, and his chin determined. His close-cropped hair was black, as were his long lashes. Though I couldn't see his eyes from my position, I knew they would be blue—the same aqua blue of the snow lakes that formed after the spring melt high in the Harndale Mountains. Which wasn't where I was born but was very similar in topography.

I frowned and tried to chase the snippet back through the ice, tried to force memory forward so I could recall my past, with little success. Which was frustrating, but there was nothing I could do except wait for the barrier to melt.

I refocused on the stranger and saw the angry-looking scar that started at the base of his ear and disappeared under his rough woolen shirt near his collarbone.

Someone had attempted to cut this man's throat. I wondered if they'd survived the encounter. Wondered how *he'd* survived, given the severity of that scar.

"Where do they take us?" I hesitated but held back the need to ask who "they" were. I didn't want to expose my lack of memory. Not yet. Not until I was more sure of where I was and who this man was.

He shrugged, a movement that had his big shoulder briefly brushing mine. "You women are more than likely bound for the flesh markets in Tendra. The rest of us will no doubt be earmarked for the mines."

Tendra was a name I recognized, though I had no awareness of flesh markets within her walls. But it did at least mean I'd crashed in Arleeon rather than elsewhere.

The woman to my left sobbed loudly. I shifted and surreptitiously squeezed her thigh. She jerked away from my hand, and as the light flashed once again, the scent of her fear and pain grew stronger. She wasn't comforted by my touch—quite the opposite, in fact.

I frowned, my gaze sweeping her. She was young—no more than fifteen or sixteen, at a guess—and very pretty. Her face was unmarked, but her clothing was in disarray; one breast was exposed and bore bruises that spoke of brutish hands, the traces of blood farther down her clothing of innocence lost.

Anger stirred again, sharper than before. But again, it was useless. I clenched gloved fingers, watched the drops of moisture leach from the leather, and imagined it as blood. The blood of our captors. The blood of those who'd raped these women and broken these men.

I might not remember who I was, but it certainly seemed I had a vengeful bent.

I returned my gaze to the warrior. "We cannot let that happen."

Even from this angle, his smile was sardonic. "We're locked inside a prison pod and held down by chains. We have no weapons, and the minute we make any untoward move, we'll be nullified."

"And yet you have a plan."

He carefully glanced around. "What makes you think that?"

I'd been right about his eyes—they were indeed the aqua blue of the melt lakes, but as cold as the ice that gave them birth.

I smiled. "You may wear the clothes of a farmer, but you're not one of their number."

His gaze swept me, impersonal and assessing. "And you wear the uniform of a long-destroyed fortress and yet have the coloring of a Mareritt ice maiden—" He stopped abruptly, his gaze narrowing. "Are you all right?"

No, I wanted to say as disbelief spun through me and my racing heart ached. *I'm not. And I'm certainly not Mareritt.* Why in the wind's name would he even think that?

But the words were stuck in my throat, and my mind was awash with so many conflicting emotions that I could barely even think.

All because of three simple words that unlocked another memory.

Long. Destroyed. Fortress.

He could only mean Zephrine—my city, my home—as our uniform, though holding the same fire-resistant properties, was different in design and color to that of Esan, our sister city. My entire life was wrapped within Zephrine's stony walls—

my father, sisters, brother, lovers, and friends all lived there. Even my mother should have been there, though she was a warrior like myself and, despite her years, was unlikely to have remained grounded if we'd been under attack.

How could it all be destroyed? How could they all be gone? The fortress had for eons successfully guarded Arleeon's western border against the marauding might of the Mareritt. Their bleak and almost inhospitable lands might encompass ours, but thanks to the turbulent seas that protected us on one side and the vast, treacherously high length of the Blue Steel Mountains on the other, there were only two points through which they could attack.

Zephrine had guarded one of those points.

It couldn't be gone. It just *couldn't*. There might be frozen patches of nothingness in my memory, and a sense of loss in my soul, but it wasn't the all-encompassing devastation that should have been present if such a calamity *had* befallen my entire family.

I couldn't believe it. *Wouldn't* believe it. Not until I saw the evidence with my own eyes.

I swallowed heavily against the tightness in my throat and chest, and said, as evenly as I could, "Is that how you came to be in this pod with these farmers? Zephrine's fall meant there were none to come to your aid?"

His gaze swept me again, but he didn't ask the questions I could see in his eyes. "In a sense, yes."

"Define 'in a sense.'"

He raised an eyebrow, those questions stronger. "Why? The answers you seek are something any Arleeon soul should know."

I hesitated but very much suspected if I wanted to gain this man's trust, then I at least had to be somewhat honest.

"Perhaps *this* Arleeon soul has a very patchy memory, thanks to a bump on the head."

Though I was more than sure it *wasn't* the reason for the ice fracturing my memories, it was a reasonably believable answer.

"Zephrine's fall was hardly recent."

So he'd said earlier. Problem was, I couldn't accept it as fact. Not until I saw her ruins for myself—or indeed, regained memories of such destruction. "Were you part of a detail assigned to protect the Talien farmlands?"

And if he had been, how had he *and* these farmers ended up in a prison pod?

His gaze rose to my forehead. Judging me. Judging my words. "No. Quite the opposite."

I frowned. "You were *attacking* them?"

"Not the farmers or their lands, but the Mareritt supply train passing through them to Karlia. Unfortunately, our source failed to mention the full unit of soldiers running protection detail."

None of which made *any* sense. The Talien farmlands lay deep in the heart of Arleeon, and Karlia was the central hub of that community. Unless Esan, the fortress that guarded the eastern pass, had also fallen, there was no way known the Mareritt should have gotten anywhere near that area. Even if Zephrine *had* been destroyed, Esan would have relocated enough of its forces to keep the frost scum at bay while we rebuilt.

I scrubbed a gloved hand across my eyes. It almost felt as if I'd stepped into some sort of time slip. The world of this stranger didn't appear to be mine, and I didn't think the gaps in my memory lay at the heart of that feeling. There was something not quite right with these people and this place—

not that I could remember seeing much of either beyond the metal walls of this prison.

"If you were part of an attack, where are your people?" My gaze swept those chained nearby. None of them were warriors, of that I was sure.

Another sardonic smile touched his lips. "And why would I tell an ice maiden that?"

I frowned, unsure why he kept calling me that when the hue of my skin was as rich as his. "If you truly thought I was a spy, you wouldn't have spoken as you have."

One dark eyebrow rose. "I've told you nothing a spy wouldn't already know."

"Why would a spy be placed in a prison pod? That makes no sense."

"The Mareritt do many things that make no sense to the rest of us."

Which almost sounded as if they were now *living* within Arleeon, but that surely wasn't possible. Even if both fortresses *had* been decimated, it was hard to believe Arleeon's people would have gone down without a fight.

Maybe this was all some sort of weird, waking dream. Or rather, nightmare. It'd certainly make more sense than the entire world as I knew it having been turned upside down.

"I'm no Mareritt spy, you can be assured of that."

Amusement twitched his lips but failed to melt the ice in his eyes. "I wouldn't expect a spy to say anything else."

"True." I hesitated. "How long have we been in this pod?"

"Close to eight hours. I suspect they'll stop overnight at Break Point Pass—they've cells there to accommodate prisoners."

Break Point Pass? Where in the wind's name was that?

Until I knew, there was little hope of understanding where I'd fallen in this topsy-turvy world.

"Is that where you plan to escape?"

He raised an eyebrow and didn't reply. Which was frustrating but understandable, given his distrust. Truth be told, had our positions been reversed, I wouldn't even have said as much as he had.

Silence fell, and time ticked by very slowly. The air in the pod grew colder, suggesting night was drawing in. Eventually, from beyond the metal confines of our prison, came the rise and fall of conversation, though what they were saying was muted and garbled. But the accent came through loud and clear, and it held none of the more rhythmic lilt of the Arleeon. It was instead filled with the guttural sharpness of the Mareritt.

Tension wound through me. I had to be mishearing. The ice scum couldn't have succeeded in their quest to claim *any* part of Arleeon. Zephrine might have fallen, but why would Esan have also capitulated? The might of the drakkon had held the Mareritt at bay for as long as drakkons and their riders had existed—why would their strength have failed now? What had happened? What couldn't I remember?

Our transport came to a halt. Metal rattled as the other captives moved restlessly, their gazes darting to the sharper end of the pod. The guttural tones grew louder, closer. I clenched my fists against the growing tension, but fire burned deep within and it was begging for release—and *that* was impractical in this crowded prison pod. I breathed deep in an effort to relax. It didn't help.

A crack of light appeared at the base of the pod's nose and spread in a sweeping arc—it was a door, one that slowly moved forward and then up.

The other men and women in the pod stilled, but the rush of their fear and uncertainty swamped me. The latter emotion was one I shared. It very much felt like I was teetering on the edge of a precipice, about to fall into a darkness that was deep and unending.

A figure stepped into the doorway. With the bright hues of a golden sunset behind him, he was little more than a silhouette—one with shoulders almost too wide for the door and a build so chunky he could have been a deep-earth miner. But there were six fingers on his hands rather than five, and the tips of his short, spiky hair gleamed like blue ice against the warmer colors of the sunset.

Mareritt.

Anger and hatred hit so hard that, for an instant, I could barely breathe. Heat burned through me, around me, and all I saw was red. Instinct had me rising, but a hand came down on my leg, pressing me back. Holding me still.

"Don't," the warrior hissed. "Keep your eyes down, and don't react to *anything* if you want to live."

I could feel his gaze on me.

Knew the Mareritt was also watching.

I swallowed my anger and fought for control. Reacting on instinct and emotion might have gotten me out of trouble in the past, but in this case, it would only get me *into* it. Aside from the fact that I was chained hand and foot to the warrior, I had no idea where I was. Both common sense *and* training suggested I bide my time and get the lay of the land before I did anything.

But common sense was hard to grip when I remembered all those who'd been tortured and killed at the hands of the frost scum.

And if I could remember *that*, why in the wind's name couldn't I remember how I'd gotten here or who I was?

I dropped my head and took another deep breath. Tried to ignore the thick scent of musk that was the Mareritt. Tried to act as broken as everyone else in this pod when all I wanted to do was flame and cinder.

"Up," the Mareritt growled. "Fall into two-by-two formation."

Chains rattled as everyone obeyed. I pushed to my feet, felt the cuff around my ankle bite into my skin as the warrior did the same. The Mareritt pressed a panel to the left of the door, and the shackles around our ankles unclasped, rattling loudly as they hit the floor.

"Follow the yellow line," he continued. "Eyes down. No talking. No straying."

The farmers and the women began shuffling out of the pod. I kept my eyes down as ordered but was very aware of both the frost scum and the growing tension in the man walking by my side. The closer I drew to the Mareritt, the stronger his stink became. My heart was beating so fiercely, so loudly, it sounded like a battle drum. I wanted to reach out, to grasp his thick neck and squeeze it until his dark eyes popped from his head. But that was the fire within my soul speaking, not the human who knew better.

Closer still... Heat surged, a force so fierce the air briefly shimmered. I held on tight to the power burning through my veins. Now was not the time to release—and not just because there would be more than one Mareritt soldier in this place. I was chained to the warrior and walked too close to the farmers and the women. Any action on my part would rebound back to them. My internal fires might not affect me, but these people had been abused enough; I dared not add to their suffering.

I clenched my hands and kept my eyes down. The Mareritt's stink clogged every breath and made the fire in my blood burn brighter. I wanted to strike; wanted to cinder his ass and leave nothing behind but the smoking remnants of his thick leather boots. Somehow, I forced one foot after the other, moving past him and onto the metal ramp that linked the pod to the ground.

The need to flame didn't ease. There were too many other Mareritt in this place. I could feel them—smell them.

I continued forcing one foot in front of the other. The metal ramp gave way to shiny blue-black stone; it was a substance found in the Blue Steel Mountains, the "spine" portion of the vast range that ran from Zephrine to Esan, separating Arleeon from Mareritten. The stone was prized for its strength and its imperviousness to weather, but it was so difficult to mine that few in Arleeon used it. Obviously, the Mareritt had succeeded where we'd failed—and were now using Arleeon prisoners as their workforce, if the previous comments by the man walking next to me were anything to go by.

The yellow line appeared. The other prisoners dutifully followed it but were nevertheless watched by quite a number of Mareritt if the boots I was seeing were anything to go by. I wished I dared look up; I desperately wanted to see Break Point Pass. Was it Esan, renamed? And yet how was that even remotely possible? I couldn't believe both fortresses had fallen—and even if they *had*, why would they rename it and not Zephrine? And why would an Arleeon warrior use the term?

The wind drifted past my nostrils, carrying distant scents to me. It spoke of a large settlement, one that was used by both Arleeon and the frost scum, and the confusion within me grew. Why would anyone willingly live side by side with the Mareritt? It made no sense given what I knew about either race and only made the disconnect between my admittedly fragmented memories and what I was sensing and seeing stronger.

The yellow line curved to the left. I raised my gaze a little; the buildings around me were as squat as the men who'd no doubt built them and clung in layers to the smooth sides of a mountain that rose almost vertically from the ground. None of the buildings were very deep—perhaps they were the preface of a larger settlement lying within the heart of the mountain. It wasn't Esan, but that realization didn't ease my fear. Quite the opposite, in fact.

To my right lay a vast wall and gates made of a metal that gleamed like rusted blood in the fading light of the evening. Those gates were open; the road beyond led the eye to a land that was broken but green and then arrowed on toward snow-capped mountains.

I knew that landscape, even if the city around me was unfamiliar. It was Mareritten, the home of the frost scum—a land that was a vast subarctic wilderness, and one in which the conditions were so harsh that for nine months of the year its people sought shelter in underground cities and drew on the heat of distant volcanoes to survive. And yet how was that possible if we were still in Arleeon? Had the warrior misled me? Had we been in Mareritten all the time, and Break Point Pass was merely an overnight stop on the way to Frio, the Mareritten capital?

No, some inner instinct whispered.

The yellow line now ran in the same direction of the blood-colored metal wall. Despite the number of Mareritt watching us, there were no guards on that wall, which was odd—why build it at all if you weren't going to keep watch? Mareritten might be a harsh and inhospitable land for a good part of the year, but that had never stopped those from beyond our continent seeking to control its mineral wealth.

Up ahead, a vast metal door began to open, revealing a space that was as black as the sheer sides of the mountain that now reared above us. Our prison, it seemed, was a deep cavern rather than any kind of regular cell.

Old fears stirred at the thought of being locked in underground darkness. I took another of those deep breaths that did little to help and raised my gaze to the fading but still glorious sunset. As I did, a bugle echoed. It was a deep and haunting sound, one that came not from any man-made instrument but rather a creature who'd ruled the skies since time immemorial.

My heart leapt and joy swept through me.

High above us, perched on an outcrop of rock that jutted out from the otherwise sheer sides of the mountain, was a drakkon. Her leathery wings were outstretched, dwarfing her body, the membrane between the four main phalanges glowing gold. Her long tail draped down the rock face like liquid fire, and her broad head was raised as she called in the arrival of night.

But as her haunting cry echoed around us once more, I noticed the figure standing beside her.

Shock coursed through me, and I stopped abruptly.

No, I thought. *No.*

I could perhaps accept Zephrine's destruction. I could even contemplate the possibility that the Mareritt now controlled vast sections of Arleeon.

But never, ever could I accept what I was now seeing.

A drakkon in the hands of a Mareritt.

TWO

This had to be a nightmare. *Had* to be.

If ever there was a universally accepted fact, it was that the Mareritt could not withstand the melding of minds required to become drakkon riders.

They'd certainly tried—Zephrine's libraries were littered with reports of their raids on the aeries, some of which had been successful, many not. If the stolen eggs *had* remained viable in Mareritten's subarctic clime, then those drakkons existed in a place far beyond the watchful eye of Arleeon's many graces—the collective name for groups of drakkons. It was certainly possible, given the Mareritt lived underground for a good part of the year. Maybe they'd taken the time to build a viable fighting force *before* they'd unleashed them against Arleeon's own drakkons.

But if that *was* what had happened, where were Arleeon's riders? Why would they allow the frost scum to gain *any* sort of toehold within our lands?

None of this made sense. Absolutely none of it.

The farmer behind me thrust a hand into the middle of my back and sent me stumbling. I would have fallen had not the warrior yanked back on the chain that still bound us, holding me upright, steadying me.

"Thanks," I muttered.

He didn't respond. A wise move, given the nearest Mareritt had raised his weapon in warning and was now watching us both a little too closely.

But I didn't lower my gaze. I couldn't. It was almost as if, by continuing to stare, what I was actually seeing would somehow dissolve into what I was *supposed* to be seeing—a Zephrine warrior on the back of her drakkon, heralding the attack of a full grace.

Unfortunately, that didn't happen. But as the drakkon bugled a third time, I noticed something else—her size. Full-grown drakkons were massive beasts—just over twelve feet tall and sixty feet long, with a wingspan close to one hundred and fifty feet. This drakkon was half that size—in fact, she was little bigger than the long-horned bovine that roamed across major parts of both the Baknurn and Garmain territories. There was no way known that Mareritt could ride her—she was simply too small to carry someone of his density. Hell, she might even struggle to lift *me* from the ground, and I'd been born to ride drakkons.

What in the wind's name was going on?

It was tempting, so very tempting, to reach out to the drakkon and seek answers to the questions pounding through my soul. But I didn't dare—if the Mareritt *had* somehow figured out a means of telepathically communicating with the drakkons, I'd basically be announcing my presence not only to her but also her handler.

I lowered my gaze and walked on into the cellblock. It had been carved out of the mountain's blue-black stone and was oblong in shape. The fading light behind us lifted the shadows enough to reveal tiered benches of stone lining the wall to the right; to the left, halfway down the room, were a couple of privies. These were partially shielded by a single straight wall that was barely three feet tall; it wouldn't have offered much in the way of privacy, especially if you were tall. Which I was—a long and lanky build was something of a necessity for drakkon riders.

Or it had been, until the Mareritt had somehow gained control of the drakkons.

I pushed back the confusion and the questions that rose with the thought and continued studying our prison. A small fountain to the left of the privy area provided some water, but there was little else. There were no blankets, pillows, or anything else that could have eased the discomfort of this place. And while that was no surprise given it was a prison cell, even the most rudimentary cell in Zephrine offered blankets and a basic mattress. Or they had, before the world turned upside down.

The warrior tugged on the chain to capture my attention and then motioned toward a low bench closest to the door. I followed him across and sat next to him, my back against the wall and my knees drawn up close to my chest. I wasn't cold—the fire in my veins was more than enough to chase away the chill of this place—but the guard at the door continued to watch me. Giving the appearance of defeat rather than defiance was the wiser option right now.

Once the last of the farmers had filed into the cavern, several small tubs were carried into the room and placed in the middle of the floor. The delicious aroma of bread and cheese permeated the room, and my stomach rumbled noisily. No one moved toward the food, however—not even when the Mareritt motioned to the tubs with his gun. He snorted, the sound one of contempt, and backed out. The door immediately slammed shut. Two spots of pale light began to glow, one above the door and one down the far end of the room. They didn't turn night into day, but they did at least provide enough light for people to move around without fear of running into someone or something.

But for several more minutes, everyone remained where they were. Then, one after the other, the farmers shuffled toward the food. My stomach continued rumbling, but I did my best to ignore it. I might be hungry, but there was no way known I'd eat anything provided by the Mareritt.

I looked away from them and spotted a lone monitor on the wall above the privy area. It was doing slow sweeps of the entire cavern, from the door to the deepest point of the oblong.

"We're being watched," I murmured.

"Yes. The Mareritt have little trust for anyone but their own."

"Why, when they very much appear to have the upper hand?"

He shrugged. "Because resistance still exists, for all their efforts to extinguish it."

"You have no idea how happy I am to hear that." I pulled my gaze from the camera and watched a couple of the older men take control of the tubs and start divvying out the food. It was all done in utter silence, with motions to convey directions rather than words. "I take it these men and women are not part of that resistance?"

"No. The Tarlien capital lies well within the occupied territories, and that gives us only two choices—either accept Mareritt rule, or die. There is no in-between."

"There obviously *is*, if you're a part of the resistance."

He glanced at me, a warning in his bright eyes. Of what, I wasn't entirely sure. "None of us are part of the resistance

—we're farmers. Nothing more, nothing less. You place words into my mouth, ice maiden."

"Why do you insist on calling me that?" The annoyance in my voice was real enough. "I'm no Mareritt—and the fact that I'm here, chained to you, should be evidence enough of that."

He raised a dark eyebrow, disbelief evident. "As I've said previously, the Mareritt work in mysterious ways. But if you make enough denials, I might be tempted to not only believe you but trust you."

He might not believe my denials, but, rather weirdly, I had an odd sense that he did now trust me. Up to a point, anyway. I had no idea why, but I wasn't about to question the change. If I was to have any chance of escaping the Mareritt and uncovering the truth of what was going on, then I needed an ally—someone who at least understood the world I seemed to have fallen into.

"If none here are part of the resistance, why are they prisoners? It makes no sense given how vital the farmlands —and experienced workers—are."

"There was an attack on a supply train. The raiders escaped, but we now pay the price for being in the wrong place at the wrong time."

Which was a variation of what he'd already said in the prison pod, only this time with him being placed in the role of a farmer rather than aggressor. I opened my mouth to ask why, then closed it again as the warning in his eyes got stronger.

We're being listened to, that look seemed to say. *Change the subject.*

Which was a rather odd perception on my part. That sort of unspoken understanding generally only existed between kin and their drakkons, and he couldn't be kin

21

simply because he was male. The ability to bond with drakkons had only been ceded to the *females* of the first ancestor's line.

I frowned and glanced back at the camera. After a second, I saw the bulbous lump underneath it. A sound receiver, though one far sleeker than anything I'd ever seen.

One of the farmers cleared his throat, then, when we glanced across, tossed a small loaf of bread and a bit of cheese our way.

"Hungry?" the warrior asked as he caught the two items.

"No."

"Neither am I." His gaze flicked from mine to the monitor and then back. "But given we have no idea when we'll get the next meal, I suggest we at least try to eat."

I frowned. "I don't think—"

"Eat." He tore off a chunk of bread and handed it to me. "Trust me, you'll regret it later."

And regret it if I *did*. My frown deepened, but he began to eat. Or, at least, pretend to. The minute the camera was off us, he spat it out and tucked it in his pants pocket. And that meant he did indeed have an escape plan, even if getting out of this cell—let alone a drakkon-guarded settlement filled with Mareritt—was going to be difficult in the extreme.

I didn't give voice to questions crowding my mind. I simply repeated his actions and hoped that if the Mareritt had placed something in the bread, it wouldn't have any effect in the brief time it was in my mouth. Eventually, he closed his eyes and appeared to go to sleep, but he remained very much awake and alert. I could feel it. Sense it.

Time ticked by. The farmers consumed their food and then rapidly fell asleep—too rapidly, in my opinion. The bread had obviously been laced with some sort of sleeping draught. It would certainly be one way to ensure a peaceful, drama-free night, even if none of these farmers were likely to cause a problem.

Eventually, the warrior nudged my shoulder, then leaned close, his breath warm against my ear as he whispered, "Next sweep, we move across to the privy and take the monitor and audio out."

"The chains will give our movement away," I murmured.

"That's not a concern—they'll just think someone is using the facilities."

Up until the point where we destroyed the monitor, anyway. "But they laced the bread—"

"Only enough to ensure a light sleep. They don't want us comatose, because they don't want to clean up the mess that might ensue."

I nodded and surreptitiously watched the device. It rolled back toward us, paused when it was pointed at the door, and then began its sweep back to the rear of the cavern.

The minute it had passed our bench, we rose and walked toward the privy, making little attempt to hide the noise. Once there, he did indeed use the facilities and then flushed it. As the rush of water echoed through the silence, he opened the cistern, pulled what looked to be a long but slender screwdriver from the water, and handed it to me.

He might claim not to be part of the resistance, but the mere fact that he knew there'd be a screwdriver in the cistern disputed that.

He cupped his hands and looked at me expectantly. The minute I stepped into his palms, he boosted me up until the chain that bound the two of us was taut. I swapped the screwdriver over to my free hand, making sure all my fingers were on the rubber grip rather than the metal. I didn't know a whole lot about electronics, but I was well aware that metal and electricity were a damn dangerous mix. I drew back my hand and then, with all the force I could muster, thrust it into the bulbous lump. Sparks flew, bright in the darkness; as smoke rose, the camera came to a grinding halt.

I jumped down. The screwdriver was quickly placed back into the cistern, the top replaced, and then we hurried back to our bench. We'd barely resumed our position when the door was wrenched open and five Mareritt swept in, their guns raised and expressions intent. Light speared the room, blinding in the semidarkness. I closed my eyes a heartbeat before the beam hit my face, my heart racing as I fought to keep still, to *not* react.

Several very long seconds passed, and then one of them moved toward us. I kept my eyes closed and my limbs relaxed—no easy task when all I wanted to do was jump up and cinder. He stopped in front of us, his stink so strong it filled every breath. I continued to breathe evenly and hoped like hell the overly fast pounding of my heart wasn't as audible to him as it was to me.

After a pause, he placed a hand on my left arm and shoved me sideways. Hard. Given I was supposed to be as drugged as the rest of them, I had no choice but to go with the movement—which by necessity meant I took the warrior with me. I hit the bench with shoulder-bruising force and then was hit by him. I didn't react. Didn't dare.

The Mareritt grunted and moved away. I remained where I was, my pulse rate flying and the warrior a dead weight leaning over me. The beam of light finally shifted from my face, its brightness no doubt following the Mareritt as he checked everyone else.

"Nothing?" came a guttural comment from near the door.

"No." The reply came from the privy area. "Something has definitely pierced the listening device, though."

"Could we have missed a weapon?"

The other Mareritt snorted. "We searched them. Thoroughly. They ain't got nothing but clothes and skin."

The man at the door grunted. "Tech can fix the thing in the morning. We're not going to get any problems from this lot tonight."

The Mareritt retreated. The door slammed shut again, a hollow sound that echoed. I didn't move, not for several minutes. But as my shoulder began to protest my awkward position, I carefully opened an eye. There were no Mareritt in the room, waiting to catch the unwary.

The warrior pushed upright, forcing me to do the same. I gingerly rubbed my shoulder in an effort to ease the ache and said, "Do you have a name, stranger? Because I'm getting rather tired of mentally referring to you as 'the warrior.'"

His teeth flashed, bright in the darkness. I wasn't entirely sure if it was a smile or a snarl. "Kai. You?"

I opened my mouth in the vague hope it would appear on demand, only to close it again in disappointment. "I undoubtedly have one, but I can't recall it right now."

"How convenient."

"Annoying would be a better word." I hesitated. "How did I come to be in the pod? I'm pretty sure I wasn't a part of the raid."

"You weren't. I believe we were diverted to pick you up."

"But from where?"

"That I can't tell you."

Couldn't? Or wouldn't? Either way, it was frustrating, this not knowing. That vague memory of falling from the back of a drakkon slipped past the ice again, but if the only drakkons in this land were the same size as the one who guarded this fortress, then *that* was surely a false memory.

Wait, false memories? Was that something the Mareritt could even do? I struggled—and failed—to recall the snippet of information and had to restrain the urge to knock my head against the wall in an effort to shake the ice loose. Why in the wind's name couldn't I just remember it *all*?

I scrubbed a hand across my eyes and then said, "I take it you have a plan to get us out of here?"

"Yes."

"And does that rescue include everyone in this cell?"

"No, simply because that's beyond our capability right now." He studied me for a moment. "You are included by necessity, but betray me and you'll regret it."

My smile held little in the way of humor. "If you trust me so little, why include me at all? Why not simply knock me out, undo the shackles, and leave me behind?"

"For one reason: chaining prisoners together is a new ploy, and one we were not prepared for."

"And the second reason?" Because there obviously was one.

He hesitated. "It was your reaction to the drakkon. No Mareritt spy, no matter how skillful, would have reacted to her presence the way you did. I have no idea what game you play, but I'm willing to let it roll and see what eventuates."

"How very generous of you."

"Red, you have no idea."

The grimness in his tone not only had unease rising but

also visions of white-haired, black-eyed men and women being executed. They weren't images from my past but rather *his.*

How those visions related to me I had no idea—and no immediate intention of finding out. "Why call me Red, then?"

"Because of this." He raised his hand and lightly tapped the corner creases of his right eye. "The spot in your eye gleams like bloody fire, even in this darkness."

Of course it did—the crimson mote was the sign of a drakkon rider. It was said to have come from the time when the first ancestor shared blood with the first drakkon to save both their people. The process not only made them kin but gave the females of her line the strength and fast healing abilities of the drakkons and drakkons the ability to control and use flame. It was a union that had echoed successfully down through the generations.

"And you're aware of the reason for that mote, aren't you?"

"I'm aware that it no longer applies."

How could it not apply? You were born kin or not. What had happened here to erase that?

But now was not the time to ask such a question—better to concentrate on simply getting free before I worried about anything else. "How do you plan to get us out of here?"

"I've done my part. Our escape is now dependent on others."

Which meant I'd guessed right; the resistance he supposedly wasn't a part of had people in Break Point Pass. It would certainly explain the screwdriver in the cistern. It'd also explain why he'd been angry but *not* overly concerned about being captured.

I hoped said resistance moved sooner rather than later.

Waiting wasn't something I'd ever been good at... a thought that made me wish I could remember the important stuff as easily as I did the random.

"And the drakkon?" I said. "I take it there's more than one in this place?"

"Actually, no. They tend to keep their main stock guarding the more troublesome territories."

Stock. How could drakkons—half size or not—be considered nothing more than stock?

It just didn't make sense. *None* of this made sense. I scrubbed a hand across my eyes again and wished the ice would hurry up and melt. The answer to all this had to be in my still out-of-reach memories somewhere... didn't it?

"How many drakkons do the Mareritt have?"

"At last count, they had a fighting force of twenty-five."

So just over two graces—and *that* meant they had indeed been successful in raising drakkons from stolen eggs. There was no other way to explain that number— Zephrine's aeries had only contained three eggs and five drakklings. Even if they'd somehow managed to gain control of all eight, that still left a large gap. "What about Esan? And her aeries?"

"Esan exists, but aeries don't." His voice was flat, and yet his anger surged, a thick wave that damn near stole my breath. "The Mareritt didn't overrun us as they did Zephrine, but they nevertheless ensured we had no means to fight them from the air."

My breath momentarily caught in my throat—its cause, his anger and my growing horror. "How did they destroy the aeries if Esan never fell?"

He shrugged, a casual movement that belied the dark wave. "With ice, of course. Both those on guard and the breeding drakkons were frozen and then shattered; two eggs and three drakklings were taken. We have no idea if any survived."

Tears stung my eyes. While drakkons were generally long lived, they only bred once or twice in their lifetimes. To lose so many in one hit would have been catastrophic even when the fortress had a full complement of drakkons. To lose them when the graces had already been decimated by the coruscations...

I briefly closed my eyes against the rise of grief even as another piece of the puzzle fell into place. The "coruscations" was the name we'd given the Mareritt-created icy spheres of magic that had threatened Arleeon, and against which the combined might of both Esan's and Zephrine's graces had flown.

I drew in a deep breath and then said, "If Esan survived, why did it never mount—"

"Esan exists, no more, no less." His voice was curt. "Where did you get that uniform?"

"Where do you think I got it? From Zephrine."

"Old Zephrine lies in ruins. There's little left but broken remnants of what it once was."

"So you keep saying." I hesitated. "How was it destroyed?"

"When the drakkons disappeared—"

"They *didn't* disappear," I cut in again. "They're still here, in the hands of the Mareritt."

"And are little more than shadows of the might they once held."

"Yes, but why?" It was but one of many questions that burned inside of me, and I had a suspicion solving what had happened to them might—at least in part—solve the conundrum of what had happened to me. "What caused such a calamitous size change?"

He grimaced. "They already had a number of the smaller drakkons under their control—"

"Which had to have been unleashed *after* the coruscations had done their work." We certainly hadn't seen any sign of them before we'd flown into icy disaster.

"Yes." He hesitated. That dark wave of anger rose and then fell as he regained control. "We believe they're culling the larger drakkons in favor of the smaller ones."

Culling drakkons. Two words that sent a chill racing through my veins. "But *why*? No one can ride a drakkon that's little bigger than a longhorn."

"But they *can* control them, whereas they seemingly couldn't the larger ones."

"Have you any idea *how* they're being controlled?" Because they couldn't have been using a mind link like the kin—the name given to the women who could communicate with and ride the drakkons. The Mareritt might be masters when it came to magic, but there'd never been any indication they were also capable of mind speech.

"We've never managed to capture a drakkon, and it would be pointless if we did, given there are none alive who can communicate with them."

How was that even possible? How could the first ancestor's line be so entirely erased? I shook my head. "When did all this—"

I stopped as he held up a hand and cocked his head to one side.

After a moment, I heard it—the soft "churring" of a Nightjar. Unless their habitat preference—which was generally almost any tree-studded area rather than stark mountainside—had changed as drastically as the size of the drakkons, it was way out of its usual hunting area.

Kai immediately rose, forcing me to do the same. We

walked across to the door, and he repeated the soft call. After a moment, the rattle of keys sounded. The door swung open just enough for the two of us to slip through and was then locked again.

Three figures waited in the shadows beyond, one of them facing us and the other two on watch. Their heads were swathed in material and their clothes dark.

"Changeover lasts for another two minutes. That's all the time you have to get into the forecourt and tunnel." The speaker—a woman—shoved a cloth-wrapped package into Kai's hands. "Pickup will wait twenty-five minutes, no longer."

Twenty-five minutes seemed an extraordinarily dangerous amount of time to wait—how long was the tunnel?

"That's fine," Kai said. "Thank you."

The woman nodded. "Good luck. With those chains, you're going to need it."

Then, with barely a look my way, the three of them melted into the darkness. Kai quickly unwrapped the parcel; inside was a handgun the likes of which I'd not seen before and a couple of clips—none of which would go far if we were discovered.

He shoved the clips into his pocket and then checked the gun. With a soft grunt of approval, he motioned me to follow and then padded toward the main courtyard, keeping close to the wall and well away from the yellow line. The Mareritt who'd filled the area earlier were absent, but there were now a couple of guards on the wall. Thankfully, they were all looking out rather than in. I glanced around, and up. The drakkon remained on the outcrop, a forbidding shadow against the starry sky.

Again, the urge rose to contact her. Again, I ignored it.

31

Kai paused as we neared the courtyard. I crowded closer and studied the buildings opposite. The U-shaped courtyard was empty, and there was no sign of movement, but I had no doubt there were guards we couldn't see.

"See that guardhouse down the end?" Kai whispered.

My gaze followed the line of his finger. Sitting to the left of another big metal door was the building in question. It wasn't overly large, but it didn't really have to be if its only purpose was to protect those on duty from the elements.

"That's where we're going," he added.

I narrowed my gaze, judging the distance and the time we had left. It was going to be close. "The rattle of the chains will give us away in seconds."

"Not if we remain far enough apart to keep them taut. Ready?"

I nodded. We'd already wasted close to a minute.

"Good. Go."

We moved as one, fanning out until the chain that bound us was stretched tight and less likely to rattle.

Twelve seconds.

That's all it took for the Mareritt soldiers to react.

Lights came on, lifting the shadows, and the sharp sound of rifle fire bit across the night. Multiple rounds of bullets chased our heels as we raced toward the guardhouse. Mareritt poured out of the nearby buildings, some half dressed but all with weapons raised. Kai fired left and right, but we were greatly outnumbered and the guardhouse still too far away.

Heat burned through my blood, and this time I didn't control it. I raised my free hand and unleashed.

Flames spurted from my gloved fingertips and spread in an arc across the Mareritt to my right. They lit up like torches; flesh instantly peeled from their bodies, and their screams echoed around the courtyard for barely a heartbeat before death snatched the sound away.

I twisted and threw fire at the Mareritt on the wall, setting them alight, melting their bones. High above, the drakkon screamed and launched into the air; there was no one on her back, but the metal band encircling her rear leg had an unnatural sheen in the glowing embers of those I'd destroyed.

She swooped toward us, her mouth open as she sucked in air, getting ready to unleash in much the same manner as I had. I clenched a fist and punched upward with fire, hitting her under her chin. The blow flung her sideways and her screech echoed loudly, a sound that was both surprise and fury. She crashed into a building three stories up, her weight shattering the structure and sending a deadly rain of stone into the courtyard.

I leaped over a number of boulders, my head pounding in time with my heart. There was always a cost to using blood heat—always a price to pay in strength. I wasn't at my limits yet, but the pounding was an indicator I was roaring toward it.

It didn't matter. Nothing did, beyond escaping.

A bullet clipped my calf and sent me stumbling. Kai cursed and yanked the chain upward, almost wrenching my shoulder out of its socket but keeping me upright.

Up ahead, the guardhouse door flung open; Kai swore again and swept his weapon around. But the gun was blinking red, and only two bullets sped from the chamber before it fell silent. There was no time—and no space—to reload.

"Faster," he yelled, even though both us were going at full tilt.

I sprayed fire left and right; moisture filled my right eye, blurring my vision as it dribbled over my lashes. The mote in my eye was bleeding. I was close, *so* very close, to the wall.

A screech echoed across the night. I glanced up and saw the drakkon pull free of the building, spilling more stone into the courtyard. I kept on running, my eyes on the guard-house door as I prayed—with everything I had—for the wind to gift our feet wings. She must have been listening, because as another roar signaled the drakkon's attack, we hit the darkness of the guardhouse. I grabbed the metal door, pulled it shut, and then quickly fused the lock. A heartbeat later, the drakkon's flames hit the door; it had obviously been fortified against such fire, because it didn't instantly melt. But the edges glowed with heat; it wouldn't hold for long.

Kai quickly reloaded his weapon and then swung around to face me. "Why the fuck didn't you tell me you could use flame?"

"Why do you think I didn't?" I touched the middle link of the chain tying us together and sent a burst of heat through my finger. The metal melted in seconds, leaving us cuffed but finally able to move independently. "You don't trust me, and I didn't want to be left behind."

His gaze narrowed but his expression was hard to read, and the odd connection that sometimes flared between us was inert, giving me no hint as to what he might be thinking.

"This way," he growled, then spun and stalked away.

I swept up a guard's rifle and followed. Again, the shape of the weapon was unlike anything I'd ever seen, but it had a muzzle, a trigger, and a chamber that appeared to be full. Right now, that's all that mattered.

We moved through the guardhouse into a wider

chamber that held a table, a couple of chairs, and a bench on which a kettle steamed. At the end of the bench was another door. Kai gripped the handle lightly but didn't immediately open it, instead pressing an ear against the metal.

"Do you know where we're going?" I asked softly.

"Yes."

"Have you been here before?"

"No, but I've seen floor plans." He glanced at me. "There's a large forecourt beyond this door and six men approaching. I'll go left, you go right. All right?"

I nodded and raised the rifle. His grip tightened briefly on the handle, then he flung the door open and flowed left, his movements smooth and quick. I followed him through, darted right, and fired. There was no recoil from the weapon, and the shots flew as true as any could when unsighted and on the move. Three men went down; the others threw themselves sideways and came up shooting. Kai grunted, then dropped and rapidly returned fire, disintegrating the face of one Mareritt. I took the other two out.

Kai thrust to his feet, his face grim and blood pouring from a deep graze near his left shoulder. His gaze briefly swept me, reminding me of a general checking the state of his soldiers before raising the call to war.

He didn't say anything; instead, he strode over to the nearest body. With a grunt of effort, he picked the man up and hauled him over his shoulder.

"Why do we need him?" I asked.

"Fingerprints. Would have been easier to just take off his hand, but I haven't a knife and we need to conserve bullets. This way."

I had no idea why fingerprints were required, but now was not the time to admit ignorance. I collected the rifles from the other bodies and then hurried after him. The fore-court—like our prison—had been carved out of the mountain and seemed to be little more than a parking bay. There were at least a dozen vehicles present, including the pod that had brought us here, and several caterpillar tanks. The latter would have been a good choice for getting out of here *if* we'd been able to access and start one.

At the far end of the cavern, in a direct line with the metal gates behind us, was the tunnel entrance. It was high, wide, and dark, but the air flowing from it was fresh and held the hint of spicy citrus—a scent generally associated with blacknut trees. The tunnel obviously exited either into or close to a large forest of them.

To the right of the tunnel's entrance were a number of open carts—the sort of things mines used to ferry their workers to and from the surface. They were lined up in single file and attached by what looked like rolling clamps to a ribbon of metal that snaked into the darkness of the tunnel.

A soft clanking broke the silence. I half swung around; a crack of light now separated the two halves of the big metal door dividing this area from the main courtyard. It was being opened; we'd just run out of time.

Kai threw the body into the first cart, then jumped in. I followed, taking the rear seat and raising the rifle in readiness. Kai pressed a couple of switches, and the cart began to power up. Blue light flickered along the metal ribbon, as if in readiness. As lights across the control board flicked from red to green, Kai grabbed the Mareritt's hand and slapped it onto what looked to be a black pane of glass. Light swept the dead man's hand, and the remaining red light on the board switched to green. The brakes on the cart released, and the vehicle slowly trundled forward. Kai kept the dead man's hand firmly pressed on the screen, which suggested contact was necessary for movement.

The crack in the door was now a foot wide; ice scum gathered beyond it.

"At this rate," I commented, "the forecourt will be flooded with Mareritt before we get anywhere near the mouth of the tunnel."

"Then you'd better make sure you're ready to shoot the bastards, hadn't you?"

Despite the situation—or perhaps even because of it—amusement bubbled. "You're sounding a wee bit testy."

"That's because I am." He paused. "But don't take it personally."

I didn't. I raised the rifle and sighted on the door. As the cart picked up speed, the first Mareritt squeezed through the widening gap. I fired. His brains splattered across the face of the next man, who I also shot. The third man was cannier—he jumped back behind the door, stuck one hand out, and started firing. It might have been random, but random could be just as deadly as systematic.

The cart rounded the corner, picking up more speed as it entered the tunnel's mouth. As the darkness gathered around us, I shifted position, squatting behind the cart's rear wall for protection even though most of the returning fire didn't come anywhere near us. But the gap in the door was now wide enough to reveal the presence of a vehicle—one that seemed to have a rather long and deadly cannon at the front of it.

"Kai, there's some sort of armored vehicle about to enter the forecourt."

He glanced around and swore. "That's a needle tank."

"A what?"

"They're designed to maneuver in small spaces but have

almost as much power as the larger ones parked in the forecourt."

"Would the Mareritt risk using it in the tunnel and possibly cave the place in?"

"Yes, because their mages could clear the rubble easily enough."

Mages. The word had my pulse rate leaping several notches, and I had no idea why. Mages and magic had existed as long as drakkons, and it wasn't like I'd never confronted either. I had, plenty of times, and I'd survived every encounter thanks in part to my connection with Emri and the inability of magic to kill drakkons.

Emri...

I froze as a portion of ice fell away, giving me a small but precious nugget of memory.

Emri. My drakkon, and the missing part of my soul. The part that had been torn away when the riding harness had shattered and I'd fallen.

Fear crashed through me. Fear, hurt, and pain. For several seconds, I couldn't breathe, couldn't think. Couldn't do anything except silently repeat, over and over, *In the wind's name, please don't let her be lying at the bottom of the lake. Please don't let her be dead...*

Even though common sense and everything I'd learned so far suggested that's exactly what her fate might have been.

A bullet pinged off the metal strut in front of me, spraying sparks across my face. I blinked, took a deep breath, then raised the rifle and fired. And kept firing, needing to see Mareritt go down even though it did little to ease the ice now settling into my soul.

Our speed continued to increase, and the screech of metal rollers running against the ribbon grew so loud it wiped out the noise of gunfire—both mine and that of the Mareritt. Wind tore at my clothes and hair, and the cart swayed dangerously. I braced my back against one side of it and my foot against the other, holding steady as I continued to fire.

A red light started blinking on the rifle, lending the darkness a bloody glow. I hoped it wasn't an omen of what was to come.

But the tank was now trundling toward the door, and the cart's screaming wheels suggested we were at full speed.

I exchanged the rifle for another, but I didn't bother firing—the Mareritt had retreated behind the tank. It would only waste bullets.

Then, with a loud, echoing clang, the doors locked open. The tank surged across the forecourt, its speed frightening. It wouldn't take long for that thing to catch us—if catching us was its goal. Given the gun was now being cranked into firing position, I doubted it was.

"We've got a metal tail." I had to shout to be heard.

"We're at full speed," Kai replied. "There's nothing else I can do."

"How long is this tunnel?"

"It runs the width of the Blue Steel Mountains."

I blinked. "The Mareritt have direct access into Arleeon? Since when?"

"Since forever." He glanced at me, eyes blue chips in the soft glow coming from the control panel. "This tunnel was created soon after Zephrine fell."

Why would Esan have allowed such a thing to happen? Drakkons might be of no use in an underground fight, but both Esan and Zephrine had well-equipped ground forces. Unless, of course, there'd been a catastrophic failure of *all* defenses—not just Zephrine's but Esan's as well.

But I once again shoved the questions aside and said, "We only had twenty-five minutes to meet the pickup—will we make it?"

"Maybe. Maybe not."

"What happens if we don't?"

"Then you'd better hope the Mareritt only have a partial guard at the other end of this thing."

My gaze went back to the blot of darkness that was the tank. We were in trouble anyway—it was getting too close, too fast.

"What's the firing range of that tank?"

Kai glanced over his shoulder. "We're almost within it."

Even as he spoke, fire flashed from the tank's gun, and the air whistled. I instinctively ducked, even though the cart wasn't going to offer much protection if we were hit.

With a deafening *whoomph*, the missile hit the side of the wall twenty or so feet behind the cart. Debris and heat spun through the air, pummeling the cart and tearing holes in metal and skin. The cart rocked violently, but somehow the rollers clung on, and we sped on into the darkness.

Another flash of fire. Another *whoomph*.

This time, the missile hit the wall just behind the cart. The force of the explosion not only blew apart a massive section of mountain but sent the cart tumbling end over end. I tried to grip on, tried to hunker down and use the cart as protection against the sheer mass of stone and dirt rolling with us, but the force was such that it simply ripped my grip away.

Then darkness hit, and I knew no more.

THREE

I woke to the awareness of blood and pain. Warmth dribbled down my face, my head hurt, and my ears rang. Instinct had me pushing upright, but there was something lying across my butt and legs—a weight that pinned rather than crushed. While my feet *were* going numb, I could at least move my toes, and that meant there was no life-changing damage.

The air was thick and heavy with dust, and every breath left the inside of my mouth and throat coated with muck. The darkness was absolute—either the exit remained a long way off or it was not only guarded but also blocked by another rusted metal door. Thankfully, there was no immediate indication that guards had been sent back down the tunnel to investigate whether or not we'd survived the explosion.

All around me, rocks groaned as they settled into position. The metal track lay scattered across the floor in variously sized chunks, and the bulk of cart was who knew where.

I twisted around to check what had happened behind

us. My back and shoulder muscles protested the movement, but again, the rising weight of pain suggested bruising rather than major damage.

The tunnel had gone. In its place was a mountain of rock and dirt. The explosion had not only blown out the side of the tunnel but also caused the roof to collapse. It gave us some time to escape, although the faint sounds of movement coming from the other side of the barrier suggested we only had hours rather than days to get out of here.

But it at least meant I could safely produce flame and more thoroughly examine the rock that pinned me. I raised a hand and called fire to the tips of two fingers. It was little more than a splutter of warmth—a warning that even though my strength regenerated at a rapid rate, my reserves were still low. The slab of stone was four feet long and a good six inches thick. The only thing that had stopped it crushing my body was the rubble lying on either side of my hips—it was just high enough to support the bulk of the slab's weight. While the goddess of luck might not be giving us much of a break tonight, she hadn't totally abandoned us. But Túxn didn't throw her favors around lightly, and that meant there'd be a cost for this piece of luck. There always was.

I frowned and cast my flame a little higher. As the shadows peeled farther away, I saw Kai. He lay on the other side of the tunnel, his body covered by chunks of stone and the remnants of the cart. The back of his head and neck were bloody, he wasn't moving, and I couldn't tell if he was breathing.

He *had* to be alive. Flame might be able to knock a drakkon off her course, but it couldn't melt or move stone. Not without so much effort it would render me unconscious for days—and *that* certainly wasn't practical in this situation.

I picked up a small stone and tossed it at him. As much as I wanted to wake him, I didn't dare speak. The flame wasn't bright enough to be visible through the mountain of rubble behind us, but the Mareritt had keen hearing. While it was unlikely they'd hear a whisper, I didn't want to risk it. The longer they thought us dead, the more chance we had of getting away.

The stone hit the bottom half of Kai's right leg and bounced away. There was no immediate response. I frowned and tried again; we needed to get out of here, and we needed to do so soon. Not just because the Mareritt were already working on a means to clear the tunnel but also because we were running out of time. We couldn't have more than six or seven minutes left before the rescue party departed. And if they *did*, it would take something close to a miracle for us to get away.

The third stone hit Kai on the shoulder and, this time, elicited a response. His body shifted fractionally, then, with a half grunt, half growl, he surged upright, shaking stone and metal from his body as he swung around and raised his weapon.

For an instant, all I saw was death. Death and hatred.

For *me*.

Then he blinked, and the hatred was quickly shuttered. But it was a blatant reminder that I knew absolutely nothing about this man; as much as I needed his help, I also needed to keep alert and aware.

He checked the rifle, swung it across his shoulder, and then walked over to me. Without comment, he squatted at the top end of the slab and then raised one eyebrow in query.

I nodded. His grip tightened on the edges of the stone, and then, with another grunt, he thrust upright. The minute the stone was off my legs, I dragged myself out from under its shadow. My feet were barely clear when his grip slipped and the stone smashed back down, crushing the rubble that had saved me and sending sharp shards of debris slicing through air and skin.

But those cuts were minor compared to what the Mareritt would inflict if they caught us. We had to move—now.

I dragged the collar of my undershirt over my mouth and nose in an effort to filter out the muck and then pushed into a sitting position. Agony bloomed, and I gritted my teeth against the scream that tore up my throat. The pain wasn't the result of injury—it was simply the tingling agony that came with blood rushing through limbs that had been restricted for a little too long. It did at least make the throbbing in my head seemed less intense, though the latter would undoubtedly last longer.

I swiped at the blood still running down my face, then glanced up as a hand appeared in front of my nose. Again, there was little emotion to be seen in Kai's expression, and his eyes—though bright in the light of my flame—remained icy. Ungiving.

I let him haul me up, then stepped around him and moved deeper into the tunnel. Once we were clear of debris, we upped our speed. But our footsteps echoed lightly across the silence and would provide ample warning of our approach to the guards who undoubtedly waited ahead.

The inner countdown hit red territory; we had one minute left and the gateway was nowhere in sight. But there was little point in saying anything. I was already running as fast as I could; there was nothing else I could do.

The vital minute came and went; frustration rose, but I thrust it aside and concentrated on keeping up with Kai—who, despite the two-inch-long cut on the back of his head, seemed totally unaffected and full of strength.

I rather suspected that he was more than just a mere soldier. There was something in his manner and the way he moved that spoke not only of deadly experience but also someone well used to commanding others. My sister had the same air—it was the reason she led the graces and I'd been happy to be just another of her soldiers. She'd been born to lead; this man had been too. It made me wonder if, despite our allotted time having passed, the people waiting for us at the far end of this tunnel would risk remaining until we got there.

But even if they didn't, we'd find that miracle and somehow escape.

We had to.

There was too much I needed to understand. Too much I needed to know—like, where in wind's name were the kin who'd followed my sister into the coruscation? Were they also prisoners, perhaps already en route to Frio? And what had happened to Emri after the harness had snapped? She *couldn't* be dead, no matter what common sense might be saying, as it was very hard to kill a drakkon without sending her rider insane. The fact I *was* here—and apparently lucid despite the strangeness all around me—meant she should be too. But I couldn't feel her presence—not in the skies and certainly not in my thoughts.

And yet, despite the initial rush of fear, I really didn't think she was dead. Maybe that was wishful thinking—maybe this whole escape was nothing but the nightmare of a mind no longer able to deal with reality. Or maybe *I* was dead, and this was a form of eternal punishment for supporting my sister's bold plan to attack the coruscation spheres with the full might of both fortresses—a plan that might well have led us all into a trap... but had it also led to their death? I didn't know, because the events of that day were locked behind the ice.

I silently cursed. These fragments were more infuriating than enlightening, if only because they raised more questions than they solved.

Especially when they made *no* sense.

Once again, the urge to get to Zephrine rose. Maybe if I saw her for myself, I'd understand what was going on. But to do that, we first had to escape this tunnel and the Mareritt.

We ran on... and on. The ache in my head now beat in time with my footsteps, but my eye had at least stopped bleeding. The inner fires might be depleted, but they weren't as yet extinguished.

It was another ten minutes before the slightest glimmer of light appeared ahead. I instantly doused my flame and drew in the air; underneath the crisp scent of night ran the spicy citrus of blacknut trees and the musk of the Mareritt. There were guards up ahead, even if they weren't immediately visible. We slowed our pace to ease the noise of our steps, and gradually the ink of the tunnel gave way to the brightness of a moon-clad night. My gaze swept from the very large gate and the trees beyond it that promised freedom to the buildings that stood on either side. They were far larger than the one that had guarded the entrance into the forecourt and were both dark. I didn't trust that darkness. If there was one thing that could be said about Mareritt soldiers, it was that they were well trained and well disciplined. They wouldn't have abandoned their posts or even gone to sleep—not until they were given the all clear, at any rate.

"What's the plan?" Though I kept the question soft, it still seemed abnormally loud in the silence.

He glanced at me, his expression ungiving and the rifle raised. I had a suspicion that if I took one step out of line, the last bullet in that gun would be aimed my way. "We each tackle one guardhouse. Ready?"

I nodded in answer to both what he'd said and what he hadn't. He studied me a second longer, then turned and moved to the right. I went left, keeping close to the wall, hoping the shadows were thick enough to conceal my presence. I knew from years of playing hide-and-seek with my brothers that brown skin and black hair was harder to spot in shadows. The problem in *this* situation was the gold-and-red uniform I wore. It had never been designed for concealment, simply because there was little point when you were astride a drakkon with a wingspan of over one hundred and fifty feet. But the stronger the moonlight got the closer we moved to the exit, the brighter the red threading decorating the uniform would glow.

I clenched my fingers against the need to take out the Mareritt before they attacked. As tempting as it was, I really needed to conserve my strength *and* my fire. But attack first, ask questions later had been something of a mantra for me when it came to the Mareritt—and it was one that had rarely led me astray.

I let my breath hiss through clenched teeth and padded on. My heart raced and sweat trickled down my spine, but nothing stirred in the darkness within the guardhouse, and there was no sign of weapons being trained my way. Which might or might not mean anything, given the weapons both

Kai and the Mareritt used were of a design I'd never seen before.

Then, finally, the shadows moved within the guard-house, swiftly followed by a short, sharp rattle.

Machine gun.

I dropped to the ground and hurled a lance of fire at the window and my unseen assailant. Bullets pinged off the wall and ground all around me, sending sharp shards of stone spearing through the air. I swore and threw up a hand in a vague effort to protect my face. My fire streamed into the open window of the guard's box, and a heartbeat later, the screaming began. It didn't last long. It never did.

As more gunfire rang out from the second guard's box, I scrambled upright and ran forward. The thick stench of burned flesh assaulted my nostrils, as sharp as the agony that still rode the air. I grabbed the edge of the open window and leaped inside. All that remained of the guards were still-burning remnants of bone and flesh.

Relief stirred, but we weren't out of the woods yet. I carefully stepped across the remains and moved to the rear wall. The weapons stores hadn't been locked—a move I'd normally consider careless if it wasn't for the fact that they apparently controlled this entire region. Perhaps security wasn't a major problem for them, despite the presence of the resistance in this outpost. I threw a rifle over my shoulder, gripped a second, and then shoved as many ammo clips as I could into my pockets. I'd half turned to walk across to the door when a flicker of blue caught my attention. It belonged to a knife—one that had an intricately carved blue-glass handle and a matching blade. It was an Ithican hunting knife, and why it was even here in a Mareritt armory I had no idea. They were extremely rare in Arleeon, even though Ithica had for many years been one of our major trade partners. The blades were nigh on destructible —not even drakkon fire could destroy them—and yet despite this, the Mareritt had never used them against us. Weapons such as knives and long swords generally required close-in fighting, and the Mareritt had never been flight capable.

I plucked the knife from the cabinet and hefted it lightly in my right hand. Once again, blue light ran down the blade, making me wonder if perhaps magic had been a part of its creation. Not that it mattered to me; the balance was perfect and the blade light. Even if it hadn't been, there was no way known I was about to leave such a weapon in the hands of an enemy. I shoved the blade into the empty sheath strapped to my leg and continued on. Kai gave me a nod as he left the other guardhouse and motioned toward the exit. I slipped out the door and, with my back pressed against the wall of the building, made my way to the massive gate. The strip of cleared land that separated us from the trees was just wide enough to allow a small drakkon to sweep in and flame. I studied the trees, seeing no one, sensing no one, then edged past the gate's stanchion and peered up. I couldn't see her silhouette against the night sky, but I had no doubt she was up there somewhere.

The soft call of a Nightjar ran across the silence. I glanced at Kai, but his attention was on the forest. After several seconds of silence, he repeated the sound.

This time, the call was answered.

Our rescue party hadn't left, despite the fact we were well past the nominated deadline.

A mix of relief and uncertainty ran through me. Freedom from the Mareritt now seemed assured—but was I about to walk into an even worse situation? Kai might have needed me to escape captivity, but the utter hatred I'd glimpsed in the tunnel had shaken my earlier belief that he could be trusted.

He lowered his gun and glanced at me. "Let's go."

I hesitated briefly and then followed him into the open space, angling across until I was directly behind him. It probably wouldn't stop those in the trees shooting me if that was what Kai intended, but it at least gave me the illusion of safety.

We were in the middle of the open area when I heard a familiar whistle of air—a drakkon, sweeping in.

I glanced up and saw her—a fiery spark against the brightness of the stars.

"Drakkon incoming!" a male shouted from the trees.

Kai slid to a stop and raised his rifle.

"Don't shoot her," I said and dove toward him.

I hit him at the same time the shot rang out. Heard the screech of her pain even as he grabbed me and tossed me to one side. I scrambled to my feet; saw the gun pointed my way. Froze, even as two men appeared out of the trees and began shooting. At the drakkon, not me.

Bullets generally couldn't penetrate a drakkon's tough hide; the only part of them that was susceptible to damage was the membrane between each of the phalanges when stretched out in full flight. And even then, it took a lot of shots to shred it. But *this* drakkon was half the size of Emri, and surely a drakkon's body structure couldn't be altered so brutally without there being other effects—effects that might well make her vulnerable to regular weapons.

The screams that now echoed across the night certainly seemed to indicate just that.

"Don't kill her," I yelled. "I need to speak to her!"

They didn't listen, and the barrage of shots continued. I twisted around, saw the bullets now shredding the membrane on her left wing. Saw her spiraling downward, her unbroken wing cutting the air furiously in an effort to remain aloft. But even a drakkon as small as she needed both wings to remain mobile.

"In the wind's name, Kai, make them stop! I need to speak to her!"

He didn't lower his weapon. Didn't order the other men to lower theirs. And his eyes... I shivered.

"No one can speak to drakkons," he said, voice flat and cold. "No one but Mareritt."

"And *kin*. What calamity has happened here that all knowledge of drakkon *kin* has been erased?" My voice was filled with desperation. The agony of that drakkon was so strong I could practically taste it. "She's no immediate threat to any of you—"

"She's a *drakkon*—she can cinder our bones and scatter our ashes to the four winds."

So could I, and it was damn tempting to do just that right now. "Drakkon fire has distance limits—"

"And both us *and* that forest are well within her range. We cannot risk it."

"Then go—leave! I'll distract her, and you can be safe and escape."

Something flashed across his expression—something that was both surprise and suspicion. "I'm not going anywhere until I solve the puzzle you present."

There was a decided grimness to his tone that suggested the outcome would *not* be good if, in solving that puzzle, he found me wanting. But that was the least of my problems. I glanced over my shoulder. The drakkon's blood now rained onto the ground, staining it black and filling the air with its stink. "You've trusted me this far, Kai. Let me talk to her. *Please.*"

He studied me for what seemed an eternity, then raised his rifle and motioned the others to stop firing. "You have five minutes; any longer, and we finish her."

And perhaps me with her...

I pushed the thought away, handed him the two rifles I carried, then spun and raced toward the drakkon. She hit the ground with an audible thump, the claws at the end of her good wing digging a deep ditch in the soil as she fought to remain upright. Her injured wing dragged behind her, bent, useless, and bloody. Tears welled in my eyes, but I blinked them away. This drakkon was not *my* drakkon. She didn't even belong to any of the graces I'd grown up with. She was an unknown, and that made her dangerous. I might be somewhat immune to drakkon fire—long exposure *would* eventually kill me, but my uniform was fireproof and I could use my own flames as a shield to protect my head when I wasn't wearing a helmet—but I was as vulnerable to teeth and claws as anyone else.

I reached out to her mentally but hit an impregnable wall. It wasn't one raised by pain. It wasn't even a result of the mind blindness a rare few drakkons were born with. This was different; it almost felt unnatural—as if it were something being *forced* onto her.

She shifted her body to brace herself further, and the metal band on her rear leg came into view. Blue light flashed across its surface, a rhythmic pulse that matched the ebb and flow of static in her mind. She roared in fury and pain, her leg muscles twitching as she tossed her head from side to side, as if in denial.

The band, I suspected, wasn't only causing her pain but was the means by which the Mareritt controlled her.

I slid to a halt twenty feet away. Her head snaked around, and her dark gaze pinned me. There was fury in that gaze—fury, hatred, and pain. It was the hatred I didn't understand; something had seriously gone wrong when a *drakkon* didn't recognize kin.

I raised a hand. "Easy, easy, little one. I'm not going to hurt you."

She opened her mouth and sucked in air. I called to my own fire and let it burn across my fingers. "I know you can understand me, so heed this warning well. Your flames cannot hurt me, but if you try to burn those behind me, I *will* finish what they started."

Something flickered through the fury in her dark gaze— a spark of understanding, perhaps. Then the band flared brighter and that spark fled. She flamed. At me, not at the men. Somewhere behind the Mareritt-induced pain, she'd understood my warning.

I braced my feet and threw my flames in front of me, forming them into a shield. Blood dribbled from my eye once again, but there was nothing I could do but ignore it. Her fire hit with the force of a thousand hammers, pushing me back several feet. The heat behind it was even fiercer than mine and would have instantly cindered anyone else. Every breath felt like liquid fire, and sweat poured down my spine, face, and body. But the shield did its work; it forced her flames over my head, leaving my hair dripping and my face burning with effort rather than simply burning.

Her fire died. I extinguished my own and ran straight at her. She bellowed and snapped at me, her teeth razor sharp and coming altogether too close. I dodged sideways and then leaped high, catching the edge of one nostril and flipping up, over her head and through the horns on either side before landing heavily on her neck. She reared in shock; I gripped tight with my thighs as she bellowed and threw her head from side to side, then lunged forward and grabbed her horns, hanging on grimly as her movements became more violent. I had to ride them out; only then would I have any hope of restraining her.

She became even more frantic, and her desperation stung the air. Every breath was fast but shallow, and her scales were beginning to lose their sheen—a sure sign blood loss was taking its toll. She rose up and her good wing began to beat; a storm of dust erupted, making it hard to breathe and impossible to see. Slowly, awkwardly, she rose from the ground. A few feet, no more. Then she crashed back down and threw herself sideways in a last, desperate effort to dislodge me. As her head and neck smashed against the ground, I tore off my flight jacket and scrambled forward, sitting on her cheek and using my weight to hold her down. It had taken a number of us to hold down the bigger drakkons, but this one had neither their size nor weight, and was close to exhaustion besides. I threw my jacket over her visible eye; ideally, it would have been better to blind both, but at least the other was locked against the ground.

With a defeated groan, her frantic struggles ceased. I gently scratched the ridge above her eye and crooned softly. After a few minutes, she relaxed. The danger was far from over but she'd at least ceded to my control. How long that would last was anyone's guess—lightning continued to flicker across the band on her leg, and her skin twitched ever more violently in response.

"Kai? You still there?"

"Yes." There was something close to astonishment in his voice.

"I need you over here."

"Red, you're out of your ever-loving mind if you think—"

"She hasn't the strength left to flame," I cut in, "and she won't smell you if you approach from the side."

"And may I ask why you want me to approach? Because that *isn't* what any normal, sane, and sensible person would be doing right now."

"I need you to take the band off her leg." I risked a look across the clearing. The other two men were standing either side of him, and their expressions were a mix of uncertainty, surprise, and suspicion. "I think it's how the Mareritt are controlling the drakkon. Take it off, and we may be able to switch her allegiance."

Or not, given the glimpse of hatred I'd seen. But I had to at least try. She deserved a chance at freedom.

"If your rescue party has a medikit handy," I continued, "bring that too."

"Kaiden, it's not going to take the Mareritt more than a few hours to break through the collapse point," the thick-set man said. "We need to be well gone by then."

Kaiden, not Kai, I noted.

"I know," Kai—Kaiden—said. "Go across to the gate and keep watch. Holt, get me the kit."

The drakkon briefly attempted to raise her head. But with my weight on it and her good wing underneath her, she had little hope—especially when her strength was leaching from her as fast her blood was staining the soil. If I didn't stem that flow soon, she'd die. Of course, that might be a better option than her falling back into the hands of the Mareritt.

I continued to caress the bony ridge but kept on eye on Kaiden's careful approach. Once he was close enough, I drew the knife and threw it into the ground in front of him. "Use that to pry open the band."

He drew it out of the soil and whistled softly. "An Ithican blade. I've heard of them but never seen one."

"That's because we used to drop the things deep into the ocean whenever we found them. Weapons that could injure drakkons weren't something we wanted readily available."

His gaze flashed to mine; once again I saw the questions in his eyes. Once again, he didn't give them voice. He simply moved forward, the knife held at the ready. He ducked under the injured wing, carefully avoiding the broken phalanges and dripping blood. I shifted slightly to keep him out of sight. The drakkon moved with me, and her wing claw dug a trench into the ground only feet from him. I crooned softly, and her clawing stopped. Kaiden waited another second and then edged to the back of her leg. "The band is a good two inches thick—I'm not sure the knife will be strong enough to break it."

"It will. Just find the clasp point and pry it apart."

He grunted—a disbelieving sound if ever there was one —but nevertheless stepped closer. After another brief pause, he shoved the knife's slender point into the band's seam. Blue lightning flew across the metal's surface, though whether it was in response to Kaiden's actions or whether the Mareritt were simply trying to force the drakkon back into action, I couldn't say. I had no idea if the device was simply one of control or whether it gave them an electronic version of the mind link we kin were born with. Either way, she groaned and twitched, forcing Kaiden to jump out of the way or risk being gored.

He tried again; this time, the knife went deeper, and with a grunt of effort, he managed to twist the blade sideways and force the edges of the band apart. Then, with a loud click, the bracelet fell away, freeing her from its evil.

Kaiden clipped it to his belt and then retreated. I attempted the mind meld again. This time, there was no static, only pain, confusion, and hatred. The latter wasn't specifically aimed at me but rather everyone and everything. But that was unsurprising if she'd known nothing but pain and submission since the day she'd hatched.

Can you hear me? I silently asked.

Yes. Her reply was uncertain and filled with confusion. *Why?*

I'm kin.

Know not kin.

No surprise, but the admission still cut deep. *Kin are women who bonded with the drakkon and rode them to war.*

Ah. Kaieke.

Kaieke was a Mareritt slur for kin that basically meant "daughters of trulls"—a trull being the term for a lady who sold her wares on the streets. They held none of the esteem of the Danseuse, many of whom could count royalty amongst their clients, and who used a mix of sensuality and dance magic to pleasure. In the Arleeon I'd known, there hadn't been many active Danseuse, though I had no idea why that had been.

Interestingly, the way she used the term was in no way derogatory—quite the opposite, in fact.

Yes, and I'm here to help you.

You shot me. She paused. *Not you. Others.*

Yes, and I'm sorry. I can fix the damage but only if you do not attack.

Attack is all they want.

They no longer control you. The decision is yours to make.

She considered this silently, her mind a myriad of conflicting thoughts and emotions.

Mental pain has gone. They *are gone.* Relief and wonder mixed with disbelief. *For that, I will not attack.*

Thank you, little one.

Oma. I am Oma.

Do you wish the blind left on your eye, Oma?

No. Wish to see. Have been blind too long.

Meaning mentally, I knew, not physically. I pulled my jacket from her eye, then gave the ridge a final scratch and slipped from her cheek to the ground. She raised her head and turned to follow my movements.

I ducked under her injured wing and then held out my hand. "I need the medikit."

Kaiden warily walked closer and handed it me. "I think this is the first time in a very long time a field kit has been used on a drakkon."

I grunted, concentrating more on finding what I needed than what he was saying. "We used to carry specialized kits with us whenever we went out. Ah, here we go." I plucked out the bone straps and a bottle of wound sealer, then handed the kit back to Kaiden and glanced at Oma. "I'll have to spread your wing out to patch it. It'll hurt."

Uncertainty flashed through her thoughts, followed swiftly by the heat of fear. But she gave none of it voice and silently assented.

I returned my gaze to Kaiden. "I'll take the shoulder area—you take the wing tip."

"If she flames me, me and my burned butt will come back to haunt you."

"That threat might or might not be worrying." I walked over to her shoulder and gently placed my hands either side of her wing claw. "Depending on whether or not said butt is a good one. I haven't actually had the time to notice."

He snorted, a sound that was a mix of amusement and

disbelief. "I'd prefer it if you didn't stop to do so right now. This drakkon is giving me the evil eye."

I glanced across at her. She was indeed studying Kaiden rather intensely, but not with any immediate intention of flaming him. "You're safe. She's fascinated, not annoyed."

"I'm not sure I like the sound of that, either."

I smiled, even as an odd sort of uncertainty ran through me. Something pretty drastic really *had* happened in Arleeon for drakkons to become such an unknown quantity —something *other* than the Mareritt gaining control of Zephrine's aeries. Even if they'd lost all their drakkons, they should still have had the libraries as well as those who'd retired from flight and could still remember... The thought died. Those who retired most often ended up working in the aeries alongside the older drakkons, keeping the eggs safe and warm and the drakklings under watchful eyes.

But even if they'd all fallen victim to the ice, did no one read anymore? Did no one share the knowledge of what once had been?

The wing clicked into full spread. I glanced across to Kaiden. "Hold her steady while I repair the broken phalanges."

He nodded. I released her wing claw and moved into the center of her broken wing, avoiding some but not all of the blood drips. While its strong metallic scent had my nose wrinkling, its dark staining did at least erase some of the uniform's brightness.

Three vital sections of her wing were broken—two along one phalange, one on the other. I carefully pushed each one back into position, aware of her restless stirring and the haze of pain running through her mind, then placed and activated each of the bone straps. Once the broken sections were braced, I flipped off the sealer's lid and began to patch the bigger sections of torn membrane. Even with the force each sweep of her wing would place on the repairs, they should hold long enough for her to find somewhere safe to rest and recuperate. Drakkons, like those of us who rode them, healed extraordinarily fast; she wouldn't be out of action for very long.

"It sounds like they've brought in machinery to clear the rubble," the soldier stationed near the exit said. "We need to get going."

"You finished?" Kaiden immediately asked.

I nodded. "I'll join you in few minutes. I need a final word with her."

He hesitated, then handed me the knife and cautiously retreated. I shoved the knife back into its sheath, then ducked under her wing and walked over to her head. She shifted slightly, presenting her eye ridge for a scratch. I obliged.

Your wing should hold long enough to get free from this place. Find somewhere hidden and safe to recover.

And you?

The Mareritt come after us. We must run.

Mareritt?

Those who held you prisoner.

Deep in her chest, thunder rumbled, and fire rolled briefly around the edges of her nostrils. A hint of what waited for any frost scum who tried to recapture her.

I leave. She paused. *Owe you.*

No. Be free and be safe. With that, I stepped away, giving her the freedom to move.

With a grunt of effort, she dug her patched wing into the ground and dragged herself upright. Then she pushed to her feet and started beating both wings, slowly at first and then with more confidence as the patches held. She crouched and leaped, her wings pumping but her body dipping a little to one side, thanks to a few remaining tears in her wing. Gradually, though, she gained height and speed.

Then, with a joyous bellow, she was gone.

Free.

Her thought, not mine.

Once again, tears stung my eyes; once again, I blinked them away. She might be free, but many more drakkon were still in the hands of the frost scum. But until I knew just what had happened—to Arleeon, and to me—there was really nothing I could, or even should, do.

I spun around on a heel and marched across the clearing. Kaiden was waiting at the edge of the forest. His two companions were nowhere in sight.

"This way." He returned one of the rifles to me and then led the way into the trees.

"Where are the other two?"

"They have tasks elsewhere."

"So we're on our own?"

"For the moment, yes."

"And do I call you Kai or Kaiden?"

He glanced around, the half smile on his lips doing little to counter the coldness in his eyes. "Kaiden when alone. Kai when we're in Mareritten cities or towns."

"And do you have a last name? Or is that to remain a secret until you trust me?"

"Guess."

"Thanks for the vote of confidence."

"I'll share once you start sharing."

I snorted softly but didn't bother replying. The darkness closed in as we entered the forest. Leaves crunched under our feet, the soft sound echoing around us. But there was little other noise to be heard—if there were night creatures here, they were in hiding. Even the shrill, shrieking noise made by spittlebugs was absent, and that was unusual in a forest this dense.

The spicy citrus scent of the blacknut trees became more intense the deeper we moved into the forest, overriding the metallic stink that covered my uniform. Many of the trees had begun their autumn shed, allowing moonbeams to filter through half-cloaked branches, highlighting the deep furrows of black in the trunks of the older trees—such staining was an indicator of age. The fact that there was so much suggested this area had not seen much in the way of drakkon fire, and that meant either the resistance had been more successful in breaking other prisoners out than they had us, or simply that the freedom had never lasted past the exit gates or open field. Perhaps if I'd studied the ground between the gate and the trees a little longer, I might have spotted the cindered patches of soil that spoke of past escape attempts.

I flexed my fingers and said, "Where are we going?"

"We've transport waiting on the other side of this forest."

"Once we get there, what then?"

He half hitched a shoulder. "Not sure yet. Depends."

"On what?"

"On you answering a few more questions." He glanced over his shoulder, suspicion darkening his expression. "I want to know who you are. I want to know why you know so much about drakkons and yet so little about Arleeon."

"Trust me, I probably have as many questions needing answers as you. But until my memories come back fully, that's not going to happen."

"Amnesia is a pretty convenient excuse."

"It's not an excuse, and it's not amnesia." I hesitated. "Not exactly."

"Then what is it?"

"This is going to sound strange, but it almost feels as if portions of my brain are covered in a sheet of ice that's slowly thawing out. I know some stuff, I'm remembering other random bits, but a whole lot more remains locked behind that ice."

"Perhaps the first thing we need to do once we escape is find a reader and see if they can get past this ice of yours."

Reader was the common term for those gifted with the ability to slip into the minds of others and uncover their thoughts and memories via a simple touch. Earth and air mages might be somewhat rare in Arleeon, but those gifted with psychic abilities—or even personal magics such as healing—were not. Kin might naturally heal fast, but even we couldn't heal major injuries in a matter of hours, and that's where healers came in handy.

"There's a reader at Zephrine—" I stopped. Zephrine didn't exist—at least, not as I'd known it.

"And there're plenty within Esan."

"Is that where we're heading?"

He snorted—a sound of disbelief if ever I'd heard one. "Would *you* take me there if our positions were reversed?"

"Yes, because you'd be strapped to the leg of a drakkon and unlikely to cause any problems until we got answers."

He stopped so abruptly I had to do a quick step sideways to avoid running into him. His expression, when his gaze met mine, was angry. "*That* is exactly the reason I don't trust you."

I frowned. "I don't understand what you mean—"

"Drakkons—fighting drakkons who bore kin aloft—no longer exist—"

"Yes, but—"

"There *are* no buts," he went on relentlessly. "The day the graces made their futile attack against the coruscations was the day the Mareritt stole both our strength and the will to fight. It was the day Arleeon became a Mareritten territory."

I let his words wash over me and simply stared at him. My heart raced, and the pounding in my head increased until the ache was so bad it felt like my brain was about to explode. Not because of what he'd said, but what he *hadn't*.

Part of me wanted to cover my ears—to run from whatever else he was about to say. But I needed answers, however unpleasant. I swallowed against the dryness in my throat, but it didn't really help.

"And?" I asked, my voice hoarse.

"And," he replied heavily, "it all happened over two *hundred* years ago."

FOUR

I stared at him for several seconds, his words echoing but making no sense. Two hundred years? If anything was impossible, it was *that*.

"You *can't* have ridden a fighting drakkon, Red, because they haven't existed for two hundred years. No matter what you believe to the contrary, *that* is simply the truth."

His expression remained grim, but there was an undertone of anger in his voice now. It wasn't aimed so much at me but rather at history itself. At the events that had led to so much loss, and at the woman who'd been central to it all —my sister.

"No—" I somehow ground out.

"You can deny it all you want, but that doesn't change a thing." His voice remained relentless. Ungiving. "I don't know what's happened to you. I don't know why your memories seem stuck in a time long past, but there's no possible way I'm taking you anywhere near the last free city until we uncover who you truly are and what's happened to you."

The last free city... Four words that had me reeling even

65

more. The drakkons all but gone, Zephrine destroyed, Esan standing alone, and the Mareritt in control of the majority of Arleeon? How was all that even possible?

How could everything I *did* remember be so totally and utterly out of step with *this* reality? Or was there a far darker purpose behind those memories?

Was *he* the problem and not me? Had he been placed in my path to confuse and subvert? But even as that thought rose, I rejected it. There was simply too much about this world that was very obviously different to the one I remembered for it to be a part of some gigantic charade. Besides, every instinct within suggested I trust this man, and given the lack of recent memory, instinct was all I really had.

I shoved a gloved hand through my short hair. "I think, perhaps, we need to find a reader ASAP."

"With that, I agree. Let's move."

He continued on, striding through the trees with an assurance that suggested familiarity with this area. I followed silently, barely watching my steps, my mind awhirl with so many conflicting emotions it was hard to think. And maybe *that* was a good thing, because I really didn't want to dwell on the fact that everyone I'd ever known was not only *dead* but not even dust on the wind, given the length of time that had elapsed.

So how did I get here?

What had happened within the coruscations to throw me—and no one else—two hundred years into the future?

What was the ice hiding?

Or was the ice itself nothing more than a deliberate attempt on my part *not* to confront painful memories or shocking truths?

I didn't know, and that was both frustrating *and* frightening. I flexed my fingers and said, "I take it you come from Esan?"

"Yes."

It was curtly said, but I ignored the unspoken warning within it. He might not want to talk right now, but I *needed* to.

"Are you of kin blood? Because you don't smell like it."

He snorted. "I wasn't aware kin came with a specific smell."

"When you hang around drakkons long enough, their musk becomes somewhat entrenched."

"We have no drakkons to hang around, remember. I'll also point out that for all your words about being kin and riding drakkons, you don't hold such a musk."

I didn't? Given I certainly *should*, it was yet another question needing to be answered. "You said Esan was the last free city—but Esan is a fortress. It was never designed or meant to be a city."

"Well, it's both now." Again, that mix of grimness and anger rode his voice. "We had little other choice."

It was a statement that chilled, if only because it suggested Esan and Arleeon had both been caught unawares. But if Zephrine had fallen first, why would that be the case? None of this was making much sense.

"How much of Arleeon do the Mareritt now hold?"

"Too damn much." He glanced over his shoulder, his blue eyes glittering. "Can we hold the questions until we get out of this forest? They do run patrols through this area— the last thing we need is your chatter alerting them to our presence."

A smile twisted my lips, though it contained little in the way of amusement. The possibility of Mareritt patrols— while no doubt valid—was simply a means to avoid answering my questions. The truth was, the crunch of leaves underfoot was probably making more noise than *anything* I was saying.

We marched on. Weariness and hunger were now biting deep, but I resolutely ignored it. There was no other option; aside from the fact that we had no rations, this area wasn't safe. Until we were, we had to keep moving.

The moon had made its way through the stars, and the flags of sunrise were just beginning to spread across the sky when Kaiden held up a hand and stopped.

I halted behind him and cocked my head to one side, listening intently. There was nothing that immediately suggested danger to me, but this wasn't an area I knew. Even if it *had* been, the dangers I'd been familiar with would have changed in two hundred years.

Again, disbelief rose. Or maybe it was more the *desire* to disbelieve rather than anything else. Because honestly, how was something like time travel even remotely possible? Magic could do the seemingly impossible at times—the Mareritt and the coruscation spheres had certainly proven that—but I seriously doubted even *they* were capable of such a feat. Besides, why would they want to throw even one of us so far into the future—a future they now controlled? It made no sense.

But if it wasn't magic, then what?

I scrubbed a hand across my face, sending small flakes of dried blood flying. Maybe this really *was* one big nightmare. Maybe I'd wake up tomorrow safe and sound in my own apartment within Zephrine and have a good laugh about the absurdity of it all over a tankard or two with my friends.

After another few seconds, Kaiden moved forward again. The trees thinned out, revealing a sweeping meadow of barely existing yellow grass and a broken farmhouse that had been more than half claimed by autumn-colored snake vines. Behind it were several outbuildings—one was more or less upright, but the smaller of the two leaned on such a precarious angle that the next big storm would surely blow it over.

"I take it our transport's waiting in one of those buildings?" I asked.

"Yes."

Again, it was a curt response. I rather suspected it would be easier to get information out of stone than the warrior ahead of me right now. "If the Mareritt patrol this area, why wouldn't they regularly check those buildings? It seems an obvious stop point for escapees."

"They do check, but the vehicles we use wouldn't raise much in the way of alarms."

Which didn't fill me with a whole lot of confidence in our upcoming mode of transport. But then, I was kin. *Any* form of ground transport made me uncomfortable—especially if it was enclosed.

I glanced at the brightening sky, half searching for the flash of red that would indicate a drakkon aloft. But there was nothing, and that was surprising. The first thing I'd have done in their situation was order all available drakkons into the area. But if their supply was limited and used more to control Arleeon's population in fractious areas, then maybe they didn't want to take the risk. Or perhaps they simply figured it would be easier to deploy the tanks and speeders once the tunnel had been cleared.

At least the ground here was hard and the grass near dead; whether they used drakkons aloft or vehicles, our trail would be difficult to spot.

The old farmhouse had been constructed out of greenstone, a hard-wearing rock that had been plentiful in the

Argon region. Was that where we were? I didn't know the area well, as it was located in the east of Arleeon, closer to Esan than Zephrine. It was—or had been—a cropping region, but the dryness of the soil and the fact that this vast field was abandoned suggested no crops had been grown in this area for years. Maybe even centuries.

The wind sighed through the building's broken windows and tugged at the remnants of metal sheeting that had once covered the entire roof. The sound echoed forlornly through the gathering brightness of the morning, emphasizing the lonely nature of this building out in the middle of nowhere. I wondered what had happened to the people who'd once lived and farmed this vast stretch of land. Wondered if the Mareritt had forced them elsewhere or if they'd fled to the safety of Esan. Like many other things right now, they were questions I had no answers to.

"You'll find clothing and food in the kitchen," Kaiden said. "Go change while I check the vehicle."

I nodded and walked around the broken end of the building to the still-standing portion. The door was unlocked and scraped against the floor as I opened it. The sound bit across the silence, and deep in the shadows, tiny feet skittered away. I had no idea whether they were rodents or overly large bugs, but it did at least mean this area wasn't as barren as it first seemed.

I walked through the first room, past broken furniture and the remnants of an ornate mirror, into a kitchen that held little more than an old stove and a few cupboards. After a brief hesitation, I moved across to the sink and turned on the tap, which resulted in a loud, somewhat thumping squeal and brownish water spluttering out. I waited until it ran a little clearer, then rinsed the blood from my face and used my jacket sleeve to dry it. I checked the cupboards and then inside the old stove for the clothes Kaiden had mentioned, with no success. I frowned and glanced around again, studying the floor for anything that suggested there might be a concealed storage area, and then the roof. A small portion of plaster above the stove had come down, and there were a number of spiderweb-like cracks fanning out from it that suggested further collapse was imminent. I frowned and stepped a little closer. A small triangular portion of those cracks seemed less random than the others.

I climbed onto the stove, threw a hand against the wall to steady myself as the thing rocked sideways under my weight, and then reached up and pressed my fingertips against the suspicious area. There was a soft click, and a section of wall slid silently to one side. I jumped down and discovered a storage area had been built within a largish cavity in the wall dividing the two rooms. Inside were not only neatly stacked piles of clothing, but dried rations, weapons, and ammunition.

Footsteps echoed in the other room. I swung around and reached for the knife rather than my fire; in a place this old, and a region this dry, any spark could be disastrous. Kaiden appeared, his gaze sweeping me before coming to a halt on the hand clasping the knife. He raised an eyebrow, amusement briefly warming the chill from his eyes. "You were expecting someone else?"

I released my grip and flexed my fingers. "Given I'm in a land that has altered beyond anything I recognize, caution is definitely warranted. Is the transport there?"

He nodded. "It's an old skid, though, so it's going to be a slow journey anywhere."

I had no idea what a skid was and didn't bother asking; I'd find out soon enough. I stepped back to give him room to enter the store, but his arm still brushed mine and an undefined sensation ran through me. It wasn't so much awareness or even attraction—it was both more nebulous and yet far stronger than either of those. It certainly wasn't something I'd felt before, and I had no idea what it meant. No idea whether it was a warning of some sort or simply a random reaction due to nothing more than the situation I'd quite literally fallen into.

I frowned and followed him into the room. "How do you keep this place operational if the Mareritt run constant patrols through the area?"

"We get regular updates on patrol positions, which enables us to work around them. It helps that the place looks and feels deserted."

He picked up what looked to be a miniature knife—one that had a grip little wider than half an inch and a thin blade with an odd hook at the end—and motioned toward my left wrist. I raised it and watched as he shoved the knife into the cuff's old-fashioned keyhole and then pressed a button at the top of it. The cuff unlocked and clattered to the floor; once he'd repeated the process with his own, he picked up both cuffs and dumped them onto a shelf that held multiple others. No matter what I might have thought earlier, there'd obviously been plenty of escapees from Break Point Pass.

"But if I found the entrance for this room so easily," I said, "surely the likelihood of them doing so is—"

"Quite low," he cut in. "You had enough nous to expect a hidden room; they do not. And the vehicles we leave here can't be started until the wiring is reattached. They wouldn't think to do that."

"None of which sounds like the Mareritt I fought against."

"Presuming, of course, your memories of fighting against them are real rather than implanted."

False memories... A snippet escaped—that of a rescued kin whose story belied her later actions, resulting in chaos within Zephrine and her eventual death. What her actions were, I couldn't say, but the fear in me increased. Her memories had proven to be false and her destructive actions devised by the Mareritt. "Is that what you think has happened? You think the Mareritt have replaced my memories in an effort to infiltrate Esan? Because you know how ridiculous that sounds, don't you?"

"Almost as ridiculous as you having been flung forward two hundred years through time."

Which was a good point. "Even if I was a plant—and I'm not, whether you want to believe it or not—why wouldn't they rejig my memories for *this* time rather than a point so long ago?"

He shrugged. "The Mareritt often do things that make no sense to the rest of us—like subverting Argon's major water courses to use in the fishery farms and all but dooming what was once prime farmland to a slow death."

Meaning I'd guessed our location right. But fishery farms out here in Argon? Why not just use major fishing hubs like Holton? Or did they not control those centers? Not knowing this sort of stuff was possibly even more frustrating than the lack of full memory.

"It's still hard to believe they'd go to the trouble of reconstructing memories that would automatically engage distrust—"

"Except there's been a lot of unusual activity happening in the last few months," he cut in again. "We've only vague reports to go on, as none of our informants live within the White Zone—"

"The what?"

"White Zone—it's a restricted area totally occupied by the Mareritt. None of us can get anywhere near it—the Mareritt have a shoot-to-kill policy for any Arleeon found within its boundaries."

"How large is this White Zone?"

"Large enough." He glanced at me briefly. "New Zephrine lies within its boundaries."

"Why would they bother to rebuild Zephrine when *it* was built to guard against *them*?"

He shrugged. "We presume it's because they wanted a trade and dispersing hub close to both a seaport and Mareritten."

That seaport being Kriton, which—despite its closeness to the Mareritten border—had never been attacked, thanks in part to the presence of the aerie and drakkons but also the Mareritt's aversion to sea travel.

I frowned. "Zephrine had a full complement of land soldiers; it's hard to believe they were overrun so easily."

"They weren't. From what was gleaned from the few survivors, it was magic, not fighting numbers, that made the difference."

"Meaning they unleashed more coruscations?"

"No. It was said that the air became so cold it froze everyone on the spot. The Mareritt then simply walked in and shattered each warrior."

Ice, it seemed, had been the Mareritt weapon of choice.

"Was New Zephrine built on the remains of the old city? Or did they erase her entirely and start anew?"

"It was rebuilt." He hesitated. "Why?"

"Just how destroyed is she?"

"That I can't say, because we can't get into the White Zone."

"So it *is* possible the structures within the mountain and her foundations still exist."

"I guess—again why?"

I shrugged. "Curiosity, and perhaps an unwillingness to believe that the place and the people so vivid in my memories were totally and utterly annihilated."

He grunted and pulled a shirt and a pair of trousers free from one of the stacks. "You'd better change out of that uniform and into these. It'll garner too much attention even if people aren't aware of its origin."

"Another fact that surprises me—why didn't the Mareritt, at the very least, recognize the standard flight uniform of the kin?"

He tossed the clothes toward me. "The Mareritt care not for history as far as I can see, so perhaps minor details such as the coloring of their enemy's uniform are not as important as the fact they were defeated."

I caught the clothes and dumped them onto the nearby shelf. "Then what's the point of me changing?"

"No Arleeon living within occupied territories wears leather these days, let alone gold leather."

Which explained what he was wearing; it was camouflage. I stripped off my flight jacket and said, "Just so you know, my clothes are coming with me."

He frowned. "Why? It's not like you're ever going to need them again."

"Maybe." I caught the end of my right glove and began to tug it off. The water had shrunk the leather, so it was somewhat tighter than usual. "But the uniform is fireproofed and that might yet come—"

The glove came off and the rest of the words froze in my throat. My hand was white. Not brown. *White.*

Disbelief and shock stormed through me. For a moment,

I could only stare at it. Then I hastily pulled off the other glove. That hand, too, was white.

What in the wind's name was going on?

My expression must have matched my surging horror, because Kaiden quickly said, "What's wrong?"

I didn't answer. I just spun and raced through the kitchen into the other room. Dust stirred with every step, creating an angry storm of brown that matched my confusion and growing sense of wrongness. Not just with this world, but with *me*. I slid to a halt next to one of the mirror shards and scooped it up. One edge sliced into my palm and red blood welled. At least *that* hadn't changed.

But everything else had.

Because while the facial features in the mirror *were* mine, the skin, the hair, even the eyes of the person staring back were not. My coloring *should* have been the same as Kaiden's, but the reflection was white-skinned, with blue-white hair and eyes such a pale blue there was only a small difference between the white and the iris. The crimson mote was the only thing that remained the same.

It couldn't be me. It just *couldn't*...

I reached out with a shaking finger; the reflection did the same. Fingertips met, separated only by glass.

It wasn't a joke. It wasn't a game. The image in the mirror *was* me.

The shard fell out of nerveless fingers, and my knees gave way. I staggered back and would have fallen if Kaiden hadn't somehow moved fast enough to catch me.

He lowered me to the floor and then squatted in front of me.

"Deep breaths, Red." He grabbed my hands, pressed them together, and started rubbing them. "You're hyperventilating. You need to calm down."

"Can't." Not when all I could feel—all I could hear—was the roar of disbelief. "It's wrong. It's all wrong—"

"And becoming unconscious isn't going to make it better." His voice was calm. Soothing. Gone was the abrupt terseness of before. "Just listen to me and concentrate on slowing your breathing. Take a deep breath in and hold." He paused. "And now release."

I closed my eyes and rested the back of my head against the wall, listening to the soothing resonance of his voice and gradually managing to match my breathing to his.

"Now," he continued softly, "without getting all hysterical again, tell me what's wrong."

"I wasn't hysterical. Just shocked." I opened my eyes but for several seconds did nothing more than stare at him. The words were stuck in my throat; as silly as it seemed, part of me just didn't want to utter the unbelievable, as if by doing so, I'd somehow make the change irrevocable. I swallowed heavily and said, "I'm white. Actually, not just white, but *Mareritt* white."

"Yes, I know." His dark brows drew down. "Why do you think I thought you were a Mareritt spy?"

"I really had no idea, and it confused the hell out of me." I drew in a somewhat shuddery breath. "I guess it does explain why the woman in the pod drew back when I touched her."

"Yes." He paused. "Don't take this the wrong way, but... while it *is* possible for readers with enough psychic skill to implant or erase memories, utterly changing someone's skin color is a different matter."

"Then why has it happened?"

"I can't tell you that." His voice remained gentle; perhaps he feared anything louder might just break me.

Truth be told, I definitely *was* feeling more than a

little brittle. But the cause wasn't anything he'd said or done; it was being hit by one impossibility after another. His presence was probably the only thing keeping me grounded.

"But I'm a soldier not a doctor," he continued. "It's possible there's some disease I don't know about that can cause—"

"This isn't the result of some disease." Of that I was sure, if nothing else. "I went into the coruscation one color and came out another, so something obviously happened within that place."

He stared at me for a long moment, then said, his voice as neutral as his expression, "*You* went into the coruscation?"

"Everyone did. Everyone who could fly." I hesitated. In truth, I couldn't actually remember doing so. I *could* remember the ice that had surrounded Emri and me, but what if that hadn't happened in the coruscation? What if we hadn't been part of that main attack force? But if that were true, then what had changed? I'd certainly been part of it all when my sister had broached the idea to the council... I licked my lips and somehow said, "But you already knew that."

"Yes, but this is the first time you've said you were one of their number—and again, we're presuming your memories are correct. We both know how unlikely *that* really is."

"I'm not a spy, Kaiden. I'm not Mareritt."

He hesitated again. "Look, I believe something very traumatic has happened to you. I believe the cut on your head hasn't helped your memories. As to the rest—" He shrugged. "While it's extremely rare—given the Mareritt aversion to our color and lack of extra fingers—there *have* been instances of half-breeds. They're not treated kindly by *any* of us, so maybe abuse lies behind what you remember and what you don't."

Annoyance surged, and I pulled my hands from his. But in truth, would I have said or acted any different had our positions been reversed? If I were being at all honest, no. Despite my earlier threat to tie him to Emri's leg and haul him into Zephrine, we'd had plenty of problems with the Mareritt and their magically leashed spies—

The thought ground to a halt. False memories. Implanted orders. Was that what had happened to me? Had I somehow been caught by the Mareritt and turned into some kind of weapon against my own people?

It certainly made just as much sense as anything else right now.

I ran a hand across my eyes, smearing sticky warmth. I swore softly and scrubbed the blood from my face with the sleeve of my undershirt. Then, in a probably futile effort to find some remnant of my true color, pushed it all the way up my arm. The skin to my elbow was white, but it changed to a murky cream past that, and then gradually became a darker shade near my shoulder. I hastily tugged the end of the shirt free from my pants and saw brown skin patched with splotches of lighter brown and cream.

"At least some of me retains the color I was born with," I muttered.

"Which to me suggests a medical problem rather than outside intervention." He rose and offered me his hand again. "We need to get moving."

I let him pull me upright. He didn't immediately release me; instead, his gaze scanned me critically before he said, "Are you all right?"

I couldn't help a somewhat bitter smile. "No, but I'm not going to collapse on you again."

"Good. Let's go get changed."

He stepped to one side and motioned me to proceed. I rather suspected he didn't really believe my statement that I wasn't about to faint—and that only made me wonder if the strength of Esan's fighting women had disappeared right along with the drakkons they rode. Maybe there were in fact no true kin left; if the Mareritt had gone after both kin and drakkons, I guessed it was possible, given it was only ever women who bonded with and rode the drakkons—a fact that had been true since the first ancestor had shared blood and fire with the drakkons and had forever bound her line to theirs.

And yet, Kaiden knew about the eye mote, so there had to be some kin blood left in this age.

Once back in the storeroom, I grabbed a medikit from the shelf and tended to the cut on my hand as well as the various other wounds scattered about my body. Then I shucked off my boots and stripped off my pants and tried to ignore the deepening sense of disbelief when I saw a similar gradient of color slipping up my legs from my toes. Once I'd pulled on the rough woolen pants, I reached for the knife, but before I could strap the sheath on, Kaiden said, "Don't."

I glanced at him, one eyebrow raised in query.

"Any sort of visible weaponry will get you arrested," he added.

I frowned. "So how did you attack the supply train if you didn't have weapons?"

"Even I'm not reckless enough to move into the occupied territory without access to guns." His amusement was evident in the creases that briefly touched the corners of his blue eyes. "We have caches and safe houses placed in strategic locations."

And no doubt those locations would be strategically

changed on a regular basis in an effort to prevent informants causing major damage to the supply depots.

I tucked the knife sheath into the waistband of my pants close to my spine, tightened the drawstring to ensure it stayed in place, and then tugged the shirt over the top to hide it.

Kaiden plucked a small tub from a shelf holding a number of hand tools and tossed it to me. "Use this on your hair."

I pried the lid open. The stuff inside was foul smelling and pitch-black. "What is it?"

"Grease. The smell will fade after a few hours."

"What is the point of staining my hair when my skin color gives the game away?"

"Black hair suggests a generational gap; quarter bloods are treated a little more kindly than half-bloods."

I grunted, scooped some up, and carefully applied it. He tossed me a towel to wipe the excess off and nodded in satisfaction at the result. "At least now you're not going to instantly alienate everyone."

His tone suggested that even with the staining, I wasn't going to be welcome in many establishments. I plucked a bedroll from the shelf, rolled my pants and jacket into it, and then tied it off and tossed it over my shoulder. Kaiden repeated the process to conceal the band we'd pried off Oma.

He must have sensed my curiosity, because he said, "We had no idea the bands were the means by which the Mareritt controlled the drakkons. Now that we *do* know, we might be able to find a means of disrupting the signal between the devices and the Mareritt. It could just give us the edge we've desperately needed."

"Then we'd better hope that if we're pulled over by a

Mareritt patrol, they don't think to inspect the maggoty-looking bedrolls."

"They generally don't." He reached for a backpack and tossed extra clothes and rations in it. "But if they do, we deal with it."

Meaning *I'd* deal with it, given he didn't take any of the weapons in the store, leaving us with only the one gun and the knife.

Once the storeroom had again been concealed and the footprints I'd left on the stove covered with more dust, we made our way across to the outbuilding that leaned precariously. Inside was a mess of cobwebs and nesting skites, their crimson and blue plumage the only bright spots in the gloom. There were a few old farm machines—most of them in rusted bits that looked unsalvageable—and a long, needle-nosed vehicle that sat on a couple of brown metal skids—hence the name, I suspected. A control unit was situated at its midpoint, and behind that a bench seat that obviously *wasn't* designed for two. A metal frame swept over the top of both, and probably supported the thick canvas bunched behind the seat. As vehicles went, it was pretty damn basic.

"You sure this thing is safe?" I asked, eyeing it rather dubiously.

His smile flashed, bright in the gloom. "Nope, but it's our only option, so climb aboard."

I sat astride, then pushed back to the rear of the bench to give Kaiden room. He handed me the backpack, then climbed on board. The whole machine settled lower. It was a tight fit—my legs were pressed either side of his, and my breasts were squashed against his back. It all felt a little too intimate for my liking.

I softly cleared my throat and said, "How is this thing powered?"

"With batteries that are charged at night via either sun panels or wind turbines."

"Is it going to be powerful enough to move the two of us?"

"Yes, although it won't be capable of its usual speed. But that may not be a bad thing, given slow movement is less likely to attract attention."

He pressed a button and the skid came to life; it might be battery powered, but it wasn't silent. Its rumbling filled the shed, and the skites rose as one, creating a feathery cloud of crimson and blue as they abandoned their nests and headed out of the building.

"Do you want the cover up?" Kaiden asked.

"Not unless it's necessary."

"Unless it rains, it won't be. But it means you'll have to hang on to me."

I was pretty sure my thighs—which were used to gripping the back of a drakkon—would keep me upright, but I nevertheless held his waist. The heat of him warmed my fingertips, even through the thick roughness of his shirt.

He carefully maneuvered the skid out of the shed and then through the yard. Once we were in the open field, he pushed the control stick all the way forward. The skid didn't exactly lurch forward, but it did rise up and increase its speed. Fractionally. What was possibly worse, however, were the vibrations that ran through the thing. When combined with Kaiden's closeness, it had a rather arousing effect.

Not something I wanted to be feeling, given the situation I'd fallen into and the fact that I knew so very little about him. Instinct might trust him, but he certainly didn't trust me. Not entirely, at any rate. And, despite the flashes of understanding that sometimes ran between us, he certainly hadn't seemed in any way attracted.

"Where are we headed?" I almost had to shout to be heard over the rush of wind and the racket the skid was making.

"Renton."

Vague memories of a pretty city made of soaring stone buildings and tree-lined streets rose. "You've people there?"

"Not as many as we once had. The Mareritt have had a good run of luck when it comes to ferreting out insurgents."

Suggesting, perhaps, they'd been getting insider help. No wonder he was so damn suspicious of me.

"How long will it take us to get there?"

"At this speed? It'll probably be nightfall."

"Won't the guards think that suspicious?"

"The Mareritt tend to think everything is suspicious these days—another pointer to them planning something big, in my opinion."

I frowned. "If they're planning to mobilize against Esan, wouldn't you have seen evidence of it by now?"

"Not if they're massing within the White Zone." He glanced around briefly. "And it's not as if we had any warning two hundred years ago, when the coruscations and subsequent ice storms were unleashed."

"We'd had more than enough warning to get the graces from both fortresses into the air to attack," I said. "Surely if they're planning something along those lines again, there'd be a similar warning time frame."

"Except we no longer control the skies—the Mareritt do."

"But the coruscations were huge—we spotted them the minute they entered Arleeon. Surely if they were creating more of them, you'd see them from beyond the boundaries of the White Zone?"

"The White Zone is a large area, so not necessarily."

I frowned. "Which begs the question, why haven't they created them before now? Why wait two hundred years to wipe out the last Arleeon city?"

"We don't know. And until we can somehow get more information from either our people close to the White Zone or from our scouting forays, we remain very much in the dark."

"I take it you're not just responsible for supply raids but also scouting forays?"

He glanced over his shoulder again, one dark eyebrow rising. "What makes you think that?"

"You have that air."

It was dryly said, and amusement twitched his lips. "I'd ask what sort of air that might be, but I'm a little afraid of the answer."

I snorted. "I very much doubt that."

His smile grew. "You think me incapable of fear?"

"No, because anyone with common sense knows fear is neither here nor there—it's how you *react* to it that matters. You, Kaiden, have reacted as any good leader should up to this point—with calm efficiency."

"Thank you for the compliment." He paused. "It sounds like you're familiar with leadership."

"I've never led anyone or anything." Unless it was into trouble—*that* I'd definitely been good at—and my sister had been very good at pulling me out of it. "I was considered a little too reckless for such a position. But my sister did."

"And your sister was?"

I hesitated, battling against the ice in an effort to remember her name. That I couldn't was troubling—why would I be able to remember that I had sisters and brothers but not remember the name of the one who'd been my commander? A woman who'd saved my life twice?

"You can't remember your own sister's name?" he said, that touch of disbelief riding his voice again.

"No." I hesitated again, half fearing how he'd react to the information I *could* supply given the anger that had washed through his voice earlier when he'd spoken of the woman who'd led the graces into the coruscations. "I *do* know she led the attack, though."

The surge of his contempt was so strong it almost felt like mine. And yet within that rush of fierce emotion came a flare of something far more undefined—something that almost walked the edge of hope.

"Sorrel? *She* was your sister?"

Sorrel. Once again, an image flashed through my mind, this time of the happy creases lining the corners of her eyes and the warm sound of her laughter as we drank mead after a particularly sweet victory over the Mareritt—one that had been meticulous and daring and planned entirely by her. Strategy and precision were her thing—always had been. So what had gone so desperately wrong at the coruscations?

"Yes—and if you're blaming her for an action the combined war council agreed to, then you're out of line."

His silence stretched for too many minutes, but his continued disbelief and anger surged around me, so sharp it felt like I was being wrapped in fire. Then he took a deep breath and that wave was gone, leaving nothing but empty neutrality. Which I wasn't sure I liked, because it gave me no idea as to where his thoughts and emotions were.

"If Sorrel *was* your sister, that means you're Nara. They were the only two members of the Velez line who were drakkon riders at the time."

I blinked. Another name that felt right, even if there was no immediate certainty stirring from behind the ice. "I take it from the edge in your voice that I've now been added to your hate list?"

"Given you didn't lead an unauthorized attack into the coruscations, no."

"That's not what—"

"It's what the reports made after the attack state happened."

"Then the reports are wrong."

"All joint council decisions were recorded as a matter of fact," he said. "There is no record of such a decision being made, by either Zephrine's council or ours."

"I was there, Kaiden. I don't know why your records show otherwise, but trust me, it was a joint decision. Why else would Esan's graces abandon their posts?"

Though I couldn't see his skepticism, I felt it. "Because Sorrel was apparently a charismatic and powerful leader."

That was true enough. Even if she hadn't been my sister, I would have followed her into the deepest depths of the underworld itself—and, from the looks of things, probably had. Or at least the Mareritt's icy version of it.

"No one could have convinced Esan's graces to abandon their posts to follow an unapproved mission," I bit back. "You do your ancestors a great disservice by even *thinking* that."

He grunted. It was difficult to say whether he agreed on that point or not. Silence fell, but this time I was in no mood to break it. Until we found a reader to either prove or disprove my memories, there was little point. But at least now I had a name—Nara. Whether it was mine or not, I'd soon find out, but in the meantime, I certainly intended to use it.

It was late afternoon by the time the first signs we were approaching a major city appeared. Houses dotted the fields around us, gradually growing in number. There were no lights visible in any of them, however, which suggested they'd been abandoned. Either that or the Mareritt had cut their power—a task I would have thought difficult given that even in my time, power for regional areas was provided via individually owned wind generators and sun collection panels. It was usually only the major cities that were connected to the grid—a system that used a mix of sun generation, wind power, and energy drawn from the earth itself.

Our rough roadway soon joined a wider, better-kept one. The dust blooming around the skids fell away and the ride smoothed out. Our speed didn't increase, however. I suspected the old vehicle had nothing more to give.

The sky was a riot of orange and gold and the chill of the oncoming night beginning to bite by the time we neared Renton—a vast city whose stone buildings shone a deep green in the fading brilliance of the day. Aside from them, Renton seemed an otherwise drab city. Gone were the trees and the brightly colored flags that had once topped many of the buildings here. Maybe the Mareritt had ordered them cleared—it'd be the sort of move they'd make to cow or break the people they were trying to control.

But perhaps the most gut-wrenching sight of all was the metal towers that dominated the city's outer ring and cast deep shadows over all the houses. Guard platforms and guns topped three of those towers, but the fourth strangely empty.

It wasn't hard to guess why.

"Where's the drakkon that usually guards this city?" I

asked. "We haven't sighted her at all during the day, which is odd considering how close Renton is to Break Point."

Kaiden shrugged. "Perhaps two fugitive farmhands aren't worth the trouble of unleashing a drakkon."

"If that was the case, she'd still be here. Besides, I seriously doubt they still believe we're farmhands, given the efficiency we showed with guns and the means by which we escaped."

Not to mention my use of fire—that alone should have had them scrambling after us, given kin were all but dead in this time.

"Except the drakkons usually do a final patrol before the night sets in."

Which made it even odder that they hadn't set her flight zone to target the area between the pass and here. "Why don't the drakkons patrol at night? They're not night blind, are they?"

"As far as we're aware, no." He shrugged. "With travel restrictions and the difficulties involved in moving from one town to another, the general population mostly stays put. And that, in turn, means there's little cause for night patrols unless there's been a major problem."

"Is that why you timed our arrival for dusk?"

His smile was something I felt rather than saw—a heat that swirled deep within. "Not deliberately—I had no control over the vehicle left at the farmhouse, remember."

Our speed increased fractionally as we continued down the hill toward Renton, and the old vehicle shook violently. The noise was so bad that half of Renton probably heard our approach. Hopefully it'd make the Mareritt less suspicious of us—after all, why would fugitives make so much damn noise?

Kaiden slowed the skid as we drew closer to the city.

Lights were now visible in many of the taller buildings, but those in the outer ring remained in shadows.

"Is there a problem with the electricity supply here?"

"Only in that all citizens have set weekly allocations and tend to reserve it for cooking, heating, and other necessities rather than lights."

"I would have thought light to be a necessity."

"Many in the outer circles use candles—they're cheap to make and easy to replace."

I snorted. "Candles went out with the dark ages."

"And the dark ages came charging back the day the Mareritt took over."

"But wouldn't it be easier to control the population if they ensured living conditions were at a comfortable standard?"

"As I've said before, the Mareritt don't think like the rest of us. And they certainly don't care about Arleeon's population other than what use they are in the fields, mines, and factories."

I frowned. "Factories?"

He nodded. "Huge buildings in which they process meats, fish, grains, and vegetables for transport back into Mareritten."

"So they're basically stripping Arleeon of its resources?"

"Indeed."

"If they've been bleeding us dry for hundreds of years without proper soil management, it's a wonder the entire continent isn't barren."

"At least 45 percent of occupied Arleeon *is* on the cusp of being irredeemable." His voice was grim. "I suspect that's what's behind the recent reports of unknown activity in the White Zone. Esan still controls a third of Arleeon, and they want our wealth of soil and minerals."

There was movement on the tower closest to the road we were using, and a heartbeat later, light speared through the gathering dusk and spotlighted us.

I pulled the hood over my head, then raised a hand to protect my eyes against the brightness. A metal box slowly descended from the top of the platform to the small building at its base.

"We'll be stopped by guards up ahead," Kaiden said softly. "Let me do the talking."

"Given I'd rather kill the bastards than talk to them, that's probably a good idea."

He snorted softly. "Trust me, it's a desire I share but one that's not practical in this situation. Say or do nothing that'll raise suspicion."

"I'm not stupid, Kaiden."

"I know you're not. But I also witnessed your battle for control when we left that pod in Break Point, and I'm well aware just how close to the wire it was."

Which suggested he was reading me as well as I was reading him.

The metal box disappeared into the building at the base of the tower, and several seconds later, a doorway opened and two men appeared. Their guns were held loosely by their sides, suggesting they weren't really expecting trouble —although the large gun atop of the tower continued tracking our progress and would no doubt do a whole lot more damage than the ones either guard carried.

The oldest of the two stepped into the middle of the road and held up a hand. The other stayed to one side, one arm resting casually on the barrel of his rifle.

Kaiden stopped. "Is there a problem, officer?"

"There's a curfew currently active in Renton," came the gruff reply. "Why are you out?"

"Sorry, we came up from Hornton to visit a friend and weren't advised of the curfew." The deep rumble of authority had left Kaiden's voice; in its place was a high note of both nervousness and contrition. The man could act. "I'd planned to be here by midafternoon, but the skid is having engine problems."

The Mareritt grunted, his gaze moving past Kaiden and catching mine. I bit down on my lip and lowered my head, hoping he took it for nerves rather than an attempt to control the flames stirring within.

"Name and address of your friend?"

Kaiden provided both and then said, "He said he'd notify the appropriate authorities about our arrival if it looked like we were going to be late."

"Ren? Check it."

The other Mareritt spun and walked back into the building at the base of the tower. After a few seconds he returned, this time holding some kind of flat tablet. "You Kai Jenkins and spouse?"

"Yes, officer."

The Mareritt grunted and held the tablet out to Kaiden. "Thumbprint."

Kaiden dutifully pressed his thumb onto the screen. There was a flare of light, and after a pause, a green light flashed. "Approval given."

The man in front of us stepped to one side. "Hurry on up and get inside. No movement until the morning or you'll be incarcerated."

"Thank you, officer." Again, Kaiden's voice held just the right mix of contrition and relief.

It drew a contemptuous smirk from both soldiers and had me clenching and unclenching my fists. Thankfully, they weren't paying me any attention.

Kaiden carefully drove around them and continued on up the street. I resisted the urge to look back and concentrated on calming the inner fires. The slightest spark right now would not only give the game away but also unleash the tower gun that still tracked our movements.

The rumble of the skid's engine echoed through the narrow street. Ramshackle houses lined either side, their front doors almost within touching distance. There was little noise or light coming from any of them, but there *was* life—curtains twitched, indicating we were being watched. At the midway point between the tower behind and the one ahead, Kaiden turned left and pulled into an old lean-to attached to a small building. Like all the others we'd passed, it was little wider than the door and the two small windows that sat either side of it. An old brick chimney dominated the lean-to end of the building and at least meant we could take the chill out of the air once we got inside. If, of course, the people here were allowed firewood or coal.

Kaiden switched the engine off, and the vehicle settled back onto its skids. "We're here."

"So I see." I eyed the multitude of barely patched holes littering either side of the chimney. If we couldn't get the fire going, it was going to be a cold night. "Will your friend be home? It sounds rather quiet inside."

"It does." Kaiden climbed off and then pulled a long cord from off the wall. After opening the front of the vehicle, he pressed the cord onto some sort of control unit attached to several rows of thin batteries and then flicked a switch. A light on the unit began to blink orange.

With that done, he turned and offered me a hand. He pulled me upright, then nodded toward the rear of the lean-to. After a moment, I saw the gleam of metal. Not a camera this time but a simple listening device. They really *didn't* trust anyone.

I nodded and concentrated on keeping upright. My legs were stiff and sore after being held in the one position for so long, and my back was aching something fierce. I needed painkillers, and the sooner the better.

"Brock did say he'd go visit a lover if we didn't arrive on time," he said, "so it's possible he's staying the night and giving us some privacy."

He didn't release my hand. Instead, he guided me to the front of the house. The door wasn't locked; Kaiden pushed it open, then stepped to one side and ushered me in.

The moonlight filtering through the somewhat grimy windows provided enough light to see the interior was as basic as the exterior. The main room held a kitchen and a small living area, while to the right there was a bedroom, and directly opposite the front door was another lean-to that contained basic bathing and privy facilities. Furniture consisted of little more than a table with a couple of chairs, a number of old cloudsaks —large, wool-filled leather bags that were roughly sewn into the shape of a chair—and a double bed. Rather weirdly, despite the fact someone had to be living here on a part-time basis to give credence to Kaiden's story, there was very little evidence of it. Certainly there was nothing in the way of the personal items or adornments that usually crept into any home.

The old fireplace dominated the left wall and would have provided enough heat to warm ten rooms rather than the three here. There was no kindling set in the hearth, but there were at least a few scraps of both wood and coal in the nearby box. It mightn't last more than a few hours, but it would at least take away the worst of the night's bite.

Kaiden closed and locked the door, then moved across

to the table. On it was a small candle, a box of strikes, and a note. He picked up the strikes, ran one stick against the rough edge to set the tip alight, and lit the candle. I could have very easily done it for him had he but asked, but it was possible the device out in the lean-to wasn't the only one in this place.

The pale light from the candle danced through the darkness, highlighting the dust and the cobwebs. Kaiden didn't immediately pick up the note. Instead, he dumped the sleeping roll and backpack on the table, then moved across to the small kitchen area. After pulling a pot out of the cupboard under the sink, he filled it with water, then put it on the small cooker and hit two switches. A warm glow immediately appeared under the pot.

"Right," he said. "I've just activated the ambient noise generator. It should stop the device outside hearing little more than the murmur of voices."

"Won't that raise their suspicions?"

"No, as most people simply whisper when needed."

"I'm surprised they haven't placed them inside homes, then."

"They did, initially, but it provided them with no benefit because people resorted to using hand signals."

I crossed my arms against the increasing bite in the air. "Does anyone actually live here? Because it really doesn't look like it."

"They do when it's not required as a safe house." He moved back to the table and picked up the note, quickly unfolding it and then leaning closer to the candle to read it. "Lindale, a reader who's affiliated with the resistance, will be here in the morning."

"What time is the curfew lifted?"

"Probably with dawn—too many living in the inner three circles rely on Arleeon labor."

"Is it just the Mareritt who live there?"

"No. There's also a few hybrid serfs and some Arleeons who've switched allegiance in order to get ahead." The grim note in his voice did not bode well for these traitorous souls should the Mareritt ever be driven from our lands. He motioned toward the back lean-to. "Facilities are basic, but the shower works if you want to clean up while I make us a meal."

"I will. Thanks."

I dumped the sleeping roll and knife on the table beside his stuff and moved into the bathroom. Facilities-wise, there was a privy, a basin, and a shower that looked almost old enough to have come from my era. There was also a stack of old but clean towels sitting on the shelf above the basin, along with several bars of unused soap that smelled faintly of lemongrass. I stripped off, turned on the shower, and stepped under the water. It was surprisingly hot and made me long for a bath so I could fully soak my aching body.

Once I'd washed both my underclothes and me, I pulled on the shirt and trousers and headed out. The fire had been lit, warming the air and lending additional light to the small room. "I hope you're not offended by the sight of ladies' undergarments hanging about."

He motioned me to the newly cleared table. "I've got five younger sisters, so hardly."

"Are any of them kin?"

He shrugged. "Three have the mote but certainly not the fire."

I frowned. "How old are they? Because the blood heat doesn't really appear until bonding time, and that's usually after puberty."

"If there are no drakkons to bond with, there is no heat."

My confusion grew. "Whether or not there are drakkons to bond with shouldn't matter. The blood heat runs through the first ancestor's line; it had nothing to do with the drakkons."

"Except that when the drakkon and kin were erased by the coruscations—"

"They can't have been erased," I cut in. "The fact I'm here proves that."

"Just because you somehow survived doesn't mean others did."

His disbelief remained apparent—and maybe that wouldn't change even after Lindale either confirmed or denied my story. But then, who could blame him? I was having a hard time accepting the situation, and I was the one who'd been thrown two hundred years into the future. I waved him on.

"Only the very young and the infirm remained. It not only weakened the bloodline but left few to teach." He placed the pot on the table; inside was what looked to be a vegetable soup into which he'd broken pieces of the dried meat. "It's reconstituted, but it doesn't taste too bad, considering."

I sat down opposite him, scooped some soup into a bowl, and tried it. Declaring the concoction "not too bad" might have been pushing it, but it was at least edible. "If Esan is still free, why haven't more of Arleeon's folk fled there?"

He shrugged. "For many, it's impractical—they've kids or family they can't move for one reason or another. Or the journey is too far or too dangerous. The Mareritt patrol the Grand Alkan River—which is now the border between occupied lands and free—and any escapees they catch are dealt with harshly."

I munched on a chewy bit of meat for a minute. "But if Esan also patrols, why don't they come to the aid of those in trouble?"

"We do, but the border wall runs the full length of the river, and while we patrol at regular intervals, it's almost impossible to save everyone who flees. Many no longer even try to do so."

"I guess after two hundred years of occupation, there's little point."

"There is *always* a point." His expression was suddenly fierce. "This is *our* land, not theirs. We *have* to keep fighting the ice scum until they're driven out of Arleeon or there's none of us left to fight."

And he'd already admitted the latter was a closer eventuality than the former.

I finished the first bowl and helped myself to a second. And would have taken a third except for the fact that there was little enough left for Kaiden if he wanted another. I leaned back in the chair and rubbed my eyes wearily. The ache was still there, but the soup and the relative quiet had at least eased it to a background murmur.

"What happens when Lindale clears me?" I asked.

"Perhaps you should ask what happens if she *doesn't.*"

I opened my eyes and studied him. His expression once again gave little away but that odd connection between us flared enough to suggest that while he didn't believe me, he didn't entirely disbelieve, either. At the very least, he didn't think I was working for the Mareritt, and that was an improvement.

"I presume an attempt at incarceration and interrogation would follow."

"Attempt? If Lindale believes you are, in any way, a threat to either of us or the resistance, your mind will be rendered inert so fast you won't have time to draw breath, let alone fire."

I smiled. It wasn't a pleasant sort of smile, and his eyes narrowed. "There *is* nothing faster than the instinctive rush of protective fire, so I'd advise her against trying that, if I were you. Unless, of course, she fancies being crisped."

Something very deadly entered his expression. "You'd kill an innocent person?"

"She's hardly innocent if she's attempting to fry my brain." I met his gaze evenly. "I *will* find out what has happened to me, Kaiden, and if that means going through Lindale or you or a thousand damn Mareritt to do so, then I will."

He studied me for a few seconds longer, then rose, collected the bowls, and moved over to the sink. After washing up, he set a kettle on the stove and reached into a cupboard, drew out a small medikit, then tossed it over. "You'll find painkillers inside."

"Thanks." I was a little surprised by his thoughtfulness, given the anger I could still sense. I found the tablets and swallowed them dry.

Once the kettle had boiled, he made two cups of what smelled like shamoke—a somewhat bitter brown bean that, when crushed and mixed with cane crystals, made a surprisingly pleasant hot drink—and brought them over, placing one in front of me before resuming his position.

The anger, I noted, had gone. Or, at the very least, had been fully leashed.

"If you *are* deemed to be telling the truth," he said in a voice so even it was as if the whole other conversation hadn't happened, "then we have two choices—we either go back to Esan and report in, or we try to find how and why you escaped the coruscations."

"And whether there might be others like me." Others like my sister and Emri—surely I couldn't have been the only one to have survived.

"If there'd been others like you, we would have heard about it."

"I can't believe I'm the only one to have escaped. That makes no sense at all."

"Red, *none* of this makes sense."

That was an undeniable truth. "Do the coruscations still exist?"

"The larger one does."

"Meaning they might still be frozen."

"If they are, I have no idea how we'll correct that situation without killing them."

"There has to be a way—I came out of the coruscation alive, so it's definitely possible."

"And things would be a whole lot easier if you could just remember how that all happened."

Another undeniable truth. "What happened to the other coruscation?"

"We think it simply melted away."

I stared at him for a moment, my throat suddenly dry. *No,* I thought. *That isn't possible.*

And yet, it made perfectly good sense, given that in this time, the larger drakkons had disappeared, the Mareritt controlled Zephrine's aerie, and the abilities of those who were kin had all but been forgotten.

If the coruscation *had* melted—or otherwise disappeared—then it could only mean one thing.

I might be the only true kin left in Arleeon.

FIVE

I gulped down the shamoke, burning my throat in the process, and somehow croaked, "The coruscations are *magic*. Magic doesn't melt."

But even as I said that, I remembered again the utter cold that had hit Emri and me. It had not only encased us but had also frozen any ability to move. What happened after that—or how I'd gotten from there to here—I had no idea, thanks to the ice still holding my memories captive. But if we *had* been part of the attack force—and I refused to believe we weren't—then surely it meant others *must* have survived the cold and the time that had passed. Neither Emri nor I had been the biggest or strongest of those who flew with my sister that day. In fact, aside from a number of my friends, we were probably the *youngest* amongst the three graces she'd led.

Which meant there very definitely could be others out there... so why hadn't anyone seen them? Drakkons weren't something you could hide very easily—or at least the full-size ones weren't.

"We actually think the coruscations are a combination

of both," Kaiden said. "The larger one remains in West Laminium, but a lake now sits under it."

Meaning the coruscations hadn't really moved since we'd attacked them—and the lake could explain my wet uniform. "I take it this lake formed as the smaller coruscation melted?"

He nodded. "If there *had* been kin and drakkon trapped inside, they would have been spotted floating on top of the water. But there've been no such sightings."

"Would there be though, given the area is controlled by Mareritt?"

Once again his smile held little humor. "They may control the area, but we patrol it, under various guises. The coruscations have caused enough grief—we have no option but to keep eyes on the one that remains."

So if no other drakkons or kin had appeared as the smaller coruscation melted, what had happened to them?

Was it possible, perhaps, that the freezing had not only included motion but also flesh? Had we simply been frozen —become nothing more than ice within ice—and then left to melt away along with the spheres?

It was an idea that filled me with utter horror—and one I refused to believe. After all, if that *were* the case, why was I here?

And given I *was*, surely that meant it was possible for everyone else to have survived as well.

Kaiden shrugged. "If the reader can uncover what has happened to you, then maybe we'll find out what happened to the others."

If there were others. The unspoken words seemed to hover in the air.

I took another drink. Despite its heat, it didn't do much to warm the chill gathering within. The fact was, if the ice in my mind *was* part of the magic that had consumed both kin and drakkon whole, then what were the chances of a reader getting past it?

And what if that magic was somehow still active? It was possible, given a coruscation still survived. What if in trying to get past it, she somehow triggered it?

I tried to ignore the pulse of foreboding and said, "Once she does the reading, I'll need to get to West Laminium. If you could at least give me a map of the areas I'll have to avoid—"

"Red, if you *are* who you say you are, do you really think I'm going to let you go anywhere without guidance—specifically, *my* guidance?" His tone held the slightest hint of amusement, despite the seriousness in his eyes. "If there *are* other remnants of the old graces and kin in that area, we need to get to them, and fast."

"On that we at least agree." But given I'd been picked up by a Mareritt patrol, what were the odds of any others escaping such a fate? I had to get to the coruscation, had to find out what had happened to my sister—not only because she might be the only family I had left, but because her military nous might be the difference between saving Arleeon and losing it. "And I guess you *are* a better option than a map. At least you can hold a conversation—when you're not coming over all grumpy, that is."

He snorted softly and drained his cup. "We'd best grab some sleep, because no matter what the outcome tomorrow, we have a long day ahead of us. Unfortunately, there's only the one bed, so I'll bunk down—"

"I'm not about to jump the bones of someone who doesn't fully trust me," I said mildly.

He raised a dark eyebrow, amusement evident. "Does that mean you *will* jump me once I do?"

I pursed my lips and let my gaze sweep across his shoulders and chest. They were, it had to be said, perfectly proportioned. "Perhaps. Perhaps not. I tend to be rather choosy about my partners, and you, warrior, have not fully proven your worth as yet."

The amusement got stronger. "I hauled your butt out of Break Point Pass *and* gave way to your insane desire to free that drakkon. I think that speaks *volumes* about my character."

"And I think it speaks more to the fact that A, you had no other choice, and B, you didn't want to lose someone who'd revealed she had a very handy weapon at her fingertips."

"Also possible." He grinned and rose. "I apologize in advance for any untoward and unintended attention you might get from certain portions of my body during the night."

"Apology accepted. But if you snore, expect to find yourself on the floor."

He laughed, a warm, rich sound that stirred the embers of desire. "I'll go have a shower and give you a little privacy to get into bed."

"Privacy isn't necessary, but if I'm sharing a bed with you, clean-smelling skin is."

He laughed again and headed into the bathroom. I finished the shamoke and then headed into the bedroom, stripping off before climbing into the bed. He joined me ten minutes later, his body warm and the heady scent of his masculinity filling my nostrils. But desire had little hope against the tide of weariness.

Thankfully, the man didn't snore.

I did wake at some point during the night to find his body tucked close and the heat of his erection pressing against my buttocks. But, stranger or no, I didn't really mind. If nothing else, it proved the man wasn't made of ice.

And that, no matter what had happened to me, neither was I.

Lindale was a short, stout woman with a heavily lined face and a mane of hair that ran like a silver waterfall down her back.

She motioned me to sit at the table, then claimed the seat opposite. Her gaze was wary, no doubt due to the fact that I looked like a half-blood. "You know how this works?"

I nodded. "You take my hand and invade my mind."

She made a sharp clucking sound. "Invade is such a crude word for what we do."

"But still the truth."

She didn't refute it. "You just need to relax. You'll feel a slight pressure within your thoughts and memories—that'll be me. It shouldn't hurt or cause you any sort of distress, but if does, squeeze my fingers immediately."

I nodded again. While I hadn't been the subject of a reading before now, I knew well enough how they worked. I'd seen enough Mareritt captives being read over the years, although they'd never reacted well to the process. Of course, *that* was no doubt due to the fact the readers had never tried to take it easy on them.

Lindale held out her hands. I placed mine in hers and watched her face. For several seconds, nothing happened; then, gradually, awareness left her brown eyes. A heartbeat later, the pressure began. Gently at first, then with increasing force.

I closed my eyes and concentrated on not reacting. But

it was a rather weird sensation, having someone else's mind in mine, knowing she was rifling through my thoughts and memories and completely unable to do anything about it.

The pressure intensified. My head began to ache, and heat flared within, a force determined to protect. I held it at bay, knowing from watching Mareritt interrogations that forcing her out before she was ready could have disastrous consequences for us both.

Deeper still she dove, until she finally hit the ice. She didn't break it. Didn't get past it. She never got the chance. At her first touch, energy surged; that energy wasn't my fires, but something else. Something that was cold, dark, and *old*.

It exploded through me, through her, tearing her mind from mine and blasting us apart.

I tumbled backward and hit the floor hard. Breath whooshed from my lungs, and for several minutes, I didn't move. I *couldn't* move. I could barely even breathe. Everything was black. Everything was silent. Everything except the vicious drumbeat echoing through my brain.

Fear surged, and fire flickered across my fingertips, a heat I felt rather than saw. I clenched my fist, pushed down the fear, and concentrated on my breathing rather than panicking over what that explosion might mean.

Gradually, the blackness cleared, and the ache in my head retreated. But the ice remained. Untouched. Unaltered.

Terrifying.

I swallowed to ease the dryness in my throat and forced my eyes open. Kaiden was on the other side of the table, kneeling beside Lindale.

"Is she all right?" I croaked.

His head snapped around. Distrust and anger gleamed

in his blue eyes. "Why in the wind's name did you attack her like that? I thought you wanted answers?"

"I do, but—"

"Then why blast her away? What are you trying to hide?"

"Nothing!" I sucked in a breath in a vague effort to calm down. "I'm not sure what happened, but that blast wasn't me, Kaiden. You have to believe that."

He stared at me for several seconds, then rose, got a blanket from the bed, and wrapped it around Lindale. His disbelief hung heavily in the air, and I couldn't really blame him. In his shoes, I'd be wary of me, too.

I sucked in another breath, then pushed upright and hugged my knees close. Fear continued to pound through me, as rapid as the beat of my heart. But I didn't want to think about what had happened—or what it might mean.

Lindale's face was pale, and both the tip of her nose and the tops of her ears were red—it very much looked like she'd been frostbitten. *Ice magic*, a voice inside whispered. *Coruscation magic*. I shivered despite the fires that raged inside.

After a few more seconds, her eyes flickered open and she groaned softly. "It feels like I've been hit by a ton of ice."

Ice, not fire. Another indicator the surge had been magical and icy in nature.

"You were torn from Red's mind. Keep still until I can get a medic—"

"I don't need a medic. I'm fine, if cold. Help me up."

Somewhat reluctantly, he did. Lindale studied me, her gaze an odd mix of uncertainty, distrust, and hope. "Do you remember what happened?"

"You tried to probe the ice."

"That ice is some form of magic—but old magic, not new."

"Meaning what?" Kaiden's question was sharp. Terse.

"It means that while there's no sign of mental interference and no indication of false memories, a portion of her brain is locked behind a wall of ice-based magic." She ran a somewhat shaky hand through her long hair, her fingertips as red as her nose. "By all accounts, she *is* who she says she is; two hundred years ago, she was part of the force that flew into the coruscations. There is no memory after that—nothing until she wakes in the pod with you. Those memories may be locked behind the barrier; whether that is something we should be worried about or not, I can't say."

"Meaning she could be a Mareritt spy?"

Lindale hesitated. "It's always a possibility, but personally, I doubt it. I'm not sure what that ice is or why it's there, but the memories that *do* exist hold no falsehood."

"Could the ice be part of whatever magic the coruscation was made out of?" I said.

"Possibly. It certainly has the taint of Mareritt magic."

"So you've come across magically altered minds before?"

"Yes, but none of them had the feel of the magic that lives within you. It's very old, and yet it remains active. *Why* is a question I can't answer." She hugged the blanket a little tighter around her body. "Kai, do you want me to make a report to your father?"

He nodded. "Let him know we're headed back to the Talien farmlands."

Lindale frowned. "Why there?"

"That's where Red was found, so it makes sense to go back and check if any others have appeared."

"I'll pass it on, but I suspect your father won't be pleased."

"He never is." It was flatly said and suggested there was a history of tension between father and son.

"Ah, well, you know I'm not one to comment on private family matters, but you both need to pull your heads in."

Kaiden's expression was somewhat wry. "So much for not commenting."

She patted his arm. "Whatever you do next, be careful."

Of me. Of what I might do. She didn't actually say that, but she didn't need to.

Once she'd left, I said, "For your own safety, it's probably better if—"

"No." It was sharply said. "Until we know the truth of what has happened to you, I'm going nowhere."

"You heard what Lindale said—"

"Whatever magic lies in your mind doesn't negate the fact that there's no lie in what you *do* remember. You *are* who claim to be, and that fact raises the possibility that others might have also survived." He moved into the kitchen. "That being the case, we continue on as planned."

The determined note in his voice suggested there was no arguing with him. And really, I didn't want to. For all my bluster about going on alone, I didn't know enough about this time to move anywhere without running a huge risk of being caught.

And yet, a greater risk might lie within me.

"Kai, if the ice in my mind takes over, if I start acting strangely or become a threat..." I let the sentence trail off.

"Have no fear in that regard." He glanced over, his smile oddly comforting. "But know also that I won't act against you until I'm absolutely positive there is no other choice."

"That could put your life—and others—at risk."

"Perhaps. But acting rashly is what got us into this mess. I'm not about to repeat the mistakes of the past."

Attacking the coruscations wasn't a mistake, but there was little point in arguing. We would never see eye to eye on it simply because we viewed the attack from very different angles—and times. "Why did you lie to Lindale about where we're headed?"

"For safety. We think at least some of our transmissions are being monitored, which could account for the number of missions that have gone wrong of late."

Meaning if the Mareritt *did* go hunting for us in Talien, we'd at least have some breathing space. "If you were made aware of that possibility, why did the attack on the supply train proceed?"

"It wasn't supposed to—my father had ordered us to stand down when we were advised of the possibility."

"Then why didn't you?"

"Because there's been a red fever outbreak in Esan and we desperately needed the medical supplies the train was supposedly carrying."

I frowned. "Red fever usually only happens when the food or water has been contaminated."

"Yes, and we believe it came from a shipment of infected food inadvertently brought in." He grimaced. "By the time anyone realized what had happened, it was already too late. We've run out of drugs, and the healers can't fix a bacterial infection."

"You springing what was obviously a trap wouldn't have helped anyone."

"I thought the risk was worth it." He half shrugged. "But at least we spotted them before it was too late."

"For the majority," I noted. "You were caught."

"Deliberately. It gave the others time to escape."

I raised an eyebrow. "I wouldn't have taken you for a martyr."

He walked back with a knot of bread, a thick slab of cheese, and a serrated knife. "I'm not, but it was my stubbornness that got those men into that situation. I had no choice but to get them out."

He had plenty of other choices, but he'd chosen the most honorable, if foolish, one. A man after my own heart.

"Why didn't the Mareritt kill you on the spot, then?"

"They were probably taking me back to either Break Point or Frio for interrogation."

Given I'd been chained to him, did that mean I was also being transported there for interrogation? Or was I simply being sent to the Tendra flesh markets with the other women—an action that suggested they didn't know what I was, despite the fact I'd been wearing a kin uniform?

He grimaced and added, "Of course, I'm now hoping our people there don't pay the price for our escape."

"Wouldn't Lindale—or whoever manages communications here—have been advised if that were the case?"

He cut thick slices of bread and cheese. "Communications can be hit and miss—we're using the old comms system in the occupied territories rather than tapping into the Mareritt's. Maintenance, as you can imagine, is a trifle hard."

I picked up a thick slab of bread and cheese; both were surprisingly fresh. "How long is it going to take us to get to West Laminium?"

"On the skid? Probably about five days."

"We can't swap it for something faster?"

"Anything faster will attract too much attention. It's going to be dangerous enough moving from town to town."

"So why don't we just avoid towns?"

"Because we'll have to leave a forwarding address when we leave Renton."

I frowned. "Surely the Mareritt don't have the time or manpower to monitor the movements of all Arleeon's people?"

"They don't, simply because most don't travel."

"Then how are you getting away with it?"

His smile flashed. "I'm listed as a bladesmith—it's one of the few crafts that can move around with relative impunity, thanks to the scarcity of the skill amongst the Mareritt."

My frown deepened. "Why, when from what I've seen, no one even uses knives or swords anymore?"

"They're used for ceremonial purposes." He paused, and something cold entered his expression. "And for executions."

It made me wonder who he'd lost—someone close, that much was evident. If the anger tainting the air was anything to go by, he held himself at least partly responsible for that death. My gaze went to the scar on his neck, and I wondered if he'd gained it in the battle that had resulted in the execution of someone he cared about.

"Which still doesn't explain why they don't use their own smiths," I said. "I would have thought bladesmiths would be the one trade they *wouldn't* allow to roam the countryside willy-nilly."

"One man—or even a hundred—armed with a sword and knife isn't going to do much damage to a foe armed with guns." He shrugged. "The Mareritt are skilled workers of stone, and their mages can manipulate earth with their magic and cause the air to freeze, but they've never shown any capacity for smithing silver or metal."

"And yet they have tanks and guns, so they're not totally unfamiliar with the substance."

"The tanks and—for the most part—the guns are imported, not made."

My gaze briefly dropped to the muscular arms that had held me so gently last night. "Can you actually smith?"

"I'm proficient enough for the purposes of this identity."

"Is that identity the reason why your people at Break Point risked getting you out?"

He nodded. "While my fake ID holds up under normal scrutiny, full interrogation would have revealed the truth. Kai Jenkins has been too useful to waste him in such a manner."

"And yet by getting you out, haven't they all but destroyed that identity anyway?"

"No, because they never scanned for IDs before they placed us into the prison pod."

"That makes no sense."

"As I said, the Mareritt do a lot of things that make no sense." He shrugged. "A lot of it comes from the confidence of ruling over a foe that has shown little more than a fading spark of fight."

I reached for another slab of bread and cheese. "I gather you spend a lot of time in Esan, so how do you explain your alter ego going missing for long periods of time?"

"The Mareritt only check IDs coming in and out of official gateways. We have a few nonofficial ones we use."

"They don't perform random ID checks of the local population?"

He shook his head. "They couldn't care less about our movements within the towns—not as long as we're obeying the local rules."

"So what's our next port of call?"

"Husk." He must have seen my frown, because he added, "It's a small town that's been built around the fish farming complexes. It sits on the border between Argon and Nyssia."

"Even if they fear the sea, they control the ports, don't they? Why wouldn't they use Arleeon labor to run sea boats rather than set up new fishing avenues inland? Isn't that a waste of resources and time?"

"Not from the Mareritt point of view." He gathered the rest of the bread and cheese and then rose. "Their fear of the sea has for centuries forced them to import fish."

"Which doesn't explain why they simply didn't set up farms in their own land." Or why they didn't even *try* trading with us rather than go the conquering route.

"*That* is a question I can't answer. We depart in ten."

It didn't take us that long to clean up and leave. The drakkon, I noted, was back on her perch. Her scales were afire in the daylight, and her gaze was centered on something distant rather than the movement beneath her. But her tail flicked back and forth, suggesting agitation even if there was no sign of it in her expression or eyes.

Again, the urge to reach out rose, and again I battered it down. She wore the same silver band as Oma; until it was removed, or until Kaiden's people found a way of disrupting the signal between her Mareritt controller and that band, there was little point.

We were stopped at the exit on the opposite side of the city. Kaiden advised them of our destination, was signed out, and was told he had to be in Husk by nightfall. Once the Mareritt stepped aside, Kaiden gunned the skid and we headed out, following a road that cut through the barren countryside in a long, straight line.

Once we were far enough away from Renton, I leaned forward and said, "Why have they never asked for my ID?"

"Because we listed you as my spouse."

"Meaning what? That as a spouse, I neither provide a threat nor have need of an identity?"

"If you had Arleeon coloring, you'd be both registered and checked. But even with your hair stained black, you obviously have Mareritt in your background." He half shrugged. "As I said, half-bloods and, to a lesser extent, those with a quarter or less Mareritt blood, are not well tolerated by either race."

"So if I wasn't accompanied by you..."

"You most likely would have been arrested."

"And after that?"

He hesitated. "It would depend on the mood of the magistrate, but many are forced to spy on their own people."

Which was why he'd thought me one of them. "And those who don't or won't agree?"

He shrugged. "Most are shipped off to the manufacturing units, but there are a rare few who are sterilized to serve as trulls to the Mareritt hierarchy."

"Why would they bother, given what you said about them hating half-bloods?" I asked. "They rule a good portion of Arleeon—why wouldn't they just bring their own women here?"

"Because none have acclimatized. Most spend three months here and are rotated back."

"After two hundred years of occupation, at least *some* of them should have become used to our warmer clime. Mareritten does have a three-month season of summer, so heat isn't unknown to them."

"Their summers are nowhere near as warm as ours."

"We're still talking about two hundred years. Surely that's more than enough time—"

"*If* they were so inclined. They are not."

115

"What of the women in the pod? If Arleeon women so disgust them, why were they raped?"

"For the same reason the men were beaten—it's a means of both cowing and punishing them."

Which only inflamed the fires of rage anew and made me even more determined to free Arleeon from the murderous grip of the Mareritt.

"And Arleeon's trading partners?" I asked. "Were they ever asked for help?"

Though I couldn't see the grimness of his smile, I felt it. It stabbed through me as sharp as any knife, and it made me wonder yet again why we seemed so in tune despite the fact we were strangers.

And strangers from two very different times, at that.

"Yes, but those who traded with us also traded with Mareritten. They don't care who they deal with, as long as the supply lines are kept open."

"But surely if you explained the situation..." My voice faded. If anyone were going to come to Arleeon's aid, they would have done so in those first few vital months after Zephrine had fallen. But I knew enough about both Cannamore's kings and our other trading partners to understand they wouldn't interfere in what they'd see as the internal conflicts of another continent.

"We're on our own in this fight," he said. "And it is one we are slowly losing."

"Maybe that's why I've suddenly appeared. Maybe I'm meant to be the fairy godmother that grants your wish for freedom." It was lightly said and something I didn't really believe. Whatever might be happening, it was something more than the gods of earth and air suddenly feeling sorry for the plight of Arleeons.

He laughed, a sound that ran over the noise of the skid

and warmed me deep inside. "You're too young to be a fairy godmother."

"Well, technically I'm not, given I'm over two hundred years old."

"True." He paused and then added, with a hint of huskiness that echoed the desire I'd felt last night, "Although the body I snuggled into did *not* feel that old."

"I bet you wouldn't have snuggled so close if it had."

"A truth I cannot deny."

"Does this mean that double beds are likely to remain a fixture in our journey?"

"Sadly for you, yes. Requesting separate beds when we are supposed to be married would only raise suspicions."

"Not necessarily. Couples do fight, after all."

"Not when one partner holds Mareritt heritage." His voice lost much of its amusement. "Those who survive into adulthood have generally learned to keep their heads down and make no waves. Any form of fire from you—emotional *or* physical—would not only be unexpected but also have the Mareritt looking at you more closely."

"I hate what Arleeon has become, Kaiden."

"So do we," he said grimly. "So do we."

Silence fell after that. The miles and the hours ran on, and the barren fields gave way to trees and then a broken landscape filled with stone. We stopped midafternoon to stretch our legs and grab something to eat.

After unwrapping and then slicing bread, cheese, and hard meats, he said, "Silva."

I glanced at him. "What?"

"You asked me what my last name was. It's Silva."

Silva was one of the first ancestor's descendant lines, and in my time, Silva women had led three of Esan's five graces. A smile teased my lips. "Does imparting that information mean your distrust has faded?"

He hesitated. "Lindale is one of our strongest readers. She found no lie in your words; I trust that."

"But?" Because there obviously was one.

"I also fear what she couldn't find—the barrier she couldn't cross—and what you can't remember."

"So do I."

He studied me for a second, blue eyes giving little away and the tenuous link developing between us still. "Tell me about your life in Zephrine. Or what you remember of it, at least."

I perched on a rock and then helped myself to the food. "Why?"

"Aside from curiosity, talking about your past might just shake something loose."

I doubted it, but I guessed it was worth a try. So I told him what I remembered—about Zephrine, about Sorrel's daring raid into the heart of Mareritten to rescue fallen kin, and then, finally, about Emri.

"So just how deep is the bond between drakkon and rider?" he asked.

"It's not just a bond—it's a merging of mind and soul. She knew my thoughts, my hopes and my dreams, and I knew hers." A smile twisted my lips. "I can't tell you how many times she either comforted or chastised me over a breakup with a lover."

"Seriously?"

"Yes. There's no such thing as privacy when you share life with a drakkon."

Just for an instant, I heard the rumble of her voice, telling me in no uncertain terms that Jak wasn't worth my time or tears, and that what I needed was a good damn flight. We'd flown high that night—high and long. By the time we returned, the heartache had eased. She'd been right —but then, she usually was.

"So if she was dead," Kaiden said softly, "you'd know?"

"If she was dead, I'd more than likely be the same."

"Because of that bond?"

I nodded. "If a kin loses her drakkon, she loses half her mind and her soul. Few have the strength to survive it."

"But some obviously have."

"Some. Not many."

He studied me for a second. "Then why can't you feel her?"

"I don't know."

Perhaps the inner turmoil echoed in that brief reply, because he leaned forward and clasped my hand. His face— his lips—were close to mine, and for one brief—undoubtedly insane—second, I thought he was going to kiss me. He didn't, and I wasn't sure how I felt about that.

"If you survived," he said softly, "surely Emri did as well."

"Logically, I know that, but it doesn't stop me worrying." Didn't stop the fear.

"All the more reason to get to West Laminium as soon as possible."

"Then you'd better release me so we can get moving again."

He glanced down at our still-clasped hands, an indefinable emotion flickering through his expression. Then he released me and rose. We packed up the remains of our meal, then got back onto the skid and continued on, but the tension of distrust and disbelief that had been so evident only a few hours ago had definitely eased.

As dusk was just beginning to stain the sky, drifting lines of smoke appeared on the horizon.

"Where's all that coming from?" I asked.

"Probably from the smokers."

"Smokers?"

"The Mareritt salt and then smoke much of their meat and fish to make it keep over the winter months. Husk is a major production zone, thanks to its proximity to the fish farms."

"Which we haven't yet sighted."

"They lie on the other side of the city. You'll see them when we leave tomorrow."

I eyed the smoke-stained sky somewhat dubiously. "The air quality must be pretty bad inside the walls."

"It's generally blown away on the breeze, but today has been abnormally still." He shrugged. "It's the smell of drying fish that you'll notice more than the smoke."

"Something to look forward to, to be sure." I studied the buildings growing ever more visible. "There are no watch-towers here."

"No. They do keep a military presence, but for the most part, the citizens here are better off than many and cause few problems."

"How can they be better off when they're kept from moving about freely and are under constant guard?"

"Compared to many other cities that contain manufacturing sites, their work is relatively easy." Again I felt his grimness. "The conditions in the mining developments, for instance, are extreme."

"I'm gathering that means a high turnover rate, which is why the men in our pod were destined for the mines?"

"Yes. The Mareritt seek the glimmer stone veins that lie deep within the Blue Steel Mountains."

Glimmer stones were a black rock that sucked in light and shone like a star at night. "I take it most of the stone is shipped back to Mareritten?"

"Almost 90 percent of it is, though what use it would be during their long winters is anyone's guess." He shrugged. "The rest is distributed for Mareritt use here."

"They really are treating us like second-class citizens, aren't they?"

"That's because, in their eyes, we are."

Because of our skin color. Because of our lack of that extra digit on each hand. Both were the reason behind their relentless attacks even back in my day—they couldn't abide the fact that beings they saw as less worthy held a land far richer in resources than their own.

The closer we got to the city, the stronger the scent of smoke became. It was a mix of mesquite and bloodwood—two scents I normally didn't mind—but underneath them both ran a very strong fishy aroma. A shudder ran through me, and my stomach stirred uneasily. I'd never been a huge fan of fish, and I wasn't entirely sure how I was going to get through the night without losing the contents of my stomach if that smell got any stronger.

"It won't be as bad within the walls," Kaiden commented, obviously feeling my shudder. "They've planted a lot of orange clamberers and mint sprays, which combats the worst of the stench."

"Are we staying in another safe house here?"

"No, though the manager of the tavern we're staying in is not unsympathetic to our cause."

I snorted. "Which suggests he'd hand us over in a heart-beat should a problem arise."

"Perhaps, but you're forgetting there's now been at least two generations born and raised under Mareritt rule."

Kaiden's voice held an edge. "Many *do* chafe under the yoke of servitude, but they also prefer that than to risk death or being shipped off to somewhere less salubrious. You can't really blame them either, given how little success we've had at ousting the Mareritt."

Which was a rather sad but true statement. Had I been born into this way of life, would I have thought any differently to those within Husk or any of Arleeon's other cities?

Probably not.

"Would any of that change if Esan started driving the Mareritt from these lands?"

"I think for the majority to be rousted, we'd first have to prove ourselves worthy of them risking it all."

"And how would you do that?"

"The only way I can see is by destroying the heart of Mareritt occupation here in Arleeon—the White Zone."

"Which you've already said is an impossible task."

"Not for kin and drakkon," he said. "Which is why I'm not about to let you out of my sight, Red. Even if no other drakkon or kin survived the coruscations, you're here, and you can converse with the drakkons of *this* time. If we can free them, the advantage switches to us."

"Your drakkons can be killed far easier than mine, Kaiden. Oma is evidence enough of that."

"Yes, but it took three guns and a number of rounds to bring her down. It takes a hell of a lot more to kill one."

"Speaking from experience, I take it?"

I couldn't help the flat edge in my voice. The drakkons in this time had as little freedom or choice as Arleeon's human population, and part of me just couldn't understand why anyone who came from Esan and who probably had the blood of kin running through their veins wouldn't at least *try* to uncover the reason behind their allegiance switch.

"Yes and no."

He glanced over his shoulder; his blue eyes gleamed with not only understanding but also determination. He wasn't about to apologize for his or anyone else's actions, and I could accept that, even if grudgingly. I might not like what had happened to the drakkons or the generations of kin that had come after us, but the reality was, they were fighting for survival in a world that had turned upside down in a matter of days.

"I'm sure we've mortally wounded more than a few drakkons," he continued, "but we've never recovered the body of one. We believe they're programmed to fly back into the White Zone if they're injured or near death."

"Which at least partly explains why you weren't aware the drakkons were controlled by that band."

"Yes." He paused. "You have no idea of the chaos that resulted after the disappearance of the graces and the failure to recapture Zephrine, Red. To be honest, I suspect the only reason the Mareritt were held at the Grand Alkan River was because the wave of ice that accompanied their forces had finally faded."

"Suggesting the strength of their mages had also faded."

"We believe so." He half shrugged again and returned his gaze to the road. "It at least gave us time to rebuild."

"Which is what surprises me the most, I think. Given Mareritten's determination to utterly control this land, why wait two hundred years to have another crack at Esan? That makes no sense at *all*."

"Perhaps not, but I'm not about to question fate smiling favorably on us."

"Fate isn't generally that smiley. Not two hundred years' worth of it, at any rate."

"It's not as if peace has reigned during that time."

"No, but the point remains; the Mareritt had the advantage and they didn't push it. Instead, they gave Esan time to regroup and build a wall. In no war book I've ever read does that make sense."

He hesitated. "I personally believe they had little other choice."

"Why?"

"All magic costs. Perhaps in raising both the coruscations *and* the ice storm that accompanied their forces, they drained their mages unto death."

"*That* I can believe." They'd always cared more for the result than the price to be paid. "But why would it take several generations to replace them?"

"I don't know enough about Mareritt society *or* their mages, but what if—much like the kin bloodlines here—there are only a limited number of families who are capable of the ice magic?"

"It's possible—but *that* only makes it even more imperative we find a way to uncover what's happening in the White Zone."

"Yes, because if they're now constructing a coruscation large enough to consume Esan..."

His voice faded, but I had more than enough imagination to fill in what he'd left unsaid.

I drew the hood over my head once we were near Husk. Kaiden's ID was again checked and then we were allowed inside. The buildings here were not only newer but larger than the ones in Renton. They were made of a mix of wood and stone; there was no tin in sight, new or old. I guess that wasn't surprising, given the Mareritt had built this town for a purpose and couldn't actually harness metal as they did stone and earth.

The deeper we moved into town, the fainter the smell of fish became. Orange clamberer covered most of the houses, and the bell-like flowers bobbed lightly in the breeze that teased the deeper scent notes from their throats.

Kaiden stopped the skid out the front of a longhouse, then killed the engine and climbed off. I followed suit, shaking my legs to ease the ache in my muscles. Once he'd unwound the cord and connected the skid to a nearby power source, he caught my hand and tugged me close.

"Keep the hood on," he warned softly, his breath so warm against my lips. "And your hands concealed as much as possible."

"I have the gloves—"

"Unfortunately, in this place, they'll attract far more attention than your skin."

"Then why come here?"

"Because this is the only tavern in Husk that has a recharge station approved for visitor use." A spark of bedevilment touched his eyes, and a heartbeat later, his lips brushed mine, a barely there caress that nevertheless sent delight shimmering through me.

Even so, I couldn't help asking, "Why?"

"Because, after a long day of having your body pressed so snugly against mine, I desperately needed to."

"Your desperation isn't immediately obvious."

"That's because I'm a man with fierce control."

I laughed softly. He grinned and stepped back. "Keep close."

"I have little other choice, given the grip you have on my hand."

His smile flashed but there was tension in his eyes. "And a very nice fit it is too. Once inside, no sarcasm."

"Can I talk?"

He hesitated. "It would be better if you didn't. Most in your position would be afraid to in this sort of establishment."

"So much for those having only a squirt of Mareritt blood being more accepted."

"In this place, thanks to the relative peace and how little interference there is to daily life, they are. But you'll always get the odd one or two who might react." He gripped the door handle, then glanced at me. "Ready?"

I nodded as the embers deep within stirred to life. I'd faced all manner of threats in my years as a drakkon rider, but this was the first time I'd ever had to face a threat born out of something as simple as my skin color.

A blast of heated air hit as soon as we entered; it was a wave filled not only with the raw scent of masculinity but also the aroma of the meat being roasted over low flames in the fireplace to the left. My stomach rumbled, but the sound was thankfully lost to the babble of conversation and the clink of tankards.

Kaiden closed the door then led me deftly through the maze of tables. Though the level of noise didn't alter, a number of people openly turned and looked at us. Some of their expressions held little more than curiosity. A few edged toward hostility.

The embers deep within shone a little brighter.

As we neared the bar at the far end of the room, a stout man with silver-shot black hair and an almost ginger mustache that curled several times at its ends walked over. "What can I do for you folks?"

"We need a room for the night and some of that long-horn meat when it's ready."

The man nodded, his gaze briefly flickering to me. His expression didn't alter. "It's twenty credits for the meat and fifty for the room."

"Prices have certainly gone up since I was last here." Kaiden released my hand and swung the pack from his back. He undid the front pocket, then withdrew a number of coins and placed them on the bar.

The man picked them up and then slid an old-fashioned register across to Kaiden. "That's because the situation has changed since you were last here. Name and origin details on the next free line."

Kaiden picked up the nearby stylus and sighed in with his Kai identity; his writing was small and close together—the scratchings of a man who was in a constant state of intimidation.

But instead of handing back the pen, he also filled in the next line; this time, his signature was as bold as the man himself, but the name he used was Jon Baker.

Another of his registered identities, or an utter fake to throw any Mareritt who might come calling off our trail? I suspected the latter, but it was a dangerous ploy—especially given his earlier suggestion that the manager might as easily betray as protect us.

He placed the stylus on the book and pushed it back toward the manager, who immediately snapped it shut and placed it under the bar.

"Are there any changes we need to be aware of?" Kaiden asked. "The last thing we need is to be getting into trouble."

"The Mareritt have been on edge since yesterday." The manager pulled a key off the board behind him and dropped it into Kaiden's hand. "As long as you make no trouble, you'll be fine."

"Rest assured, trouble is the last thing we need. How long before the meat is ready?"

"Ten minutes, give or take." The man's gaze returned to me. "We'll bring it up when it's ready."

Which meant he didn't want me down here—understandable, given the hostility swirling through a small portion of the crowd behind us.

Kaiden caught my hand again and squeezed my fingers —a silent warning not to react. "Thanks."

We headed up the stairs. Gazes followed our progress. I kept my free hand well out of sight, but fire nevertheless pressed against my fingertips, aching for release. The internal flames weren't normally this hard to tamp down, but this whole situation was anything but normal.

The upstairs consisted of a long corridor with a dozen doors. The shadows crowded close, and each step echoed above the creaking of the floorboards. That made me feel a little easier; if any of the men who'd stared so hard decided to come up here for a game of "beat up the half-blood," we'd at least hear them coming.

Our room was one of two situated at the end of the hall. Kaiden slipped the key in the lock, then opened the door and ushered me inside. The room wasn't large, but it was at least clean. A couple of mint sprays hung from the ceiling, lending the air a pleasant scent, and the sheets and blankets on the double bed looked fresh and crisp. To our right, there was a window and a wooden screen, and to our left, a square table with two chairs. On the wall directly opposite the door—which would have been the end of the building itself—was a small fireplace. It wasn't lit, but it had been set, and there was a small box of firewood sitting to one side.

Kaiden locked the door, then tossed his sleeping roll and pack on the bed and walked over to the fireplace. I moved around the bed and peered out the window. There wasn't much movement on the street below, and the only noise I could hear rose from the kitchen that was obviously situated underneath us.

"Do you think those men will cause any problem?" I pushed the curtain to one side and peered to the left, past the end of the building. Lights shone in the Mareritt quarter even though most of Husk lay in shadows. And yet for some reason, I was uneasy.

"If you'd been alone, possibly." Kaiden struck a strike and slid it under the kindling. "But they won't risk it with me here—it'd cause too much of a ruckus and they'd know Jim would have to report it or face the consequences."

I dropped the curtain and glanced around. "Then we're safe for the night?"

"That depends on just how on edge the Mareritt currently are."

I swung off my bedroll and hooked it around the post at the end of the bed. "Are there bathroom facilities in this place?"

"They're basic, and behind the screen."

I walked over. Basic was not an exaggeration—there was a small basin, a tap, and a privy. I used the latter, then retreated to the bed and sat down. "Do you think there's any risk of a Mareritt patrol doing an inspection?"

"That's always a risk in Husk, but I dare say more so now."

"Because word is out about our escape?"

His gaze rose to mine, the flaring flames lending his eyes glowing specs of gold. "Yes. I think we'll need to rotate watch shifts tonight."

That was only sensible. "If they do come calling, what escape options do we have? The window?"

He shook his head. "Even if we could jump down to street without either alerting them or breaking something, we wouldn't get far."

"Which means we're trapped—"

"Do you really think I'd come here if there was any chance of us being trapped?"

His expression suggested only an idiot would think that, and I couldn't help my answering smile. "Well, you did admit to being reckless not so long ago."

"No, I admitted to being stubborn. That's very different."

I snorted softly. "So where *is* this escape route?"

"It's not so much an escape route as a means of getting into another room—which is where we'll actually be spending the night. We'll just mess up the bed here to make it look like we used it."

Hence the entry of two different names into the register. "I don't get how it helps us, though. Won't they just check all the rooms if they don't find us here?"

"Yes, but Kai was approved entry into Husk. Jon Baker was not. They may roust us, but they won't suspect us."

"I like the confidence with which you say that."

"That's because I've been through this before." His expression was one of reassurance, even if tension rode him. "Trust me, it'll be fine."

"I've done nothing *but* trust you, in case you weren't aware of it."

"And, for the most part, I you." It was softly said and held an odd sort of heat. One that was both wonder *and* desire. He was just as aware of the growing connection and was just as unsure as to what it meant.

Someone rapped on the door, a sharp sound that made me jump. Kaiden rose and walked across, unlocking and then opening the door.

"The dinner you ordered," a fresh-faced woman said. "Shall I put it on the table for you?"

Kaiden nodded and stepped to one side. The younger woman bustled in, placed the tray on the table, and then pulled off the cloth, revealing a platter piled high with freshly carved longhorn meat and freshly roasted vegetables, a cob of bread, a thick slab of butter, and some gravy. A small jug of what smelled like mead completed the meal.

"You can leave the tray outside your door," she added, with a bright if insincere smile. "We'll collect it later."

"Thanks," Kaiden said and locked the door again once she'd left.

I claimed one of the chairs and began carving thick slices of bread. Kaiden poured the mead and slid one across to me. "Once we finish this, we'll head into the other room."

"You still haven't told me where the passage is."

"It's behind the fireplace."

I frowned at the wall in question. "I take it that's a false wall?"

If so, both it and the passage must have been built *after* the tavern—if it had been done during construction, too many people would be aware of its existence.

"Yes. Three of the wall boards near the privy concertina just enough to squeeze through. The next room is a replica of this one—we'll be safe enough there."

I hoped he was right, because things could get very nasty if he wasn't.

Once we'd demolished the meal, we messed up the bed, shoved the tray outside our door, then unlatched and opened the window to make it look as if we'd climbed out. I grabbed the sleeping rolls and backpack and then followed Kaiden into the privy. He knelt next to the pan, carefully pressed a rusted nail downward, and then pushed the nearby board to one side. The next three folded together behind it, revealing a small crawl space. He shuffled back and motioned me on. I hesitated, then dropped to all fours and crawled inside. The darkness closed in and my heart hammered as once again the old fears rose. But as tempting as it was to light my way with fire, I resisted. If the floorboards in this crawlspace were anything like the ones in the bedroom, then someone in the kitchen below might just notice the light and raise the alarm.

Kaiden followed me in and, once he'd closed the door behind himself, squeezed past and repeated the process into the next room. I climbed out with a sigh of relief and brushed a cobweb away from my face, unable to contain a slight shudder.

Kaiden followed me into the room and moved across to the fireplace to light it. As the flames leapt high, he motioned to the timepiece on the small mantle. "Two-hourly rotations all right?"

I nodded and moved across to the chair. "I'll take the first one, if you like."

"You just want the pleasure of watching me undress."

"That depends on how far you strip down. Your shorts are not things of beauty."

"I'm a man and a soldier. We need comfort, not beauty. Besides, we're supposed to be married. Nakedness is required."

"Then please proceed. I shall certainly enjoy the show."

He grinned and unhurriedly stripped, revealing his lean yet muscular body in what seemed like slow motion. Desire rose between us, a thick heat that flowed over me, drowning my senses and warming my skin. He was glorious naked, and my fingers itched with the need to reach out and explore every inch of his powerful form. I crossed my arms instead.

Unlike the drakkons we rode, kin were by nature sexually free. When death is a constant possibility, you tended to celebrate life all that much harder. If things had been different—if everything I'd ever known still existed rather than being little more than dust on the wind or even water in a lake—I'd have readily accepted the unspoken invitation that gleamed in his eyes and fully indulged the fantasies I was barely keeping under control.

But the Arleeon I knew was long gone, and such indulgence wasn't wise right now.

Especially when Mareritt magic lay inside my brain.

"I hope you offer me the same sort of show later." The husky notes in his voice only strengthened my need to explore.

"That's extremely unlikely in a situation such as this." My voice was remarkably normal given the burn of desire. "We can't afford to be sidetracked when the Mareritt are likely to come a-calling."

"A sensible but disappointing statement." He climbed into the bed but only half pulled up the blanket. The firelight played almost reverently across his dark skin and had my fingers itching to do the same. "But if you change your mind, you know where to find me."

A smile touched my lips. "Prepare to be disappointed."

"Tonight, undoubtedly, but there are plenty of other nights ahead."

Only if we kept out of Mareritt hands, and to do that, I suspected we needed to keep our hands to ourselves—at least until we were out of the occupied zone.

"Go to sleep, Kaiden."

He smiled but settled down and in a matter of minutes was fast asleep. I drew my feet up onto the chair and hugged my knees, staring out at the darkness and listening to the clatter of dishes and the murmur of conversation rising from below. Normal, everyday sounds in a world that had suddenly become very abnormal—at least for me.

Tiredness pounded through my system by the time my two hours were up. I stripped off and then slipped into bed beside Kaiden, briefly drawing in his scent and heat before I poked him in the back with a stiffened finger.

He muttered something unpleasant, making me grin. "Time for you to stand watch, sunshine."

"And you're already in bed. That's cruel, Red."

"Tough. Out you get, warrior."

He grunted but nevertheless threw off the blanket and climbed out. I resisted the urge to watch him pad across to the fireplace and closed my eyes.

Only to be wakened a few hours later by a warm hand covering my mouth.

SIX

Heat speared through my veins and my eyes flew open. A musky, masculine scent swirled around me, and recognition belatedly sparked. Kaiden. It was Kaiden. But relief was short-lived.

From the next room—the one that had initially been ours—came the harsh bark of conversation.

"The sheets are cold," someone commented. "Looks like they've been gone a while."

"Window is open," another said. "It's possible they heard us coming and escaped out of it."

"We would have spotted them if they had," came a more authoritative tone. "Check the premises and IDs."

Kaiden's arm snaked around my waist and pulled me closer. This time, his body hummed with tension rather than desire. "Act frightened when they enter," he whispered. "And under no circumstances flame."

"The former isn't going to be too hard." The latter, however, was an entirely different matter.

I closed my eyes and concentrated on keeping my breathing slow and even. But it was a hard task when the heavy footsteps of the Mareritt echoed across the silence. Then, with little warning, the door was forced open and the stink of them filled the room.

"You two, wake up."

I squeaked in fright, a sound that wasn't entirely faked. Kaiden squeezed me briefly, then sat up. "What's this? What's going on? Is there a problem?"

His voice was high and held a trembling note.

"Who's in the bed with you?" came the response.

I shifted around to face him but kept the blanket up. Not so much to cover my body, but to hide my hands and the heat beginning to press at my fingertips.

There were three in the room, but only two gripped weapons. They were ready for—and wanting—trouble. Their expressions didn't alter when they saw me, nor did their stance relax. But then, if they were here looking for escapees, they were well aware that one of them had Mareritt blood.

"Name?" the one in charge said.

"Kai Jenkins," Kaiden stammered.

His hand slid across the top of mine and gently captured my fingers, a warning more than an offer of support.

The officer glanced at someone beyond the doorway. "They in the book?"

"Yes."

"And registered at the gate?"

There was a pause, then, "Yes."

He held out his hand. "Scanner."

The device was handed to him. The officer activated it and then held it out. Kaiden dutifully pressed his thumb onto the glass. Blue light swept it, and after a moment, a green light flashed.

The officer grunted and handed the scanner back to the person beyond the door. His gaze returned to us and there was no disguising his distaste as he snapped, "Stay in the room until morning, or you'll both face the consequences."

With that, he turned and marched out. The other two followed, and the door slammed shut. Kaiden released a relieved-sounding breath, then dropped back onto the mattress and turned to face me. "I told you we'd be fine."

He was so close that all I could feel was the warmth of his breath and all I could see was the aqua of his eyes. Awareness glimmered in those depths. Awareness and desire.

"We're hardly out of the woods yet."

I curled my fingers in an effort to restrain the need to reach for him—to caress the lean but powerful planes of his body. To follow with touch or tongue the smattering of dark hair down his abs to the delights hidden by the blankets.

Now was not the time to be distracted by temptation.

"And never will be when we're in a Mareritt town," he said softly, "but I think we'll be all right tonight."

"Unless the manager says something."

"He got good coin for the room—he won't jeopardize that unless absolutely necessary."

"I do like the surety with which you make these proclamations."

"Have I been wrong yet?"

"Well, no, but we've only been together for little more than forty-eight hours."

"And yet it feels far longer."

Again there was a note of wonder in his voice, but it was the desire visible in his eyes and the heat emanating from his body that had my pulse rate skipping into overdrive.

"In a good way, I hope."

It was lightly said, but I couldn't help the husky undertone. I was no stranger to either desire or need, but this was something I'd never felt before.

"In the only way that matters." He kissed my nose, a featherlike caress that had those deeper hungers quivering in anticipation. "Go to sleep, Nara. I'll wake you if anything dramatic happens."

Something within danced at his use of my name. "Aren't we supposed to be sharing watch?"

"Yes, but I've not been frozen, thawed, and then dropped into a world turned upside down." Amusement and concern creased the corners of his eyes. "You may not be inclined to admit it, but I can feel your weariness. Now that the immediate danger is over, it's better if you rest and recover."

"I'm kin, and more than capable of surviving a night or two without—"

"Then think of it like this—we need you at full strength and flame ready if I'm proven wrong and we have to make a very hasty escape from this place."

A smile twitched my lips. "I have a feeling that no matter how much I argue, you're determined to have your way on this matter."

"A major fault of mine, as you'll no doubt discover the longer we're together. Go to sleep. We've a long way to travel tomorrow, and no soft bed waiting at the end of it."

"Another fun day, in other words."

"The only thing that could make it better is rain."

I groaned. "You had to say that, didn't you? The weather gods will now think you've issued a challenge and will rise to meet it."

He laughed softly. "Which might not be a bad move. The Mareritt are less likely to hunt in inclement weather."

"Inclement weather doesn't bother drakkons."

"No, but we'll be spending a good portion of the day traveling through forests, and that'll restrict their ability to see us. Now shut up and close your eyes, woman."

I chuckled softly but nevertheless obeyed. And even though I was far too aware of his heat, his closeness, and the fact that he watched me, I slept.

We had little trouble leaving Husk the following morning. There were plenty of Mareritt out on the street, and while a few of them stopped and checked us, Kaiden's identity held.

Even so, relief surged once the blood-colored gates were well and truly behind us. Unfortunately, that only meant we were in the midst of the fish production zone, and the stench was horrendous.

I held the bunch of orange clamberer we'd picked as we were leaving the tavern close to my nose, but it wasn't doing a whole lot against the sheer density of the fish scent.

"How long before we get out of this area?"

"Another half hour or so," he said, "but looking at those skies, we may have bigger problems."

I glanced up. The gathering clouds were dark and tinged with green—a sure sign that an ice storm was headed our way.

"Do you think it's a natural or Mareritt-produced storm?"

He shrugged, a movement I felt given how closely we were pressed together. "It doesn't really matter either way, as we can't risk running the skid through it."

I frowned. "Why not? It's got a cover, hasn't it?"

"Yes, but a violent enough storm will tear through the

material in a matter of seconds. Besides, while the skid's batteries can last two days, fighting against *that* storm in combination with our weight will drain them faster."

"There's no town between Husk and our next stop?"

He shook his head. "Not without going too far out of our way."

I looked ahead. The land was rising again, and both rocks and trees were more prevalent. A deeper line of darkness lined the horizon—the Jantingle Forest, which was where Kaiden had said we'd be staying the night. Above the forest rose the Red Ochre Mountains, a range I was familiar with and one that divided Nyssia from West Laminium. According to Kaiden, there were two means of getting through those mountains without going over—the old and very winding pass that had existed in my day and was now little used, or the tunnel that had been completed a hundred years ago.

We were currently headed for the pass, though it wasn't without problems. While it offered plenty of hollows and rocky outcrops in which to hide, there were now three checkpoints to contend with. The tunnel only had a checkpoint at this end, but there was nowhere to hide once you were inside, and the Mareritt had already proven their willingness to destroy their tunnels if needed. At least the pass wouldn't collapse as easily.

"What are the chances of finding shelter anywhere nearby?" I asked.

"Pretty poor."

"Then you'd better rattle the cobwebs out of this thing and get us into that forest."

"We're already pushing it." Even so, he pressed the control stick forward, and the skid gained a fraction more speed.

But the wind had picked up, its cold bite cutting through the rough wool of my shirt and freezing my skin. There was nothing I could do about it. Not until we were out of the production zone and free from prying eyes.

By the time we were, the skid was being sent sideways by the force of the wind. I wrapped my arms around Kaiden's waist and raised the fires within just enough to send the heat running through my veins into his spine, warming him as much as I could without burning.

"Will we make it to the forest?" The wind's howl was so fierce I had to shout.

"You'd better hope so." His words barely reached me. "Those clouds suggest it's developing into a razor storm."

A razor storm was one of the worst—instead of being mere chunks of ice, they were long, thin daggers that could slice open the skin of human or animal alike in an instant. The only creatures somewhat immune were drakkons, and even *their* scales couldn't withstand a lengthy assault.

I kept my gaze on the tree line ahead and fervently hoped we made it there before the storm hit.

We didn't.

The ice began to fall when we were still a mile or so out from the forest. It bounced off our heads and the skid's body with equal abandon, and it rather felt like someone was throwing stones at us. But we were racing toward the deeper green clouds as much as the forest now, and the nearer we got to both, the harder the ice began to fall.

Then it became daggers.

They hit with deadly force, slicing through clothes, boots, and down into flesh with the ease of any blade. As red stained our wet clothes, I called to my flames and raised a hand, letting my fire flow over our heads and the skid's engines, forming a shield hot enough to ensure it was rain that hit us, not daggers.

"Dangerous," Kaiden shouted.

"Not as much as the storm—it only takes one ice dagger to hit the right spot, and we're both dead."

A point he didn't argue—not only because it was true, but because it also applied to the skid. And without it, we were in real trouble.

We raced on. The ice continued to slice all around us, destroying what little vegetation there was by the roadside. Thunder rumbled overhead, a warning the danger was far from over.

But the trees were close now... five minutes, if that, and we'd be in them and safe.

It was then I heard the bellow.

I looked up. Saw the flash of red in the sky and the spray of fire as she swept toward us. I swore and punched more fire up through my shield; the two streams met and, for an instant, did nothing more than roil around each other. Then the drakkon swept through them, causing droplets of flame to rain down amongst the ice. She bellowed again and adjusted the position of her wings, her legs stretched out before her, her long and deadly nails gleaming like white ice as she readied to rent and tear.

That's when I saw the chunky addition on her leg band —a camera. They'd added a damn camera.

While my shield might prevent them from seeing our identities, it didn't really matter. They now knew their fugitives were racing toward the Red Ochre Mountains, and it was far too late to do anything about it.

I drew on more fire, formed it into a leash, and flicked it toward the drakkon. She saw it at the last minute and banked sideways; the leash missed her legs, but in banking, she exposed too much of her wing to the ice daggers. Holes began to appear in the delicate membrane, and she screamed, the sound one of fury and frustration. Blue fire flicked across the leg band, and with another bellow, the drakkon rose, her wings pumping as she endeavored to rise above the worst of the storm. I hoped she made it.

Two minutes later, we hit the shadows of the forest. The ice still slashed down, but the thick canopy overhead reduced the daggers to icy splinters that didn't have the power to puncture our clothes, let alone skin.

I snuffed out my fire, and the pounding in my head instantly jumped into focus, its force eye-watering. I rubbed my temples wearily; it didn't help a whole lot. My fire muscles certainly needed strengthening—but that was only natural if I'd been frozen for two hundred years.

The skid's rattling was fierce, and the note of its engine didn't sound right. I leaned close to Kaiden's ear—which was bloody thanks to a gash on the side of his head—and said, "What's wrong with the skid?"

"Several daggers pierced the metal—I think they've either cut power lines or damaged some batteries."

"Will you be able to fix it?"

"Until we can find somewhere safe to stop, that's an unknown."

"*Is* there anywhere safe in this forest?"

He hesitated. "There's an old water mill about two miles ahead. It was abandoned some time ago, but we've used it occasionally."

"We" being the resistance, obviously. "Why do I get the impression it's a place you'd rather avoid?"

"Because it's an obvious stop point and with that drakkon spotting us—"

"Yeah, sorry about that."

"Don't be. The ice would have shredded us if you hadn't raised the shield."

"I know, but it just makes things harder from here on in."

"It was going to get harder anyway." He shrugged. "My preference would be to push on as long as possible and get to the foothills. The place is riddled with old caves, a number of which are used as supply warehouses. We might even find another vehicle in one."

"If you know about the caves, the Mareritt are likely to."

"This is our land, not theirs, remember. They may have occupied it for two hundred years, but they haven't bothered exploring the breadth of it."

Because Arleeon was nothing more than a place they farmed and used; it was not somewhere they ever wanted to live.

"Given you know this area and the skid's capabilities far better than me," I said, "I'll go with whatever you decide."

He nodded, and we continued on. The ferocity of the storm eased at around noon, and the ice was replaced by rain. Moisture dripped all around us, silver in the shadowy light of the forest, soaking our already wet clothes. It made me colder than I'd ever thought possible, but I couldn't risk raising my internal temperature again. Not so much because of the ache in my head, but because it was very possible that, now the ice storm had eased, the drakkons would be up and searching. And while they wouldn't see my inner flames, they might well sense my heat trail. The larger drakkons certainly could—although that ability was part and parcel of the link between drakkon and kin. It was possible *these* drakkons had not only been bred down in size but also abilities.

The day wore on; the road climbed steadily through the

trees, and the skid's rattling became so bad my entire body vibrated. Kaiden didn't appear worried, so I tried not to be, even though a very definite burning smell rose from the battery area of the vehicle now.

Dusk came and went—noticeable only by the deepening of the shadows already surrounding us. Kaiden flicked a switch and a pale light pierced the gloom ahead, highlighting the road and the trees that were gathering ever closer.

"Is that wise?" I asked. "There might be drakkons—"

"Wrong era," he said, amusement evident. "Our drakkons generally don't fly at night. Besides, I need to find the track that leads up into the caves."

"Won't the skids leave a noticeable trail if we go off-road?"

"With this rain? Unlikely."

I hoped he was right, because the last thing we needed was to be trapped in some damp old cave. It'd make it all too easy for the Mareritt to simply call up one of their ice or earth mages and lock us in. The shudder that ran through me was due as much to old fears as the chill creeping through my veins. Which was frustrating—why could I remember getting lost in a cold, slime-and-spider-filled tunnel thanks to my brothers, and yet not remember the events of the day that had not only changed my life, but that of Arleeon itself?

The pale light eventually spotlighted a break in the trees on the left edge of the road ahead. Kaiden slowed and carefully eased the skid onto what looked to be some sort of animal track. The going was tight, and more than one tree branch skidded across the machine's body and our legs. But, eventually, the trees gave way to barren ground and then to steep slabs of stone as we moved deeper into the foothills.

Finally, the light shone on what was little more than an open slash in the mountain's face. Lace moss fell across the wound like a green waterfall, all but hiding what might lie beyond. Kaiden carefully edged the skid through the gap.

The cavern beyond was cold, dank, and far longer than it was wide. The light startled the disk wings roosting within; they shrieked and rose in a black cloud that raced for the exit. I tucked my head into Kaiden's back until the last of them had gone. I wasn't particularly scared of disk wings, but I didn't want one of the leathery little creatures stuck in my hair, either.

Kaiden didn't stop. Instead, he pushed the skid on, following the twisting and ever-narrowing tunnel until there were barely inches between our legs and the walls.

But just as I was about to question his sanity, the tunnel opened into a secondary cavern. The skid's light caught the stalactites high above us, sending a crystal-like spray of color across the walls and highlighting the various boxes and sacks that sat on the rock shelf running along the left side of the cavern. Some of those boxes looked old enough to have come from my timeline, which didn't leave me with a lot of hope about the state of the contents inside.

Kaiden pulled up close to the shelf and then stopped the skid and turned off the engine, though he left the light on. The engine rattled on for several minutes and then cut out with a groan that rather sounded like the last breath of a dying beast. It was an impression deepened by the tendrils of gray smoke drifting upward and the strengthening scent of burning.

"That doesn't look or smell too good," Kaiden said.

He climbed off the skid, then turned and offered me a hand up—and kept hold as my legs threatened to buckle underneath me. How could being frozen have created such weakness in my limbs? Surely if I'd gone into the coruscation fighting fit—and I had—then that was the way I should have come out? Or did it work along similar lines as those who were bedbound for weeks or months on end, the result of which was severe muscle wastage? I was nowhere near *that* bad, but it was nevertheless frustrating that I couldn't do what I used to—especially when it only felt like days ago for me.

I took a deep breath and concentrated on locking my knees. It was pointless bitching about things I couldn't immediately change. "How far away is the pass if we have to walk?"

"Too far. Are you all right?" When I nodded, he released my hand and then motioned toward the boxes and sacks on the nearby shelf. "You want to check those and see what you can find?"

I nodded and headed toward the rough stone steps. He pried open the skid control section; smoke fled upward, and the thick stench of burning increased.

"This really *isn't* good," he muttered.

"Do you actually know anything about engines?" I pulled my stolen Ithican knife free from its sheath, pried open the first box, and discovered an assortment of clothes and jackets. The latter would have been handy during the ice storm, because although they looked like regular woolen jackets on the outside, metallic threads had been woven through the inside lining and would have lessened the force of the daggers.

"No more than the ordinary layman."

"Meaning you can fix the skid or not?" I moved on to the next box and had barely cracked it open when the smell of rot hit. I gagged and slammed the lid back down again. I had no idea if it was meat or something else inside, but it sure as hell wasn't consumable. Not when it smelled like that.

"Unless we can find parts, I don't think so. Two batteries are dead, and two more are smoking."

"Batteries aren't supposed to smoke, are they?"

"No. And until they cool down, I'm not going near them." He bounded up the steps and used the barrel of his gun to pry open another box. "Oh, this is handy."

He pulled out what looked to be some sort of assault rifle and ran a check on it. "In working condition, too."

"I take it there's ammo inside as well?"

He nodded. "Several loops, from the look of it."

"Handy indeed." I opened a sack that held more clothes, then moved to a larger stack of boxes. As I moved a smaller box off the top to check it, a gleam of silver caught my eye. I put the box down and walked around. Behind the stack, close to the wall, was what I'd known as a scooter. Unlike the vehicles Arleeon produced, these Gallion-designed ones used a mix of magic and electromagnetic repulsion technology that drew on the earth's crisscrossing energy lines to move. Those same lines also provided coordinates for the navigation systems. They were fast, fairly silent, and shaped like fat tadpoles that could, at a push, fit two people in them. Zephrine might have had her drakkons, but they weren't exactly easy to hide, even when flying high. Our ground forces had used scooters like this whenever a quick, undercover scout mission had been necessary. Or even for a daring rescue deep in the heart of Mareritt territory.

Anxiety stirred, but I pushed it aside. If I'd survived, then surely Sorrel would have. She was stronger, fiercer, and smarter than me.

"It would seem Túxn is feeling sorry for us tonight,

because I just found a replacement vehicle." I pressed the door release button; once it had risen, I leaned in and hit the starter. The engines spluttered for several seconds, then a soft whine kicked in and the control board lit up. "Though I'd like to know why, if you've access to these things, you're still using the skids."

"Because the skids are forgettable. These are not." Kaiden pressed a cold hand against my spine and leaned into the cabin. "I'd still rather use a skid than this thing, but we have no choice. We need to get to the pass before they send reinforcements, and this is our best bet."

"They're looking for two people on a skid rather than a scooter."

"Yes, but scoots are only used within the occupied zone by the Mareritt. It'll be easy enough for them to check if there's been an authorization for scoot movement in this area."

"So we move at night?"

"Yes." He glanced at me. "Do you want to strip out of those wet clothes and tend to your wounds?"

I nodded. "You'd better do the same. And get some sealer onto that head wound, too."

"What? No offer to look after it for me?" He shook his head, his woebegone expression at odds with the amusement lurking in his bright eyes. "Where's the caring? And after I so generously let you sleep last night."

"You're a big boy," I said, amused. "I'm sure you're quite capable of taking such a task in hand."

"Only when I absolutely have to." The amusement grew stronger. "Which isn't often, let me assure you."

I laughed and nudged him out of the way with my shoulder. "I can imagine. In fact, I bet you've a whole *bevy* of beauties waiting for you in Esan who'd be more than happy to take such a task in hand."

"Indeed I have." It was lightly said but held an odd note of seriousness. "But sometimes the bevy isn't enough."

I glanced across at him, and my amusement died. "And sometimes wanting more is dangerous, especially when the road ahead is uncertain and perilous."

"Yet there are times when the risk is worth it."

I half smiled, though there was more than a little uncertainty in it. "And times when it isn't. At least not until the end is known."

He studied me, his expression shuttered. "I wouldn't have thought kin to be risk averse."

"It depends entirely on what they're risking." Which, in my case, was possibly my only remaining relative and the drakkon who was my soul. If they were still in the coruscations, then any delay—however minor—could be fatal. For them, and for the fate of Arleeon itself.

He continued to study me for several more seconds and then nodded. I wasn't entirely sure whether it was in agreement or an indication of a challenge accepted.

And not entirely sure how I felt about either.

We stripped off in silence, tended to our wounds, and then dressed in the fresh clothes we'd taken from the old farmhouse. After we'd finished checking the rest of the boxes—finding a few more ammunition packages and a couple of handguns, but little else useful—Kaiden edged the scooter from behind the stacks while I walked across to the first box I'd opened and sorted through the jackets until I'd found two of a suitable size.

Once the scooter was packed, I climbed into the rear and squashed down into the seat. The sloping rear end of the vehicle meant sitting upright wasn't exactly an option, and the position was likely to get uncomfortable as the night wore on.

Kaiden climbed into the front, shut the door, and then gently pressed the control stick forward. The soft whine of the engines filled the silence as the vehicle rose several inches off the ground and then slowly scooted forward.

Our speed didn't increase once we were out of the cavern. The underbellies of scooters were notoriously fragile, and the rough terrain of the foothills needed to be traversed carefully or we'd incapacitate the vehicle before we'd gotten too far.

Once we were back out on the main road, Kaiden unleashed the scoot's speed. The night slipped by quickly and quietly.

The red and gold flags of dawn were coloring the night sky when he finally slowed. I shifted position, wincing as my cramped legs protested, and then leaned forward. There was no obvious sign of the pass, and the landscape around us was a mix of bare, broken tree remnants and rocky red outcrops that rose skyward like stiffened fingers.

"How far ahead is the pass?"

"Half a mile, give or take." He slowed the scoot down some more. "I think it'd be wise to scout the area first and see if they've reinforced the gateway or not."

I nodded, even though no matter how many guards waited for us—be it two or twenty—taking them out would not only announce our current position but also where we were headed. Which, of course, meant that unless our attack was so fast and so furious that the first checkpoint had no chance to forewarn the others, the other two would be ready and waiting for us. How we were going to get through them I had no idea—and I suspected Kaiden didn't either. He seemed to be working on the "one thing at a time" principle.

Kaiden pulled off the main road again and followed a twisty path through the trees. After a few minutes, a cave appeared. He carefully edged inside, parked in the shadows to the left of the entrance, and then killed the engine and opened the door. I followed him out and then stretched my arms over my head in an effort to ease the cramped soreness in my back.

"It'll take twenty minutes to get to the lookout." He handed me a rifle and an ammo loop. "We can decide our next course of action once we see what the situation is."

I nodded and slung the loop over my shoulder. "And our packs? Do we leave them here or take them with us?"

He hesitated. "Leave them for now. We can always come back if necessary. Ready?"

When I nodded, he turned and led the way out of the cave. The rain was now little more than mist that silvered the nearby leaves and clung lightly to our coats and hair, but the air was cold enough to frost each breath. We made our way along the ridge, following a path that was a mix of stone and earth; the latter clung to my boots, making it feel like there were weights under each.

As the sunrise kissed the skies with ever-brighter layers of color, Kaiden moved off the path and climbed a steep hill, heading toward a thick slab of stone that jutted sideways into emptiness. As we neared the edge, he dropped onto his stomach and crab-crawled the rest of the way. I did the same and stopped beside him.

The pass lay below us—a ragged, flat-bottomed V that had been cut into the mountain by both time and the river that ran along its base. Between the two sides of the mountain lay a curved wall that shone like red glass in the growing light of day. At least six guards stood on top of the wall, and four more stood on either side of the central wooden gateway.

"How in the wind's name are we going to get through those gates without being seen?"

"I'm not sure we can." He scanned the area for a moment, his expression troubled. "There's usually only a token force of four stationed at each of the checkpoints; if this one has been boosted, the others probably have, too."

"Which isn't really surprising given this pass is the most obvious access point into West Laminium for escapees like us."

"Yes, but I didn't expect them to move so fast. They usually don't."

"I bet they don't usually get attacked by someone capable of using flame the way I do, either."

"*That* is a certainty." He pursed his lips, his gaze narrowing. "As I see it, we have two choices—we hit them hard or fast here, or we risk going through the tunnel."

"And getting blown to smithereens by another tank. I'd rather fight my way through three damn checkpoints than chance that happening again. Besides, if they've already fortified this pass, they'll surely have done similar to the tunnel."

"Undoubtedly." He paused. "Can you drive a scooter?"

I glanced at him. "I ride drakkons, remember?"

"So that would be a no?"

I grimaced. "I know how in principle, but I've only done it a couple of times. I tended to walk around Zephrine rather than use the transports."

"Then I'd better do it."

"It makes more sense anyway—you can be the distraction while I'll be the hammer."

He nodded. "The path we followed to get up here winds through the forest and then back down to the pass. You should end up a few hundred yards from the wall."

A few hundred yards which—from the look of it—was all open space. But even so, I'd be in a far safer position up until that point than Kaiden. There was no cover on the road leading to the gate.

"If they shoot first and ask questions later, you're going to be in trouble—the scooter won't offer any protection."

"Except they're expecting the skid, not a scooter. I'll be fine until they stop me and ask for identification. Let's move." He slithered down the outcrop, then rose and helped me up. "It'll take you about half an hour to get down near the gates. Wait in the trees until the Mareritt move out to stop me. Once their attention is caught, hit everyone on the wall with fire. I'll take care of the others."

I nodded. "Be careful, Kaiden. We have no idea how many other Mareritt are in there."

"I will. Make sure you do, too."

I half smiled. "I have no intention of dying until I at least get some answers."

"Good." He half raised a hand, as if to touch my cheek, then checked the movement and stepped back. "Go."

I did so. His gaze followed me—a heat that burned into my back and stirred a need that had little chance of release in the near, and perhaps even distant, future.

By the time I reached the top of the hill, my legs ached, and every breath was a short, sharp rasp. I paused to suck air into my burning lungs and studied the valley below. Three of the four gate guards now stood to the right of the entrance. Given the amount of arm waving and the guttural barks I could hear, they were either having an argument or a very animated discussion. The lone guard stood at ease but even from here looked bored. As did the six men atop the wall. All of which at least played into our favor—for the moment, at least.

I started down the hill, following the slight path as quickly as I dared. The wind remained icy, but the clouds that had dominated the sky for the better part of the last day and night appeared to be breaking up—which was both good *and* bad. There was enough ice in my body and mind already; I certainly didn't need any more in the form of storms. But they had at least provided some cover. Blue skies and sunshine just made it that much easier for the drakkons and their masters to find us.

My hair and face dripped with sweat by the time I reached the end of the forest. I leaned against a tree to catch my breath and studied the long sweep of emptiness between the wall and me. I'd be visible the minute I stepped out, so I just had to hope Kaiden's diversionary tactic worked. Otherwise, we were in all sorts of trouble.

I raised my gaze to the top of the wall. Only three Mareritt were currently visible, which was frustrating. I needed to know where all six were, because I didn't want to waste energy unnecessarily. We had no idea how many more were inside, but I had a bad feeling my fire strength was going to be put to the test yet again.

I continued on, following the tree line but keeping out of sight. I eventually spotted one of the missing men—he leaned over the parapet above the gate, obviously listening to the three arguing below—but the other two remained out of sight.

As the day grew brighter, the guttural growls of the three Mareritt increased. I couldn't help hoping the escalating argument would end in violence. It'd certainly make things a whole lot easier for us if it did.

Unfortunately, that wasn't a piece of luck Túxn appeared willing to grant. One of the arguing Mareritt spun around and stomped through the gate, and the other two resumed watch.

The drizzle had eased by the time Kaiden appeared. I flexed my fingers in a vague effort to blunt the tension humming through me. One of the guards walked into the middle of the road and raised a hand. The other two remained where they were, their pose casual and unconcerned.

I studied the top of the wall again. Four guards were visible—three on my side and one on the right. I still had no idea where the other two were, but there wasn't much I could do about it now except hope they revealed themselves sooner rather than later.

The scooter slowed. Heat burned through my blood, and my fingertips began to glow. While I was probably too far away for the guards on the wall to see the glimmer, I nevertheless clenched them. It was always better to be safe than sorry when it came to the ice scum.

The scooter came to a halt several yards shy of the guard, forcing him to walk on. As he did, the door began to rise. I reached for the heat burning through my veins and, after a deep breath to fortify nerves still unused to being ground-bound when on the attack, flung it toward those on the wall. The comet-like force of tumbling, fiery energy hit the nearest guard and cindered him in an instant. I flicked the ball sideways, running it along the length of the wall, hitting three more guards before those below even suspected something was wrong.

I bolted out of the trees and raced across the emptiness, heading for the gate and Kaiden. He leaped out of the scooter and started firing. Two men went down, then three.

A fourth came out of the gateway; a barrage of gunfire forced Kaiden to jump behind the scooter. Bullets pinged off its metal shell and tore thick gashes into its sides. I swung my fireball around and down and let it explode at the front of the gate. The guard firing at Kaiden—and anyone else in that immediate area—was ash in an instant.

Then a klaxon rang out, the strident sound harsh in the silence of the early morning.

Deep within the pass, a second siren sounded.

Then a third, even more distant.

The other two checkpoints were now alerted to our presence.

I kept running, my gaze switching constantly from the gate to the wall. No more Mareritt appeared, but there had to be other guards alive and well beyond the open maw of the gate given the still-sounding siren.

I slid to a halt on one side of the entrance. Kaiden stopped on the other; he reloaded his weapon, then glanced at me and raised an eyebrow. I unslung the rifle and then nodded at his unspoken question. As one, we stepped into the gateway. No gunfire met our appearance, but the ashy stains on the ground suggested there'd been at least three others here.

The courtyard beyond the tunnel gateway was still and silent, and there was no visible movement in any of the other buildings.

But the Mareritt were out there. I could feel them. Smell them.

I called more fire to my hand and then glanced across at Kaiden. He motioned me to the left and then held up five fingers. I watched the silent countdown and then unleashed my fire, throwing it around the corner and then following it fast and low. Screams ripped through the air, along with bullets. I raised the rifle and unleashed on the Mareritt hiding behind their burning companions. Three went down; four others backtracked and ducked inside the nearest doorway. The mote in my eye began to bleed as I caught more flame and flung it after them. This time, no screams followed my fiery lance; they simply didn't have the time.

I shifted position and scanned the immediate vicinity. No movement; no Mareritt. I swiped at the blood dribbling down my cheek, then rose and padded toward the nearby buildings to check them, the rifle held at the ready and fire burning through my blood, eager for release. There were no more guards in this area.

But in the last of the five rooms situated under the wall, I discovered what looked like a control center. I studied the various panels for a moment, found what looked to be the klaxon switch, and pressed it. The resulting silence was eerie.

I reloaded the rifle, then shouldered it and walked back out. Kaiden approached, blood staining his left thigh.

"How bad is that wound?" I asked.

"Nothing vital was hit, and I've already sealed it. We've bigger problems to worry about now that the other check-points know we're here."

"The chances of getting past this one without the others being notified was always remote, but it remains a better option than the tunnel." Especially given the Mareritt had had plenty of time to flood the Jantingle Forest with additional forces. "We're going to need better transport than the scooter, though—that thing might have the speed, but it offers zilch in the way of protection."

"Agreed." He studied the long structure that was both

the end of the checkpoint station and the exit. "Let's go investigate the machinery shed."

I followed him across the courtyard and into the building that stood to the right of the exit gate. Inside were a couple of scoots, what looked to be an armored people mover, and a tank. It was smaller than the one that had chased us into the tunnel at Break Point Pass, and its gun decidedly shorter. Still, it was a far better option than the scooters—and came with the bonus of being able to blast open the next gate if it was closed. It didn't look particularly fast, however.

"Mover or tank? Or both?" I said.

"The tank is a two-person vehicle—one to drive, one to use the weapons." Kaiden walked across to the tool racks lining the far wall. "The mover is more practical—it has the speed and will at least offer some protection from whatever armaments they throw at us."

"Which may not mean much. Even if the next checkpoint hasn't received extra men, they probably have the use of a tank." My gaze went to the mover. "And if a drakkon attacks us, that thing will act like an oven."

He picked up a large bolt cutter and walked back. "Not if you hit her with fire first."

Just thinking about that had the ache in my head intensifying. "The blood heat isn't endless, Kaiden. We do have limits; when the mote in my eye bleeds, it means I'm nearing mine."

His gaze jumped up, and his expression became concerned. "What happens if you *do* hit your limits?"

"Unconsciousness at best."

"And at worst?"

My smile held little in the way of humor. "Death."

"Well, that's certainly not an option we want."

Definitely not. "The other problem is the fact that we haven't got enough ammunition to take out a fortified checkpoint."

"Let's deal with one problem at a time."

He strode out the door but returned a few seconds later with a severed hand. Obviously, the mover required fingerprint activation. After opening the mover, he walked across to the small tank and repeated the process.

"If we're not using the tank, why are you activating it?"

"Blowing up the entry gate will at least delay any ground forces sent after us. Do you want to check the armory on the other side of the exit gate and grab anything that looks useful?"

As I headed out, he climbed into the tank and started it up. The armory wasn't particularly large—no surprise given how few people normally used this pass—but there were plenty of rifles and ammo, as well as guns that looked to be some sort of handheld cannons.

From outside came a soft *whoomph,* then a sharp explosion. I peered out the doorway and saw smoke and fire rising as the wall around the gateway collapsed inward and utterly blocked the entrance. Kaiden jumped out of the tank, then turned and ran back.

Once we'd found the armaments for the cannons, we hauled the weapons across to the mover and secured them in the gun lockers. As we rolled out of the gateway, I grabbed our backpack and sat in the front passenger seat. "Hungry?"

"Yes." His gaze, when it met mine, held a warmth that suggested he wasn't entirely speaking about food.

A smile tugged at my lips. While it wasn't an unknown phenomenon for intense military action to cause a spike in sexual drive, we were hardly out of the woods yet. In fact, we'd barely entered said woods.

I reached into the backpack and pulled out the bread and a chunk of cheese, tearing off some of each before handing it to him.

"Thanks." His voice was bland. "Just what I needed."

"How far away is the next checkpoint?"

"It sits midway through the pass, so about thirty minutes at this speed."

"How close will we get before they start attacking us?"

"That depends entirely on what weapons they have. At the very least, they'll hit us with the hand-cannons; they have enough force to damage the mover, if not destroy it."

"Excellent. Just what I needed to hear."

A smile tugged his lips. "Better to know than not."

I wasn't entirely sure about that—at least when it came to this sort of situation, where the odds were greatly against us.

Even though I was too tense to be really hungry, I nevertheless ate. I needed strength for the battle ahead, and going hungry wouldn't help that goal. What we should have done was find the medical center and look for something that would aid our recovery and boost our strength.

The road followed the twisting path of the river, and the vegetation was sparse and shrubby. The shadows grew longer the deeper we moved into the pass, and the miles rushed by. Eventually, the road ahead turned sharply left; Kaiden slowed the mover. Tension once again ran through me, as did the blood heat. But its force was far less than it should or could have been. Thirty minutes just wasn't enough recovery time.

"The road snakes around an S-bend before it straightens and runs true to the next checkpoint," he said.

"It's rougher terrain, so I'll have to lower the speed. It should be safe enough for you to open the top hatch and ready one of the hand-cannons."

I climbed from the seat and moved back to the storage bins; after pulling one of the cannons and a number of armaments out, I stacked the latter on nearby holders, then stepped onto the gunner's stand. The hatch was latched but not locked and slid back easily. The air was cool against my skin and smelled faintly of mud and Mareritt—although the latter was probably my imagination, given the checkpoint remained some distance away.

"Let me know when we're about to leave the bends." I grabbed the cannon and locked it into the holding mounts.

"Will do." He hesitated. "If they start firing, drop back into the mover."

"If I drop down before returning fire, we're in deep trouble."

"Remember the whole 'not getting dead' thing," he bit back.

Amusement stirred. "It wasn't so long ago you were ready to kill me yourself."

"Yes, but you've proven a rather useful woman to have around since then—and we have unfinished business besides."

I grinned. "I'm beginning to suspect you have a two-track mind, warrior."

"Three-track—food is as vital to the soul as fighting and sex."

I laughed but cut it off abruptly as bright shafts of sunlight began to lift the gloom up ahead. "That's the end of the bends, I take it?"

"Yes." He glanced around, his eyes aqua pools of

concern. "I'll keep as close to the middle of the road as practical to give you a straight shot at the gate."

I nodded. My heart raced a hundred miles an hour, and my palms were so sweaty I had to keep wiping them on my pants. I'd rather face a thousand Mareritt alone on drakkon back than a handful of them on the ground any day.

The road made its final turn and then straightened out. The next checkpoint lay ahead of us, the red structure a replica of the one we'd broken and left behind.

But between that checkpoint and us sat a tank, its gun raised and ready to fire.

SEVEN

I unleashed the hand-cannon. At the same time, the tank's gun boomed; air whistled as the shell arced toward us. Kaiden swore and turned the mover sharply left, throwing me sideways. My shoulder hit the edge of the hatch, and pain slithered down my arm. I cursed and grabbed at the rim to steady myself. The mover scraped the mountain's side, and metal screamed in protest. Sparks flew, fiery stars that were quickly lost to the spray of dirt and stone as the shell hit the ground to our right and exploded. But the rising cloud wasn't thick enough to cut my vision; the tank's gun was already swinging toward us.

As Kaiden pulled the mover off the mountain and angled sharply away, I fired again. I had no idea if the first shell had hit, but the second did, exploding close to the point where the gun merged with the body of the tank. It didn't appear to cause any damage.

I swore and ducked inside to grab more ammunition, only to hear the whistle of an incoming shell.

Instinct had me sliding the hatch shut and ducking behind the gunner's stand. A heartbeat later, we were hit, the force of the blast so near and strong that it not only rocked the mover off the edge of its tracks but also ripped a hole in its side. Dirt, stone, and metal flew into the cabin, a dark and dangerous cloud that shredded the seats in its path. It was only thanks to the gunner's stand that I wasn't killed.

I twisted around and peered through the smoke and dust, trying to see Kaiden. He was still in the driver seat, fighting to keep the mover upright and moving.

Another blast hit us, and the mover tilted alarmingly. I held on tight and crossed mental fingers that we remained upright.

But our luck had run out. With a metallic groan, the mover crashed onto its side. The still-moving treads dug deep into the ground and swung us around, exposing the vehicle's underbelly to the tank's gun.

Kaiden clambered out of the driver seat, his face ashen and blood smeared across his forehead from a cut above his left eye. "Out—get out."

I grabbed the sleeping rolls and a couple of rifles and then pushed open the hatch. Smoke rushed in; smoke and heat. Our tank was on fire, but that was the least of our problems right now.

The mover had settled at an angle to the pass, leaving more space at the front of the vehicle than the back. I scrambled out of the hatch and edged sideways to the rear. It was tight—damn tight—but I pushed on, trying to hurry, trying to ignore the fear pounding through my veins and the knowledge that, at any minute, the mover could be hit again and we'd end up little more than bloody smears on the mountain. Rocks scraped across my breasts and tore into my stomach, but it didn't matter. Nothing did except getting away from the mover.

Kaiden followed me out with the other cannon and a third rifle. It wasn't enough. It would never be enough. Not even against a tank, let alone a locked-down checkpoint full of Mareritt.

Again the air whistled. I pushed past the end of the mover, tearing skin and drawing more blood, and then ran, as hard as I could, away from the vehicle. Kaiden was three steps behind me, his fear as sharp and as strong as mine. It was all I could smell. All I could feel.

The shell hit the mover. This time, it exploded, sending a wave of heat and metal debris into the air. Kaiden swore and his weight hit me from behind, sending me sprawling to the ground. He fell on top of me, covering me, protecting me. Air whooshed from my lungs, and for several seconds unconsciousness loomed. I fought it with everything I had; to do anything else would be giving in to death.

A shock wave of heat and metal hit us a heartbeat later, a force that tore at our clothes and skin with equal abandon. The shattered remnants of the mover thumped all around us, some pieces so large they'd kill us in an instant if they hit. Kaiden's body shuddered several times, and the metallic scent of blood filled my nostrils. Fear surged anew—fear for him—but his fingers found mine and squeezed lightly. Hurt, but not seriously.

As the deadly rain eased and thick smoke plumed around us, he pushed off me, then sat up. I saw the jagged piece of metal puncturing his calf.

"I'm fine," he said, even though he plainly wasn't. He shoved the hand-cannon at me. "Go shoot that bastard."

If the previous hits hadn't caused the tank any damage, I doubted the two remaining shells would, but we were out of options. I hadn't recovered enough strength to turn the tank into an oven, and even if I *did* manage it, then what? We still had to get through this checkpoint, and rifle power wasn't going to achieve that.

I grabbed the hand-cannon and scrambled upright. The remains of the mover burned, and black smoke billowed skyward. I couldn't see the tank but I could hear it—it trundled toward us.

I kept low and ran to the mover's broken shell. Red flames danced and shimmered within its metal bones, their heat caressing my skin. Though I couldn't draw on them to refuel my own fires, I *could* use them.

I brushed the fire to one side; the tank appeared through the thick smoke. I had no idea if they could see me, and no desire to give them that time. I hefted the hand-cannon, sighted on the tank's gun barrel, and then, with a prayer to Túxn, fired.

She must have been listening.

The cannon's smaller shell cut through the smoke and fire and arrowed into the tank's gun barrel. It was a one-in-a-million shot, and it not only destroyed the gun but also ripped open a wide seam in the front of the tank. I hastily gathered the fire and lanced it toward the tank. It hit the seam, flooded inside, and consumed any who might have survived the blast. The tank rolled past the mover's remnants and headed toward the river.

I swung around and ran back to Kaiden. He'd torn his shirt into strips and was tying the metal dagger into place.

"Why not pull it out first?" I stepped past him and quickly gathered the scattered rifles and sleeping rolls.

"Because I have no idea if it simply sliced through muscle or hit an artery."

"If it hit an artery, you would have bled out by now."

"Unless the metal has it plugged." He finished knotting the last strip of material, then raised a hand. "Help me up."

I hooked the guns over my shoulder, then gripped his hand and hauled him upright. Pain flickered through his bright eyes, but he didn't say anything, and after a moment, he nodded.

I released him and then handed him a rifle. "The Mareritt remain locked behind their fortress."

"That's no surprise, given we've just taken out their tank." His voice was grim. "Has the hand-cannon got any ammunition left?"

"One shell."

"Then that will have to be enough."

He hobbled forward. I fell in step beside him, my gaze on the checkpoint barely visible through the smoke billowing from the two vehicles. There were no Mareritt on top of the wall and certainly none standing outside the gates. It left us with absolutely no idea how many more remained inside.

Kaiden paused several yards away from the burning mover. Though the heat was fierce this close, he gave no sign of feeling it. Perhaps pain or even adrenaline overrode any such discomfort. Or maybe it was an indicator of kin in his bloodline, even if there'd been little evidence of it so far.

"Have you enough fire strength to take out the Mareritt in this checkpoint?"

I hesitated. "Maybe, but it'll leave nothing for the last checkpoint."

"If we don't get past this one, there won't be a next." His voice was resolute. "I'll play bait. You take them as they rise to shoot."

"*That* is an insane plan."

He glanced at me, eyebrow raised. "Have you got a better one?"

"No, but I need you alive to help me navigate what is

basically a brand-new country to me." I dropped the sleeping rolls onto the ground, then handed him the hand-cannon and the other rifle. "*I'll* draw them out—"

He snorted. "What were you saying about insanity?"

"I can at least run. You shoot them, I'll flame them, and —if Túxn is still looking favorably our way—we'll both survive to bust open the gate and get inside."

He studied me for a second. "Run fast."

I smiled. "I'll pretend I'm late for a date with a flagon of mead."

He laughed softly. "If we survive this, I'll buy you one."

"I'll keep you to that, warrior."

I touched his arm lightly, needing the contact in case it was my last. His hand covered mine, and something flared between us, something that was bright and strong—a connection that was new and yet old, and far beyond the scope of physical desire, even if desire was a part of it.

Most kin believed in *Dhrukita*, even though not all of us would ever experience it. It was a belief that certain souls were destined to meet every rebirth—sometimes as antagonists, sometimes as lovers. It was a belief I'd never really subscribed to, and yet, as I looked into this man's eyes, I couldn't help but feel the deep tug of something that transcended time and emotion. Something that was meant to be.

Something that *had* been in the past.

It was both scary and exhilarating. Tempting and yet daunting. I didn't really know this man and might not even survive to explore this link that seemed to lie between us.

But I wanted to. *Needed* to. Even if something within suggested Túxn would not be that generous.

I pulled my hand from under his and stepped away. Saw the understanding in his eyes as well as the determination. No matter what Túxn's plans for us might be, Kaiden had his own—and he would not give them up easily.

"I'll blast the gate when you're close enough," he said softly. "Don't run in a straight line."

"Don't miss that gate."

His smile failed to lift the concern. I spun and walked away—from him, and from that unspoken something between us. I had a sister to rescue and a homeland to free, and both were far more important than dwelling on things that might never be.

The heat of the fire consuming the mover caressed my skin but did little to melt the ice forming in the pit of my stomach. I pushed back the flames and smoke, then squeezed through the gap between mover and mountain, doing my best to avoid the worst of the rocks but nevertheless scraping skin. Once the gap widened, I took a deep breath, then gathered the flames to me, formed them into a gigantic ball, and launched it at the checkpoint.

Then I ran. As hard and as fast as I could.

The ground was littered with vehicle and rock remains, forcing me to keep an eye on where I was going rather than the fireball. But I didn't need to see it to know where it was —I could track its position through the growing distance of its heat.

Something hit the ground near my feet, spraying dirt into the air. I swore and began to weave, even as the uselessness of the plan hit me. I was too open out here, too exposed, and far too slow. I might be long and lean, but speed was not my forte...

I cut the thought off. *That* path could only lead to despair—an emotion I couldn't afford to cultivate.

The sprays of dirt grew more numerous. I had no idea if Kaiden was returning fire—all I could hear was the pounding of blood in my ears and the soft ping of bullets all around me.

The fireball reached the wall. I looked up, splayed my fingers wide, and directed the flames left and right. Two Mareritt were hit, and another three ran. I stumbled over a rock and flailed for balance, only to crash to my knees with bruising force. Swore, then pushed upright and ran on. The fire I'd borrowed held none of the heat of my own flames, and the two Mareritt continued to burn, their agony lingering in the air even if I couldn't hear their screams.

But those who'd fled had now reappeared, and bullets once again churned the ground all around me. Whether they hit or not, I couldn't say; I felt no pain and my movements weren't curtailed, but that may have been nothing more than adrenaline and desperation.

And there was still too much distance between that wall and me.

One of the Mareritt went down. Two others took his place. Something hit my thigh and I stumbled again, my fingers brushing the ground as I fought to keep going. Desperation surged anew, as did the fire in my blood. If I wanted to survive, I had to unleash and risk depletion.

Am here. Will help.

The voice cut through my thoughts like a sunbeam through rain, and hope surged. *Oma?*

Yes. Mareritt will burn. For you. For me.

She dropped through the clouds and swooped toward the checkpoint, her scales gleaming like bloody diamonds in the morning sunshine.

I ran after her. The Mareritt were still firing, but Oma was now positioned between them and me, and most of their shots went wide. They weren't willing to hit her, and that meant they hadn't yet noticed she wasn't wearing the band and was no longer in Mareritt control.

She neared the wall, swooped upward, and then unleashed her fire. It cindered those on the wall in an instant. With a flick of her fully healed wings, she soared over the wall and sprayed flames into the courtyard.

Silver screamed past me, and a heartbeat later, the gate blew apart. I plowed past its ruins and ran into the tunnel, ignoring the smoke, the fire, and the stench of burning flesh. A Mareritt stumbled out of a doorway ahead, coughing and wheezing. Fire flared across my fingertips, and I flicked them toward him. He went up like a torch, his scream barely leaving his lips. I jagged around him and pounded on toward the courtyard. Oma hovered in the center of the open space, fingers of fire licking her nostrils as she waited for more targets.

No Mareritt left, she said, disappointment evident.

They may be hiding. Can you keep watch?

Yes.

I pushed flames to my fingertips and checked each room. We were alone in this place.

Relief hit so hard and fast that for several seconds, it was all I could do to remain upright. I bent over, my hands pressed against my knees, sucking in air as my body began to shake. Which was ridiculous. This wasn't my first fire-fight, and it certainly wasn't the first time death had come so close. But it was, perhaps, the first time I really understood just how much I stood to lose.

Once my breathing had calmed and the shaking eased, I pushed upright and walked across to Oma. She landed softly and tucked her wings close, her dark eyes shining and happiness heavy in her thoughts.

Mareritt burn good.

A smile tugged at my lips. *They do. Thanks for the rescue, Oma.*

Owed you, she said. *Help more, if wish.*

We could use the help, but the decision is yours to make.

Then I help.

She ducked her head toward me. I scratched her eye ridge, and she closed her eyes, a soft hum of contentment running through her thoughts. Emri had been similarly blissed out by a good eye rub.

Who Emri? Oma asked.

My bonded drakkon.

What bonded?

I hesitated, searching for the right words to describe a state of being that had been mine since puberty. *It's an emotional and psychological link between a kin and her drakkon.*

So we bond?

There was a hint of wistfulness in that question, and I couldn't help smiling. Bonding wasn't something that happened just because you desired it, but I wasn't about to tell Oma that. I had no desire to hurt her. *Yes, we can bond.*

Where Emri?

I don't know—we got separated.

You go find?

Yes. Find and rescue, if Túxn was willing. *Could you wait here while I get Kaiden?*

Who Kaiden?

Oma, I began to suspect, wasn't particularly old in drakkon terms, as it was usually only those in the tween years between drakkling and full adulthood who asked so many questions. Which also meant she was still growing— and might possibly end up bigger than the Mareritt would have wished. It was also perhaps why she'd so quickly shaken loose the effects of the Mareritt control band.

He's the man who helped me repair your wing.

Wing he shot.

There was a rumble of annoyance in her mental tones but no true anger. In terms of grievances, Kaiden's actions were way down the ladder compared to the Mareritt.

He's lost many to fire, Oma. Which was not something he'd ever said, but surely a truth many in this age could claim. *He didn't know the drakkon had no control over their actions.*

She considered this for a moment, then said, *You fetch. I watch.*

I spun and limped back through the gates. Kaiden limped toward the checkpoint, the rifles and sleeping rolls slung over his shoulders. His pants leg was wet with blood; he was losing too much of it. We needed to remove the dagger and heal that wound or he'd die.

I hobbled quickly toward him, grabbed the sleeping rolls and one of the rifles, and then wrapped an arm around his waist in an effort to take at least some of the weight off his injured leg. But by the time we reached the courtyard, his sweat stung the air and tremors racked his body.

"First aid," he said, his voice little more than a husk, "to the right."

I guided him that way and, a second later, saw the green sign bearing a white heart—the emblem for a first aid facility. The room itself wasn't large, but it had a number of storage units and a hospital bed over which hung some sort of complicated-looking medical machine. To one side of this stood a control screen.

I helped him onto the bed. His skin was pale and his

eyes little more than narrow aqua slits. "What do I need to do?"

"I'll do it. You go outside, prepare a vehicle, and find supplies."

I frowned. "You're not going to be in a fit state to go anywhere—"

"For four hours," he cut in. "The Mareritt have a history of spending the long nights of their winter advancing their technology, and this machine is designed to do the work of most surgeons."

"Which forces me to point out that Mareritt physiology is different to ours."

"Not as much as many think, but I'll be focusing mainly on my leg, so it won't matter," he said. "The good thing about these machines is they don't require fingerprints to activate."

"I take it you're speaking from experience?"

He nodded. "There'll be additional medical supplies in the larger cabinet—treat your wounds before you head out."

He pressed the control screen; as it came to life, I headed across to the cabinet and opened the door. It was full of bandages, sprays, and other medical stuff, much of which was totally alien to me. But after a few seconds of studying them, I spotted what looked to be antiseptic and sealing spray. I stripped off, then grabbed some swabs and began cleaning and sealing the scrapes and cuts I could reach. There were certainly plenty of them, and every single one stung like blazes, especially the deeper scrapes across my breasts. The wound on my thigh wasn't as bad as it looked or felt—the bullet had simply scoured a deep trench through the fleshy outer layers but hadn't hit anything vital in the process. Once I'd patched and sealed it, I grabbed a towel, hung it over the door, and then poured the antiseptic over my shoulder and down my spine. Then I pressed back against the towel to pad it dry and sealed those wounds as best I could.

I redressed and moved back to Kaiden. A cannula had been inserted into his arm, and he was now pressing a number of buttons on the screen. Fluid flowed down the line from the machine to his arm.

"You all right?" I asked.

"Yes—go." His attention was more on what he was doing than me. "I'll be fine."

I wasn't so sure of that, given the amount of blood he'd already lost, but there was no point arguing. Right now, repairing the wound to ensure he didn't lose any more and then getting the hell out of here remained our best option.

I headed out. *Oma, could you fly over the first check-point? We need to know what's happening there and how close the Mareritt force is. But keep high so they don't see you.*

No flaming?

Not yet. It's better if they don't know you're helping us.

Sneaky. I like.

With that, she hunkered down and then jumped high into the air, her wings a golden blur as she attempted to gain height. Dust swirled around me, a thick cloud filled with the ashy remains of the Mareritt. I dragged the collar of my undershirt over my nose and watched her slowly rise. Once she'd disappeared into the clouds, I headed over to the machine shed. It was a replica of the one we'd raided in the first checkpoint—the only thing that was missing was the tank. Unfortunately, while there *was* a mover here, in cindering the Mareritt we'd also—thanks to its position close to the doors—destroyed any hope we had of using it. I walked across to one of the scoots and crossed mental fingers as I pressed the opening lever. It responded, and relief stirred. While it didn't offer anything in the way of protection, it did at least give us speed; right now that was probably the most important thing. Besides, it wasn't as if the mover had proven very effective against tank shells.

I climbed in, hit the start button, and took several minutes to familiarize myself with the various screens and buttons. It wasn't all that different to the scooters I'd occasionally used in Zephrine—just a more modern version, basically—so I was able to maneuver the scoot out of the shed without damaging it.

When it was safely parked again, I started the search for food and clothes. I found Mareritt uniforms in the armory, but they weren't of any practical use—especially if we were forced into another town. I collected rifles, a couple of hand-cannons, and ammo for both, and carted them across to the scooter. Once it was all securely stashed, I moved on to the next building. It was a washhouse filled with tubs and drying racks, the latter half-filled with various clothing bits and pieces. I walked across to the nearest shirt and sniffed it warily. A faint, almost rotten egg aroma lingered on the material, but it smelled a whole lot cleaner and fresher than the Mareritt usually did. I stripped off the torn and bloody remnants of my clothes, then tugged a brown woolen shirt over my undershirt and slipped into a pair of trousers that were made of some sort of soft skin. I grabbed a belt to keep them up and then tucked my knife into the back of it.

Once I'd found clothing big enough to fit Kaiden, I continued on, this time looking for the mess and kitchen. I found them two buildings down from the med center and made my way through the half-dozen tables to the kitchen at the rear. It wasn't surprising to find their larder filled with newly butchered meats—most of which was hart meat, if the stack of antlers sitting in a box near the door was anything to go by. Fresh meat wasn't practical to carry, however, so I settled for flatbreads, hard cheese, and a mix of nuts and dried fruits. Once I'd found a rucksack to carry it all in, I walked across to the med center to keep an eye on Kaiden. He was totally out of it, but the machine was in automatic mode and tended to him with precision. It was pretty damn impressive to watch—I doubted a surgeon could have done any better.

The hours passed slowly. Once the wound was sealed and bandaged, the machine beeped, and a message flashed on the screen, indicating it was now safe to remove the cannula. When Kaiden didn't respond, I carefully removed it for him, dumped the needle and line into a tray, and then pressed the healing pad the machine offered via a slide-out tray against his skin and secured it.

It was a few minutes before he came to. He blinked, his expression a little confused and his pupils wider than normal. "Nara?"

"Yes." I touched his arm lightly. "How are you feeling?"

"Like I've been bowled over by a longhorn." He scrubbed a hand across his face, scraping whiskers. "How long did it take?"

"Closest reckoning? About five hours."

He grunted and pushed upright. Pain flared through his expression, but I suspected it came from the multiple minor wounds and scrapes that hadn't yet been treated. "We need to go."

"You're not going anywhere, warrior, until I treat the rest of your wounds."

He gave me a look—the type that suggested I was being ridiculous. "We've wasted enough time. We can't afford—"

"Oma is keeping an eye on the Mareritt and will report

back when they hit the other checkpoint," I said. "What we can't afford is you becoming ill—or even worse, dropping dead—because of an infection taking hold. I need to rescue Sorrel and whatever remains of the graces, and I need your help to do that. So shut up and just let me get on with it."

His eyebrows rose and a smile teased his lips. "Are you always this bossy?"

"Only when I'm faced with male stubbornness." I walked over to the medical cabinet and collected wash pads, antiseptics, and sealers.

He chuckled softly. "Shame. I quite like it."

"So bossy women are your thing?" I dumped the items onto the bed beside him, squirted the antiseptic onto one of the pads, and then motioned him to remove his shirt. His broad back was littered with cuts, and I had a suspicion most of them had been caused when he'd thrown himself on top of me.

"Generally, no. I think it's more a sum of all things when it comes to my attraction to you."

"Or simply a matter of proximity."

"We both know it's more than that."

It was, but I wasn't ready to verbally acknowledge that just yet. Not until I knew more about what had happened and how I'd gotten here. Not until I'd remembered what I couldn't and was absolutely sure the ice in my mind wasn't a danger to anyone. And certainly *not* until I'd freed all those still trapped.

If any of that was even possible.

I dressed his wounds, then offered him the clean clothes I'd found and headed out while he changed. Oma reappeared as I walked toward the scooter, doing a low sweep around the courtyard before coming to roost on top of the wall.

Mareritt at checkpoint. They work to get through gate. Kill now?

I raised my eyebrows. While it was not unusual for drakkons to have a bloody bent, Oma was decidedly more eager to kill than most. I couldn't help but wonder if it was merely the need for revenge on those who'd kept her captive for so long, or more ingrained than that. Perhaps in reducing their size, the Mareritt had heightened their violent tendencies. And while Oma was no threat to me personally, I couldn't help but wonder if the older drakkons would be less mannered and far more savage. If the Mareritt *had* been breeding drakkons from stolen eggs for centuries more than the two that had passed since my time, it was certainly possible.

"No. We need your flames to destroy the final checkpoint."

I go eat. Call when need.

"Avoid Mareritt-patrolled areas, Oma. They'll try to kill you once they realize you're free."

They try, I kill.

But they have many guns.

She considered this for a moment and then said, *I keep to peaks. They don't like peaks.*

Which perhaps explained why the Mareritt had built so many tunnels. It also meant the network of tunnels under Zephrine might have survived the rest of the city's destruction. Those tunnels—or at least the ones that riddled the peaks—had been the home of kin long before the external city had been built. They might be needed again if the graces still locked within the icy heart of the coruscation could be revived.

If they'd survived, that is. There was no guarantee that

they had, despite my inner certainty that Emri, at the very least, had to be alive.

Oma jumped into the air and flew into the clouds. I turned at the sound of steps and watched Kaiden approach. Though there was definitely some movement restriction that suggested soreness and bruising, there was no sign of a limp.

"Where's Oma going?" he said.

"To eat."

"She won't find much prey across these mountains—the red hart herds that once inhabited this area have been all but hunted out by the Mareritt."

"She's a drakkon. She can cover more ground in half an hour of flight than we could in a day." I shrugged. "How far away is the next checkpoint?"

His gaze moved past me. "Probably six or seven hours—the rougher ground will limit the scooter's speed."

Meaning we'd arrive there right on dusk. I motioned toward the vehicle. "And the gates?"

He hesitated. "Blasting it probably won't delay them long enough to be advantageous now. Besides, we've limited ammunition. I'd rather keep it for the fight ahead."

I nodded. "I'll drive. You get some rest."

He studied me for a second, no doubt internally debating the wisdom of letting someone with so little experience driving ground vehicles be in control. But I was the fresher of the two of us and carrying fewer injuries—and the ones I *did* have would be healed by sunset. Even if he was kin, he was male and therefore wasn't as fully blessed with the first ancestor's gift of fast healing as those of us who rode drakkons.

After a short nod, he stepped into the scooter's back seat. It was probably even more uncomfortable for him than it had been for me, thanks to the fact he was taller and broader.

I climbed in and shut the door, then started the vehicle and carefully accelerated through the gates. Once I'd gotten used to the vehicle's foibles, I sped up, concentrating fiercely on the ground ahead as I guided the scoot through the pass's twists and turns.

The hours sped past.

Vibrant fingers of color were spreading across the sky by the time we neared the final checkpoint. As I slowed the vehicle, Oma said, *What we do?*

The timing was no doubt deliberate. Drakkons could track the location of kin through the telepathic link, so she would have been aware of my whereabouts in relation to the next checkpoint at all times.

Can you see the next checkpoint?

Yes. Mareritt on walls. She paused. *Can flame?*

Is there a tank between the checkpoint and us?

What tank?

A metal box with a long nose.

She paused. *Yes.*

I immediately stopped the scoot. Kaiden leaned forward. "What's wrong?"

"They've put out another welcome wagon."

He swore softly, then leaned over my shoulder and quickly tapped one of the screens I'd been ignoring. After a moment, a map appeared, showing our location in relation to the checkpoint. In between the two was what looked like a shadowy blob, which meant the tank was sitting between energy lines. Otherwise, its outline would have been sharper.

"Is Oma's fire enough to take out a tank?"

"A full-sized drakkon would be able to, but I have no

idea if she can." I studied the blob for a second. "It might be better if she takes out the Mareritt on the wall first and then hits the tank. If nothing else, her fire should be hot enough to force them out—"

"And make it easier for us to pick them off." His fingers flew across a couple of screens, and the scooter began to crawl forward. "I've put it into auto mode—"

"Why didn't you do that earlier?"

"Because it only works at low speed. Once the scoot nears this point"—he pressed another shadowy area on the map, although this one didn't look anything remotely like a vehicle—"we'll grab the gear and jump out. With any luck, the Mareritt will be too busy lining up the scooter to notice us scrambling through the shadows."

"Won't they see there's no one inside through the windows?"

"Not in this light."

I passed on his plan to Oma and then added, *When I give you the word, come in from the other end of the checkpoint and cinder all those you see. Then hit the tank.*

Her anticipation surged and her thoughts became more distant as she flew away from us. Kaiden removed the guns and ammunition from the storage units, then handed me my sleeping roll. I slung it over my shoulder, then rolled my neck, trying to ease the gathering tension.

Once we were closer but still out of sight of the tank, Kaiden stopped the scoot while I opened the door and scrambled out. He handed me the weapons and ammo, then hit the resume button, followed me out, and closed the door. The scooter moved on, its silver body gaining a bloody sheen in the quickly fading light of day.

We shouldered the gear and ran toward the canyon's wall, keeping close to the shadows and moving as fast as the rock-littered ground would allow. The road held no such dangers, and the scooter crawled along unimpeded; it would soon be visible to those in the tank. We had to be in position before that happened.

Kaiden's speed increased. I followed, concentrating on the ground, on not falling over. As the scooter turned into the final curve and the road straightened, Kaiden scrambled up the rock scree and then dropped onto his stomach. I did the same and peered over the edge. The tank sat in the middle of the road, a dark spider lying in wait for its prey.

It didn't have to wait long.

The scoot appeared. With a puff of smoke and a soft *whoomph*, the tank fired. A heartbeat later, the scooter exploded into a thousand bits.

Kaiden handed me a rifle and ammunition. "Tell Oma to attack."

I did so and began loading the rifle—a process done on autopilot. My gaze was on the checkpoint.

Oma dropped out of the clouds, a streak of gleaming red. She sprayed fire across the full length of the wall, cindering everyone in a heartbeat, then banked sharply and dropped lower. Another stream of fire ripped across the courtyard.

Those in the tank must have seen what was happening, because it reversed, its gun tracking around as it headed back to the checkpoint.

Oma, the tank!

She circled around and swept toward the vehicle. The tank fired, but she flicked a wing and dipped sideways. The shell flew past her belly and hit the canyon's wall, spraying debris into the air.

They didn't get a second shot. Her fire hit the gun, then the tank. She banked around and hit them again. Her second blast didn't hold as much heat, but it didn't really need to. The men were already scrambling out of the vehicle.

I raised the rifle and started firing. I took out one; Kaiden took out two. Oma flamed the fourth and then moved back to the checkpoint. She landed on the wall, spread her wings wide, and roared her satisfaction to the darkening skies.

"You might want to tell her to move," Kaiden said. "I need to blast the gate open."

Oma, thanks again for the help.

Like burning Mareritt. Feels good.

I bet it did—especially after being their captive for so long. *We're about to blow open the gate. Do you want to find somewhere safe to roost for the night?*

What you do?

We need to keep moving.

She considered this for a moment, and then her head bobbed. *I roost. Find in morning.*

With a final roar to the fast disappearing daylight, she leaped high into the air, her wings shining gold as she rose toward the peaks.

"You know," Kaiden said, his gaze on Oma, "a drakkon working for rather than against us is something I'd once hoped for but never thought I'd live to see."

"If we can figure out a means of disrupting the signal between the Mareritt and the drakkon, you might well see more of them. You want to shoot that gate so we can keep moving?"

"There's that bossiness coming out again." He hefted the hand-cannon and pushed to his knees. "Are you sure you weren't just resting on your laurels because you didn't want to challenge Sorrel for leadership?"

"Positive." My voice was dry. "I was deemed far too reckless to ever lead a grace."

"Sounds like there's a story or two behind *that* decision." He sighted the cannon and then fired. The shell whistled toward its target and hit the gates dead center. The resulting explosion not only took out the gates but part of the wall on either side.

"I will admit to an unwise misadventure or two." I rose and then grabbed his arm, steadying him as he climbed somewhat awkwardly to his feet. No matter what he might say, the leg obviously wasn't 100 percent.

"Thanks." He pulled free. "I think our wisest course of action is to grab another vehicle and get the hell out of this area before any more reinforcements can be sent to this end of the pass."

"How far away is the nearest military encampment?"

He slid down the scree and then turned to catch my hand and help me down. "In tanks or movers? Probably somewhere between one day and three, depending on whether they're sent from the division near the coruscation or from New Zephrine itself."

"Is there a safe place anywhere near here to rest up? Or do we run straight to the coruscation?"

"My first instinct is to head straight to the coruscation, but I don't think we should risk it after the mess we've made of the checkpoints." His expression was grim. "We'll need to know what their troop movements are and what further restrictions might have been enforced within the nearby towns before we go any farther."

"But how are we going to do either of those?" I followed him across to the road, my gaze on the checkpoint more than where I was going. While I doubted there were any

Mareritt left alive in that place, I wasn't about to risk either of our lives on a doubt.

"There's a comms point three hours away. We'll rest there the night and wait for info."

"I gather it's not in another town?"

"No, although there is one close. But we can't risk entering at night."

Especially when we were wearing Mareritt clothing. They might be a whole lot more complacent than the Mareritt of my time, but I had no doubt that now they knew they were dealing with kin—or at least someone with kin-like powers—they'd be pulling out all stops in an attempt to recapture me.

We clambered over the gateway remains and moved cautiously into the final checkpoint. After ensuring there was no one left alive, we grabbed another scoot and got out of there.

It was tracking toward midnight by the time we reached Kaiden's safe place—yet another cavern, this time perched high above a valley. There were long, scattered lines of lights dotting the darkness far below, suggesting the settlement followed the valley's base rather than climbing its sides.

Kaiden switched off the scooter's engines but didn't immediately turn off the pale yellow headlamp. The cave wasn't particularly large and was split in the middle by a small spring running from the rear of the cave. There were multiple boxes, shelves that held weapons and other stuff, and several beds on the right, while a rudimentary cooking area lay to the left. The latter suggested there was power available here.

"How do you keep the wildlife out of these caves?" I asked as I followed him out. "A tunnel mouth wide enough to fit a scoot through is certainly large enough for fossa or even cardinal bears to get through."

And while the fossa—who were smallish carnivores closely related to the mongoose—did tend to stick to the treetops, cardinals were well known for raiding human camps in search of scraps.

"There's not many cardinals left these days, especially in the occupied zone—the Mareritt have a shoot-on-sight policy out on them. Fossa aren't strong enough to break open the boxes."

Kaiden moved across to the shelf and broke open half a dozen glow sticks. I turned off the headlamp, and the shadows drew closer. The sticks provided little more than pale puddles of blue light that barely caressed the rough red walls, but at least that meant they weren't likely to be seen by any soldiers patrolling the area.

Kaiden placed the sticks in several spots around the angular cave, then walked across to the kitchen. There were a couple of putrid-smelling bags and five boxes sitting against the rear wall; he moved them all to one side to reveal a niche carved into the wall. Inside were six medium-sized batteries and a panel on which sat a dozen switches and lights.

"That doesn't look like any comms station I've ever seen," I said somewhat dubiously.

His smile flashed, bright in the shadows that still surrounded us. "Technically, it's not actually comms but rather a series of switches that, when used in previously set patterns, will inform our people below that we're here and what we need."

I crossed my arms and watched, trying to remember the pattern in case we ever got separated and I needed to repeat it. Although given I now looked like a Mareritt, it was unlikely I'd get anything more than a bullet in the head if he weren't with me.

After a few minutes, the lights above the switches flashed, the pattern different to the one Kaiden had sent. He grunted in satisfaction and then shifted the rubbish and boxes back.

"They'll be here an hour after the city gates open." He rose and walked over to the cooking area, picking up two pots and handing them to me. "You want to fill both up? There's not much here in the way of rations, but there are some shamoke beans and some broth we can reconstitute."

"That sounds utterly delightful."

"Beggars can't be choosers at this point in time."

Indeed. I shoved one of the pots under the mini waterfall pouring out of a fissure in the rear wall. It didn't take long to fill. "Will they have time to uncover all the information we need before they get here in the morning?"

He nodded. "Or enough for us to get by, at least. Our biggest problem will come from the fact that the Mareritt will probably have figured out where we're headed and fortify the entire lake area."

I walked back, the movement splashing water over the rim of both pots. "Is there any place near the lake where we could view the coruscation but not be within the watch zone?"

He hesitated. "Yes."

"I hear a 'but' in that reply."

"That's because the only possible viewing area is altogether too close to the military encampment."

I frowned. "Why would they still have a major encampment near the coruscation? Esan didn't mount a secondary attack on them, did they?"

His smile held a bitter edge. "With what? Drakklings and kin too old to flame?"

"Both Esan and Zephrine had full complements of ground warriors, Kaiden. We never relied on *just* the drakkons."

"Except few of Zephrine's ground soldiers survived the ice attack, and while Esan's forces were busy attempting to regain the fort via Kriton, the Mareritt wiped out our aeries and then attacked us with their drakkons. Esan barely survived."

I scrubbed a hand across my eyes. Perhaps it was just as well I'd been flung two hundred years into the future. Even if I *had* survived the clash with the coruscation, how long would I have lasted against a Mareritt force that had obviously spent decades planning its attack?

"So why the encampment near the coruscations?"

"We suspect it was initially because they were unstable, and the Mareritt wanted to be ready to deal with any resulting problems."

"And when nothing eventuated?"

He shrugged. "The encampment is midway between the old pass and the tunnel. It's a good location to station a ready-to-move force."

"How far away is the White Zone from there?"

"A day's drive in a scoot."

So, not far. "Why would they have detoured a prison pod to pick me up rather than take me to that encampment?"

"Maybe you didn't fall into the lake. Maybe whatever gave you freedom from the coruscation jettisoned you across the mountains."

I frowned. "Even if that were true, I *still* fell some

distance into water. There's not many lakes large enough to break such a fall in the Talien farmlands."

"*If* that's where you were picked up. We have no real idea, remember."

"It's very inconvenient, this not remembering."

"Yes," he agreed dryly. "You want to grab a couple of bowls from that shelf over there?"

I did so and held them out while he filled them. The soup didn't particularly look inviting, but it was at least hot and probably more nutritious than it appeared. It was also better than dining on yet more bread, cheese, and dry meats.

"How far away is the coruscation from here?"

"Three or four hours on foot."

"We can't take the scoot?"

"We can't risk using the road, and while there *is* a path through the foothills, it's too narrow and rough for the scoot."

I nodded. While I didn't fancy the prospect of walking, we would at least be harder to spot on foot.

Once we'd finished the soup, I rinsed the bowls under the spring water, then put them back on the shelf and followed Kaiden across to the other side of the cave.

"Single beds," I commented, claiming one. "Looks like you're out of luck tonight, warrior."

"Which is probably just as well." The devilish light in his eyes had my pulse rate tripping into a higher gear. "I want to be at peak strength when we finally give in to desire."

I raised my eyebrows, amusement bubbling within. "Just so you know, I'm not really into rough lovemaking. So if you are..."

I let my voice trail off and that wicked light got stronger. "*That* is very disappointing to hear, given the many tales

I've heard of the... shall we say vigorous?... sexual exploits of the kin."

"I never said I didn't enjoy vigor." My voice was mild, at odds with my racing pulse and the surging wave of desire. There was no denying I wanted this man, but I wanted to save Sorrel more, and I really couldn't afford any complications or dalliances right now. It would only take an hour or two of inattention to not only totally upend everything we'd achieved but any hope we had of saving those still locked in the coruscation.

And the flicker in his eyes suggested he was well aware of both my reluctance and my reasons.

But all he said was "You have no idea how pleased I am to hear that. Shall I take the first watch?"

"Please do."

I stretched out and then rolled onto my side, presenting my back to him but all too aware of his heat and his desire. It was a rather delicious wave that gently rocked me to sleep.

The man who appeared the next morning was small, weather-beaten, and bald. He walked with a stoop and at no great speed, which made me wonder how he'd gotten up the mountain in the two hours since dawn had broken.

His blue eyes narrowed when he saw me sitting in the shadows, and distrust crossed his expression. But he nevertheless gave me a polite nod before returning his gaze to Kaiden.

"Well, you've sure stirred up a hornet's nest, haven't you, laddie?" His tone was sharp, but amusement lurked in his eyes. "If you'd wanted to announce your presence, it might have been easier to simply write 'I'm here' on the clouds."

"It's not like we had any real choice." Kaiden clasped the other man's hand. "Good to see you again, Jance."

The older man grunted. "In any other circumstances, I'd agree. What in the wind's name have you been doing?"

"Trying to get to the coruscation."

"Why?" He glanced at me. "Has your companion got anything to do with it? Because rumor has it there's a woman capable of spraying fire like the kin of old on the loose—and she happens to resemble an ice prick."

"I'm not," I said.

"You certainly don't sound like one, I'll give you that." Despite the amusement in his tone, his expression remained wary. "What's so damn important about the coruscation that you risk blowing your cover and that of everyone you've contacted?"

Kaiden hesitated. "We believe the magic surrounding the coruscation is disintegrating."

"And what if it is?" Jance said. "If it was at all danger-ous, you can be sure the Mareritt would have either gotten out of the area or had their ice mages strengthen the thing again."

"Have you seen it lately?" I asked. "Noticed any changes with the sphere's external or internal structure?"

His gaze flicked to me again. "You can be sure that I *haven't*, simply because I've no wish to either view the source of our downfall or to encounter the many patrols they now have around the area."

"So they *are* doing additional patrols?" Kaiden said.

Jance nodded. "They're on the hour. There's also been a lot of heated chatter on the comms lines."

Kaiden frowned. "What sort of chatter?"

"Stuff about escapees, checkpoint destruction, a woman capable of throwing flames, and an AWOL drakkon that may or may not be related." Jance studied the two of us for a moment. "I hope whatever you're up to is worth the heat you're raising, because it's going to be a difficult few months for the rest of us."

"I wouldn't be doing any of this if I didn't believe it was vital."

Jance's expression was somewhat wry. "The problem with *that* statement is the very recent—and very foolish—risk that you did indeed take."

Kaiden's smile was countered by the anger in his blue eyes. "My niece is one of those with red fever. Don't tell me you wouldn't have done the same had it been your daughter or granddaughter who was ill."

Jance gripped Kaiden's arm. "Calm down, laddie. I meant no harm."

The laddie in question didn't look mollified. "What are our chances of getting to Pike's Finger unseen?"

Jance grimaced. "About fifty-fifty. They're patrolling the roads, but if you're willing to shoe it, you should be able to get there. I'd be avoiding towns at all costs at the moment, though." His gaze came to me again. "If you do have to go in, go without your companion. There're orders out to detain all half-breeds."

"I'm surprised they didn't issue that order sooner," I said.

"They might have had a little communication trouble after your escape from Break Point." Jance's blue eyes twinkled. "That's been fixed, however, so watch your backs."

"Has the encampment below Pike's had any fortifications we need to know about?"

"They got themselves a drakkon about a week ago. She

patrols West Laminium and the Red Ochre Mountains every couple of hours."

Kaiden grunted and glanced at me. "That's not what we needed right now."

"A drakkon's eyesight might be keen, but even they can't see past trees. If we keep to the forest—"

"You mean the one that has been basically decimated by the Mareritt's logging activities?" Jance said.

"Yeah," I said, pretending knowledge when I had none. Kaiden hadn't mentioned who I was or where I'd come from, so while he obviously knew and trusted this man, it was also clear he had no intention of imparting the whole story. Whether that was to protect his friend or for some other reason, I had no idea, but I wasn't about to do or say anything that would either make the older man suspicious or a target. "But between the trees that remain and the caverns, we should be able to get through unseen, shouldn't we?"

"Possibly."

"Depending on what we find at the coruscation," Kaiden said, "we may need fast transport back to Esan. What are the options?"

Jance snorted. "Right now? Between zero and nothing."

"That's not helpful."

"Neither was blasting the crapper out of three checkpoints. How the hell did you manage that when at least two of them would have been prepared for you?"

Kaiden's smile held little humor. "We borrowed a tank."

Jance chuckled and shook his head. "Well, you've made a rod for your own back, laddie. It'd probably be best to grab a scooter, keep away from occupied areas, and head for one of the sea towns. A ship back to Esan would be the easiest option."

Kaiden's expression suggested easy wasn't something that had his vote, but he simply nodded and said, "Can you contact the team in Fiske and tell them to ready one?"

Jance nodded. "Anything else?"

Kaiden shook his head. "No. But thanks."

"Be careful out there, laddie. The scum are agitated and on high alert."

"It won't last long."

"Nor will any of us if we're not careful."

He clasped Kaiden's arm and then, with another nod toward me, turned and left.

I waited until the sound of his steps had well and truly faded, then said, "Why would they have brought in a drakkon a *week* ago? That's well before I turned up in the prison pod."

"I have no idea, but it does suggest your escape from the coruscation might have happened earlier than we thought."

I frowned. "Yes, but if I'd caused enough problems to warrant a drakkon being called in, why would they then transport me to another garrison? Why not take me to the one protecting the coruscation?"

He shrugged. "Until we can figure out how and why you escaped the coruscation, we probably won't be able to answer any of those questions."

And even then, his tone seemed to suggest, we might still be left in the dark. I crossed my arms to counter the surge of frustration. "I take it we're not actually heading toward Fiske?"

His smile lit his eyes. "It's rather scary how well you can read me, given how little time we've actually known each other."

That ability had a whole lot to do with the connection growing between us, and we both knew it. "*Why* aren't we going to Fiske? Given everything Jance said, it's the sensible option."

"Which is the precise reason we'll be avoiding the place unless we have absolutely no other choice." He walked across to the sleeping rolls and tossed mine over.

I slung it across my shoulders. "But it leaves us with only the Red Ochre tunnel, and they've undoubtedly forti-fied that by now."

"I wasn't intending to take that, either. Despite what some might think, I'm *not* that reckless."

I walked across to grab the backpack and transferred the remaining food and water from the rucksack to the pack. "If not the tunnel, the pass, or Fiske, then where?"

There weren't any other choices that I was aware of, simply because the Red Ochre Mountains basically divided Arleeon in half. It was only near Fiske that the rocky spine gave way to rolling hills and then to the flatlands that surrounded the fishing port.

He handed me a rifle and clips, then shouldered the rest and headed out of the cave. "We'll be taking the Black River pass."

"Since when was there a pass near—" I cut the comment off. "The Mareritt created it?"

"Yes, around the same time as they created Break Point. It gave them two direct avenues into Arleeon without having to go through Zephrine."

"So what you're suggesting is we take a pass that leads directly into Mareritten to escape the Mareritt."

"Yes."

"That's absolutely crazy. You know that, right?"

"Crazy enough to work."

I stared at his back for a long moment and then shook

my head. "Was it only a few minutes ago that you claimed you weren't as reckless as most presumed?"

"It's a calculated action rather than recklessness," he commented. "And that tunnel is the only one not monitored."

"That's because no sane thinking Arleeon would *ever* contemplate entering Mareritten."

"Don't tell me that, as kin, you've never ventured there."

"More than once but always on the back of a damn drakkon. We haven't that option here." And wouldn't, no matter what we found when we reached the coruscation. There was an unknown series of events between me escaping that thing and waking in the prison pod, and that meant even if the graces *were* alive and we somehow freed them, there was no guarantee they would, in any way, be conscient enough to help us, let alone attack the Mareritt.

"It's the one move they *won't* be expecting."

"Because it's insane!" I took a deep breath and concentrated on the rocky path for several minutes. The early morning sunshine wove its way through this untouched portion of the forest, giving the air a green tinge—which rather appropriately matched the way I was feeling right now. To deliberately go into Mareritten... I shuddered. "Even if we did attempt it, it'd take us months to get to Esan on foot, and we haven't enough food or water to last that length of time."

"Which is why we'll steal another scooter."

"Because the Mareritt are kind enough to leave them lying about for the resistance to acquire."

My tone was sarcastic, and he chuckled softly. "No, but there are ways and means of getting them. How do you think the resistance has gotten their hands on so many?"

"Given what you're currently planning, I dare not ask."

I thrust a hand through my hair. "Even in a scooter, it could take up to a week—and that's presuming we're not spotted and chased."

"A week if we stop." He'd obviously decided to ignore the whole "being chased" thing. "But if we drive in shifts, we could cut that time down dramatically."

"You may be able to hang the old boy out and pee into a container, but it's a touch more difficult for us women."

He flashed a smile over his shoulder. "We'd stop for privy breaks, naturally."

"Oh, that makes me feel a *whole* lot better."

"There's far less risk going through Mareritten than a fortified and alert Arleeon," he said. "Trust me on *that*, if nothing else."

I grunted but didn't bother replying. The fact was, I'd done nothing but trust his decisions, and—up until this point, at least—he hadn't really led me astray. It just went against every instinct to willingly cross into Mareritten without the might of a drakkon underneath me.

Have me, came Oma's comment. *Can burn any who chase.*

Her comment once again held the hint of anticipation, and I couldn't help my smile. She really did have vengeance on her mind.

Can you see any Mareritt movement from up there?

Some. I burn?

It'll warn them we're near, I said quickly. *It's better not to until we're discovered.*

Displeasure rumbled through her thoughts. *Burn later, then.*

Yes. I hesitated. *Can you warn us if any Mareritt approach our position? But keep out of sight—they suspect we've a drakkon helping us and might shoot at you.*

They shoot, I burn.

That was one comment I couldn't really argue with. Not when I'd probably do the exact same thing.

After a couple of hours, we reached the first of the deforested areas, which meant we were close to where the coruscation lay. My heart began to beat a little faster, and I scanned the area ahead with a mix of anticipation and trepidation. I couldn't immediately see it, which was odd given the size of the sphere—although my memories and the coruscation of *this* time might be two vastly different things.

Kaiden moved to the edge of the path and peered over the edge. "I can't see any Mareritt on the road below. It should be safe enough to cross."

Oma? I asked. *Where are the patrols?*

Other side of lake.

Thanks.

I passed the information on to Kaiden, and we immediately crossed the gutted strip of land.

"Has she flown over the coruscation yet?" he said.

"I haven't asked."

"Might be worth doing so. If nothing else, we'll get a feel for what we'll face once we get close."

I nodded and passed on the request.

What coruscation? she immediately asked.

I hesitated. *It's a cylindrical ball that's a mix of magic and ice; it looks like a moon fallen to earth.*

The moon leashed to lake?

I presume so.

Will check.

Be careful. They have another drakkon doing sweeps around the area.

Won't report. She seeking you, not me.

I frowned. *You've been in contact with her?*

Yes.

Suggesting that while the Mareritt might control and communicate with the smaller drakkons via their bands, the drakkons *did* maintain a degree of individualism. And *that* would explain why Oma had heeded my warning when she'd been shot down. She couldn't ignore the band's demand that she flame, but she'd understood my words and, perhaps instinctively, had recognized the kinship between us, even if she'd never heard of the kin.

And what if she is sent after you?

Then you free her.

It's not that easy, Oma.

Is easy. I believe.

Believed in me, she meant, and that was both warming and alarming, if only because she was setting a bar I might not be able to reach.

We made it across the first of the deforested sections, but the tension within ramped up rather than released. We had who knew how many more to go, and with every one, the chances of us being spotted by a patrol on the road below increased.

Above moon, Oma said.

Can you describe it?

Like moon.

I smiled. *Is it bright like the moon or are there darker patches?*

Bright. She paused. *But cracked.*

My heart began to beat a little faster. *Cracked where?*

At top. Wide enough to stick leg into.

If it was wide enough to fit one of *her* legs, it was wide enough for me to slip through and fall into the lake underneath—and would account for my wet clothes. But it still didn't explain how I'd gotten from West Laminium to the

Talien farmlands. Or why my clothes hadn't dried in all that time.

Can you see anything in that crack?

Ice. She paused. *Part wing. Is white.*

I clenched my fists against the surge of hope. There was no guarantee that wing belonged to Emri. No guarantee that the ice had kept her safe and whole as it had me. But the fact that it was white did at least confirm the coruscation had caused my skin bleaching.

How is the coruscation held above the lake?

Leashed. Metal. She paused. *Mareritt on move.*

To where?

Away from moon.

That didn't sound good. "Kaiden, how far away from Pike's are we?"

"About ten minutes." He glanced over his shoulder. "Why?"

"Oma just said the Mareritt are pulling back from the coruscation. I think we need to uncover why."

"Let's go."

He broke into a run, moving swiftly through the trees and into the next deforested zone. I followed, leaping over trenches that had been cut into the ground by unimpeded runoff and skirting ragged tree stumps. We raced through another small strip of forest, a third stripped section, and had barely entered the next forested zone when he jagged to the right and began scrambling up the slope.

"Why?" I asked, even as I scrambled up after him.

"Pike's Finger lies around the next bend, but it can only be accessed from above."

After a few more minutes, he went left, edged along an almost nonexistent path, and then dropped and crawled through some bushes. I followed, my heart pounding so hard it felt like it was about to tear out of my chest. I wasn't sure if it was fear or anger or a mix of both. The coruscation had taken everything from me. It had catapulted me into a place so utterly different that it might well have been an alien landscape—and I was about to see it for the first time since we'd attacked the two of them.

We were on a huge finger of stone that jutted out over a severe drop. The valley below was a green haven compared to the stripped and broken starkness of the surrounding slopes. A wide, dark lake lay at the base, and above this— sitting in a wide shallow cup supported by a thick rod of metal—was the coruscation. It did indeed resemble a moon, though on a much smaller scale and with a glow that was pale blue rather than warm white. It was as perfectly round as the day I'd first seen it but definitely smaller. This coruscation would not have held three graces. I doubted it would have held two. It was melting, just like the one that had caused the lake. The magic that had protected this one for two hundred years was finally failing.

As my gaze followed the crack over the curve of the coruscation, a memory stirred. One of blue skies viewed through ragged edges of ice. Of the caress of power— perhaps even magic—in my mind and body, a power that protected both even as it restrained. I remembered the caress of sunlight and heat slowly melting the imprisoning ice, and then a jolt as it fell away and gave me freedom. That's when I'd fallen, a cry on my lips and agony ringing in my ears and mind. But that agony was itself little more than a memory—a brief echo from the moment before magic and ice had frozen all hope. Emri hadn't come to life as I had. She remained frozen deeper within the coruscation.

Could we apply the same sort of slow melt process to rescue Sorrel, Emri, and what remained of the graces?

I hoped so. But to even attempt it, we had to get the coruscation to a far safer place.

"We have to get down there—"

"Not until we know what the Mareritt are up to." Kaiden pointed to the road that ran around the boundary of the lake. There were three people movers on it and one division of foot soldiers doing a double-time march. "They're definitely retreating."

The inner uneasiness ramped up. "It could be some sort of trap—maybe they're withdrawing enough troops in the hope we'll risk going down there."

"It's a possibility."

"But not what you think is happening."

"After what we did to the checkpoints, they should be reinforcing, *not* retreating. Besides, if they were going to set a trap, they would have done it by now. The valley is far too open, and they're all too exposed."

"So are we once we get off this section of mountain." My gaze followed the retreating Mareritt. This *wasn't* a trap. This wasn't the Mareritt being recalled into other positions. Something else was going on. "Maybe they've brought in tanks or some kind of long-range weapon and want their men out of the way."

"Could be. Can you ask Oma to do a sweep?"

I immediately did so, then added, *Is the other drakkon still patrolling?*

Has left.

Did she say why?

Ordered out.

The unease became full-blown fear. My gaze went to the coruscation, and a thick lump formed in my throat. *Oma, fly away from the moon. Fast.*

Her thoughts gained height and distance, but that thick

lump of fear increased until every breath was short, sharp pants.

"Red?" Kaiden voice seemed to be coming from a great distance. "Nara, what's wrong? What's happening?"

I couldn't answer him. I could only stare across the long length of the valley toward whatever point the Mareritt were retreating to.

That's when I saw it.

The arc of light. Not one. Not two, but five deadly streams.

They weren't incoming artillery shells. They were something else; something that cut through the air, leaving a frozen tail streaming behind it even as it propelled the round, glowing object at the nose forward.

They moved in utter silence, a force of destruction that hit the coruscation with deadly accuracy.

For a second, nothing happened. The glowing objects were simply absorbed into the coruscation.

Then, with little noise or fanfare, the coruscation exploded.

Between one heartbeat and the next, every hope I'd had and everything I'd ever known became little more than a million tiny shards of glittering, silvery blue ice that drifted gently on the breeze.

EIGHT

For several heartbeats, I could only stare at the spot where the coruscation had been.

Emri.

Gone forever.

Sorrel, as dead as those who lay far in the past.

The beauty of graces soaring through blue skies now forever nothing more than a memory.

Any hope Arleeon might have had of redemption via drakkon wing splintered into minute shards of icy destruction.

Horror surged and the shaking began. Pain hit—deep, utter, mind-destroying pain.

A scream tore through me, a scream that was soul deep and endless. I had no idea whether I gave it voice or if it remained locked inside, echoing through the void that had once contained the other half of my soul.

I could hear voices. Distant voices. Voices I recognized, voices I trusted, but they held no power and absolutely no means to call me back from the brink. I tumbled into utter darkness, blind and unresponsive, wanting death. *Needing* death.

But she refused to heed my call.

Consciousness returned in fragments as small as the ice that had shattered both my heart and my soul.

A murmur within, offering strength.

A murmur without, asking for courage. Telling me not to abandon those who yet remained.

Stone against my back. Heat surrounding me, warming skin as cold as death.

The musk of a drakkon. The earthy scent of a man.

Life, when all I wanted was death. But for whatever reason, she was not yet mine to hold.

I climbed the few final steps to full consciousness and opened my eyes. I lay in a vast cavern. Stalactites glittered high above, and somewhere in the distance water trickled, a merry sound in the deep silence that otherwise dominated. A sleeping roll padded the stone slab underneath me, and a second one covered me.

Kaiden stood to my right, his arms crossed and one shoulder resting against the edge of the cavern's entrance. A thick beard covered his chin, and his face was set in stony despair. Beyond him, stars twinkled, bright in black skies.

To my left, her bulk dominating much of the cavern's rear and with her head tucked under her tail, was Oma. Her eyes were closed and her mind silent aside from drifting dreams of flaming Mareritten. It was her body heat I'd been feeling.

Somehow, these two had called me back from darkness and insanity. It shouldn't have been possible. History—and to some extent, experience via friends who'd suffered similar losses—had taught me that when a drakkon or her rider was killed, death soon took the remaining partner. Our lives and our minds were too entwined to survive the erasure of one.

I *should* be dead.

And yet, despite the thick fist of despair and emptiness that sat like a weight in the middle of my chest, I wasn't sorry to be here. Wasn't sorry to still be alive.

I had no hope of vengeance if death *had* heeded my call.

"How long have I been out?" It came out little more than a vague croak; my throat was raw, and every word burned. My screams obviously *hadn't* been just internal.

Kaiden swung around, the force of his relief so fierce it had tears rising. I blinked them away as he strode over and squatted beside my makeshift bed.

"How are you feeling?" His voice was soft, barely reaching my ears despite his closeness.

I wasn't sure if he simply didn't want to wake Oma or if perhaps he feared I was still so fragile that any undue noise might cause me to slip back.

"Like my heart has been torn out of my chest and thrown away." Grief rose, a thick wave that closed my throat and had me battling tears. There was nothing I could do for my sister now. Nothing I could do for Emri. Nothing except give them revenge. It wouldn't ease the pain, but it at least gave me a reason to continue on. To resist the urge to just give up and join them. "Why would they destroy the coruscation like that after leaving it to melt for so long?"

"I don't know." His expression was grim. "But perhaps they suspect you came from it and wanted to ensure no others could be released."

Despair pulsed, a wave of darkness threatening to wash me away again. I blinked back the tears and the pain and said, "Which makes sense, but why wait two hundred years to do so? Why not simply destroy the coruscations the minute they'd trapped us all?"

"Perhaps they couldn't," he said. "Perhaps they've only just developed the means and the power to do so."

"But—" I paused and swallowed again. In the end, understanding their actions didn't matter. Only getting revenge did. "And the things that destroyed it? Have you ever seen missiles like that before?"

"No."

"Meaning that could be what they're developing in the White Zone." Not another coruscation but a weapon that was powerful enough to erase one—and no doubt everything else that stood in their way.

His hand touched mine—a brief but comforting caress, and one I wasn't entirely sure was meant for me but rather for him. "We can't discount the possibility they're creating another coruscation just yet, but those ice missiles are not a good development. Do you want a drink?"

"Yes. Thanks."

He rose and moved across to a portable cooking unit on the other side of the cavern. A small but lightly steaming pot sat on the top. He scooped up some of the contents with a metal cup, topped it up with fresh water, and then walked back.

"Can you sit up? Or do you want help?"

"I can sit." I pushed upright and then scooted back so my spine was pressed against the wall. The effort left me trembling.

Kaiden held the cup close to my lips. It smelled of grass and an assortment of other herbs, and I sipped it somewhat warily. There was obviously some sort of numbing agent in the concoction because my throat instantly felt better. I drank the rest of it and then leaned my head against the cavern wall and briefly closed my eyes.

"How long was I out?" I asked again.

"Just over a week."

I stared at him, unable to comprehend. A week? How was that even *possible* given the hunt that must have followed the destruction of the coruscation?

It was a thought that had the thick knot of grief stirring, but that was a hole I couldn't afford to fall down. Not again. I couldn't change what had happened, but I could certainly change this world.

Or, at least, attempt to.

And while that would never ease the knot or the pain, it would at least make living with it all that much easier.

"But haven't the Mareritt been searching for us?"

"Yes." He took my hand, his fingers warm as they twined through mine. "But we remain free thanks to a whole lot of help from Oma and a thick slab of luck."

"Meaning?"

"Meaning she dropped from the sky the minute you collapsed and carried you away from the valley. She found this cavern, stashed you, and then came back for me. Aside from one hunt, she hasn't moved from your side."

Because she was giving me her heat and her strength. Urging me not to give up, to come back, because the drakkons of this time needed me. Because *she* needed me. I wanted to reach out and touch her, thank her, but didn't. I could feel the underlying tiredness in her now; she needed to rest and recover after giving so much to me.

I returned my gaze to Kaiden. "We owe her our lives. Again."

"Yes. And I have a newfound respect for kin after being carried by a drakkon. Man was *not* meant to be borne aloft, especially when it's in the claws of a drakkon rather than on her back."

A smile touched my lips, as he no doubt intended. "How far did she carry us?"

"Across to the Balkain Mountain range. This cave is very near the Black River tunnel, in fact."

Which was a good distance for a drakkon her size, especially when she was unused to carrying anyone. Even full-sized drakkons didn't lift kin until they were at least twenty years old—which was why most bonds were formed *after* drakkons had reached that age.

"I'm surprised the Mareritt didn't immediately flood West Laminium with drakkons. It would have stopped Oma getting us out."

"They couldn't—"

"Why not? Surely they would have had spotters out after the explosion—"

"Which rained deadly shards of ice—and, I presume, whatever magic remained within the coruscation—into the entire valley for close to an hour. We were high enough to avoid it, and it allowed Oma to sweep in and out without being seen."

If we were above it, then it surely wouldn't have affected the other drakkons. But maybe the Mareritt simply didn't want to risk it; maybe they had no idea just what the aftereffects of exploding the magic encased coruscation would be. It had, after all, been created two hundred years ago, and they apparently hadn't tried to replicate the spell since.

Or was it more the fact that they *couldn't*?

I took a deep breath that did little to ease the ache inside

—an ache I would feel for the rest of my life. "What are the Mareritt doing now?"

"Swarming through Arleeon." He grimaced. "We can't risk contacting anyone for help, which basically leaves us with little choice but to chance the tunnel."

"That tunnel is probably an even bigger risk now—especially if they're pouring soldiers into Arleeon."

"You're forgetting eight days have passed. The only traffic coming through the tunnel at the moment is supply trains and the occasional scooter."

I grunted. I remained unconvinced it was the best option, but it was pointless going against his advice now. "I take it this cavern is another the rebellion uses?"

"No, but there *is* one a half a day run from here. Once the focus had shifted from the immediate area and Oma had fed, I was able to go and grab enough supplies to get us through."

"What about a scooter?"

"*That* we'll have to purloin once you're fit enough to move."

"But every second we spend here is one more they have to find us."

"I know."

"And don't care."

"Indeed." He reached out with his free hand and brushed stray strands of hair from my cheek. There was gentleness in his caress and caring in his eyes. "Right now, *nothing* is more important than you regaining strength. Arleeon's soul depends on it."

Mine depends on it. He didn't add that, but it seemed to hover between us anyway.

It was then I noticed the echo of pain in his eyes. *My*

pain. He might not have known Emri, but he'd nevertheless felt the agony of her death thanks to the growing connection between us.

I didn't say anything. I just tugged him closer and kissed him. Not sweetly, not softly, but with all the hunger of someone who'd stepped into the arms of death and yet was somehow still alive. His hand slipped to the back of my neck, holding me steady as the kiss deepened; for many minutes there was nothing but his lips and the passion that rose like a bonfire between us.

When he finally pulled back, his eyes were aglow with desire. "As much as I want, with every inch of my body, to take this further, you need to rest and regain strength."

A smile tugged at my lips. While I wanted nothing more than to celebrate being alive in the most basic way possible, he was right. Getting to Esan would take a lot of time, luck, and no doubt fire strength. If we wanted any hope of freeing Arleeon and her drakkons, we both needed to be in peak condition. And *that* unfortunately meant sex would have to wait until a more appropriate time and place.

"I don't suppose you have anything more substantial to eat than that grassy concoction you just gave me?"

"We have reconstituted soup, cheese, or some kind of flatbread that is doing a good impression of thin rock."

I snorted softly. "I think I'll stick to the soup."

He nodded and rose. I drifted off to sleep for a time, woke long enough to eat the soup, and then drifted back. That was basically the pattern of the next few days. Oma remained asleep, which wasn't unusual for a drakkon who'd expended a great amount of energy.

Dawn was just breaking across the skies outside when the awareness of being watched hit. Kaiden's body was pressed against mine, his heat stirring the distant embers of desire. But he wasn't the one watching me—he was asleep, his soft snores echoing through the cavern's vastness.

I smiled and carefully moved a hand from under the sleeping roll. Oma stretched her neck and presented an eye ridge for me to scratch. Delight rumbled through her thoughts when I complied.

You awake. Am happy.

I'm awake because of you. I owe you my life, Oma.

You free me. Right I save you. She hesitated. *Emri gone.*

That fist tightened. I blinked and nodded. *Yes.*

Am sorry.

So am I. I would have liked you to have met her.

Mareritt pay?

Indeed they will.

Another happy rumble ran through her thoughts. *Now?*

No. We need to get to Esan first.

Esan?

The fortress where Kaiden lives.

Why?

Because we need them to find a way of blocking the control bands the Mareritt use on the drakkons. If we can, they would no longer control any of you.

That good aim. We go now?

I couldn't help my chuckle. Though it was soft, Kaiden stirred and his arm snaked around my waist. "What's funny?"

His voice was a warm mix of sleepiness and desire, but he did no more than hold me close. "I told Oma why we needed to get to Esan, and she's now eager to move."

"We can't go anywhere until we know it's safe." He kissed my shoulder, then got up and padded barefoot across to the cavern's entrance. Dawn's light lovingly caressed the muscular planes of his upper body, making my fingers itch with the longing to do the same. After several minutes, he said, "The coast appears to be clear, but it might be wise for Oma to do a quick sweep before we leave our hideout."

Oma grunted and climbed to her feet, being careful to tuck her wings back so she didn't accidentally hit me. *Will fly now.*

Kaiden backed away to give her room. Once at the entrance, she crouched low and then jumped high, her wings pumping hard as she slowly climbed and disappeared from sight. I got out of bed and padded across the cavern, following the gentle sound of tumbling water until I found the stream. It was icy cold but better that than not bathing at all. To say I stunk would be something of an understatement.

Once dressed, I heated up the remains of the soup while Kaiden stripped off and quickly bathed. Once we'd eaten, we gathered everything together, slung the rifles over our shoulders, and moved across to the cavern's entrance.

There was no sign of Oma in the cloud-streaked skies, but she was close.

No Mareritt near mountain.

Where are they?

In valley of moon. They look at pieces.

No doubt ensuring the destruction of hope had been utterly complete. I closed my eyes against the stab and drew in a deep breath. It didn't really help. I suspected only time would, and even then only partially.

I repeated the news to Kaiden. He nodded and led the way down the mountain. The Black River tumbled past us, its spray drifting through the air, not only clinging to my hair and dampening my clothes but also making the path more than a little treacherous. I had to grab at nearby trees more than once during the long descent but made it down in one piece. We followed the riverbank until we found a crossing point and then, keeping to the trees, moved toward the road. The entrance of the tunnel became visible and very much looked like the maw of some ancient but monstrous animal.

Kaiden hunkered down at the edge of the forest and studied the road and the tunnel for several seconds.

"What's the—"

He held up his hand and cocked his head to one side. After a moment, I heard it—the distant rumble of a vehicle.

"That *doesn't* sound like a scooter."

"I think it's a supply train and may actually be the better option in the current circumstances."

I frowned. "A supply train doesn't sound like it'll be fast—"

"They're not scooter fast, but they can still move along at a reasonable clip. The advantage will be the fact they're less likely to stop a train."

"Up until the moment they realize there's one missing."

"Yes, but the trains have no exterior identification, so they can't use drakkons to spot the missing one. Add *that* to the fact they won't expect us to be in Mareritten, and we have a good chance of getting a clean run."

"What happens once we take the train beyond Break Point Pass? Do they still have a military encampment near Esan?"

"Yes—and I daresay it's far larger than the one that existed back in your day."

I frowned. "Which basically means they have Esan surrounded—how on earth has the city survived two hundred years, given the Mareritt ability to create ice in the air and freeze foe?"

"Their ability to freeze is dependent on the strength of their mages. It's only recently we've noticed the uptick in its use." His voice was grim. "But we've had two hundred years to figure out means to at least combat its use in Esan itself."

"What sort of technology can combat the use of air as a weapon?"

"Full protection suits and shelters with air conditioners designed to regulate and warm incoming air."

"Machines can't work when frozen."

"Yes, but their mages don't have unlimited resources or strength—otherwise, why would they have used ground forces to destroy Zephrine and the mages to assault the aeries? The only explanation is a lack of strength and the need to concentrate on what they considered their most important aim—to destroy the fighting drakkons and to claim future graces as their own."

Two aims that had been totally successful thanks to meticulous planning. And for the first time I wondered just how much Zephrine's downfall was due to arrogance—to an ingrained belief that no matter what the Mareritt threw at us, the drakkons and kin could handle it.

"Would the defenses you've developed work against something like the ice missiles?"

"Given what they did to the coruscation, I very much doubt it." He touched my arm lightly, as if to counter the wave of grief that rose within me. "Which is why we need to get back to Esan and warn them. They can't counter what they don't know about."

If there was some way of countering them. Something within suspected that might not be done easily—though *that* might be nothing more than pessimism.

But even if we did nothing more than free the drakkons and take out a couple of their mages, it would hamper their progress, perhaps for another century or two. And by then, drakkons might have regained full size and once again dominate the skies.

I returned my gaze to the tunnel. "How do you plan to stop the train?"

"I'll step out in front of it."

I gave him a long look. "Despite your protests to the contrary, you really are insane, aren't you?"

He grinned. "They won't run me over."

"Once again, I like the assurance with which you say that."

"For the most part, trains only have the driver and a guard—"

"Which only means they're less likely to stop."

"Except I won't be armed. Trust me, they *will* stop and check my ID. It's common procedure for any Arleeon found within a restricted area."

"What if they decided to run you over instead? Or simply stop and shoot you? That's going to put a serious dent in our hijack plans." My voice was dry. "And in case you've forgotten, your Kai identity has been blown."

"Yes, but while the guard is checking my ID, you can sneak into the train and take out the driver."

"Because he won't be alert for such a possibility, now will he?"

Kaiden's grin flashed. "Which is why we'll do this on a curve. Neither of them will see you until it's too late. Shall we go?"

I shook my head at the anticipation in his tone but nevertheless rose and followed him through the trees. The sound of the train grew closer; Kaiden stopped just beyond the halfway point of a sharp turn and motioned to the other side of the road.

"You hide over there—it's the same side as the control center's door. Once the guard moves out to question me, you sneak up and take out the driver."

I nodded. "Good luck."

"Good hunting."

I snorted and then cut quickly across the road. After finding a large enough tree to hide behind, I checked my rifle—just in case things didn't go according to plan—then slipped the knife into my hand. Blue light ran down the blade's sharp edges, as if in anticipation.

The growing rumble of the train suggested it wasn't far away now. I shifted my weight from one leg to the other, tension thrumming through me. After another few minutes, a silvery pod came into sight. It was long and bullet shaped and obviously used the same sort of repulsion technology as the scooters because there were no wheels or sleds in evidence. Five of the bullet-shaped pods went by; there were at least another eight that I could see. The coupling links connecting each pod were thick and heavy—if we needed to disconnect them at any point, it would not be easy *or* fast.

As the ninth pod passed my tree, the whole train came to a shuddering halt and the vehicle silently settled onto the ground. I peered out from behind my tree but couldn't see the control pod—it was already well around the corner. I ran to the side of the train and waited a second to see if I'd been spotted. When no alarm sounded, I carefully moved forward. But I'd barely traversed five pods when there was a loud hiss; a heartbeat later, the control pod's door opened up and out. I ducked into the gap between two of the pods, my knuckles white with the force of my grip on the knife. After a second, the clomp of boots on metal echoed, quickly followed by the crunch of stone as the guard moved to the front of the train. Once he'd disappeared from sight, I continued on toward the control pod, pausing briefly at the ramp to peer inside. The driver's attention was on Kaiden and the guard. I took a deep breath, silently bid Túxn to grant me luck, and then moved.

The driver didn't hear my approach—not until my arm wrapped around his neck, and by then it was too late. I stabbed him, held him still while he died, then released him and wiped the knife clean on his shirt. And felt absolutely no remorse whatsoever. In fact, there was something very satisfying in taking a Mareritt life up close and personal rather than from a distance or from drakkon back. If I could have killed them all the exact same way, I would have. Such a desire wasn't possible, practical, or even smart, I knew that, but that didn't in any way negate it.

They'd killed my family. Destroyed my sister and my drakkon. I would never, ever forgive them for that.

I unclipped the driver and hauled him out of the seat. Kaiden appeared at the bottom of the ramp. "Drag him over here—we're going to need him at the other end of the train."

"Why the other end?"

"They have control pods at front and back. Saves them turning the thing around." He grabbed the guard and hauled him over his shoulder. "Hit the door close button on your way out."

I did so, then followed him to the rear of the train. There were eighteen cargo pods in all, and concern rose. "Are you sure we're going to get enough speed out of this thing? Wouldn't it be easier to dump the cargo and just run in the control pod?"

He pressed the guard's hand against the control pad. As

the door opened, he glanced back at me. "We'll do that if it becomes necessary, but right now, those cargo pods are our ticket through Mareritten. Besides, we might be able to use their contents. You want to tell Oma we're about to head into the tunnel?"

I did so, then added, *Meet us on the other side of the mountain. Let us know if you see any patrols. And fly high, just in case they have their drakkons out.*

Drakkons out. Still hunting you, not me.

Doesn't mean they won't be, Oma, so be cautious.

Will.

I closed the door and then climbed into the passenger seat. The control board looked even more complicated than the ones on the scooters, but Kaiden didn't seem fazed. After he'd pressed a number of buttons and switches, the train rose from the ground and was soon moving forward at a reasonable clip. He then reached underneath the main panel, felt around for a few seconds, and pulled out a small metal disk.

"Locator beacon." He dropped it onto the floor and smashed it under his boot. "I've also disconnected the security features, including fingerprint access. It'll make things easier."

We entered the dark maw of the tunnel, and the forward lights came on. "How long will it take us to get through the tunnel?"

He glanced at a screen to his right, where a red dot was moving along a green line. "According to guidance, thirty-eight minutes."

I grunted. "It's one hell of a long tunnel."

"So was the one at Break Point. It just didn't feel that way because we were under threat."

"Putting it mildly." I sat sideways on the chair to study

him. "How about we fill in the time with you telling me a little more about yourself?"

He raised an eyebrow, his expression amused. "There's not all that much to know."

"You said you had five younger sisters—are they your only siblings?"

The shadow of guilt and grief ran briefly through his expression. "No—I've also three brothers, two of whom are still alive."

"The third being the one who died via the sword—the one whose death you feel responsible for?"

"Yes. It was his first raid and I was in charge. I should have taken better care of him. Should have—" He stopped and grimaced. "But I didn't, and he was caught and executed."

Which no doubt explained why he and his father were at odds. Both of them blamed him for the death.

My gaze went to his neck. "Is that where you got the scar?"

He nodded. "If we hadn't had a medic on the team, I would have bled out."

The brief flash of bleakness in his expression suggested that in the darkest hour of his darkest dreams, he sometimes wished he *had*. It went some way to explaining why he took part in so many dangerous forays into occupied Arleeon—it was a means of making his brother's sacrifice have some meaning, as much as an avenue of revenge.

"Was your brother executed straight away?" I asked softly.

He glanced at me, his expression once again carefully controlled. Which was pretty pointless when the connection between us roiled with anger and guilt. "No. He'd no doubt been thoroughly interrogated first."

"You were there. You witnessed it."

"I had to be. I couldn't save him—there was just too many of them. But I didn't want him to die alone." He paused and then added softly, "Someone had to sing his soul onward to the next life."

I wanted to reach out and touch him, to offer the comfort I suspected he needed and yet would reject. "If you *had* tried to rescue him, you'd now also be dead."

"I know. That doesn't make accepting his death or my part in it any easier."

"Nothing ever will." Not for him, not for me.

"No." He glanced at me again. "What about you? Are the tales of your family true?"

A smile twitched my lips. "That depends entirely on what you've heard about my family."

"According to the legends, the Velez line had a reputation for living as hard as they fought—and that the hardest of them all was, in fact, Hattie Velez, the ninety-three-year-old matriarch."

Memories stirred, and there seemed to be a lot more of them now. Ice remained in the deeper sections of my mind, but perhaps in shattering the coruscation, the Mareritt had diminished its magic within me. "I think she got worse the day they stopped her and Teela from flying missions—she wanted to prove to all and sundry there was still a lot of life in her old bones."

"Why did they stop them from flying?"

"Teela was losing her sight—it's a problem many drakkons have when they hit senior years. It's why so many were used to protect the aeries."

Which also meant they'd probably have been amongst those frozen and then smashed when the Mareritt had attacked Zephrine and claimed her aeries. I studied the darkness beyond the front window for a second, trying to marshal the sadness that rose. It wouldn't have been a great way for anyone to die, but for someone so vital, so full of life and love and fierceness, to be taken so easily, without any warning or the chance of taking any Mareritt down with them... At least the rest of my family would have gone down fighting. Even my youngest sister—who'd barely been fifteen at the time of the coruscation—had been proficient in weapon usage.

I hoped they made the Mareritt pay for their victory.

Hoped they didn't suffer when they died.

"I wasn't aware drakkons no longer able to fight were relegated to the aeries," Kaiden said. "I thought looking after the eggs and the drakklings was the province of the males."

"To a point yes, but drakklings are a hungry bunch and require constant feeding to ensure full development."

"So the older drakkons guarded the aeries while the males did the meal runs?"

I nodded, even as curiosity rose. "How can you not know any of this? Granted, Esan came close to falling, but she didn't, so why has so much knowledge about drakkons and kin been lost?"

"It hasn't been lost, as such," he said. "But there's little point in studying the glories of the past when we've spent two hundred years on the brink of annihilation."

An annihilation that had begun with the destruction of all I'd known. The fist in my chest briefly tightened.

"But for the first time in all that time, we have hope," he continued softly. "We have you and Oma, and that gives us a starting point."

I met his gaze. Knew he was talking more from a personal point; that the hope he held was one of a future that didn't involve fighting and death but rather love and family.

It was a hope I desperately wanted to share, and yet one I didn't dare reach for. I had no idea why Túxn had chosen me, out of all the kin to have flown into the coruscation that day, to survive, but I doubted it was to give me what had otherwise escaped me two hundred years ago. There was always a price to pay for her favors, and I had no doubt mine had yet to be revealed.

"One kin and one drakkon do not a grace make, Kaiden."

He smiled, though that determination was back in his eyes. He knew my thoughts. Knew, and was absolutely rejecting them.

"As I said, it's a starting point. And if we can free other drakkons, then hope will spread through Arleeon. That's all we need—hope."

Hope was a powerful motivator but on its own would never be enough. Even if we could free more drakkons, we still needed to uncover what the Mareritt were doing in the White Zone and then find a way to stop them. And that was before we even began the long push to remove them from our land.

Silence fell between us, and the miles hummed by. A scooter went past at the midpoint but gave no indication they noticed anything untoward—no doubt because they were as blinded by our lights as we were by theirs.

We came out of the tunnel into a landscape that was both stark and beautiful. The autumn coats of the tamarack trees contrasted sharply against the darker green of the needle pines, and a carpet of red and green summer grasses stretched as far as the eye could see. All of which would be gone soon enough, buried for another nine months under layers of snow. How either survived—and even thrived in parts of Mareritten—I had no idea.

Kaiden reset guidance, and we were soon following a road that ran parallel to the mountains. I glanced across to the screen and groaned. "Four and a half days to get there? Seriously?"

"That's if we maintain full speed. I'm not entirely sure what the road conditions are like—there could be areas where we'll have to slow."

"Great." I scrubbed a hand across my eyes. "This is going to get boring."

"Under different circumstances, I might have made several satisfying suggestions to pass the time, but given we're in enemy territory, I don't think that's wise."

"Only several?" I raised my eyebrows. "I'm disappointed, warrior."

His grin flashed. "Then perhaps you can take the lead once we're safely back at Esan."

"Once we're safely back at Esan, won't we be planning an assault into the White Zone?"

"Yes, but any such assault will have a better chance of success if we can find a means of disrupting the signal between the Mareritt and the control bands on the drakkon."

"That could take months, and we don't have—"

"It won't take months."

A smile touched my lips. "Again, such confidence."

"In this case, it's justified."

I hoped so, because the only other means we had of freeing the drakkons was to remove the band from each and every one of them, and *that* was nigh on impossible.

The day drifted on. After eight hours at the controls, Kaiden gave me a rundown, and from then on, we alternated shifts. Thankfully, the control pod did have privy facilities, and while they weren't the cleanest I'd ever used, it was certainly a better—and less risky—option than stopping the train and running behind a tree. Especially when trees were becoming scarcer the farther east we moved.

Oma reported the occasional Mareritt sighting, but for the first two days, none came near us.

On the morning of the third day, the communications panel came to life, and a gruff voice demanded all trains report in and then divert to the nearest base.

I glanced at Kaiden. "Can they use comms to track us?"

He shook his head. "But they'll no doubt send drakkons aloft. It won't be hard to find us, especially if there's no delivery programmed for the eastern encampment."

"How big is that encampment?"

"Big enough."

"Does it lie between us and Esan?"

"No, but the minute their ground radars show us leaving the road and heading toward Esan, we will become a target."

That would no doubt have happened regardless of which side of the mountain we were on. "Our biggest danger is going to be tanks—a train this size isn't exactly a hard target, and drakkon fire can only take out one tank at a time." I paused. "In fact, making the train a target might be our best option. If they think we're dead, they might call off the patrols and give us the chance to get to Esan."

He raised his eyebrows. "So you're suggesting we proceed on foot? And you call me crazy?"

"It's no less improbable than anything else we've done to date."

He laughed. "That's totally true. Let's wait and see what eventuates."

I studied the bleak landscape for several minutes. It was a place of rocks, stunted-looking shrubs, and autumn-colored grasses. There wasn't much in the way of cover, on foot or not. "What's the ground like closer to the Esan gateway?"

"We've the delightful choice of bogs or barren foothills. Neither will be easy to traverse."

"Bogs?"

"They're eons old and run from the base of the foothills to the sea." He glanced at me. "Have you never flown over this area?"

I shook my head. "It was only when additional help was needed that either fortress crossed into the other's flight zone. That didn't happen in my time—"

"Until the appearance of the coruscations."

I ignored the squeeze in my chest and nodded. "And perhaps their development is the reason we had so many seasons with little or no Mareritt activity—and why we'd felt so secure."

"Falsely so, as it turned out. The signs that something was happening within Mareritten were certainly there."

"It's very easy to look back with the benefit of hindsight and make such connections, Kaiden. It's a different matter when you're living it."

He grunted, but whether it meant he agreed or not, I couldn't say. Silence fell, and the miles continued to track past.

But as the flat landscape gave way to a long succession of rolling hills, Oma said, *Drakkon comes.*

From where?

From pass.

Meaning Break Point, no doubt. *Any sign of Mareritt?*

She paused. *No.*

Meaning the drakkon might be on a simple scouting sweep rather than being sent after us.

Let me know if Mareritt follow or if the drakkon prepares to attack.

Will. She paused again. *Know her.*

Something twisted inside. I knew what was coming. Knew that in the current situation it would be dangerous. Very dangerous. *How?*

Born same time.

Oma—

Must free her. She egg sister.

Egg sister? Twins were extremely rare in drakkons, but it did at least explain Oma's determination. *We have no safe means of bringing down a drakkon, and any delay could be deadly.*

I ground her. You free.

The determination in Oma's mental tones suggested she wasn't about to give way on this—and really, who could blame her? Hadn't I done the exact same thing? Hadn't I gone careening through Arleeon in the vague hope of rescuing Sorrel, Emri, and the trapped graces? This really wasn't any different.

Will she not sense the trap?

She trusts.

Meaning I'd guessed right—while the Mareritt did control their actions, the drakkons at least maintained some autonomy of thought. And, in the long run, that could very much play into our favor.

Fine, Oma. We'll try. As her happiness flooded my thoughts, I scrubbed a hand across my face and then glanced at Kaiden. "We have a problem."

"Mareritt?"

"Drakkon. Oma insists we free her."

Kaiden frowned. "I'm all for doing that, but now is neither the time nor the place—"

"Oma doesn't care. The incoming drakkon is an egg sister."

"Damn." His expression was grim. "Then we have no choice. If it were our kin, we wouldn't hesitate. Oma has saved our lives twice now. We owe her this."

"I'm glad you feel that way, because I've already agreed to help."

Kaiden chuckled. "What would you have done if I'd disagreed?"

"Probably jumped out of the train and tackled the situation myself."

"I'm beginning to think you have more in common with your grandmother than you ever let on."

"Which is saying something, given I did have a reputation for recklessness."

"So do I." There was a seriousness in his eyes that belied the amusement in his expression. "I think we both know there's nothing impulsive or thoughtless about our actions, despite appearances to the contrary."

I wondered just how many of his friends and family understood that; certainly there'd been no one in *my* time who'd so deeply understood me. No one, I thought with a wistful smile, except Hattie.

Kiva nears.

How do you plan to bring her down?

Will force her down and pin.

I frowned. *Why pin?*

Band gives Mareritt eyes. Will react when sees you.

Meaning two things. I needed to be bait, and I needed to get away from this train before she neared if we were to have any hope of maintaining our cover. *How far away is she?*

Close.

Within sight of the train?

Not yet.

How long?

Forty sweeps.

Which, given her wingspread and depending on how fast she was actually flying, was about ten minutes. It would have to be enough.

"There's been a slight change of plans." I pushed up from the seat and moved to the back where we'd stored our kit and weapons. "Kiva's got a camera attached, so you need to slow enough for me to get out."

He immediately powered the train down. "I'll put it into auto—"

"It's better if you stay at the controls. I have no idea how long it'll take to free Kiva, and the train remains our best chance of getting past the eastern encampment. We can't risk it getting away from us."

"A strategy that makes perfectly good sense—which is no doubt why I hate it."

I smiled. "I'll get Oma to do a fly past once we've freed Kiva, and you can come retrieve me."

He nodded. "Keep safe."

I punched the door open but didn't extend the ramp. After a deep breath to gather courage, I leaped out and stumbled away from the train for several yards before I was able to catch my balance. As the door closed and the train continued on, I adjusted the weight of the rifle on my shoulders and jogged down the road. When I looked back, the end section of the train was disappearing over the top of the hill. Relief rose. While it would still be visible to the drakkon, it was less likely that she—and any Mareritt who watched through the camera—would make the connection between it and me.

I moved off the road and into the scrub that filled the area, continuing to move in the opposite direction to the train. It was better to let them think I was heading away from any help Esan might have offered rather than toward it.

As the dusk's golden light increased, a glimmer of bloody red-gold appeared on the horizon. Kiva, not Oma.

Fire surged to my fingertips, eager for release. I flexed them and hoped like hell Oma knew what she was doing. I really didn't want to unleash my weapon on the unsuspecting drakkon—not when we'd undoubtedly need every inch of my firepower to survive whatever the eastern encampment threw at us.

Kiva's bright form drew closer. She was about the same size as Oma, but whereas the phalanges in Oma's wings were gold, Kiva's were red—a sign that one of their parents had come from Zephrine stock, the other Esan.

She spotted me and swooped low. I kept on walking, watching her leg, waiting for the moment the Mareritt gave her the kill order. It didn't take long. The control band flashed blue and Kiva screamed—a sound that echoed harshly across the empty landscape.

Oma? I halted and watched the incoming drakkon warily. *Now might be a good time to bring her down.*

Soon.

Kiva screamed again and sucked in air, readying to attack. *Soon is now, Oma.*

Not yet.

My inner fire surged, and heat burned across my fingertips in readiness. Not to attack but rather shield.

Oma—

Wait.

If she burns me, I'm not going to be pleased.

Trust.

I flexed my fingers and tried to ignore the surge of frustration. Kiva tucked her wings back and dove, her scales glittering like jewels in the fast-disappearing light. I shifted my weight, bracing for the impact of her flames, my own gleaming brightly as they dripped from my fingers.

Kiva's flight flattened out. *Here it comes,* I thought grimly, and cast my shield in front of me. At that precise moment, Oma dropped like a stone from the sky. She hit Kiva hard, driving her down, sending her tumbling. I swore and dropped as Kiva flew past only feet above me and then hit the ground in a squawking, rolling mess of legs and wings. Before she could react in any way, Oma landed and caught the other drakkon's throat in her jaws, her teeth close to the jugular. It was a killing position, and Kiva knew it. She stilled instantly.

Trust, Oma said, though not to me. *We not kill.*

The other drakkon didn't respond, but I could feel her fear and the rising tide of pain that was the Mareritt trying to enforce their will on her.

I grabbed the knife and ran toward them. Kiva saw me, and rage burned through her dark eyes. But she still held enough awareness to obey Oma.

I ducked under her wing and warily approached. Her claws flexed, digging trenches into the soft soil. One wrong move and they could very easily gut me.

Won't, Oma said. *Free her.*

I slashed the small camera from the band and then stomped on it. As metal bits went flying, I shoved the knife into the band's joint point and twisted it sideways. A small gap opened, allowing me to thrust the knife deeper. I took a deep breath, shoved the blade sideways as hard as I could, and forced the band apart. With a soft click, it undid and dropped to the ground. I picked it up and then quickly retreated.

Oma didn't immediately release Kiva, which made me wonder what she was sensing in the other drakkon's deeper thoughts.

Nara free me, she said. *Now she free Kiva. Cannot kill. Understand?*

Brown eyes studied me for several seconds. Then, in a voice that was huskier than Oma's, Kiva said, *Leg and mind no longer burn. Why?*

I walked up to her head and warily scratched her eye ridge. Surprise and perhaps a touch of suspicion flittered through her thoughts. Oma had trusted me almost instantly, but earning Kiva's trust would take longer.

Because I removed the band by which the Mareritt controlled you.

Mareritt?

The white ones, Oma said.

She white.

She kin.

Kin?

Kaieke. Warriors who rode ancestors and shared flame.

I couldn't help my growing smile. Oma had gleaned a whole lot more from our exchanges than I'd presumed.

Kaieke? Kiva eyed me pensively. *Mareritt hate Kaieke. You burn them?*

Yes. And so can you now.

Kiva's answering rumble suggested *that* was an activity she was more than ready to embrace.

You're no longer in their control, Kiva, I continued. *They can no longer force their will on you. You are free to fly where you wish, as you wish.*

Can't. Oma heavy.

I chuckled softly and stepped back to give them both room. Oma released Kiva's throat and then raised her wings, fanning enough to rise and drift sideways. But she settled between me and the other drakkon, protecting me, just in case.

Kiva pushed upright, shook out her wings, and then studied the two of us for several seconds. Uncertainty remained in her thoughts. She wasn't sure what to do next; unlike Oma, it appeared she'd never actually dreamed of freedom.

I shoved my knife away and then said, "Kiva, you're welcome to come with us if you wish."

Where go?

"To Esan—"

Home of the ancient ones, Oma finished.

Ancient ones?

"Your ancestors," I said. "Esan is where many of them once lived."

Why no longer?

Pain rose. I swallowed heavily and said, "The Mareritt killed them all."

Mareritt bad.

Yes, Oma agreed solemnly. *That why we fight.*

Will help, Kiva said. *Mareritt chained. Must pay.*

Relief swept through me, and I briefly closed my eyes. "Thank you, Kiva."

We go now? she said.

"Yes." I glanced at Oma. "Before you find somewhere safe to roost for the night, can you sweep past the train so Kaiden knows we succeeded?"

Who Kaiden? Kiva asked.

Will explain, Oma said. *Come.*

The two of them leapt high, their wings stirring enough dust to briefly block their retreat from my sight. I tugged my undershirt up to filter it from my lungs and then began the long trek back to the road. The train appeared about ten minutes later, and we were soon heading toward Esan once again.

"I gathered it all went to plan?" Kaiden said.

"Yes, although there were a few hairy moments." I studied the control screens for a moment. "Any further communications from the Mareritt?"

"No—and I don't believe it's a good sign."

I glanced at him. "You think they're suspicious of us?"

"We'd be foolish to think they aren't."

"So we head into the marsh and hope for the best?"

He hesitated. "Rather than attempt that area on foot—which would take entirely too long and give them far too much time to find us—I think it would be better to uncouple the rear control pod and use it to make a run through the bog."

"Except you've already said we'll be easy to spot—"

"I know, but there's a good chance their attention will remain on the train rather than us."

"What about their radar?"

"Won't work. There's something about the moisture content in the soil that disrupts the signal."

"And the control pod? Will it actually run through the bog, or will it simply sink?"

"The electromagnetic repulsion technology should be strong enough to pull us through. It'll only sink if we stop."

I glanced across to the guidance screen. The little green dot was now only half an hour out from a turn point in the road, and only fifty-five minutes away from the eastern encampment. If we were going to do this then we'd better do it soon. "I vote for the control pod."

"So do I." He powered down the train, then rose. "Keep her at a crawl. I'll get the control pod ready."

I nodded and slipped into the driver seat. He hit the door release, then jumped out and quickly disappeared into the night. I watched the road and the stars, briefly wondering what sort of reception the drakkons and I were going to get at Esan. Kaiden might have accepted us, but how many of his kin would? In this time of suspicion and danger, would they dare believe the drakkons could be freed? Or that I was not only kin but a surviving remnant of a now destroyed past?

Probably not.

Kaiden's two companions might have witnessed me freeing Oma, but neither they nor anyone else had witnessed her helping us. After two hundred years of being hunted by the drakkons under Mareritt rule, I suspected it would take far more than our word to shake their distrust and fear.

Besides, Túxn always claimed her pound of flesh, and what better means was there to do that than have us rejected by the one place where safety should have been guaranteed?

It was another twenty minutes before I heard the sound of returning footsteps. As I twisted around in the seat, Kaiden leaped into the pod. Sweat ran down his face and stained his shirt.

"*That* was all damn harder than I thought it would be."

"I take it you did manage to uncouple the pod?"

He nodded and leaned past me, filling every breath with his musky, sweaty scent. "I've jury-rigged a disconnect.

Once the train turns toward the encampment, we'll make our run."

"How long will it take to get to Esan from that point?"

His fingers flew across several control panels. "We could be there by dawn if we don't have any problems."

"And if we do?"

"Somewhere between midmorning and noon. Let's go."

He pushed back, caught my elbow to help me up, and then headed for the rear of the pod. After slinging my sleeping bag and weapons over my shoulder, I jumped out, this time not losing my balance. Kaiden leaped out after me and then closed the door. We waited until the rear control pod approached and then stepped inside. The door had barely closed when the train began to pick up speed again. He'd obviously preset the speed controls before we'd left.

Kaiden resumed position in the driver seat, flicked a few more buttons, and then glanced at me. "Our guidance systems won't work in the bog, so I'll need you to watch for possible problems. The pod's underbelly isn't as fragile as the scooter's, but anything big can still rip out her guts and ground us."

I nodded. "Dare we use our lights?"

He hesitated. "Not until we're some way into the bog. We need them to believe we're still on the train for this to have any chance of working."

I glanced at the guidance screen again and tension rose. Only a few more minutes to go.

The train began its slow turn. Kaiden reached down and gripped a red handle. As the pod ahead of us finally followed the rest into the turn, he pulled the handle up. There was a metallic snap and the front of the pod shuddered. Kaiden hit the power button and our pod's engines fired up. As the train pulled away from us, he sped off the road and into the black-clad bog.

I leaned forward. The sliver moon was of little use when it came to illuminating the countryside, and while the stars were far brighter, their light barely touched the shadows haunting the ground. Though bogs were tradition-ally flat, there were stumps and rocks and who knew what other obstructions scattered about—none of which would be overtly obvious until we were almost upon them.

We'd only traveled a couple of miles when a huge explo-sion lit the sky to our left. I twisted around and saw a mush-room-like cloud rising toward the stars. A long line of flickering flames was spreading either side of the cloud's origin point.

"Looks like they had fuel cells in some of those pods," Kaiden commented. "They would have been damn handy had we been able to get them back to Esan."

"I think it's more important *we* get back to Esan."

"A point with which some would disagree, at least when it comes to me. Eyes front and center, if you please."

I crossed my arms and leaned on the console again, my gaze sweeping ground littered with thick clumps of spiky swamp grass, some of which were so tall it was impossible to see what they might be hiding. "It may seem that way right now, Kaiden, but when the push comes, that line is rarely crossed. Anger and loss always make a parent say things they don't actually mean."

He looked at me, something I felt rather than saw. "Speaking from experience again, are we?"

I smiled. "I'm not a parent, if that's what you're asking."

"I wasn't." He paused. "Did you have a partner in Zephrine? Someone to fly home to?"

"No."

"Good."

I raised my eyebrows in silent query, and he grinned. "It means your heart is wholly mine to win."

"Except there's no guarantee you'll be the one to win it," I teased. "After all, I've had little chance to explore what this time offers in the way of male companionship. How do I know you are indeed a prime example?"

"You could take my word for it."

"Or I could not." I motioned to the left. "Tree stump, twenty feet."

He adjusted the steering. "I have every faith you will."

"There's that confidence again."

"In this case, it's not misplaced."

It wasn't, but I also wasn't about to admit that. It was far too soon and the future far too uncertain for any such admission.

We continued on through the night, our banter falling silent as tiredness and the constant need for alertness took its toll. But as the stars began to fade and dawn spread tentative fingers across night skies, the throat of Huskain—the far end of the nigh on impassible mountain that dominated the eastern end of Arleeon—loomed on the horizon. The pass itself was invisible from our current position, but the descriptions I'd heard of it said it was a sleek, sideways cut in the mountain—one that was supposedly the point where some ancient eruption had literally torn the mountain apart. Time and rain had given this tear point a smooth finish, making it all but impossible for anyone who couldn't fly to sneak up on the fortress that lay in the heart of the tear.

Another half hour or so, and we'd be safe.

I should have known better than to temp Túxn like that.

Something hit the ground to our right, and the earth

exploded upward; the pod shuddered and drifted sideways, scraping rock before Kaiden was able to get it back under control.

I swore and twisted around. All I saw was lights.

Dozens of lights.

They'd found us.

NINE

Another explosion rocked the pod. Kaiden cursed and punched several buttons. Light speared the fading darkness, and the pod's speed increased. He skillfully wove through the stumps and rocks littering the area, his expression one of utter concentration. There was clear ground ahead—I could see it rising to the throat—but reaching it was no guarantee of safety. The bog had to be hampering the Mareritt as much as it was us, but once clear, we'd be easy game. The speed with which they were moving upon us, even in the bog, was evidence enough of that.

Another shell hit to our left, spraying mud and peat across the viewing screen. Kaiden pressed another button, and metal arms swished water across the glass, clearing it. Rock scraped across the pod's side and metal squealed; it sounded too much like the sound made by a dying animal for my liking.

The stumps gave way to trees. Up ahead was a long line of them—a forest of deadness that stood between the foothills and us. We had to go through it—there was no visible way around it—but it would slow us more than it would slow them. The train's control pod was chunkier than the needle-nosed vehicles the Mareritt were using.

I had to stop them if we were to have any chance of reaching Esan.

I scrambled out of the seat. "Get into that forest as fast as you can."

"That's my plan—what's yours?"

"Prevent them from following us."

I punched the door release button. The door had barely reached the halfway point when it smashed into a rock and was torn off its hinges. As it spun off into the bog, I caught the grip bar and leaned out. The posse had moved into an inverted V-formation; they were trying to stop us entering the forest.

I flexed my fingers and glanced ahead. Three minutes and we'd be in the trees. Heat burned through my blood in readiness, but the bog was too damp to set alight, and there were too many vehicles in our wake to attack. I might cinder three or even four, but doing so would deplete me and leave us virtually defenseless.

Two more explosions hit; the force sent the pod skidding sideways and almost launched me out of the door. It was only my fierce grip on the bar that saved me, but the sudden stop all but ripped my shoulder out of its socket. I swore and lunged for the bar with my free hand, my body swinging wildly in time with the pod's movement and my boots digging a trench into the soft soil.

"Nara?" Kaiden shouted. "Do you need help?"

"No. Concentrate on getting through that forest."

I swung one leg up into the pod and then awkwardly hauled my butt back inside.

The first of the dead trees sped past. Branches flicked

through the open door, only to be snapped away and sent spinning when they hit the rear frame.

Another explosion. Earth and wood sprayed high and then rained down, thudding against the roof of the pod and spearing into the ground all around us.

I pushed upright, gripped the bar again, and then called to the heat in my blood.

"How long until before we leave the trees?"

"Three minutes," Kaiden replied.

Another explosion, this time to our rear. The Mareritt were closing in; it could only be a matter of seconds before they had us dead in their sights.

"Keep this thing moving," I said. "I'm about to set the world on fire."

Flames immediately erupted across my fingertips; I formed them into a lance, sprayed it across the nearby trees, and then sent it spinning behind us. Flames leapt from tree to tree, their dry and rotten carcasses quickly succumbing to the heat. Soon there was nothing to see except a wall of fire.

It would delay them, not stop them. The Mareritt hierarchy had always worked on the theory that the greater the loss, the greater the gain. They wouldn't think twice about entering an inferno if, in the process, they took us out.

All around us trees burned, and thick smoke plumed into skies that were gradually brightening. The drakkons would soon be awake...

Awake now, came Oma's thought.

Can you fly in this light? Kaiden might have said the drakkons weren't night blind, but I wasn't about to order them out if they were going to have any trouble seeing.

Can fly anytime. Problem?

The Mareritt are attacking us.

We come. Leave some to burn.

A smile twitched my lips. *I don't think that's going to be a problem.*

See smoke.

I set the forest alight.

There soon.

Good.

An explosion ripped the trees to our right apart and sent a wave of fiery wooden splinters into the open door of the pod. I cursed and threw myself out of the way. Felt the prickle of pain and the flush of warmth and saw the deep gash that ran across my hand, just below the knuckles. Evidence of just how close I'd come to more serious injury.

"The drakkons are on their way," I said. "How much longer will it be before we're out of this forest?"

"We're hitting open ground now."

The long line of fiery trees gave way to gently sloping fields, and the pod sped up once again. I braced against the wall, tore off my left shirtsleeve, and quickly wrapped it around my hand to stem the blood.

Yet another explosion. This time, it was so close the force of the blast spun the pod around and threw me sideways and down. I cursed and flung out a hand; my fingers caught the edge of the weapons locker, and I hung on tight as the pod continued to spin. Then the stabilizers kicked in, and the spinning stopped with an abruptness that had my head smacking back into the locker. Stars briefly danced, but I shook my head and scrambled over to the door.

Some Mareritt vehicles had made it out of the forest.

I gathered fire and sprayed it across the leading three. Two jagged sideways, but I hit the third front-on. Fire punched through the view glass and set everyone and everything inside alight. A heartbeat later, the entire vehicle exploded, spraying metal and bits of Mareritt into the brightening skies.

One down, over a dozen to go.

But the ache in my head was beginning. I threw another lance regardless, taking out two more vehicles, but the effort had the mote in my eye bleeding. I sucked in air, trying to calm the racing of my heart and the fear that was building into panic, and then ran to the weapons locker. Rifles weren't going to do a lot against the vehicles chasing us, but they were a better option than draining myself to the point of unconsciousness.

"Will Esan see our plight and come to our rescue?" I returned to the doorway, braced as best I could, then raised the rifle and began to fire, aiming for the view screens rather than the vehicles themselves. If I could take out a driver or two...

"Maybe," Kaiden said.

"Why maybe?" I bit back. "It seems pretty obvious to me that anyone the Mareritt are so desperately trying to kill might be someone you'd want to rescue—if only to uncover why."

"That might have been the case in your time, but the Mareritt have used the decoy ploy a number of times over the last hundred years or so. We've learned to be cautious."

"That damn caution could get us killed. Is there no way we can signal them?"

Another blast rocked the pod. As grass and dirt and heat sprayed across my body, I cursed fluently and fired every damn bullet in the chamber. It didn't do much other than waste bullets, but it made me feel a whole lot better.

Then, from out of the sky, dropped two red-gold figures of flaming destruction.

Here, Oma said, rather unnecessarily.

Burn, Kiva said. *Burn all.*

They swept down, wingtip to wingtip, their flight so precise, so beautiful, it brought tears to my eyes. As one they flamed, creating a wide line of fire from which no vehicle escaped. Some exploded instantly. Some melted. Others simply glowed so hot that staying within them was impossible. As the Mareritt within scrambled to escape, the drakkons swept up, around, and began another fire run.

No Mareritt escaped.

Check the forest, I said. *It's possible there are still vehicles coming through it.*

Kiva peeled off to do that. Oma swept toward us. *Hurt?*

No.

Movement ahead. Mareritt?

I twisted around. "Kaiden, Oma says there's movement—"

"I know." His voice was grim. "Esan has fallen out."

"That's a good thing, isn't it?"

"Not necessarily. Not when we're in the company of drakkons."

"I'm *not* losing the drakkons."

"I'm not suggesting you do. Just making you aware of a possible problem."

I snorted. "It'd be the mother of all ironies to have safely traversed the entire breadth of Mareritten only to be killed by the very city we're trying to reach."

"And it's just the sort of kick in the guts Túxn would enjoy."

Which basically echoed my earlier thoughts and deepened the trepidation. "What are we going to do?"

"I don't think they'll fire—"

"Is that another of your grand statements I need to take with a grain of salt?"

He flashed a grin over his shoulder. "Maybe. But they've seen the drakkons attacking the Mareritt vehicles and protecting *us*, so they'll be on amber alert rather than red."

"And the fact we're in a Mareritt vehicle?"

He hesitated. "Could make them trigger-happy."

I grunted and glanced around as Kiva swept down. *Mareritt burned.*

The regret in her voice was due to the fact that *she* hadn't been responsible for their death. I smiled and said, *There will be more.*

Those ahead?

Are not Mareritt. They're friends.

Don't look friendly, Oma commented.

Because we're in a Mareritt vehicle.

If hate Mareritt, won't burn, Kiva commented.

Good, because we'll need their help if we're to free other drakkons.

I pushed upright and walked to the front of the pod. The throat loomed large, and the Eastern Slit was now visible. It was indeed an angular break between the two sides of the mountain; water tumbled from the edge of the upper slice and hit the lower, becoming a leaping, silvery stream of water that plunged into the deep pool at the base of the mountain and then rushed toward the distant sea. It was the upper slice that held the aeries, and they were all but inaccessible aside from the fly-in points for the drakkons. There was one stairway that ran from Esan to the aeries—and that entrance was heavily guarded. Or at least it had been in my time; I guessed there was little point in doing so now.

But it did make me wonder just how the Mareritt gained access to the eggs, given Esan never fell. Or was that where they first used the drakkons they'd bred themselves?

I didn't know. I suspected not even those who lived in Esan really knew.

I dropped my gaze to the fortress that was barely visible through the wash of rainbow spray. The great wall rose at an angle, a thick blot of darkness as smooth as the sides of the mountain it spanned. If the Mareritt had ever attacked it with tanks—and I had no doubt they had—there was no evidence of it. Arleeon might not have been blessed with a huge number of earth mages, but those who'd survived Zephrine's fall and the Mareritt takeover of Arleeon were being put to good use here in Esan.

Five squat tanks had hunkered in front of the deep, wide pool that dominated the entrance into the pass, and at least another dozen armed men stood in front of these.

Kaiden powered down the pod. "I think it best if we stop and I go talk to them."

"I'll ask the drakkons to land and go stand with them. Maybe it'll spook your people less."

"Not when you look Mareritt. Besides, nearly everyone within Esan has lost someone to the drakkons, be it in the past or the present. It's not something they'll get over easily."

"This fortress was once manned by drakkons and kin—surely that can't have been forgotten so swiftly?"

"Two hundred years isn't exactly swift."

The control pod settled onto the ground a quarter of a mile from Esan's forces. I suspected we remained within their range.

Kaiden climbed out of the driver seat, then paused and raised a hand, gently thumbing away the last remnants of blood from my cheek. "It's rather disturbing to see your eye bleed like that."

"It's the price we pay for the blood heat." I frowned. "If

three of your sisters have the mote, why would the bleeding be foreign to you?"

"Because, as I said, no fire runs through their blood." His hand slipped to my neck, then he leaned forward and brushed his lips across mine. He tasted of sweat and desire and all that was good in this crazy world. "I'll see you soon."

"Only if they don't shoot first and ask questions later."

"That depends *entirely* on whether my father is out there or not." The twist of his lips suggested he wasn't entirely joking. "I'll wave you in when it's safe."

"And the pod?"

He hesitated. "It's probably better if you leave it here and walk. They've more time to adjust to your coloring."

"Looking like a Mareritt is not something I want or desire."

"I know, but the fact remains, it'll spook just as many as the drakkons—at least initially."

"Great," I muttered. "Tell me again why we bothered coming here?"

"Because it's our best option of finding a means to free the drakkons." He kissed me again, fiercer but altogether too briefly, then released me and jumped out of the pod. I grabbed my sleeping roll and pulled out my flight gear. The Mareritt might not have recognized the uniform, but Kaiden had, and that surely meant others in the last remaining drakkon stronghold surely would. Whether they'd believe it was actually mine or something I'd either been given or stolen, I couldn't say.

Once I'd switched clothes, I stepped out of the pod, moved to one side, and called in the drakkons. They spiraled down lazily, using the breeze more than their wings, and landed either side of me. Oma snaked her head around, offering her eye ridge for a scratch. I complied, and she rumbled happily.

What happen? Kiva said.

Esan is uncertain of our presence. Kaiden goes to talk to them.

Easier to burn, she grumbled. Smoke puffed out of her nostrils, though it was little more than show. If she'd intended to burn, she wouldn't have given such a warning.

You burn and we might not be able to free other drakkons.

She sighed. Heavily. *You no fun.*

I laughed and reached up to scratch her ridge. A delighted rumble rose before she could stop it. *Mareritt no touch like this.*

Mareritt are bastards.

Bastards? Oma said. *What that?*

I hesitated. *In this case, it's another word for evil.*

You no bastard, Kiva said. *Must scratch more.*

My lips twitched. *I will.*

Two men had moved out from the main force and were now striding toward Kaiden. My gaze went to the tanks stationed in front of the pass; all five guns were aimed our way rather than Kaiden's. It would only take one of those itchy fingers, and we could be in trouble.

No, Oma said. *Can lift.*

I glanced up at her. *I'm too heavy for you to lift very far.*

More lift, stronger get.

It was certainly possible—especially if my guess was right and Oma was still growing.

Am, she said. *Emri gone, but I here.*

I smiled despite the thick knot of pain. *Thanks, Oma.*

Up ahead, the two men approaching Kaiden had stopped. He did the same and the conversation began. I wished I could hear what was being said—given their animated gestures, it would have been interesting.

Eventually, the two men moved back to the tanks. Kaiden turned and walked back.

"Is something wrong?" I asked, concerned.

"The captain refuses to give you and the drakkons entry until it's cleared by the base commander."

"Who is your father," I guessed, seeing the annoyance in his expression.

He nodded and scrubbed a hand across his bearded chin. "It's a ridiculous, and somewhat petty, delay."

I hesitated and then touched his arm. "Given the situation, it's also understandable."

He snorted. "He undoubtedly believes my head has been turned by a pretty face—that I'm thinking with my loins rather than my brains."

"I look like a Mareritt—I doubt he thinks *that* unless you've shown a past preference for half-breeds."

"Half- or quarter-breeds have never been my thing, but a pretty face? Totally different."

My lips twitched. "If you're trying to get into my bed, it'll take more than a compliment or two."

"I've already been in your bed. It's your body I'm after."

"This body has very exacting standards when it comes to lovers."

"And we both know I'm well up to those standards."

"You were certainly well up for *something* the few times we've shared a bed. I'm surprised you haven't had to take matters into your own hands."

He laughed. "I just might have to if a certain woman doesn't acquiesce to the heat that burns between us."

"Then if I were you, I'd be preparing to fly solo."

"*That* is disappointing news." He glanced back to the

pass, and his amusement faded. An open-top people mover drove toward us. Two men and three women stood inside—the latter bearing guns.

Today's equivalent of kin, perhaps?

Kaiden turned to face them; his arms were clasped behind his back and his face was a mask of indifference. But the link between us was alive, and it told a very different story.

The mover stopped several yards ahead of us. The drakkons raised their wings and fanned lightly. It was a warning of unease, of caution, and the guards in the mover braced and raised their rifles.

"Don't," Kaiden said, voice flat. "You make any attempt to shoot these drakkons, and they *will* respond."

"What the hell is going on here, Kaiden?"

The man who spoke was broad shouldered and well-built, with steel-gray hair cut close to his head and a lined face that spoke of deep grief. Kaiden's father—and a man who'd lost far more than one son.

"You're well aware what is going on, Commander." Kaiden's voice was clipped. "You've no doubt received Lindale's report by now."

"Which *did* mention the possibility that this could be nothing more than a well-developed Mareritt plot—"

"Lindale *didn't* believe that, and you well know it, Commander."

"An old Zephrine uniform, missing memories, and a mind filled with magic does not a kin make, Kaiden."

"But the ability to communicate mind-to-mind with drakkons *does*, Commander." I kept my voice polite but firm. "You don't have to believe my story, but you should at least believe the evidence in front of your eyes."

His gaze cut to mine. His eyes were the same azure

color as Kaiden's but colder. Harder. "What I see is a Mareritt woman standing next to my son in front of two drakkons. It's a sight that'll cause more than one itchy trigger finger within Esan if I allow any of you near her walls."

A smile touched my lips, even as annoyance flicked through me. "Those drakkons saved us from the Mareritt, Commander. Trust me when I say their only desire right now is to seek vengeance on those who kept them prisoner for so long. Esan is safe from them *unless* Esan attacks them."

The threat had ice glittering in his eyes. "These drakkons are Mareritt-bred. They are raised to obey—"

"Why on earth would a city manned by those whose ancestors once rode drakkon believe such a lie?" Incredulousness dominated my voice. "How could you have forgotten so much in a mere two hundred years?"

The commander's gaze narrowed, and Kaiden touched my arm. A warning as much as a silent plea to keep calm.

"The Mareritt don't communicate with the drakkons in the same manner as kin did—as *she* does," he said. "They control them via the metal bands on their legs. Remove them—as we have with Oma and Kiva—and the Mareritt lose their ability to control."

"Bands?" the commander snapped.

"Leg bands," I explained. "They're some sort of either electrical or magical device that allows the Mareritt to communicate orders and then enforces those orders with increasing levels of pain if the drakkons do not comply."

"If the Mareritt are capable of such treachery," he said, "how do we know they have not also enforced such things on you?"

Kaiden shook his head and promptly stripped off. I hesitated and then did the same. Their reaction to the changes in my skin color was brief but nevertheless present. I had no idea whether it meant they were more inclined to believe me or not.

"As you can see," Kaiden growled, "no bands, no restraints. Now, can we cut the crap, Commander—"

"The drakkons," he cut in harshly. "If you do indeed command them, have them rise."

"Oma, Kiva, rise high enough for them to see your legs. Commander, tell your people to keep their guns down. If they fire, they won't have to worry about drakkons. I'll kill them all myself."

"Trust me," Kaiden said, "she has the firepower to do so. She's kin, so I do mean that *literally*."

The commander raised an eyebrow but nevertheless motioned to his people. The guns lowered.

We gathered our clothes and then moved forward to give the drakkons room to launch. They crouched in unison and then leapt high, wings fanning hard, sending dirt swirling as they rose skyward.

"Check their legs, Commander," I said. "No bands."

His gaze remained on the drakkons. He wasn't stupid. He understood the implications of what we'd done. "However monumental this discovery might be, it's impractical to physically remove the restraints on all—"

"Agreed," Kaiden said. "But we don't have to. All we need to do is find a means of disrupting the signal between drakkons and Mareritt."

"You have these drakkons' bands?"

"Yes."

The commander's gaze flicked to me. "Are you willing to submit to a full mind read?"

"You won't uncover anything more than Lindale—"

"If you do not agree," the commander continued, overriding Kaiden, "neither you nor the drakkon will get near Esan. I'd rather kill you all than risk the city's security."

"*My* entire city is destroyed, everyone I've ever known is little more than dust, and the one chance we had of bringing the graces back is now gone," I snapped. "Don't preach security to me, Commander. I've literally given everything I have—"

"Then you, more than anyone, should be able to understand my concern."

I studied him for a minute, my hands on my hips and fire dancing across my fingertips. His gaze narrowed once again, but he didn't say anything.

"I want a guarantee the drakkons won't be fired on, Commander."

"Keep them out of the city and they won't be."

I snorted and shook my head. "It's a sad state of affairs when the blood of kin treat drakkons so poorly. Your ancestors would be hiding their faces in shame right now."

His anger flared. "Don't attempt to lecture me on what *my* ancestors might or—"

"I knew them," I cut in harshly. "I *flew* with them. I saw their courage and their bravery when faced with unthinkable odds. I see no such courage or bravery here this morning, but rather a man locked behind the walls of fear and loss—"

"Enough, both of you." Kaiden's voice was whip firm. "We haven't run the entire length of Mareritten and stirred up a hornet's nest for nothing, Commander. Esan *is* in grave danger, but it doesn't come from anyone standing in front of you this morning."

The commander studied him for several seconds and then nodded once. "Order the drakkons to the aeries, but warn them not to swoop the city. If they're hungry, the old herds of capras still roam the peaks."

Capras were agile, longhaired ruminants who could survive in conditions and terrain few other animals could. Esan of old had semidomesticated them to ensure a constant supply of ready meat for drakkon and kin alike. It was nice to know that not everything about the fortress had changed.

"Thank you, Commander," I said, more for Kaiden's sake than his father's.

He nodded and glanced at his son. "Wait here until I've given stand-down orders and the entry flag is issued."

As the mover returned to the city, I said, voice dry, "Well, *that* went a whole lot differently than I'd thought."

"Yes." Kaiden shook his head. "Though I really shouldn't be surprised. Far too many have suffered losses to the drakkons to ever readily welcome them."

Only kill because ordered, Oma commented. *No choice.*

I know. Kaiden knows. It'll just take others more time.

Is no time, Kiva commented.

My gaze shot to her. The two of them were circling lazily on the breeze, their scales shining bright in the golden light spreading across the skies. *Why?*

Mareritt kill Esan.

I blinked. *How do you know they plan to do that?*

I hear.

How?

Was shot. Returned to aerie. Heard them.

My heart began to pound a whole lot harder. *Zephrine's aeries? They do still exist?*

Yes, Oma said. *Most hatched there now. Easier.*

Of that, I had no doubt. Drakkon eggs required certain levels of heat to hatch, and though our section of the Balkain volcanic range had been dormant for centuries, the steam vents remained active. They provided the perfect microclimate for hatching drakkons.

"I take it," Kaiden said, his voice dry, "that given your somewhat absent expression, you're in a conversation with the drakkons?"

I blinked again and quickly told him what Kiva had said. He frowned. "That is *not* good news."

"No." If only because it meant we had even less time to find a way of blocking the signal to the drakkons. "But the Mareritt still using Zephrine's aeries is."

"Why?"

I gripped his arm, an odd fierceness running through me —a fierceness that was born from a twisted mix of the need for revenge and utter joy. From a realization that not everything I'd known had been lost to the dust of time, and that it *was* possible for us to get into the White Zone without being seen.

"Because Zephrine's aeries were also designed as a means of escape should the fortress ever fall—"

"Yes," he cut in, "but as I've already said, Kriton's very well guarded these days."

"The seaport was *never* the designated rendezvous point. It was never considered secure enough because it *was* a port and far too close to the Mareritten border."

His frown deepened. "But there're no other cities close enough to be considered a safe option should the evacuation order be given—and if there *had* been, why wasn't it used?"

"Perhaps they simply had no time," I said. "Especially if the air itself became a weapon and froze people on the spot."

"So where—"

The rest of his sentence was cut off by Oma's screech. A heartbeat later, something hit my shoulder and spun me around and then down. Moisture flooded my shirt. Warm moisture. Blood.

I'd been *shot*.

Esan shoot us. Oma's voice was filled with fury. *Shall burn?*

No, I said urgently, fighting the rising tide of pain and looming darkness. *Are you hurt?*

No. Burn now?

No. Rise high and keep out of sight.

You hurt. Should burn.

No, please. I'll be all right. There were hands on my shoulder and curses filling the air. *We need Esan's help, Oma. This is not the action of the city but rather one person bent on revenge.*

I had to believe that. *Had* to.

I didn't want to believe a father would betray his son so easily.

You and Kiva keep to the peaks and out of their way.

Not happy.

Please. This is important.

Dissatisfaction rumbled through her thoughts, but she and Kiva nevertheless flicked their wings and disappeared into skies filled with red and gold.

Relief surged. I closed my eyes and let the tide of pain sweep me into unconsciousness.

I woke to a soft but steady beeping. The warm air smelled faintly of antiseptic, and there was a bed rather than ground under my body. My shoulder felt tight, but I could move my fingers, and that at least meant the shot hadn't caused any lasting damage.

I opened my eyes. The first thing I saw was Kaiden. He was asleep in an uncomfortable-looking chair, his feet propped on the end of the bed and his arms crossed. He'd obviously showered and shaved in the time I'd been unconscious, though the bristles now lining his jaw suggested at least twenty-four hours had passed since then.

The room itself was small and held only one bed—mine. A device similar to the Mareritt medical machine that had healed Kaiden's leg lay to my right, although this one had a metal arm that hovered above me; for what purpose, I had no idea. There were a number of lines in my arm that ran back to the machine, and monitors of some kind stuck onto my chest. The metallic beeping matched the rhythm of my heartbeat.

Happy you awake, came Oma's thought.

So am I. Where are you and Kiva?

In aerie. Is night.

And you haven't been attacked?

No. Have hunted. Plenty food here.

No doubt because the capras had been untroubled by drakkon for over two hundred years. I shifted to get a little more comfortable, and the movement woke Kaiden.

His gaze swept me, and relief stirred, but there were new lines around his eyes that spoke of just how deep his concern had been. It warmed but at the same time scared me. I'd obviously been pretty close to death.

"Where am I?"

"In an Esan hospital ward."

I raised my eyebrows. "And the shooter?"

"Dead."

I blinked. *That* certainly wasn't an answer I'd been expecting. "Did you...?"

"No. I was beaten to it."

"Who by?"

"Kiva."

Didn't order me not to flame, came Kiva's comment. *He shot you. I burn him. Fair.*

It certainly was, but it wouldn't have endeared either of them to the general population. "And how did your father—and Esan in general—react to that?"

"Not well." He grimaced. "And to be honest, even if most are now aware of *why* they're here, deep pockets of distrust remain—especially amongst those who are refugees from greater Arleeon."

"That's not something we can change in a hurry."

"No." He lifted his boots off the bed and then rose and reached for the long flask sitting on the nearby table. "The medics have ordered that you drink their concoction the minute you wake."

"I gather it's another one of those muddy herbal things?"

"The muddy herbal things smelled a whole lot more pleasant."

"Fabulous."

"They assure me it'll have you back on your feet in hours."

"Probably because I'll be running to the privy." I accepted the tumbler of greeny-gray liquid with something close to trepidation, then held my nose and quickly downed the lot. A shudder ran through me. "You'd think after all the centuries of brewing those things they'd have found a way of making them palatable."

"I suspect they could if they wanted—they just get a macabre kick out of watching our reactions." He refilled the tumbler. "My father wants to meet with you ASAP."

I gulped the second tumbler down; for some damn

reason, it tasted even worse. "Why do you call him Commander in public?"

"Because when we're in public, that's what he is."

"Who else has he lost besides your brother?"

Kaiden's eyebrows rose. "And just how did you reach that conclusion?"

"He wears his grief like a cloak. It may not be obvious to any of you, but it certainly is to an outsider."

He reached for the chair and dragged it closer. "We lost Mom five years ago."

"How?"

"She was in the wrong place at the wrong time during a Mareritt attack on the walls." He grimaced. "My father continually ordered her to the bunkers, and she continually ignored him. She was weapon-trained and refused to flee or let others fight in her stead."

"Did she have the mote in her eye?"

"Yes. And she was one of the few who believed drakkons would one day return to Esan." His expression held a touch of wistfulness. "I wish she could have been here to meet you, Oma, and Kiva."

I reached out a hand. His fingers twined through mine, but he didn't say anything. He didn't need to. The grief we both shared—mine new and raw, his older but no less painful—swirled between us. This had to be *Dhrukita*. Had to be. I might not have believed in it, but it was the only explanation for the strengthening bond. Kin might share thoughts and emotions with their drakkon, but that ability had never crossed over to allow such communication kin to kin.

"Is he still demanding I undergo another reading?"

"That was done while you were unconscious." He paused. "Against my wishes, let me tell you."

And with good reason—reading the mind of the unconscious was dangerous to *both* parties. Not only did the reader risk being swept up in the pain or darkness holding court in the mind of the unconscious soul and utterly losing his or her way out, but in the process of trying to withdraw, could destroy that person's mind.

"Did the reader discover anything new or different to Lindale?"

"Not much. The ice in your mind has receded, allowing more of your memories to be read, but nuggets of magic remain."

"So your father believes us now?"

A smile twisted his lips. "Even if he didn't, I think the sheer number of Mareritt who have been combing Arleeon for you would have convinced him you hold *some* value."

I grunted. "What about the drakkon bands? Any success on them?"

"Yes and no." He grimaced. "The good news is that they've pulled one apart and found the receiver. The bad news is, they haven't yet found a means of blocking the signal over a broad area, which is what we actually need if we're to have any hope of freeing the majority of the drakkons."

"Do they think it's possible?"

He hesitated. "They're actually thinking it might be a better idea to boost the signal to the point where it blows the receiver apart."

"Doing *that* will cause the drakkon a lot of pain."

"Not if the communications channel is used rather than the pain one."

"There's two separate channels?"

"Three, although we're not sure what the third channel is for."

That kill, came Oma's comment.

What?

It kills, she repeated. *Fries mind.*

Are bastards, Kiva said.

I swore and scrubbed a hand across my face. "Oma says that third channel is used to kill them."

"Which means we'd better make damn sure that when we fry the receiver, it takes out *all* the channels."

"The other option is to destroy the relays they're using to send the signals."

He frowned. "That wouldn't be a long-term option though—they'd rebuild."

"We don't need long term. By destroying the signal relays, we're destroying the means by which the Mareritt control the drakkons. It gives *us* the chance—via Oma and Kiva—to order them away from the Mareritt so we can remove the bands from those who'll let us near. It also means your people have more time to work on a means of either blocking or destroying the receivers on the bands of any drakkons *not* currently in Arleeon."

I like this plan, came Oma's comment. *Should do.*

A smile touched my lips. Emri had always listened in on conversations too, especially during preflight councils.

Kaiden grunted. "It could also help throw them off the scent of what else we're trying to do."

Which was find the mages or whoever else was responsible for that ice weapon and destroy them. "Do we know where the relay towers are? Is it possible to even get to them?"

"There are three. Two we can certainly access even though they're heavily guarded by soldiers and anti-armament tanks. But the third is in the White Zone—and it's the largest."

"Is the force around the towers the reason they've never been attacked before?"

"Our attacks are the reason they're now heavily guarded." A smile twisted his lips. "Of course, we weren't aware that the towers *also* controlled the drakkons via the leg bands or we would have continued the attacks."

"Given there's no kin currently capable of talking to the drakkons, it probably wouldn't have made any difference." I frowned. "What actually happened when the towers did go down?"

"There was no discernable difference in how the drakkons reacted," he said. "But we were never able to hit the tower in the White Zone."

"Which means it's probably the main one."

"Sounds like it, but a coordinated assault on all three would be the best option. Otherwise, they'll just ramp up security around the one in the White Zone." He glanced around as the door swished open and a medic in a white uniform stepped into the room. "The patient's finally awake, Zina."

The blonde's expression was wry. "So I can see. You want to step outside while I do a release scan?"

Kaiden squeezed my fingers, then rose and left. Zina moved to the machine and punched a few buttons. The arm above me came online and slowly slid from the top of my head to my toes. Numbers came up on the screen; she grunted, pressed a few more buttons, and then removed the needles from my arms.

"You're good to go," she said. "Just take it easy on that shoulder for a few days—the muscles are healed, but they'll be a little tender. Your uniform has been cleaned and is hanging in the locker, and there's a shower in the privy room if you wish to use it."

"Thanks."

She nodded, her attention on the machine more than me. I climbed somewhat warily out of the bed, but other than a slight twinge in my arm, everything worked. I grabbed my knife and clothes—which included new under-clothing, I was pleased to see—and then headed into the privy.

When I came back out, the medic was gone and Kaiden was waiting. "My father's been informed you're awake. He wants to see us immediately."

I nodded and fell in step beside him. "Did you tell him what Kiva said?"

"Yes. I also described the attack on the coruscation and the weapon used. He agrees with the urgent need to uncover what they're developing in the White Zone. If Zephrine *did* have an escape route none of us knew about—"

"Then it's our best chance of getting in there without getting captured." Our footsteps echoed through silent corridors of metal. I had no doubt there were people—even guards—within the hospital complex, but there was no visible evidence of them. Maybe I'd been kept in an isola-tion ward. Perhaps the combination of my Mareritt coloring and the fact that Kiva had incinerated one of their soldiers—

Have no regrets, Kiva cut in. *They hurt you. I burn them. Simple.*

But it would still be better if you didn't make a habit of burning our allies. Keep it for the Mareritt.

She harrumphed at me.

"Where in Zephrine was the escape tunnel's entrance?" Kaiden said.

"In the aerie—"

"Which is now Mareritt controlled *and* protected by drakkons."

"Yes, and that means we'll need some way of smashing the receivers in the control bands on the drakkons guarding the aerie *before* we can attempt anything else."

He scrubbed a hand across his jaw, his expression one of frustration. "They're hoping to have developed a short-term, short-range means of doing that within the next forty-eight hours, but I'll give them a hurry along."

He must have sought an update when he'd been sent out of the room by Zina.

The doors up ahead swished open, revealing a wider corridor and multiple doors. The area behind me might have been lacking in movement and personnel, but that wasn't the case here. Few appeared to pay us any attention, but I was nevertheless aware of the gazes that stabbed into my back and the whispers that haunted our steps. It was to be expected, given I looked Mareritt rather than kin, but it nevertheless worried me.

We walked through a mind-numbing number of corridors but eventually entered another stark, steel-clad area with a door at the far end. The two men standing on either side came to attention at our approach.

"The commander is expecting us," Kaiden said, voice clipped.

One guard nodded and pressed his hand against the nearby scanner to open the door. Kaiden's gaze briefly met mine, and I nodded once, even though it felt as if a major storm brewed in my stomach. I might not have ever wanted to lead a grace or an attack, but I was the last true kin. There was no one else to do this. Certainly there was no one left with the knowledge I had of both the drakkons and Zephrine of old.

The room was long and wide, with windows that ran the full length of the two longer sides. One looked over Esan's great wall, and from this height, her soldiers looked minute. Beyond it, Mareritten lay stretched out like a map; the commander would have been able to see our flight through the bog long before we'd gotten anywhere near the pass.

And had done nothing to help us.

Anger rose, even though it was pointless. He had his reasons and a city to protect. I could understand that even if I didn't agree with it.

The other window looked over the old Esan fortress, newer extensions, and then out into Arleeon. Another great wall was evident in the distance, though from here it looked as tiny as the men on the wall to our left. It was undoubtedly the wall that separated Greater Esan from the rest of Arleeon.

The room itself mirrored Zephrine's war room. A long table dominated the center of the room, and a series of screens and communications points ran the length of both windows. They were dark at the moment, but I knew, come an attack, this room would be filled with people and those screens active.

Aside from Kaiden's father, there was another man and a woman in the room. The latter wore the colors of Esan's kin, which was the reverse of ours—red with gold stitching. She also had a mote in the white of her eye, which strengthened the likelihood she was kin even if, as Kaiden had said, none so marked knew how to use their inner fires. The man held an air of authority—an impression enforced by his short white hair and the ragged scar running down his right cheek—but his uniform, like the commander's, was black leather with silver stitching. In my time, it had been the dress uniform of Esan's ground forces rather than one used every day. Maybe it was now used within Esan walls to differentiate those who were kin and those who were "regular" ground forces. I had no doubt *both* used civvies when beyond her walls—as evidenced by what Kaiden had been wearing in the prison pod.

He stopped and stood with his hands behind his back. "Reporting as ordered, Commander."

The commander nodded and motioned us to both sit. Once we had, he said in a clipped and cold voice, "Kaiden tells me it's possible one of Zephrine's old emergency tunnels survived the fortress's destruction—and that it *isn't* Kriton, as we'd always presumed."

"No," I said. "The Balkain Mountains are the surviving remnant of a larger volcanic range that once dominated the area, and we put many of the old lava tubes to good use."

"There's no mention of tubes being used as escapes routes in the records we've gone through," the second man said.

"I'm also told there's no record of the attack on the coruscations being a joint decision, but it certainly *was*."

"Given your sister *led* that attack," the woman said, "you're unlikely to have claimed anything else."

"I was there." I kept my voice mild, even as anger fired inside. "You were not. I have no reason to lie when two centuries have passed and no one can alter what happened."

"And yet if such a decision *had* been made, we surely would have—"

"Enough, Lila." The commander shot her warning look. "As she said, we can no more change what happened than we can bring back the graces. Let's concentrate on what we *can* do. Where does this tunnel of yours exit, Nara?"

"Near Old Carlula."

"Which isn't a town I'm familiar with." The commander glanced at the second man. "Kemp, do we have any of the old maps on the system?"

"I'll check." The shorter man rose and moved across to one of the screens. After a few minutes, a map flashed up on the nearby wall. "This is the oldest we have—it comes from just over a hundred years ago, but I believe the cartographers of the time used the older maps as a basis and simply added to them as required."

I studied the map with a frown. It bore the names of towns and areas I simply didn't know, and yet the underlying topography was familiar—and had obviously been created by someone whose viewpoint had come from drakkon back. After several seconds, I spotted a familiar crack in the landscape. I rose, moved around to the map, and pointed to an area on the outskirts of what was now a town called Hardwick.

"In my time, Old Carlula—a city destroyed by a long-ago eruption—lay here. Depending on how accurate this map still is, the main exit point lies a mile or so north of this town."

"Which puts it right on the edge of the White Zone," the commander said. "It's highly unlikely they wouldn't have found and dealt with such a tunnel *if* such still existed."

"Does Hardwick itself still exist?" I asked.

"It exists, but no one lives there now," Kaiden said. "The farmlands to the east of it remain in use, but these days they simply ship workers in and out every day."

Which made sense if they wanted to keep people away from the White Zone but needed production to continue. The area around Old Carlula might have been pocked with the remnants of volcanic destruction, but the soil itself had become rich and moist thanks to the area's high rainfall. It had been mostly forest in my day, but even then there'd been farms springing up around its eastern edges.

"Have the Mareritt completely stripped the area of the forest, or does some of it remain?" I asked.

Kaiden rose and joined me. "This area here"—he pointed to a long strip of land between Hardwick and the port town of Redding—"remains."

"Which means if we can get to Redding, we have cover."

"Except the Mareritt have grounded all fishing fleets in all ports," Lila said. "There are standing orders to destroy any vessel attempting to enter or exit said ports."

"Which still leaves us a *lot* of coastline."

"It might be possible to slip a small enough boat in here." Kaiden pointed to an area beyond Redding. There were no towns marked on the map, and the coastline rose sharply into the mountainous terrain beyond. "It wouldn't be an easy region to traverse, which means there's less likelihood of it being patrolled."

"They don't need patrols when they have the drakkons," Lila commented. "Your two won't be of much use if they're sighted by those still under Mareritt control and then come under heavy attack from whatever ground forces they do have nearby."

"Which is where the device to break the connection between the Mareritt and their drakkons comes into play," I said.

"*If* such can be devised." Lila's voice was edged. "Even then, there's no guarantee it'll succeed."

I rather suspected Lila didn't like my presence here—not because my being kin of old jeopardized her position in Esan, but because it highlighted her own inadequacies.

Something she shouldn't have been feeling given the situation, and yet one I might have shared had our positions been reversed.

"Then *our* drakkons will force any others down," I replied evenly, "and we'll free them manually."

"Even if we *can* get you into that area," the commander said, with another warning look at Lila, "the Mareritt have poured vast numbers into *all* Arleeon in their search for the two of you. Getting anywhere is not easy at the moment."

"This isn't the first time their military forces have flooded Arleeon," Kaiden said. "We move at night, as we did each of those times."

The commander grunted. "And what happens if the exit isn't viable?"

"The Mareritt would have no reason to believe that an old lava tube would give anyone access into the aeries," I said. "Even if they *have* collapsed the main entrance, there are others. Those who planned and built Zephrine might never have imagined the city would fall, but they certainly catered for the possibility."

The commander's expression remained skeptical. "Getting into the aeries is only part of the problem—"

"Zephrine was my home," I cut in softly. "If any of her still remains—and I'm told the new city uses the foundations of the old—then rest assured I can get through her without being seen."

His gaze narrowed. Judging me, judging my words. I had no idea what he was thinking beyond his evident skepticism, and no immediate chance to find out.

A siren rang out. Two short blasts and then one long one—a signal I recognized from my time in Zephrine.

Esan was under attack.

TEN

The commander rose and strode over to one of the consoles. He tapped the screen a number of times, and the ones to our right came alive. Information and images scrolled across them so fast that from where I was standing it was impossible to read.

The commander obviously had no such problem. "Tower seven is being hit. Unknown number of Mareritt." He glanced at the other man. "Kemp, inform the earth witches to fall out in case of a breakthrough. Lila, get to your station. Kaiden, tower eight. Immediately."

Kaiden glanced at me—a silent order to follow—and then raced out the door after Lila. We bolted through a myriad of corridors, down a series of long stairs, and eventually came out into a courtyard that was long, wide, and filled with trains, pods, and people. It was organized chaos and so familiar, my heart raced. I knew this, loved this. Except *this* time, there would be no drakkon sweeping in for kin to mount. No graces to fly wingtip to wingtip, their bellows echoing through the darkness as they swept up into starlit skies in perfect formation. No bellies rumbling in fiery readiness as wings swung toward the enemy.

I pushed back the sadness and the pain that rose with the images and followed Kaiden across to ammunitions. Once we were both kitted out, we jumped into one of the many trains ferrying soldiers out of the inner courtyard.

An outer wall quickly came into sight. It was of stone construction—at least on this side—and pockmarked by both artillery hits and time. The arched gateway was set slightly off-center, and both the portcullis and the heavy metal gate were open. The gate was new—the rest was part of Esan's original fortress wall.

The train swept through the gateway and rapidly picked up speed. The surrounding buildings became little more than a blur, so it was good to see the streets were empty. Either everyone had hunkered down inside their homes or they'd moved with lightning speed into the shelters.

"How far away is the Esan barricade?"

"Seven minutes." Kaiden placed a Q-shaped device around his ear and tucked the longer tail into the canal. It was obviously some sort of comms.

"And the reason we're heading to tower eight rather than the one under attack?"

He pointed to the small monitor situated in the corner of the train's pod. "Tower seven might be taking the brunt of the attack, but eight and six are also being hit."

I frowned up at the screen. It was crisscrossed with irregular lines, meaning the system was using the earth's energy as a means to locate both friend and foe. A large circle of red sat on the other side of tower seven, but smaller circles now massed in front of the other two. There were also two farther clumps of red: one in the forest beyond the river and another in the long valleys that swept away from Esan.

Thin streams of green moved toward the three towers under attack, while smaller blobs gathered at the more distant ones. "I take it the green circles are Esan's forces?"

He nodded. "There are five companies at tower seven— three on the wall itself, and two more standing ready."

"And at eight?"

"One, and the company that's on this train."

Meaning each train had a set destination. It was certainly an efficient means of quickly ferrying soldiers into position. "Is this your company?"

A humorless smile touched his lips. "I'm infiltration, so no. I'm simply assigned a position when I'm here."

The great wall came into sight. It was a deep, bloody red in the darkness—a hulking beast of stone that dominated the skyline. The two towers immediately visible were vast things topped by multiple lights, and not only shone along the wall itself but also into the land beyond it.

Smoke rose from several points, although what there was to burn aside from flesh on a wall of stone I had no idea. There were no shells arcing through the darkness, either, and definitely no explosions shattering the ground on this side of the wall. And while a battery of noise—the shouts of men, the rattle of gunfire, the *whoomph* of cannons being unleashed—filled the air, it was coming more from *this* side than the other.

Which made no sense. Why would the Mareritt half-heartedly attack? Was it some kind of decoy maneuver? Were they also massing within Mareritten, intent on a two-prong charge?

But surely if that *had* been their intent, they would have

been spotted, given the glorious view over the bogs and foothills the command center had.

Or were they, perhaps, intent on using the drakkons from that point once Esan's forces were fully occupied here?

It was a definite possibility.

Oma, can you let me know if drakkons approach from Mareritten?

Yes. She paused. *Want help at wall?*

I hesitated. *Let's see what the situation is first.*

Hurry, came Kiva's comment. *Need to burn.*

The train came to a shuddering halt. Men and women clambered out of the vehicle and up the stairs on either side of the tower. We followed, taking the steps two at a time, moving as fast as the people ahead allowed. Orders were barked as we neared the top of the wall. Those on the other stairs went left, we went right.

We ran along the walkway until we found vacant crenels. I unslung my cannon and fixed it into position. Bullets pinged off the parapet near my head, showering stone sparks into the darkness. I swore and unleashed on the Mareritt in the distance. They'd hunkered down on the other side of the river, using whatever rocks and fallen trees were in the area as cover. They were also using rifles rather than cannons, and that had unease stirring.

Even if this *was* a decoy attack, why waste men and effort by not bringing in heavy artillery?

"Something doesn't feel right." Kaiden had to shout to be heard above all the noise.

"I agree." I scanned the area beyond the line of Mareritt. While the monitor had indicated there were a high number of them in the trees, they weren't immediately visible. Were they waiting for the drakkons to attack? Or something else? "It might be an idea to gain some eyes in the sky."

Kaiden nodded. "It will also prove to those on the walls that the drakkons *are* on our side."

Oma, Kiva? Can one of you do a flame run at the Mareritt attacking the river wall, and the other do a high sweep and see what the Mareritt in the trees or valleys beyond are doing?

I seek. Kiva flame. Needs to kill more.

Thanks. I glanced at Kaiden. "Can you get the word passed along that the drakkons are about to do a fire run, and that no one is to shoot at them?"

He tapped the comms device and immediately did so. The drakkons bugled—a furious sound that ran clearly across the night and the noise—and then swept down from the aerie, one high, one low, their scales gleaming in the cold light of the moon and the stars. Kiva soared over the wall and began her run, spreading fire and chaos across the Mareritt line. A cheer went up from those manning the towers either side of us, but it was too soon. Far too soon. As Kiva swung around to begin another sweep, five lights appeared on the horizon. Lights that were fronted by a blue-white sphere and left a trail of frozen air behind them. They were coming straight at the wall between our tower and seven.

My heart flipped into overdrive. "Kaiden—"

"I see them, I see them." He tapped the ear device again and said, "Lila, get your people off the wall. Immediately. Those incoming spheres are the things that destroyed the coruscations."

A heartbeat later, a siren sounded, this one three short blasts. A murmur of disbelief ran along the wall, but the soldiers closest to Kaiden and me immediately began disconnecting their cannons and moving toward the stairs in an orderly fashion.

But they had no understanding of the danger those spheres represented, and they were nowhere near fast enough. If they didn't hurry, if they didn't get off this wall, then they were dead. As dead as the graces who'd been held within the coruscation. As dead as Sorrel and Emri.

I quickly unhooked my cannon. *Oma, can you see where those spheres came from? Kiva, fly high and see if your fires can stop those things.*

Kiva immediately swooped upward, her scales appearing to drip fire in the light streaming from the spots. As the siren sounded again and a sense of urgency crept into those leaving their posts, I called to my flames and threw a thick lance at the first sphere. Fire met ice and the sphere came to a juddering halt—the force of which echoed through me and physically pushed me backward. Kaiden swore and lunged for both my arm and the parapet, anchoring me, stopping me from sliding over the edge.

I dug deep and forced more energy into the lance, even as Kiva swooped and hit the next two. The final two spheres shot past and began their descent toward the wall; it was then that I saw the tank shell trailing behind them.

We were going to be hit no matter what we did. It was now just a matter of how much damage we'd suffer.

I swore and threw every last scrap of energy I had into my lance of fire. The mote in my eye popped and blood poured over my lashes. I ignored it, concentrating on the sphere. A faint spot of red-gold finally appeared at the contact point and quickly spread. Then, with startlingly little noise, the sphere shattered. Kiva's two quickly followed, but the force of their explosion—though silent—was so strong it sent her tumbling.

Kiva? I all but screamed.

Not hurt, she said after a moment.

Relief swept through me. *Are you able to fly high? Can you warn me if the Mareritt rush the wall?*

Will. Can flame.

Only if it doesn't put you in danger.

Won't.

"We need to get off this wall. *Now,*" Kaiden said and left me with no choice by tightening his grip on my arm and all but hauling me toward the stairs.

Mareritt in valley hidden, Oma said.

We joined the crush of people hurtling down the stairs. *Hidden how?*

In ground. Flame won't reach them.

If they'd bunkered in, it meant they'd expected our drakkons to be brought into any counterattack. It also meant they might have taken other measures against them. *Are there tanks or some other kind of machinery in that valley?*

The air was thick with raw uncertainty and disbelief; despite the urgency, despite the ringing of the sirens and the fast-approaching spheres, Esan's soldiers didn't believe the danger. Didn't believe the wall would fall.

Not tank, came Oma's comment. *Something else.*

Can you describe it?

She hesitated. *Can only see nose. It long, like tank. Shall swoop lower?*

No! I swallowed the flare of panic and added more calmly, *No. They now know you and Kiva are helping us, and they could have set a trap to recapture you. Keep high, out of their sight, but let me know if there's any movement from either the Mareritt or whatever they're hiding in the ground.*

Someone hit me from behind, sending me stumbling

into the back of the woman in front. She flung a curse over her shoulder even as a gruff "sorry" came from behind. It didn't matter. Nothing did except getting off these steps and away from the wall.

I risked a glance over my shoulder. Saw the two spheres. We weren't going to get off the wall—off these steps—in time. They were too damn close...

A heartbeat later, they hit. As with the coruscations, nothing immediately happened. Not for several seconds. Then a soft rumbling began, and the stone under our feet became so cold it radiated up through the soles of our boots. Fat fingers of ice appeared, forcing their way into minute cracks and stone joints. Breaking the adhesion, forcing them apart.

Then the tank shell hit. The wall exploded, sending stone and bodies flying. Kaiden somehow swung around and wrapped his body around mine even as we were blown off the steps and high into air filled with debris and destruction.

Save!

Kiva appeared out of nowhere, swooping past and then under us. We hit her hard and between her wings, a position that wasn't ideal for any control of flight. She plummeted downward, her muscles working furiously underneath my spine as she fought to control the descent. Slowly, steadily, she did and carefully wove through the rain of destruction, avoiding sudden moves to keep us on her back as she headed for safer ground.

Mareritt in forest move toward wall, Oma said. *Flame?*

Yes. In fact, set the whole forest alight. It would burn for days, given the sheer size of it, and that in turn would give Esan time to repair the wall and, hopefully, find a means of countering the ice shells.

Will do. She paused. *Five more drakkons come.*

Where from?

White Zone. Protect retreat of tanks hidden by earth.

I swore softly. I needed to get out there, needed to see what their new weapon looked like before they could drag the thing back into the no-go zone.

Can fly you, came Kiva's thought. *Dump Kaiden first. Too heavy.*

We were skimming the ground now. She could land if she wanted, but to have any hope of lifting me back over the wall, she had to remain in the air. She didn't have the strength of the bigger drakkons and wouldn't be able to lift me from a jump-start.

Oma, how far away are the other drakkons?

One hundred sweeps?

Which gave me time to grab a vehicle but nowhere near enough to fight my way through the Mareritt flooding toward the break in the wall. It left me with no choice.

Kiva, can you hover so Kaiden can get off? When she immediately did so, I added, "Kaiden, roll off me and jump down."

He did and then stepped back to give me room. Kiva kicked her wing sweeps into a higher gear and took off again. Kaiden shouted after me, but the words were lost to the scream of wind and the rattle of gunfire from those now scrambling to protect the breakpoint.

I twisted around so I was facing in the right direction and then inched forward, carefully lifting myself over the first couple of spine plates that ran up her neck until I was sitting between two of the larger ones—a position that put me in front of her wings and one that was somewhat perilous when she wasn't wearing either a breastplate or tack. My legs and thighs were well used to gripping drakkon back, but without the tack straps to loop my legs through and hold me in place, any sudden movement could see me dislodged.

Won't, Kiva said. *Safe.*

We soared over the wall and across the river, the wind sharp and cold on my face and hands. But it felt good—so good—to be on drakkon back again.

The plain below was alive with movement. The Mareritt weren't hiding now—they were flooding from the burning forest on foot and in tanks, heading for the thick breach in the wall. There were many more in the forest itself; hopefully Oma's fire would take care of them.

But it made me wonder why they were now intent on retreating with the weapons that had caused all the damage —why do that when they had the advantage? Why not utterly shatter the wall and bring Esan to its knees? It made no tactical sense to retreat when you had the enemy in such a vulnerable position.

Unless, of course, the weapon was limited in what it could do. I doubted it was a coincidence that five ice spheres had destroyed both the coruscation *and* part of Esan's wall. Then another thought occurred. What if all this was nothing more than a means to draw out the last surviving kin in Arleeon?

Fear pulsed and my heart rate leapt several notches. *Oma, are there mages with the sphere tanks?*

What mage?

I hesitated. How could I describe a mage when they looked no different to any other Mareritt? It was only their eyes—their pupils were as white as the sclera—and the shimmer of energy they wore like a cloak that differentiated them from their fellow Mareritt.

Can you ask one of the drakkons who approach?

Only know one. There was a pause, and then she said, *Ineke doesn't know mages.*

I swore, uncertain what to do next. I didn't want to put any of us into deeper danger, but I couldn't lose the chance of seeing what those weapons looked like, either. If we *did* manage to get into the White Zone, we needed to know what to look for. Otherwise, we'd be scrambling around wasting time and risking capture.

Mareritt know here, Oma said.

Us or you?

Me. Must leave or Ineke and others attack.

Then leave. Kiva, can you get me close to that valley?

Can. Tired.

I knew that. I could feel it rippling through her mind. But we were nearing the end of the forest now and the ground stretched out before us, a night-cloaked series of rolling, tree-lined hills that randomly plunged into deeper valleys.

How far away are the drakkons, Oma?

Twenty sweeps.

Meaning we had five minutes, if that, before we were in their line of sight. I swore and rubbed my forehead. I still had the rifle strapped across my back, but my inner fires were dangerously low. If this *was* a trap, I was in deep trouble.

Can help, Oma said.

No. Risking my safety was one thing. Risking theirs, after everything they'd been through, was something else entirely.

Which left me with one—very stupid—option.

An action that *wouldn't* have surprised my sister or anyone else who'd flown with me.

Kiva, can you swing to the right, away from the valley that holds the Mareritt? Fly low so they don't see you.

What do?

I'm going to jump off, and you're going to return to Esan.

No like this.

Neither did I, to be honest. I hesitated and then unstrapped my knife. After cutting a portion of gold cloth from my jacket, I pricked my finger and used the blood to write four simple words—*follow Oma if caught.*

Can burn Mareritt on way? Kiva asked.

Yes.

Will burn, then eat. Happy.

Whether she meant she'd eat the Mareritt or more capras, I had no idea—and really *didn't* want to find out.

I gripped the spine plate in front of me as she swooped low, her wingtips skimming inches above the ground and leaving little dust devils swirling in our wake.

We approached a long, shallow valley that ran alongside the one in which the Mareritt were currently bunkered. I asked Kiva to hover and then, with a deep breath, swung my leg over the front spine plate and dropped down. After brushing my fingers across the ground to steady myself, I turned and held up the sheathed glass blade with the note tucked inside.

Can you find Kaiden and drop this to him?

Yes. She gripped it tight, then turned and headed away. *Call if need.*

I will. Just remember, guns can bring a drakkon down.

Know. Will be safe.

A comment that very much echoed what I kept telling them and it brought a short-lived smile to my lips. I was now alone in enemy territory. This could all go very wrong, very quickly.

Can come if need, Oma said.

No. I ran into the trees and then scrambled up the slope, every sense I had alert for any sound or scent that would indicate I wasn't alone. The Mareritt might be in the next valley, but that didn't mean there were no scouts in this one.

Emri would have, Oma said.

It was a comment that cut through me, if only because it suggested I thought less of her than my bonded drakkon. *Even Emri would have been brought down by five drakkons, Oma. I would have no more risked her safety than I will yours.*

Her grumble ran through my thoughts. *Don't like not helping.*

I know. My lungs were beginning to burn, and sweat trickled down my face and spine. The night might be cool, but this uniform was designed to counter the chill that came with flying high by keeping body heat locked within the layers of material. It was never meant to be worn during vigorous activity, and scrambling up this steep hillside was certainly that. *Can you ask Ineke what's happening in that valley?*

There was a pause, then, *Earth over strange tanks being removed.*

I swore and increased my speed, slipping and sliding as I surged up the steepening slope. If there were patrols in this area, I was all but shouting my location. But I had to see those weapons before they were taken from the area.

The top of the ridge finally came into sight. My legs burned, and I couldn't get enough air into my lungs, no matter how quickly I breathed. It didn't matter; nothing did except getting to the ridge and seeing the ice weapons.

The trees abruptly thinned, providing less cover. I dropped to hands and knees, scrambled forward the last few yards, and came out on a ridge that overlooked the entire valley. Either I'd been lucky or Kiva had placed me well.

The five drakkons circled high above, their scales glimmering whenever touched by moonlight. Their movements were casual, with no suggestion they were on lookout for intruders—but to believe that would be foolish.

There was at least a squadron of Mareritt on the valley floor, but it was the two who stood, hands raised, at the back of the semi-dismantled earth mounds that protected the ice tanks who caught my attention.

Mages.

I didn't need to see their eyes to know that. The crawl of their power stung the air and pulsed through the ground under my stomach.

There were three ice tanks here in all—although, aside from the long, needlelike gun, none of them bore any real resemblance to tanks. Or indeed, any other vehicle or weapon I'd seen up until this point. Their fat, round bodies sat on two metal skids, with some sort of chain anchoring them at the rear—a counterpoint to the weight of the nose, presumably. I wasn't sure if they were constructed out of metal or something else, as it seemed to have a frosty sheen in the cold light of the moon. If it was metal, then Kaiden's belief they couldn't work the substance was a false one.

Movement at the far end of the valley caught my attention. Two vehicles entered; they were podlike up front with a long, flat tray at the back. Obviously, the weapons weren't mobile...

The crack of a twig had my head snapping around. I scanned the trees to my right, seeing nothing, sensing nothing. The slight breeze ran past me rather than toward and gave no hint of what had made that noise. It could have been nothing more than one of the tiny honey bears who inhabited these lowland forest areas out foraging for food.

Or it could be a Mareritt patrol attempting to sneak up on me.

I carefully edged down the ridge until I was back in the thick cover of the trees, then stood and scanned the hillside again, tension flooding fire through my veins.

Still no sign of Mareritt, or, indeed, anything else, but I couldn't escape the notion that Túxn was about to claim her pound of flesh.

Oma, can you ask Ineke if the Mareritt patrol my valley?

There was a pause, then, *Know you there. Coming. Shall flame?*

No, because then you'll be attacked by Ineke and the others. We can't risk that, Oma. I swung the rifle from my shoulder, checked it was fully loaded, and then ran with all the speed I could muster down the slope.

What if captured?

Tree branches whipped across my face and stone skittered from under my feet. It didn't matter. They knew I was here and had eyes in the sky, so there was little point in hiding. *If they capture me, follow from a safe distance and see where they take me.*

No help knowing. Can't talk to Kaiden.

No. But you can lead him to me. Or if that doesn't work, you can tell me where I am, and that might help me escape.

She grumbled. Loudly. *Unhappy. Rather flame now.*

I know, but sometimes it's better to be patient.

No like patient.

I smiled and leaped over a log, landing heavily and rather awkwardly on the other side. Pain shot around my ankle, but I ignored it and kept on running.

I could hear the Mareritt now, and there were a *lot* of them.

Drakkons leaving with strange tanks, came Oma's comment.

Which didn't really help me right now. *Does Ineke know where they're taking them?*

No. Oma paused. *Will tell when knows.*

Thank her for me.

Will. Have.

The noise of pursuit grew louder. They were so damn close now...

Fire burned across my fingertips. I slid to a halt, swung around, and flung it in a wide arc. Flame leapt from tree to tree until the entire area was alight. It would stop this lot, but there were others. Many others.

I turned and bolted in the opposite direction, slipping and sliding on various patches of scree and rotting leaves. The harsh rasp of my breathing echoed across the night, mingling with the screams and shouts of those caught in the firestorm behind me. But from up ahead came the sound of a vehicle; one that moved toward the forest rather than away.

It was a trap, just as I feared.

I swore and changed direction, scrambling back up the hill. If I could make it to the other valley, if the Mareritt there were indeed leaving rather than simply repositioning their weapons, I had a chance. A slight chance, but a chance nonetheless.

The rumble of another vehicle came from the tree line above. No escape that way. I swore, abandoned any thought of reaching the other valley, and headed across the hill instead—running toward the tank on the plain rather than away from it.

I still had some fire left. If I could blast the tank, inca-pacitate it... The thought died. It wouldn't help me. Nothing would. I'd be captured no matter what I did, but I'd be damned if I'd make it easy for them.

Something pinged past my ear and smashed into the tree a few yards ahead. Bark speared into my face as I raced past, drawing blood. I swore again and spun around. Saw the Mareritt in the trees farther up the hill and raised the rifle, unleashing metal hell on them. Gunshots ran across the night, and several Mareritt went down. Bullets pounded into the trees all around me, but none hit me.

They wanted me alive.

I wanted them all dead.

I continued to shoot until the chamber-empty light flashed in warning, then flung fire into the trees, creating another barrier between them and me. My eye started bleeding again, and the pounding in my head increased; I was now roaring toward empty unconsciousness but didn't really care. I shoved a fresh clip into the rifle, then turned and ran. The heat of nearby flames shimmered across my back, and the stench of burned flesh stained the crisp air. But it hadn't stopped them. Nothing would. Not until they'd achieved their goal.

I leaped over another log. Saw movement to my right. Raised the rifle and fired indiscriminately. One Mareritt went down, and two others ducked behind trees.

Movement, this time to my left. More soldiers. In the trees, shadowing me but not firing.

They had me surrounded.

I was theirs. They knew it. I knew it.

But I'd still be damned if I'd go down easily.

I reached for more flames. But even as they answered, even as more Mareritt burned, something snapped inside.

Pain unlike anything I'd ever felt sent me stumbling. I hit the ground hard and slid for several feet, skinning hands and chin before coming to a halt hard up against a tree.

I tried to rise but couldn't. My limbs were heavy and unresponsive, my vision was black, and there was nothing beyond a fierce roaring in my ears. Nothing beyond the fire in my brain and the agony in my soul.

It was over.

ELEVEN

I drifted in a dark sea of unending pain. It burned through my heart, my soul, and my brain. It came from losing all that I held dear and from doing too much, pushing too hard. The occasional strange sound or smell had consciousness flickering, but it was never enough to hold me above that sea. To wake me.

I'm not entirely sure what eventually did.

Certainly it *wasn't* the absence of agony. My limbs were stretched to breaking point and ablaze with pain, my head thumped so hard that tears dribbled from under closed eyelids, and my heart felt ready to explode out of my chest. Which made no sense. I was captive and unmoving—why would it be pumping so hard?

There was metal on my wrists, metal around my ankles, and stone at my back. The air was icy, and every breath felt cold against my lips. The scents that ran around me were dominated by the musky stink of the Mareritt, but underneath it ran hints of age and mustiness that stirred memories I couldn't quite catch.

There was no sound in this place—no sound other than the harsh rasp of labored breathing.

Mine.

Something was *very* wrong.

Fear surged, but there was no accompanying rise of fire. My flames were a twisting, churning mass of heat and anger, but they were somehow chained. I could feel them, but I couldn't call on them.

Somehow, the Mareritt had cut access to my one and only weapon.

How was that possible? How could they retard something that was so innate in every kin? Something that was built into our very DNA?

I tried to reach for Oma or Kiva, but there was nothing but an odd sort of static. My ability to communicate with the drakkons had also been silenced.

Perhaps that's why my head thumped and my heart hurt. Perhaps whatever they were doing to curtail either ability was physically destroying me.

Was that what they wanted? To destroy me?

But why bring me here—wherever here was—if that were their intent? Why not simply kill me in the forest, where they had me totally and utterly outnumbered?

I covertly drew in a deeper breath in an effort to quell the surging fear. If I wanted *any* hope of getting out of this situation, I needed to keep a calm, clear head. And while my head *did* feel like it was trapped in a vise and being squeezed ever tighter, I could at least *think*.

The first question I needed to answer was, where in the wind's name was I?

There was no way of telling without opening my eyes, and something within suggested doing so would *not* be a good idea. I had no idea why, given this room appeared empty, but until I knew more about the situation and what had happened to me, I wasn't inclined to ignore it.

Instead, I turned my attention inward. Not so much on the pain, but the reason for it. The cause of the agony in my limbs was obviously the fact that my arms and legs were stretched wide and locked in place by cuffs. I wasn't hanging by them—there was a small shelf of stone under each foot, which suggested that while they might be trying to break me mentally, they weren't intending to do so physically. Not yet, anyway.

This belief was underscored by the fact that I didn't appear to have any broken bones. There was also nothing to suggest I'd been badly beaten or even raped, as the women in that pod had been.

But maybe they were saving all *that* for when I woke— which was a perfectly good reason to keep pretending unconsciousness.

There was a bandage of some sort around my right arm, just below the inner part of my elbow. It appeared to be holding something in place, because if I twitched slightly, metal moved inside my vein. A needle—and no doubt the entry point of whatever drug they were pumping into me.

Were those drugs the cause of the thumping in my head and the galloping of my heart? The reason I couldn't reach either of my abilities?

Maybe. It still made no sense, though. I'd cindered hundreds of their men, had caused untold damage to their carefully maintained front of invincibility, and had freed a couple of their drakkons. The Mareritt I knew would not have kept me alive—not unless they had other plans for me... The thought trailed off, and suddenly I knew.

They were trying to *turn* me.

Trying, via a mix of drugs and magic, to make me a

weapon against my own people. They'd done it to us more than once. In fact, part of the reason Zephrine hadn't noticed the coruscations until they were in Arleeon was the chaos and confusion caused by two kin who'd somehow escaped the madness that came with a drakkon's death, and who'd been found wandering through Mareritten close to death a few days after.

Just like me, they'd been thoroughly examined by readers.

Just like me, there'd been no indication of false memories having been inserted.

And, just like me, they'd been cleared of any interference.

Had Kaiden's initial fears about me been right? Was I an unwilling—unknowing—partner in some hideous, Mareritt-designed plot? If not from this time, then from mine? What if my memories of falling from Emri weren't from the coruscation but rather from a time before they'd even entered Arleeon?

Just because I remembered flying into the coruscation after Sorrel didn't mean those fears were pointless, because my presence might have triggered the trap.

What if the reason I was here now, alive and relatively unhurt, was because they wanted me to be? Because they'd realized their reprogramed weapon was faulty and needed a retune before she returned to wreak havoc on those who now called her friend?

I couldn't answer any of those questions, and that was perhaps the scariest thing of all.

From somewhere beyond my cell came the sound of footsteps. Keys rattled within a lock, and then the door opened. Two Mareritt walked toward me. It took every ounce of control I had to keep pretending unconsciousness.

"Bio readout?" The voice was gruff, and his heavy accent one I'd only heard a few times in my life. He'd come from the deep south of Mareritten—an area that was riddled with both snow and volcanoes.

"Acute." The reply came from the right side of the room and *not* from either of the men who'd entered. The third man had obviously been here the entire time, meaning my instincts had been right. "Respiratory distress, blood pressure, and heart rate at dangerous levels."

"Any sign of awareness?"

The other man hesitated. "There is some level of consciousness evident."

"And her psi talents?"

"Successfully restrained."

The gruff man grunted. "Mage? Opinion?"

Someone stepped forward, and then fingers touched my forehead. Fingers that were cold and pulsed with power.

Magic, not ice. Slithering into my brain, riffling through my thoughts.

May the wind help me...

I held still, fighting instinct and the need to react, to kill. My life might well depend on them *not* knowing I was fully conscious.

But it was a damn hard task when those skeletal fingers of darkness clawed further and further into my brain. What was he seeking? I really had no idea, because it didn't feel anything like the process of being read. He didn't appear to be mining or even *altering* my memories.

Whatever he was doing, it went on and on.

The pounding in my head became steadily worse. Every breath was now short and shallow, and my heart ached. Literally ached.

The mage continued to delve, poking and probing the

remaining area of ice in my brain; his magic swirled around it, testing and tasting it. That ice and his power were very similar in feel, and it made me wonder if the ice in my brain had in fact been caused by the magic within the coruscation.

What if it was a product of *this* time? What if he was now adjusting whatever commands or memories lay behind it?

Would I even be thinking this way if he were?

I didn't know. I just didn't *know*.

"She's about to go into cardiac arrest," came the monotone voice to my right.

"Get the infusion ready," the gruff voice said. "Mage? Anything?"

"If she has been reprogrammed, whatever her task was has been accomplished. I see no remnants of it."

Oh God... had I been right? Had I been the trigger that had trapped and destroyed Sorrel and all the graces? I didn't want to believe it, but there was no escaping the possibility.

"Meaning the magic remaining is Mareritt in origin?"

"Yes, but it is old, not new, and has the feel of the coruscation."

His words made me feel no better. Just because he couldn't feel any reprogramming didn't mean I hadn't been. Didn't mean I couldn't be once again.

The man in charge grunted again. It was not a happy sound. "Suggesting she's not, as some believe, a half-breed born with the kin ability to flame but rather an escapee from the coruscation?"

"Again, unclear."

"Do you have an opinion either way?" There was something in the commander's tone that suggested he and this mage did *not* get along.

"Her mottled skin is one of the inherent signs of a half-breed—"

"I'm aware of that, mage." The commander's voice was curt. "That's not what I asked."

"The blood of kin still runs through many today. It would not be unexpected for their ability to flame and even communicate with drakkons to make a reappearance in a new generation."

"Even in a half-breed?"

"Yes." The mage hesitated. "As to whether she's an escapee—none who flew into the coruscations on the Day of Victory would have had this mottling. Half-breeds simply did *not* exist back then."

How ironic, I thought distantly, that the one thing I hated might be the one thing that saved me.

Not that survival was in any way guaranteed. Pain radiated down both my spine and my arm now, and my gut churned. Breathing was almost impossible, and the voices of the Mareritt appeared to be getting farther and farther away.

"Then how do you explain the remnants of old magic in her mind?"

"I can't; the possibility she's an escapee remains—and she certainly matches the description of the woman in the strange uniform found within the Red Ochre tunnel."

His words had memories stirring... Stumbling along a roadway that seemed to go on forever, and rain. Never-ending rain that soaked me to the skin and made me shiver despite my inner heat. A mountain soaring above me, deep red against blue, blue skies. Then a tunnel entrance, half hidden by sheeting water that was colder than ice. Stagger-ing, delirious with tiredness, along the dark road that cut through the heart of the mountain. Then lights, bright lights pinning me, capturing me.

The commander snorted. "If she'd been transferred to the coruscation watchtower rather than the prison pod, we might not be facing the current problems."

"The pod contained the warrior who attacked the supply train being transported to Frio for interrogation," the mage snapped back. "It made sense to divert it for her. The Helmer would have sorted them both out."

The Helmer? I had no idea what that was—and a deep suspicion I didn't ever want to.

But the commander's comments at least explained how I'd ended up in the prison pod. They simply hadn't suspected who I was or where I'd come from, and it had been the easiest option.

"I take it her escape is the reason why we were ordered to destroy the coruscation—to negate the risk of others breaking free," the commander said. "If so, we should have destroyed it far earlier. We would not now be facing the possibility of free drakkons and a revitalized enemy."

"If we'd been capable of destroying it earlier, we would have." The mage's fingers withdrew from my forehead, yet the chill of his touch remained. It felt as if I'd been branded. "But regular munitions would not have worked against the magic within. In their efforts to finally entrap and destroy the Kaieke, the mages of old poured all their energy and expertise into the coruscations, making them immune to all known magic and ammunitions at the time."

The commander grunted. "It would seem the mages of old had far more knowledge than those of you alive today."

"Those mages lost their lives in the development of the coruscations, and it left us bereft of magical expertise for well over a century," the mage snapped again. "Only the foolish would wish a repeat."

The commander was either oblivious to the anger in the mage's tone or he simply didn't care. "What do you want done with her?"

"The Helmer wishes her kept on ice. Kroon will be here within the next day or so. She will decide whether this Kaieke can be turned to our advantage or is best destroyed..."

Whatever else he might have said faded. All I could hear was the too-fast pounding of my pulse in my ears, and all I could feel was pain. Pain in my chest, my spine, and my arm. Then it all collapsed in on me and I knew no more.

The second time around, there was no gentle climb into wakefulness. It hit fiercely and abruptly, accompanied by the rapid pounding of my heart and the thick taste of fear in my throat.

For several minutes, I didn't move. I barely dared to breathe. I just waited for the hammer to fall, for death to fully claim me.

She didn't.

I was *alive*—and, more importantly perhaps, relatively unbroken. *That* was so damn unexpected, a sob escaped before I could stop it. The sound echoed softly, but thankfully, nothing came from it.

I took a deep but careful breath. No pain flared in response, and the pounding in my head had receded to little more than a background murmur. My fires, however, remained beyond reach. I hoped it wasn't permanent—

hoped it was simply an effect of whatever they'd been pumping into my system.

But only time—and the fading of whatever magic or drug they'd used—would tell.

I was no longer vertically chained to a wall of very cold stone but rather lying naked on a bed of one. The cuffs remained on my wrists and ankles, but there was no bandage around my arm and no needle in my vein. I shifted one leg a fraction; chains rattled between the two, but there didn't seem to be anything securing me to the wall or even the base of the bed.

Nor did the scent of the ice scum linger. The silence in the immediate area was thick and heavy, and the air touching my flesh as icy as the stone under my back. But I wasn't cold. My fires may have been leashed beyond reach, but it hadn't stopped them from keeping the chill from my skin.

I wondered if *that* was the reason I'd woken. I suspected I wasn't meant to, given the mage's comment about keeping me on ice.

The odd, almost dank mustiness I'd noticed earlier was back, and somewhere in the distance beyond this cell, water dripped. Thirst hit, along with the rumblings of hunger. I doubted, however, that either food or water would come my way anytime soon. Not until they'd decided what to do with me—and maybe not even then.

I carefully cracked my eyes open. It wasn't completely dark—a small globe just above the heavy-looking door washed a pale blue light through the cell. Aside from a hole in the stone floor that I presumed was a privy, and the chains dangling from the wall to the right of my stone bed, there was nothing else here. Whatever machine the Mareritt had used to monitor my vital signs had gone, and there didn't appear to be any cameras or listening devices. Which struck me as odd despite the fact that the air was so cold it swirled visibly from the vent on the other side of the room.

It really *was* damn cold in here.

I shivered, though I suspected it was more psychosomatic than any real feeling of cold. My body heat was now high enough that the ice covering the stone underneath me had started to melt.

I shifted fractionally and studied the door. It, like the rest of this room, appeared to be solid stone. No surprise there; my fires couldn't affect it—not without using so much strength I'd basically incapacitate myself.

After another look around to ensure I hadn't missed a camera, I sat up. Vague twinges ran through my arms and legs—no doubt remnants of the pain that had come from them being stretched so far apart—but otherwise, I was surprisingly unhurt. My mind also felt clear, but that wasn't likely to last once Kroon—whoever she might be—got here. While the fear that I was the reason Arleeon's graces had been trapped within the coruscation remained, the mage's statements pretty much confirmed I wasn't currently under Mareritt influence.

But there was absolutely no doubt they *would* attempt to reprogram me. And if they did manage to do so, I could cause untold damage to Esan, just as the kin who'd been turned in my time had to Zephrine.

I had to get out before that happened.

Had to.

But how? This place was stone—nothing but stone. Sure, there was the vent, but it wasn't big enough to shove an arm into, let alone the rest of me. I rose, then held still as dizziness hit. Once it had passed, I bent to lift the chain off the floor so it didn't rattle and then shuffled over to the door.

Unsurprisingly, the seals were tight—there was little point of pumping cold air into the room if it just leaked out again. So why was the frosty air swirling? That suggested there *was* a source of air coming into this room other than the vent.

The door hinges and lock were also made of stone, but of a different type. They were green-gray in color, with swirls of red and black through them. Metamorphic rocks, I knew, and very similar to the ones Zephrine had mined from the old volcanoes scattered throughout the region. We'd used it for everything, from tankards and bowls to beautifully handcrafted furniture.

I ran my fingers across the top hinge and briefly wished I had the ability to hear the whispers of the earth. Perhaps then I might have pulled forth the stone's secrets and learned whether this room—and the hallway beyond— was in fact a surviving part of old Zephrine incorporated in the redesign. Because if that *were* the case, there was hope.

It also meant that maybe, just maybe, my brothers had done me a huge favor by leading me into the old tunnels and then totally abandoning and forgetting about me all those years—centuries—ago.

I shuffled around and drew in a deep breath. It damn near froze my lungs—at least until the inner heat surged in defense. But the fact that it responded so quickly perhaps meant whatever drugs they'd used were now clearing my system. It also suggested the Mareritt weren't aware of the kin's faster healing abilities—no doubt thanks to the fact that so few of us had ever been caught. Generally, when drakkons were killed, grief hit their riders so hard they took their own lives—and long before the Mareritt could get to them.

I'd been lucky. I'd had Oma to fight the grief and Kaiden to protect me when I'd been totally and utterly unable to do either.

The mustiness I'd smelled when I was on the bed wasn't evident near the door, so it had to be coming from *that* side of the room. I moved over, drew in another breath, and found it. I could again hear the drip of water, even though the sound had some distance to it. This cell was definitely close to the old tunnels—now I just had to hope it had one of the old food hatches built in.

I carefully shuffled forward and studied the area between the bed and the wall onto which I'd been chained. And there, sitting between the two, was the rusting metal remnant of an old food hatch. As escape routes went, it came with a couple of problems—the first being the fact that it wasn't large; it was roughly thirteen by nineteen inches, which was just big enough to fit a standard serving tray filled with food. I'd followed my brothers through that space easily enough as a scrawny child, but it was debatable whether I'd do so now.

The other problem was the fact that, in this part of old Zephrine, the walls were reasonably thick. I was about to force my body through what amounted to a small stone tunnel.

I knelt and tentatively probed the remains of the hatch; metal flaked away at my touch, and it didn't take much effort to remove it entirely. These hatches had been in a bad enough state when my brothers had led me into the tunnels. The two hundred years that had passed since then had only added to their deterioration.

I lay on the floor and piled all the metal remnants onto

my stomach. It would have been easier to go belly first, but given there was only a few inches wriggle room, at best, it basically meant scraping my breasts against the rough stone. Better my back any day.

I braced my feet against the floor, raised my arms above my head so they wouldn't be trapped against my sides, and then pushed back into the hatch tunnel. The cold stone tore at my skin, and my shoulders barely fit. I sucked in a breath and pushed again, gaining deeper cuts on arms and back from the metal remnants still lodged in the stone. Another push. More skin lost. I swore but kept going until I was able to grab the far end of the hatch and pull the rest of my body out. It hurt—a *lot*—but I was finally free.

I didn't immediately move. I just lay on my back in the darkness, listening to that distant dripping while I sucked in air that was dank and old but still far warmer than in the cell. Memories surged, and for a minute I was eight years old again, lost and alone and afraid. The hell my brothers had gotten from my parents when I'd eventually reemerged... I closed my eyes against the sting of tears. There was nothing I could do to save my family, but there were plenty of families in present-day Arleeon who could be saved.

I scooped up the few remnants of metal that lay on my stomach and then pushed up onto my knees. Pain slithered across my abused back, and moisture trickled down my arms; some of the scrapes were obviously quite deep. I swore again and then reached back into the hatch, shoving some of the metal bits back into the edge slots and scattering the remainder around. It wouldn't stand up to a close inspection—especially given the amount of blood and skin I'd lost—but it didn't need to. I just needed it to fool a casual glance long enough for me to get away from this area. The problem *then* would be finding my way back to the main part of old Zephrine and somehow escaping.

I glanced left and then right; both options were utterly dark, but the dripping sound came from the right, as did the slight movement of air.

I headed that way, keeping my fingers on the wall as a guide. Progress was by necessity slow—not only because of the chains and the fact it was ink dark but also because I was barefoot. The stone was either wet or slimy—sometimes both—and the last thing I needed after getting out of the cell was to slip and break something.

The tunnel wove through the darkness but never seemed to get any closer to the source of that steady dripping. The drifting air sometimes held pockets of warmth or the scent of baking bread, but they were little more than teasing remnants that faded as quickly as they appeared.

I had no idea how much time passed; it seemed like ages, but that could simply have been a product of my growing pain and tiredness. I needed to rest, but I also needed food and water.

To get either, I had to find a way out of here.

Then, from up ahead, came the faintest shimmer of light. My pulse kicked into a higher gear and I stopped. The light was static, and there was no sound to suggest anyone waited up ahead. It was simply a pale green glow that barely lifted the darkness; I had no idea if it came from a natural source or was man-made. I hesitated and then moved forward again. As I drew closer, I realized what it was, and once again my pulse skipped. I'd come across a similar patch of bioluminescent fungi when I'd originally gotten lost in these tunnels, though whether it was the same patch or a different one I had no idea. But what were the chances of there being two such places within this tunnel system?

Probably far higher than I'd want, I thought somewhat wryly.

The fungi grew in a round chamber that was the intersection of five different tunnels. Water dripped from the ceiling, and a mini stream came out of a tunnel to my left and disappeared into one on my immediate right. The air was far warmer here than in the tunnel behind me, which suggested that at least one of these exits either ran past a heat source or had an outside egress. The question was, which one?

I scanned the chamber, looking for clues, looking for anything that set off a memory. But I'd only been a kid when I'd last been here, and two hundred years had passed since then. If there *had* been clues here, they were long eroded.

I hesitated, then walked across to the small stream and squatted beside it. After scooping up some water, I gave it a careful sniff. It held no scent—certainly there was nothing to suggest it was in any way fouled—but I nevertheless stuck in a finger and carefully tasted it. It was cold and crisp, with a slightly bitter taste that suggested there was at least some sulfate in it. If that *was* the only element it contained, then it was probably safe. Even so, I only drank enough to ease the burning in my throat and clear a little of the light-headedness. After washing down my arms and hips, and then dribbling water down my throbbing back, I rose, stepped across the stream, and shuffled toward the tunnel almost directly opposite. Maybe it was a memory I couldn't quite snare, but something about the tunnel called to me.

Once again, I kept my fingers against the wall. The floor was at least flat here and free from the moisture and slime that had hampered my movements in the other tunnel. It didn't mean I could travel any faster, however. The inky darkness had returned.

It quickly became evident that it wasn't memory that had drawn me into this tunnel. Nothing about it seemed in any way familiar—not the growing feeling of space, the increasingly rough walls that suggested I'd left the man-made tunnel system far behind, or the number of what I suspected were stalagmites I kept running into.

After a while, a soft sound reverberated through the darkness. I paused, cocking my head to one side, listening intently.

Footsteps.

Four sets, walking toward me.

I thrust a hand through my wet and tangled hair. Could Túxn not give me a break? I was naked, tired, and aching. My fire remained out of reach, and I was lost in a maze of dark tunnels somewhere under Zephrine. Surely I'd given enough skin and blood to satisfy even the goddess's demands of compensation?

The footsteps grew louder. I took a deep breath, then picked up the leg chains so they didn't rattle and carefully retraced my steps until I found the mini forest of stalagmites I'd fumbled my way around earlier. It wasn't much cover, but it was all I had.

Once I'd squatted behind them, there was nothing more I could do but hope whoever approached didn't see me.

The four were close now. My heart hammered and sweat dribbled down the side of my face. I swiped it in annoyance and then stilled the movement as light speared the darkness ahead. May the wind help me—they had flashlights...

In the brightness of that light, the stalactites and stalagmites shone a deep and bloody red. The tunnel was high and rounded, and the walls etched deep with ripples that reminded me of waves. Lava waves, I knew. This was one of the old tubes I'd told Kaiden about.

Four shadowy figures stepped around the corner. My breath caught in my throat and I held still, despite the gathering urge to run. The light hit the small forest of stalagmites I was tucked behind, and the footsteps abruptly stopped.

Then an all too familiar voice said, "Nara?"

Kaiden.

I sucked in a deep breath and rose, raising one hand against the brightness of the light. "How the hell did you find your way into this place? And where *is* this place?"

"If it's not the lava tube you mentioned in Esan, then it's one close to it." His expression was hard to make out, but I heard the emotion in his voice. It was relief, concern, and caring, all wrapped in one heartwarming mix. "Are you all right?"

"I'm tired, thirsty, and hungry, but otherwise fine." Though my voice was even, it nevertheless held an underlying tremor. We were as far from safe as we could get, but I was no longer alone in this underground maze, and the relief that surged was so damn strong I was all but shaking.

Kaiden continued to walk toward me, but his three companions stopped. They were little more than black shadows thanks to the flashlights, but they appeared to be loaded down with supplies and weapons.

Kaiden propped the flashlight on one of the stalagmites, directing the beam onto the ceiling rather than at me. His face was etched deep with weariness, but his eyes shone with so much emotion it made my heart skip.

The others might be here for tactical purposes, but Kaiden had come here for *me*.

And he would have gone into the heart of Mareritten itself if that's what it had taken to rescue me.

The knowledge made my breath catch and my stomach twist. I barely knew this man, but the connection between us was already so deep and strong that I suspected there was no escaping it.

Not that I wanted to.

"I hate to be the bearer of bad news," he said softly, "but you look like shit."

A smile twisted my lips. "Way to boost someone's morale, warrior."

He didn't reply. He simply drew me into his arms and held me close. It felt as if he never intended to let me go.

Felt like *home*.

I rested my cheek against his chest, listening to the steady beat of his heart and reveling in the strength of the arms that held me so tenderly.

Two hundred years and the destruction of everything I'd ever known and everyone I cared about—that's what it had taken to find the *one* thing that had been missing from my life in Zephrine.

I blinked back tears that were a weird mix of pain and joy, then said, "How did you find me?"

"Before we get into all that, let's get you out of these chains."

He kissed the top of my head and then slid the pack from his back. From one of the smaller pockets at the front, he plucked a key lock similar to the one he'd used in the old farmhouse. He unlatched the leg cuffs first, then the wrist ones, and tossed both into the nearby stalagmites. I rubbed my wrists in relief but didn't dare touch my ankles. The skin there was red and raw from all the walking.

Kaiden waved one of his companions across. "Loretta's a field medic. Once she's tended to all your wounds, we'll set up a temporary camp."

I frowned. "Is that safe? I have no precise idea of where we are, but I do know we're close to the old tunnels that run under Zephrine. If the Mareritt are using them—"

"We'll deal with all that if and when it happens." He raised a hand and lightly touched my cheek. "I wasn't kidding when I said you look like shit. We don't move until you're back to something resembling full strength."

The depth of concern in his eyes had my innards trembling again. It was just further confirmation that this nebulous link went both ways.

Loretta—who was tall and muscular, with a lined face that suggested she was in her fifties—stopped beside him and gave me a brief, impersonal smile. "Righto," she said, balancing her pack on the stalagmites. "Let's have a look at you."

Kaiden stepped out of her way. She did a quick but thorough examination, making unhappy noises when she saw the state of my back. After dragging a medikit from her pack, she proceeded to wash down and then tend the wounds scattered around my body. It wasn't pleasant, but she did at least use a numbing agent when she got to the deeper wounds on my back. Apparently not only were there metal bits still embedded, but several of the cuts were deep enough to need both butterfly bandages to hold them together and sealant spray to cover and protect them.

Once she'd finished, she shoved the medikit back, gave Kaiden a nod, and walked back to the others. Kaiden took off his coat and placed it around my shoulders, holding it steady while I shoved my arms in. Once he'd done up the buttons, he caught the collar, tugged me close, and kissed me. It was little more than a gentle brush of lips against lips, but it held all the passion and caring that had been so evident in his eyes.

"I'm glad you're alive and relatively unhurt, both physically *and* mentally," he murmured.

"How can you tell the latter?"

A smile twisted his lips. "Do you really need to ask that?"

"No." I raised a hand and brushed the hair out of his eyes, needing to drown unhindered in those glorious aqua depths, if only for another second or two. "If I hadn't escaped, it might not have remained that way."

"I'm surprised they didn't question you when they were bringing you here."

"I was unconscious. I doubt they would have attempted to question me anyway, because even in the cell, they had to use a combination of drugs and magic to read me." I hesitated and then glanced at his companions. As much as I wanted to confide my fears over the ice in my mind and my possible part in the fall of the graces, I had no desire to do so within the hearing range of those who didn't know—and likely didn't entirely trust—me.

"Why drugs? Especially if they had mages or even readers on hand?" He caught my hand and led me toward the others. The two men had set up a camp stove and were currently pouring water and what looked to be dried vegetables and meat into a pot.

"Kin are somewhat immune to magic thanks to our link with the drakkon, and I don't think the gift of reading is one they share. Every time we saw someone turned, it was via a mix of drugs *and* magic." I carefully sat down but kept an inch or two between my back and the wall. The salve might have numbed everything, but I wasn't about to push it. "But Túxn gave me another break—the cell they put me in was one of the originals."

"Originals?" He squatted beside me, unzipping his pack and tugging free a flask and a metal cup. "Do you mean it was part of the old tunnel system?"

"In a way, yes. Just as the Mareritt built on the remains of *my* Zephrine, we built on the remnants of another civilization—one so old we had no record of it. But we think the ancient tunnels were used by the serving class to move to and from various rooms without having to use the main halls."

Kaiden poured what looked like liquid mud out of the flask and then handed me the cup. I gulped it down in the vague hope it would somehow taste better that way and then returned the empty cup. Unfortunately, he refilled it.

One of the two men standing near the small stove stepped toward me and held out a hand. He was typical Arleeon in looks, but his golden eyes shone with power. An earth mage, I suspected, and an inclusion that made sense in this sort of raid. Without him to talk to the collective consciousness and guide their steps, Kaiden and the other two could have been wandering around through the tunnel maze for weeks.

"I'm Harrod." His handshake was firm and his voice gravelly but warm. "And it's a damn pleasure to meet you. I think you brought more hope to Esan in a couple of hours than anything we've done for more than a century."

"I wouldn't overhype my presence," I said wryly. "One person can only do so much."

"But it's not just you, is it?" the other man said. "I'm Randal, by the way."

He was taller and thinner than Harrod, with short-cropped gray hair and pale blue eyes. A scar ran down the side of his weatherworn face, and his hands looked rough and gnarled. A career soldier, I suspected.

"It's the drakkons," he continued. "There may be only two, but their presence in the aerie is not something any of us thought we'd see again."

Which at least suggested the fear and uncertainty that had met their arrival in Esan was now fading. I had no doubt Kiva's actions during the attack were responsible for turning that tide. I drank more of the tonic, shuddered, and then glanced at Kaiden. "I take it the Mareritt made no ingress into Esan?"

"No," Kaiden said. "Kiva's final fire sweep took out a good portion of them, and our charge did the rest."

"At least that's something." I hesitated and finished the revolting tonic. "And the wall? Is it fully repaired?"

"Aye," Harrod said, "and we're currently looking for a means of bracing it against that damn ice weapon of theirs."

"Is that even possible?"

He shrugged. "We're not sure as yet, but there's talk of at least weaving metal through the entire structure, as it's not pervious and won't react in the same way. It might even be possible to heat the wall."

The latter would probably take far more time than the Mareritt would ever give them, but it was pointless commenting. He'd be as aware of the drawbacks as me—probably more so, given the earth would be called in to assist with either task.

My gaze returned to Kaiden. "I take it from your presence here that you *did* understand the note I gave Kiva."

"Ah, now there's a story," Loretta murmured, amusement crinkling the corners of her brown eyes. "One I daresay will entertain countless generations to come."

I raised an eyebrow. "Really? Why?"

"Because while I may have kin blood, I'm not capable of mind speech," Kaiden said, voice bland.

"Which is why I gave you the note."

"Yes, but it took a bit to work out what your message said. The blood had spread across the cloth and made the words almost incomprehensible."

"Sorry, but I didn't have anything else to use."

"I gathered that." His shoulder brushed mine lightly, a brief contact that nevertheless sent warmth shivering through me. "Oma returned to Esan once you'd entered New Zephrine, as near as I can gather. What followed *then* was a somewhat comical series of questions from me, and head shaking and foot stamping from Oma."

"It was quite a sight, let me tell you," Randal said. "There was even smoke drifting from the drakkon's nostrils. We were placing bets on whether she'd crisp him in frustration."

"She was worried," Kaiden said with a shrug. "I was never in any danger, no matter what some might have thought."

"So how did you get into this area? By boat?"

"Yes," Kaiden said. "Once we made our way through to Hardwick, it was simply a matter of Harrod talking to the earth and finding the most likely candidate for the tunnel you mentioned."

Which meant that, no matter what had happened to them in the days after the graces had disappeared into the coruscations, the souls of the earth mages in my Zephrine had at least joined the greater consciousness—there was no other way the earth could have held that knowledge. And that was nice to know.

I just had to hope the souls of my family, friends, and everyone else who'd been destroyed that day had been granted a similar gift.

"And our drakkons?" I asked. "Where are they now?"

Kaiden's gaze shot to mine, something close to alarm in his expression. "You don't know?"

I shook my head. "As I said, the Mareritt pumped me full of drugs. One of them not only restricts all my abilities but damn near killed me."

"Do you think it's permanent?"

There was an edge in his voice—an edge that spoke of anger. For me, rather than the weapon Esan might have lost. I smiled and shook my head. "My fires are returning, albeit far too slowly for my liking."

"Good." He touched my arm lightly, relief evident. "I gather from Oma that they'll be waiting somewhere near Zephrine's aeries."

Concern ran through me. "Won't that be dangerous? The Mareritt drakkons will undoubtedly have been ordered to keep an eye out for them."

"I did ask that, but I gather she didn't think it'd be a problem." His tone was wry. "I get the impression she's a very opinioned drakkon."

"That comes with the territory." Certainly Emri had never been backward when it came to expressing her thoughts on various matters—up to and including my love life. Tears stung my eyes, and I blinked them away rapidly. I might have lost the drakkon half of my soul, but I now had Oma and Kiva. And it was totally possible that as our association deepened, the connection between us would grow. Just because there'd never been a case of a kin attaching psychically to another drakkon—let alone two—after the death of her own *didn't* mean it *couldn't* happen. "So what's the plan from here? Retreat or attack?"

"Given who's leading this motley group, what do you think?" Loretta's expression was bland, but amusement creased the corners of her eyes.

"May I point out that everyone here is a volunteer," Kaiden said. "There was absolutely no coercion involved."

"In fact," Randal said, "he actively tried to *discourage* participation. But, for my part, I figured any incursion into the White Zone that had the ultimate goal of blowing shit up was not something I could miss out on."

"Ditto," Harrod said. "Although I *am* sadly missing out on a good portion of the whole blowing up shit—at least until my task is complete and I rejoin you. Hopefully there'll be some Mareritt left to kill by then."

"Given the size of the White Zone, I think there'll be plenty." Randal's voice was dry.

"Which is just as fucking well," Loretta said. "We need to make them pay for the untold number of people who have died needlessly under their rule."

Those deaths obviously included people close to her, if the savage determination in her eyes was anything to go by.

"While I wholeheartedly agree with *that* sentiment," I said, "there is one problem—five people will have more than a little trouble doing much damage."

"Which is why it isn't just us five," Kaiden said. "There's several divisions positioned in the Red Ochre Mountains, ready to attack both the tunnel and the Coruscation Fort."

I frowned. "How did you manage that? Surely the Mareritt are now monitoring all movement?"

"Distractions," Kaiden said. "We moved at night and

simply drew their gaze away from those areas with skirmishes elsewhere."

"And those divisions aren't all we have on standby," Randal said. "Boats carrying another two divisions sit just beyond the Black Claw; once clearance is given, they'll hit Kriton and take out the Mareritt there."

"Both of which are diversions for what we're going to be doing, I gather," I said.

Kaiden nodded. "Harrod will head deep into the tunnel maze and place a jammer—"

"A what?" I cut in.

"Esan's engineers found a means of jamming the frequencies being used to both control *and* kill the drakkons." His grin flashed. "And that means the Mareritt's best weapon *cannot* be used against us in this attack."

"Of course, they've only made three of them so far," Harrod added. "So they'll take out the two comms towers in Arleeon to complement the jammers. Between both, we should render the control bands inert over Esan, a good chunk of central Arleeon, and most of the White Zone."

Excitement surged, and my heart began to beat a whole lot faster. "So if we're in the aerie when those things go online, we can de-band the drakkons and *totally* free them."

And while not all of Mareritten's drakkons were kept within Zephrine's aerie, a good proportion of them apparently were. That, in turn, meant most—if not all, given Oma's earlier comments—would join us in the fight against the Mareritt.

"Exactly," Kaiden said. "A simultaneous assault on the Coruscation Watchtower *and* Kriton will draw the Mareritt's attention away from Zephrine itself."

My excitement dimmed a little. "Even with the help of the drakkons, there are still only five of us—"

"Here, yes," Harrod said. "But there's a third force—led by another mage—working their way through a different lava tunnel. When clearance is given, the mage will break through to the surface and the rest will attack."

"Our task," Kaiden said, "is to free the drakkons and have them rain hellfire onto the Mareritt while we make use of the chaos to find and destroy those damn ice weapons."

None of which was going to be easy. I hesitated. "It sounds like you've put a lot of military resources into this attack—isn't that dangerous?"

Weren't they all but repeating the mistake *we'd* made when we'd thrown everything into the coruscation attack and had subsequently robbed future generations of all hope?

"We *are* pushing resources into this, but we're not leaving Esan unprotected," Kaiden said. "If we fail, then the status quo remains. But if we succeed—if only in part—then we push the scales in our favor. And from there, the long war will finally be ours to win."

His voice was calm and confident, his expression determined. An image slipped past the ice in my brain—one of Sorrel addressing the graces in the final minutes before we'd taken off on our fatal attack. Though her words had been very different, her voice and her expression had been the same as Kaiden's. I really hoped the results *here* were not.

"This *is* our best chance," Randal said. "They're in disarray thanks to the amount of men they lost to the drakkon fire at Esan."

"And the fact that they withdrew their ice weapons," Loretta said, "has to mean that, despite their destructive power, their use is somewhat limited—"

"Not necessarily," I cut in. "That attack might well have

been little more than a test run that was also meant to draw me out—and in that, they succeeded."

"No matter what the true reason for the attack," Kaiden said, "it resulted in a massive loss of manpower. Their command will undoubtedly be working on a response as we speak, and that means we only have a small window in which to hit them."

With that, I agreed. "Their time frame for any planned secondary attack will probably accelerate once they realize I've escaped."

"Yes, which is why you need to eat and rest up. We have to be in position to attack at twenty-two hundred hours, whether or not you've regained your flames."

Harrod handed me a bowl of the reconstituted stew. I thanked him and then said, "I take it there's a preset and unchangeable timetable?"

"Yes," Kaiden said. "It was happening whether or not we found you."

There was a note in his voice—and a light in his eyes— that said while that may have been his orders, it *wasn't* what he'd personally intended.

"This whole process is just a *lot* easier with you," Loretta commented, her voice dry. "Or will be, once you get your fire back."

"Which will be soon." I *hoped*.

"In the meantime," Kaiden said, "eat up and rest. Loretta and Harrod, you take first watch."

They nodded, and the conversation moved on. I let it run over me, finding the noise soothing as I finished the stew and the rest of the awful tonic. Then I lay down on my side and, despite the hardness of the stone, quickly went to sleep.

A gentle prodding woke me some hours later, but it

wasn't a physical touch, and a fierce mix of relief and joy swept through me.

My connection with the drakkons had returned.

And that wasn't all—my fires once again burned unrestricted through my bloodstream, their force so fierce it felt as if I'd erupt into flame at any moment.

I took a deep breath and gently eased the heat down to a more sustainable level, even as Oma said, *Happy you awake. Missed talking.*

So had I—it was truly amazing how quickly she'd stepped into the breach made by Emri's absence. *Are you and Kiva all right?*

Yes, came Kiva's comment. *Ready to burn.*

I couldn't help smiling. *You'll get plenty of chances soon enough, but our immediate priority is freeing as many drakkons as we can.*

Agree with this, Oma said, even as Kiva added, *They can help burn. Cause chaos. Chaos good.*

In this case, it certainly would be. *Where are you both?*

At claw, near boats, Oma said.

Protect them, came Kiva's comment. *If attacked.*

Isn't that dangerous? Won't the Mareritt see you and order their drakkons to attack?

Ineke will warn.

Is she in the aerie?

Yes.

How many others are with her?

Ten.

Which meant, if we did free them, we'd have taken half of Mareritt's drakkon force. And if the jammers worked as expected, then they'd be unable to control their remaining drakkons over a large portion of Arleeon. As Kaiden had said, that was a very good start.

Did she see where the ice tanks were taken?

Yes. She gave me a description and then added, *Twenty Mareritt in aerie now. Numbers boosted after we freed.*

Meaning they'd probably send in even more troops once they'd realized I'd escaped. *How many of the drakkons are likely to report our presence in the aerie?*

Another pause. *If remain leashed, two. Male drakkons not smart.*

It was said with such contempt that I couldn't help but smile. *Will they help us if we manage to free them?*

Yes.

The certainty in her voice had my eyebrows rising even as I hoped she was right. The more drakkons we had on our side, the better it would be for this attack. *Is it night out there yet?*

Sun sets, Kiva said. *When attack happen?*

Obviously her flame runs at Esan had done nothing to ease her desire for revenge. *Soon. We first need to plant the devices that will jam the signal to the control bands.*

I help after, Oma said. *Can command drakkons to obey.*

That had my eyebrows rising all over again. While it did explain her certainty, it was rather odd, as drakkon generally *didn't* have an overall queen. Or hadn't, in my time.

Last born but first free, Oma said. *They respect and obey.*

I second, Kiva said. *Also obeyed.*

Suggesting the Mareritt drakkons had developed some sort of hierarchy system. I wondered if it had somehow been forced on them, or if it had developed naturally out of the military ranking of each drakkon's handler—the higher the ranking, the more esteem in which that drakkon was held.

Both, Oma said.

Will the drakkons currently in charge challenge your rule?

No, Oma said. *First free. Chosen by Kaieke. Will obey.*

So while Esan blamed the actions of the kin for everything that was currently wrong in their world—and with justification—the drakkons—who'd lost just as much—had chosen to do the opposite. It was an interesting divergence.

I opened my eyes and looked for Kaiden. With the flashlights off, the utter darkness had returned, but I nevertheless sensed he was standing close to the stalagmites I'd hidden behind. I pushed to my feet, wincing a little as the still-healing cuts in my back protested. Before I could move any farther, a light came on, its glow muted, providing just enough light to guide me across to Kaiden.

"You all right?" He lightly brushed the hair from my eyes, his fingers cool against my skin—yet another sign that my inner fires had returned full force.

I nodded. "I'm back in contact with the drakkons."

"And your flames?"

I raised a hand and let fire dance lightly across my fingertips. "All present and accounted for."

"Excellent." His gaze returned to mine. "How are you feeling?"

"My back's stiff, but other than that, fine." I gave him the directions Ineke had passed on and then added, "There's also twenty new guards stationed within the aerie."

"Which may or may not be a problem." He studied me for a minute. "What's troubling you?"

I hesitated, then softly told him everything the Mareritt had said in the cell, and everything I feared. When I finished, he didn't immediately reply, and the silence felt sharp and filled with uncertainty.

Then, finally, he took my hands in his and spoke. "We'll never know if you were the key to that trap. No one but you survived, and your memories of that day remain unreliable. The best we can take out of what was said in that cell is the fact that the mage couldn't find any remnant of Mareritt orders or control in your mind."

"But the magic—"

"Comes from the coruscation. He said that, you believe that, *I* believe that. If it turns out we're wrong, I will make good the promise I made in Renton."

"Killing me won't help if it's done too late."

A smile touched his lips. "You forget our link, Nara. It might not be mind-to-mind, but it is soul-to-soul, and strengthening fast. I see no evil or evidence of interference within you."

Would he, though? I didn't know enough about *Dhrukita* to answer that question, but I hoped with all my heart that he was right. That even if I was responsible for the first catastrophe, I wouldn't be responsible for a second.

He squeezed my hands and then glanced past me as Harrod walked up.

"Just got word from Jeanie—who's the earth mage leading the second underground assault party," Harrod added, glancing at me. "She's about an hour from her designated position."

"Then wake the others. We might as well get moving, just in case we hit problems getting into the aerie."

He nodded and moved away. Kaiden's gaze returned to me. "Will you be able to control the drakkons once the bands are rendered inert?"

"Oma can. While I can speak to individual drakkons, I'm not entirely sure I can blanket broadcast."

He raised his eyebrows. "Don't you speak to both Oma and Kiva at the same time?"

"Yes, but I don't know why." I hesitated. "I suspect it

has something to do with Emri's loss, and the fact that Oma stepped into the breach and pulled me from grief's death spiral. And Kiva is her egg sister."

"Ah." He caught the edges of the coat, tugged me close, and kissed me. It was an all too brief promise of a future still too far away. "We do have one major problem, however—and that's you running around barefoot in a coat that swims on your tall frame. It's not a look that'll avoid notice."

A smile twisted my lips. "At least I look half Mareritt. None of you do."

The sound of steps had me glancing over my shoulder. Randal handed me a rifle and an ammo loop. "Just in case there's certain areas in which you *can't* use your flames."

"Thanks."

"And you'd better have one of these." Loretta handed me one of the Q-shaped comms devices. "Just tap it once to connect and talk to any of us, twice to disconnect."

I nodded and slipped the device on, my inner ear tingling when I inserted the tail. It was a rather weird sensation, but at least there was no discomfort.

"Right," Kaiden said, "Randal, lead position. Harrod, warn us if you sense any movement. Loretta, rear guard."

As everyone moved out, Kaiden handed me my knife and its sheath. I strapped it on and felt oddly comforted by its weight—which was insane given a knife wouldn't be of much use against armed Mareritt. Still, this knife had helped me free both Oma and Kiva and may yet save others.

We made good time through the stalagmite maze and the tunnel beyond. Eventually, Harrod said, "We're approaching a tunnel junction. I need to head right. The earth is saying the quickest route into Zephrine lies to the left. Just follow the water—it'll get you into what she thinks is an ancient bathing area. From there, you'll be able to access the newer sections of Zephrine. Our drakkon rider should be able to get you to the aerie from there."

"Thanks, Harrod," Kaiden said. "And good luck."

His grin flashed. "It's not me that needs the luck. I'm surrounded by all the lovely power of the earth; you're the ones that'll be out in the open with only the weapons on your backs."

"Set that device up right," Randal said, "and our weapons will be the *least* of the Mareritt's problems."

"Amen to that, brother," Harrod said cheerfully.

He peeled off into the tunnel on the right and quickly disappeared. In single file, with Kaiden taking over the lead and me right behind him, we headed into the smaller tunnel, following the trickling stream into the sloping darkness. Despite the water, the walls and floor were free of the moss strings that had plagued my progress in the other tunnel, and the stirring air felt fresher.

We'd been moving for almost an hour when we hit a junction with three exits. The little stream split into two, heading into the tunnels on the left and the right.

Kaiden stopped and swept the light across the three entrances. "Best guess, anyone?"

"Harrod said to follow the water, but that ain't of much use when there's two options."

"No." Kaiden glanced at me. "Anything look familiar to you?"

My gaze was drawn to the middle one. It was the smallest of the three, but there was something about the keystone—and the barely visible engravings on it—that stirred a memory. I'd been here before and had chosen that tunnel; every instinct suggested we needed to do so again.

"Contrary to Harrod's advice," I said, "I'm going to suggest the tunnel directly ahead."

"So we either listen to the advice of an earth mage," Loretta said, amusement evident, "or a Zephrine native. Hard choice."

"Given we could very easily choose the wrong stream," Randal said, "I vote we follow the native."

Kaiden handed me the flashlight and motioned me on. I shone the light on the keystone as I neared the entrance. Though the symbols on it were even harder to see now than they had been before, I could still make out the odd-shaped jug sitting above three slashes and the bulbous-bottomed cross sitting to the left of this. Following a tunnel similarly marked had led me into a large room in which ale barrels had been stored.

The gentle slope of the tunnel flattened out, and the scent of malt began to touch the air. Relief rose; it *was* the same tunnel.

"Is it my imagination," Randal said, "or is that ale I'm smelling?"

"The room we're heading toward was an ale storeroom when I was a kid. Looks like the Mareritt are still using it as such."

"Ha," he said. "Shame we haven't got more time. I wouldn't have minded a tankard or two—ale is one of the few things the Mareritt do better than us."

"You can drink as much of it as you want once we free Zephrine from the Mareritt's grip." Kaiden's voice was dry. "For now, let's concentrate on getting out of this tunnel and into the aerie. We've less than an hour before the attack happens."

Which might not be enough time, given the layout of this place would have vastly changed since I'd last been here.

The tunnel came to another junction. I followed my

nose and my memories to the left. Within a couple of minutes, we came to an ancient-looking door covered in a thick sheet of rust. I flicked off the flashlight, then gripped the doorknob. Despite the rust, the door didn't even creak. They'd built things to last in that ancient civilization.

When no one challenged our entry, Kaiden uncovered one of the flashlights and swept it around. The room beyond was narrow, high, and dark. The wall to our right was lined with barrels of various sizes and age, but on the left, there was nothing more than lifting machinery. A large double door was situated halfway down the room; it was currently closed, and I was too far away to see if it was also locked.

The air was cool but filled with a rich riot of scents—while I couldn't make them all out, the aromas of sweet gale, ginger, and cinnamon were the strongest. My stomach rumbled in response; it seemed the stew hadn't really filled the hole.

The only sound to be heard was the soft scurry of rodents. There were no guards here, but that didn't mean there weren't any in the hall beyond.

Kaiden motioned Loretta and Randal toward the barrel side of the room and me to follow him. We moved across to the left wall, our footsteps echoing softly in the vast silence. While there were no cameras or listening devices here, I had no doubt they'd make an appearance once we neared the sections of Zephrine that had been rebuilt or repurposed by the Mareritt.

As we neared the double doors, the side closest to us opened, forcing Kaiden to quickly switch off the flashlight and jump silently back to avoid being smacked in the face. My breath caught in my throat even as Kaiden reached for his handgun.

A Mareritt soldier stepped into the room, a light in his

right hand. The bright beam swept through the shadows, briefly pinning Loretta and Randal before moving on.

Then it jerked back, and the soldier made a surprised noise.

He had no chance to say or do anything else. Kaiden stepped up and smashed the butt of his gun against the soldier's head. The blow was hard enough—precise enough —that if he weren't already dead, he soon would be.

Kaiden dragged him behind the door. No other soldiers followed him into the room, and no sound came from the hallway beyond. He'd obviously been doing a solo patrol. Relief stirred. Túxn remained on our side.

Kaiden motioned the other two across to the opposite side of the door and then stripped the uniform from the soldier and handed it to me.

I wrinkled my nose at the scent emanating from the material, but nevertheless took off Kaiden's coat and pulled on the uniform. The man's shoes were tight—he had tiny feet for someone his size—but they were still a better option than walking around barefoot. A half-breed in a Mareritt uniform at least had *some* chance of being overlooked; a semi-naked, barefoot one in an Arleeon military coat did not.

I picked up the guard's fallen gun and then took the lead. The stone corridor beyond the storeroom was silent and empty. I hesitated, looking right and left, trying to remember where we were. After a moment, I turned and headed left. The shadows drew close again, and the chill of night hung in the air. I brushed my fingers against the cool stone of the wall; if memory served me right, there was a semi-concealed doorway up here somewhere—one that led into an old stairwell that curled up the length of the mountain to the aerie.

"How much longer?" Kaiden asked softly. "Control's just given the fifteen-minute warning."

"Honestly? I don't know. We rarely used the entrance in this area, so I'm working on—" I stopped as my fingers hit an indent in the wall. After following the shallow indentation up, I found the lever and hauled it down. With a harsh rumble, a section of stone slid aside just wide enough to slip through.

I flicked on the flashlight and directed its muted light into the darkness; the small room beyond held little more than cobwebs, dust, and an old stone staircase that curled around a central core. "From here, we're looking at least at twenty minutes, if we run. But these old stairwells tend to be echo chambers, so running might give us away."

"It'd be better to arrive late anyway," Loretta commented. "The other attacks will hopefully pull the guards out of the aerie."

"I wouldn't bank on that, especially once the Mareritt discover I've escaped. They'll surely guess my first port of call will be the drakkons." I slipped into the small room.

Kaiden followed, then Loretta.

In the hall behind us, Randal swore—a soft sound immediately overrun by the rattle of gunfire.

The Mareritt had found us.

TWELVE

E ven as I spun around, Loretta dropped low and used the doorframe for cover as she returned fire. Bullets pinged off the walls around her, spraying sparks and chips of stone into the air. Randal lay on the ground in the hall beyond, firing left-handed. Blood poured from a wound on his cheek, and his right arm was a broken and bloody mess.

I couldn't see the Mareritt from where I stood, but I didn't need to. I called to my flames and flung them around the corner, fanning them high and wide once they were past Loretta and Randal. The screaming began a heartbeat later.

Loretta scrambled to her feet and ran out to help Randal. Kaiden stepped into her position, his gun trained on the opposite end of the hall to my fire. I didn't move; I just pushed my flames farther along in an effort to erase any Mareritt who'd survived the initial assault.

Loretta hauled Randal upright and helped him into the stair room. As Kaiden backed into the room, gunfire erupted, this time coming from the left. I flung my firewall from the right to the left.

More screams followed.

Kaiden shoved his weight against the door and slammed it shut. As the sound echoed, I thrust the lever home and then shot it to ensure it couldn't be used. It probably wouldn't stop them for very long, but even a few minutes could make the difference now.

We *had* to get to the aerie. We might not be any safer there, but we'd at least have the drakkons.

If the jammers worked, that is.

As Loretta tended Randal's shattered arm, I followed Kaiden across to the stairs and shone the light up. There wasn't much to see; the steps were unevenly spaced and wound up into the darkness.

"It's not going to be an easy climb," Kaiden muttered.

"They weren't designed to be. This is one of the remnants from the old civilization, and their escape routes were designed to make it difficult for attackers to climb *and* fight."

"I understand their thinking, but I can't imagine it'd be any easier for defenders—" He cut the rest off as a siren sounded.

It was loud, sharp, and close.

Then, from the hall beyond the sealed door—and barely audible above the screech of the siren—came the heavy sound of steps and voices. The Mareritt were now out there, and in growing numbers. They mightn't know the exact location of this stairwell, but it surely wouldn't take them long to uncover it—not when Randal's blood pooled on the stone, giving them some idea of direction

"May Túxn help us," Loretta muttered as she finished tying the ends of the sling around Randal's neck.

"If Túxn won't, maybe the drakkons will," Randal said. "Let's just pray to the gods of earth and air that the damn jammers work."

If they didn't, our gooses were cooked. And quite literally, if the drakkons were unleashed on us.

After jabbing a final needle into Randal's shoulder, Loretta packed up and then helped him rise. Randal's face was ashen, but his expression was pure determination.

"Nara, go," Kaiden said. "I'll take rear."

Loretta opened her mouth as if to argue, then shut it again as Kaiden's steely gaze met hers. I raced up the narrow steps, taking them two and three at a time, the flashlight's pale glow catching the specks of quartz in the old bluestone and making it seem as if distant stars surrounded us.

We were eight spirals up when, after a massive bang, the stairwell shuddered and stone dust rose around us, a thick cloud that caught in my throat and made me cough.

"And that would be the Mareritt blasting open the wall." Kaiden's voice was matter-of-fact. "Go faster."

The chase was now on, and the knowledge sent fresh energy to my legs. But my lungs were burning, and each breath was little more than a short, sharp, rasp. I was flight fit rather than *fighting* fit, and that difference was beginning to tell.

The siren cut out, and the silence was eerie. It didn't last long. Footsteps echoed up the stairwell—not just one or two, but at least a dozen, if not more. And they were moving a whole lot faster than we were.

Fire surged to my fingertips and cast a bloody glow across the immediate shadows. "Kaiden, do you want me to—"

"No—the narrowness of the stairwell will restrict them to a one-by-one formation. Conventional weapons will cope with that just fine."

"Unless they're planning to sandwich us between two forces." Randal's comment was little more than a wheeze.

"Given they blew open the wall to get in here, it's unlikely they know where it exits." I crossed mental fingers even as I said that.

The stairs got narrower the higher we went, but there seemed to be no end in sight. My heart hammered so hard I swore it was about to tear out of my chest, and the burst of energy had left my legs.

I kept going. I had no other choice.

"How much longer do we have?" It came out a hoarse whisper, but Kaiden nevertheless heard it.

"One minute. How much farther?"

"Unknown."

"Will the Mareritt react against the drakkons when they realize they're not obeying orders?"

"I wouldn't think so. Over half their force currently roosts in the aerie—they couldn't afford to lose that many drakkons."

But even as I said that, dread rose. What they *couldn't* afford was to lose that many drakkons to *us*. The Mareritt were bloody-minded enough to consider culling over half their "stock" a far better option.

I silently reached for Oma. *The second the jammers go online, I want you to order the drakkons to kill the Mareritt guarding them.*

Have. Make easier for you.

I smiled, but it quickly faded as my foot slipped and I went down, smashing my knee on the edge of the stone step. Pain shuddered through me, but I pushed up and limped on.

The Mareritt below were closing in—fast. There was no

time to stop and inspect the damage. I could walk; that was all that mattered right now.

You close, Kiva said.

How can you tell?

Ineke hears you, Oma replied. *Once there, safe.*

Not necessarily. Not if the jammers didn't work and the Mareritt attacked with both drakkon and gunfire. And they surely would have been warned about my use of flame by now. Given they had an aerie full of drakkons who hated them, they must have developed a means of coping with "accidental" flaming incidents. They'd already proven they *could* contain my fires.

Will be there, Oma said. *Will flame any who attempt to hurt.*

It's not safe for you to be there until the jammers—

I cut the thought off as another siren sounded—this time three short blasts followed by one long.

"Our three-pronged attack just hit them," Kaiden said through the ear comm. "And jammer one is now online."

"And jammer one is?" Anxiety made the comment sharp.

"Middle Arleeon." He paused. "Harrod's just got his up and working."

Oma? I immediately said. *The jammers just—*

Know, she said. *The Mareritt ordered drakkons to sky. Ineke and others crisped them instead.*

And the male drakkons? How did they respond to suddenly being free of the Mareritt?

Are confused. Will listen, though.

Good. The smell of smoke and burned flesh touched the air. I raised the flashlight but couldn't see any indication of a door, despite the fact both the drakkons and my nose were telling me we were close.

Unfortunately, the Mareritt chasing us were even closer.

A sharp burst of gunfire bit through the noise echoing up the stairwell; bullets pinged off the walls and sparks flew.

"Run," Kaiden said, even as he stopped and swung off his backpack.

I bolted up the steep steps, keeping a grip on the central support in an effort to stop another fall. The musk of the drakkons sharpened. We were close. *So* close.

There was another explosion, and the shaking in the stone under our feet grew more violent. This time, it wasn't just dust that rained down but also chunks of stone. I flung my free hand over my head in a vague effort at protection and raced on.

The steps finally gave away to a ramp that rose up to another stone doorway. I lunged for the lever and hauled it down. For a second, nothing happened; then, with an almost human-sounding groan, the door began to open. But slowly. Far too slowly. I thrust my weight against it to hasten the process; a heartbeat later, Loretta joined me.

When the gap was wide enough to squeeze through, I said, "Wait here," and went in.

The only thing moving in the aerie were the ashen remains of the guards caught in the breeze that swirled through the main chamber. The drakkons watched me with varying degrees of interest but made no move toward me. My gaze swept the rest of the vast space, and my stomach twisted even as something deep in my soul rejoiced. This place was home, perhaps even more so than Zephrine itself. I'd spent so much of my time here as a newly chosen teenager, not only getting to know and understand Emri but also learning to ride. There'd been many times—especially during the winter months, when the heavy snows fell and the path down to the city became unusable—when I'd slept here for two or three or even more nights, safely curled up against Emri's neck and kept toasty warm by her body heat.

I swallowed heavily and tried to concentrate on the present rather than the wash of memories. Lights now dotted the walls, an electric glow that gave the stone a deep and bloody shimmer. There were also metal pipes running across the chamber's ceiling, with round water taps attached at regular intervals. I guessed that was one way to deal with the threat of fire, though how it helped against drakkon fire —which could cinder in an instant—I had no idea.

The twelve rooms that ran off the main chamber—areas of deeper warmth in which eggs could safely hatch—were also lit, although only one appeared to have hatchlings within. Oma was positioned close to the main entrance on the right-hand side of the chamber. From there, she'd be able to see the entire city. To my left was the secondary entrance, which overlooked the Black Claw Sea. Kiva waited just inside the arch, her scales glistening in the moonlight.

The drakkon standing closest to me shifted, and it was then I spotted the thick, heavy chains around her leg. My gaze shot to the others—every drakkon here was similarly chained, which meant their movements were restricted to a space little bigger than their bodies. I glanced across to the room holding the drakklings; if they'd also been chained, it could have dire consequences for their development.

Drakklings have no chains, Oma said, fury in her mental tones. *Just bands. Is very wrong.*

Yes. But it also wasn't surprising given it was the only way the Mareritt had any hope of controlling them. Even though drakklings weren't capable of fire at such a young age, they *could* tear off a limb or two.

I took a deep breath, then pressed the ear comms and said, "The area is secure."

Although how long it would remain that way once the Mareritt in the stairwell realized the exit led into the aerie was anyone's guess.

Loretta stepped into the chamber and was quickly followed by Randal and Kaiden. As the two men pushed their weight against the door to close it again, she said, her eyes wide, "Are you *sure* it's safe? Because there's a whole lot of drakkon flesh in here, and none of them are looking too friendly."

"As long as the jammers hold, we're—"

I cut the sentence off as gunfire rattled. Bullets pinged off the wall near my head and sparks flew. I flung fire through the door's decreasing gap and then threw my weight against it. Once it had slammed shut, Randal stepped back and shot the lock to pieces.

"I doubt that's going to hold them for long." His voice was grim, his expression even grimmer.

"The drakkons will take care of them when they do break through," I said. "The bigger problem—"

Something ticks within wall, a drakkon cut in. *Mareritt retreat*.

Fear twisted my gut. There could be only one reason for the Mareritt to be moving *away* from the door. "Everybody run—*now*."

We scattered, but I'd barely gone more than a few yards when, with a muffled *whoomph*, the door and part of the wall exploded. The force sent me flying even as rocks and deadly shards of stone sprayed through the chamber. A drakkon screamed in fury and pain, and then heat rippled across the air. I twisted around and saw a deadly stream of fire crisping the first wave of Mareritt coming up the ramp.

Whether they realized it was a drakkon or not, I couldn't say because, a heartbeat later, a small round object bounced into the room.

Grenade.

I swore, scrambled upright, and ran. Saw, out of the corner of my eye, the injured drakkon twist around and hit the grenade with the tip of her tail. It hurtled back into the stairwell and exploded. As more dirt and stone plumed into the aerie, there was a deepening rumble followed by a series of crashes and another thick cloud of debris.

"Soldiers, report." Kaiden's voice crackled in my ear.

I wiggled the ear comm and said, "Here, and fine."

"Also fine," Loretta said.

There was no response from Randal.

I pushed to my feet and quickly looked around. After a second, I spotted him. The force of the explosion had flung him halfway across the chamber. He'd landed face-first, and while that might have been survivable, the huge stone lying across his back and shoulders was not. The weight of it would have crushed him in an instant.

I briefly closed my eyes and said a silent prayer for the soldier I'd barely known. And hoped no more would follow him into the next life, even though I knew it was an impossible ask. Freedom was rarely won without blood being shed.

I hobbled across the chamber and joined Kaiden near the breach point. The ramp and the first few stair turns were gone. I gripped the wall's broken edge and leaned a little farther out; there was nothing more than a deep drop into darkness. The other two explosions had obviously weakened the structure enough that the final grenade had caused a collapse.

"At least they won't be using *this* access point any time soon." Kaiden glanced at me. "How many others are there?"

"There's the vehicle access up from Zephrine and at least three other stair points which they may or may not know about."

"*That's* not something we dare count on." He swung off his pack and pulled a lockpick out of the front pocket. "Will the drakkons warn you if they hear anyone approaching?"

I nodded. "You undo the chains. I'll tackle the control bands with the knife."

I spun around and hobbled across to the one who'd saved us all.

Mareritt move up main path, Oma said.

Warn us when they get halfway.

The drakkon bobbed her head at me, as if in deference, and then said, *Am Ineke.*

She was the drakkon who'd warned me of the ticking. *We owe you a great debt, Ineke. Your actions saved our lives.*

You free us, she replied. *Even.*

I smiled and ducked under her wing. The thick silver chain that constrained her movements had been looped around her leg and sat just above the control band. Given how new the chain looked, I had to wonder if *this* was a response to me freeing Oma and Kiva.

While Kaiden worked on the chain, I unlocked the control band, then pulled the knifelike shards of stone out of her chest. Thankfully, the wounds were neither deep nor dangerous.

Once she was freed, Ineke shuffled away from the wall and us, then rose to her full height and bugled. It was a high, fierce sound filled with joy, but it was also a declaration of intent.

The drakkons were going to war.

Not for us.

For vengeance.

One by one, we released the other drakkons. One by one, they stepped into the center of the chamber and joined their voices to Ineke's. The deafening sound had fire boiling through my veins and the fierce need to fight quivering through my body.

I clenched my fists against the urgency beating through my soul and said, *Oma, what happens?*

Tanks come.

Which suggested they were now planning to destroy the aerie. I swore and walked across to Kaiden.

"What?" he said immediately. Once I repeated what Oma had said, he added, "What's our best option for getting out of here? One of the hidden stairwells?"

"It'll take too long to get back down to Zephrine on foot. We need transportation." I held up a hand to cut off his question and silently added, *Oma, how many drakklings are there here?*

Two, she said. *One egg.*

Can you ask the males and one of the smaller drakkons to fly them across to Black Claw and keep them safe?

There was a pause, then, *Done. The others?*

I hesitated. Now that the Mareritt knew we were here, getting to a bunker situated deep in the White Zone would be nigh on impossible on foot *or* in a vehicle.

Which left us with one option.

Kiva, are you willing to carry Kaiden?

Can, she grumbled. *But flame after?*

Yes. Ineke, are you also willing to carry someone?

Not done before, she said, doubt in her mental tone.

Just keep on an even keel and don't make any sudden movements.

Will.

Thanks. Oma, tell the other drakkons to use the main entrance and take out those tanks as they sweep down.

The drakkons bugled in response and the sound echoed off the walls. I motioned Kaiden and Loretta out of their way and, as the drakkons raised their wings and hurried toward the main entrance, said, "The quickest way out of here is via drakkon back. Kiva and Ineke have volunteered to carry you both down to the bunker—"

"Has the wind stolen your wits?" Loretta cut in. "Neither of us are damn drakkon riders. There's no way known—"

"You won't fall off—not if you hang on properly."

"Like I wouldn't be?" Her tone was alarmed. "And you're forgetting one major problem—these drakkons are half the size of the ones *you're* used to riding."

Half size, Kiva grumbled, *but still strong.*

"Kiva carried both Kaiden and me in Esan. Ineke is almost the same size, so she won't have any problem with your weight."

Loretta's expression suggested she wasn't convinced, but she didn't argue any further. The roar of the drakkons rose from beyond the cavern and was followed swiftly by a number of explosions. The tanks, I guessed, and crossed mental fingers that none of the drakkons had been hurt in the process.

I helped Loretta mount Ineke, showing her where to sit and what to hold even as Kiva gave Ineke some advice on how to fly with "lump on back," as she ever so politely put it.

Once I repeated the process with Kaiden, I climbed onto Oma. She rose on her hind legs, her wings flapping hard, sending my hair flying across my face as her battle cry rang out across the night.

It was both a warning to the Mareritt and a signal to the other drakkons that we were coming.

She launched off the ledge and plummeted down. I held on tight, well used to the sensation of falling, a big grin on my face despite the danger we were flying into. This was what I was born to do. This was where I was meant to be.

Oma gained control of our descent and our flight evened out. From behind us came a long, drawn-out scream —Ineke had just dived off the edge. Kiva followed, and once they'd caught up, we flew in V-formation through the pass. Far below, tanks burned; others were moving back down the path. Either they realized it was now pointless to attack the aerie or they were being relocated to other battles.

We swept past Zephrine's old gates and over the rebuilt fortress. The layout remained the same, though most of the buildings were topped with earth or stone rather than the metal sheets that had been prominent in my time. Portions of the main city beyond the fortress were also familiar, but there were many other buildings—vast ones that stretched on for blocks—that were new. Some of those were already alight, and there were plenty of Mareritt on the ground; some were scrambling to put out the fires while others raised weapons. Bullets zinged through the air in ever-increasing numbers, presenting a danger to fragile wing membranes. I gripped onto the front spine plate and ordered Oma higher. She immediately swept up, her wings pumping hard as she fought to rise beyond the range of the bullets.

A drakkon appeared underneath us and sprayed fire across the street below, taking out the immediate threat.

Oma tipped slightly to one side in silent thanks, and the drakkon bellowed and peeled off to attack somewhere else.

Half the city was alight now, and on the horizon, close to the wall that divided the White Zone from the rest of Arleeon, more fires glowed. But our destination was the bunker that hid the biggest threat of them all—the ice weapons. We had to get there—had to destroy them—before they could be deployed against us again.

The main city fell behind, and a network of roads and industrial-looking buildings appeared. Gone were the rolling forests that had once dotted this area. The Mareritt seemed pretty damned determined to destroy the richness they'd coveted for so long.

But trees could grow back. Land could be restored. Drakkons could once again fly free across Arleeon.

We just had to destroy their new weapons first. Driving them from our land *would* take more than just this attack, but this *was* at least a beginning.

And it held up the possibility of hope to those who'd all but given up.

Ahead, hugging the mountain's jagged rock face, was the dome Ineke had described. No guards were visible, but a massive metal door now barred the wide entrance. I couldn't immediately see Harrod, which meant he was probably hunkered down underground, waiting our arrival.

Oma began her descent. I hooked a leg over the front spine plate, ready to jump off when we neared the ground. Just because I couldn't see any Mareritt didn't mean they weren't here.

Oma's flight slowed to a hover. I jumped, then ducked low to avoid her wing sweeps as I moved out from underneath her. She immediately rose to give the others room.

Call if need to fly out, she said. *Will be near*.

You're not going to flame with Kiva and Ineke?

No, Oma said. *In charge. Will keep high and watch movements. Safer for all.*

Which, again, wasn't instinctive behavior, and yet another pointer to the differences between the drakkons of my generation and these. I couldn't help but think that, while there might be a noticeable size difference, *this* generation of drakkons had learned a lot more from their captors than the Mareritt might have wished.

I unslung my stolen rifle and then moved across to the door. There were no cameras on the outside and no lock pad or other means of entry. The bunker had been sealed from inside; if Harrod couldn't get us in, our mission would end before it had even really started.

Dust swirled as Kiva hovered close. Kaiden jumped off and ran toward me, one finger pressed lightly against his ear comm. "Harrod, we're here."

The earth rumbled in response, and soil began to shift. Harrod, making his way to the surface.

"It seems rather odd that they haven't fortified this area," I said as Ineke swept toward us.

"Not really." Kaiden's voice was distracted. Listening to the ear comm, I suspected. "We're deep in the heart of the White Zone; under normal circumstances—and in normal vehicles—we'd have been killed long before we got anywhere near this place."

"They would have seen us on the drakkons, though."

"Which is why it's even more important we get inside the bunker ASAP."

Ineke's flight pattern wasn't as smooth as either Oma's or Kiva's, and her hover more of an abrupt stop. Loretta fell rather than jumped and hit the ground awkwardly. She scrambled to her feet and stumbled away through the dust storm raised by Ineke's rise.

Thanks, Ineke, I said. *Be safe out there. Keep your flame runs as high as possible to avoid the gunfire.*

Will burn guns and those who hold. Her mental tone was savage.

Follow me, came Kiva's comment. *I attack Mareritt who come here.*

Alarm swept through me. I'd expected a response, but that was damn fast. *How far away are they?*

Forty sweeps?

So, ten minutes. But even if Kiva and Ineke took care of this lot, more would come—especially once we broke inside the bunker. The drakkons didn't have unlimited fire capacity—even they would eventually flame out.

And when they did, we were in trouble.

"Well, wasn't that a fucking nightmare." Loretta stopped beside Kaiden and thrust a still-shaking hand through her hair. "From now on, my feet stay on the ground, even if I have to battle ten squadrons of the ice scum to get back into Arleeon."

"Given the drakkons aren't big enough to lift us from a standing start, that may be our only option." I glanced at Kaiden. "The Mareritt know we're here. Kiva and Ineke are about to attack a force that's ten minutes away, but more are sure to be sent."

Kaiden turned on his heel and walked across to where the earth had risen. Harrod stepped out of his newly created tunnel and brushed the dirt from his hair. "Greetings, all," he said cheerfully. "Have I missed much?"

"Multiple attacks, a number of explosions, and a fucking drakkon flight," Loretta said. "Other than that, no."

Harrod's eyebrows rose but his gaze swept us, and concern touched his expression. "Randal?"

"Didn't make it." Kaiden's reply was terse, his anger aimed at himself even though no one could have predicted or even prevented Randal's death.

"Shame. He was a good man." Harrod took a breath. "I got a general layout of the place from the earth while I was waiting. There's one tunnel running from this dome to what I think is a development and construction zone deeper underground."

"And that's where the ice weapons are?"

"I would think so."

Kaiden grunted and motioned toward the curved wall. "We've now less than nine minutes before we have Mareritt company—you'd better get us in there."

"That I can do, no problem, but there's at least a squad of Mareritt bunkered inside."

"Any chance of bypassing the dome and going straight into the tunnel?"

Harrod hesitated, his gaze narrowing as he studied the mountain. "It'd take too long and drain me of all strength. I'd rather save some energy for whatever surprises the Mareritt have waiting inside."

Kaiden glanced at me. "How fast can you hit that squad once Harrod breaks through?"

"Speed won't be the problem; fire alarms will."

"I rather suspect alarms will be the *least* of our problems." His gaze returned to Harrod. "Do it."

Harrod pressed both hands against the dome; for several seconds, nothing happened. Then, with a somewhat muffled boom, a six-foot section of the dome's wall blew inward. Harrod immediately crouched low, and I threw fire high, lancing into the opening and then swirling around until it became a maelstrom that cindered every living thing in its path.

But, as I'd feared, it also set off alarms.

And the water taps.

Kaiden moved quickly into the breach. I followed, my gun held at the ready. While I was nowhere near exhaustion, I had to be careful with my fire usage. As Harrod had said, there would be surprises ahead; I needed to keep a reserve of fire.

The klaxon echoed through the high chamber and water poured down, drenching us in an instant. There were a number of vehicles parked to the left, and a long line of stacked wooden boxes—many of them scorched and steaming—to our right. Down the far end of the vast dome, barely visible thanks to the sheeting water, was the tunnel entrance.

Once Harrod had raised the earth and closed off our entry point, we moved toward the tunnel, using the vehicles as cover as much as practical. But we were barely halfway there when two metal doors appeared out of the cavities on either side of the tunnel entrance and tracked toward each other.

"Harrod," Kaiden snapped. "Stop those things."

Soldiers appeared in the doorway and unleashed a metal storm. I swore and leapt behind the nearest vehicle, then dropped low and crawled underneath it. Bullets sprayed around the hauler, and chips of stone and metal flew into the air. I shuffled forward until I could see the Mareritt and then threw flame their way. Three cindered, and two more went down under a barrage of bullets. The rest retreated. I doubted they went far.

I scrambled out from under the hauler and pounded after Kaiden, Harrod, and Loretta. In the steadily decreasing gap between the doors, the earth cracked, and thick fingers of rock thrust upward. They severed the tracks and stopped the doors dead.

Kaiden slid to a halt, pressed his back against the metal door, and then glanced at Harrod. The big man raised four fingers. Kaiden unpacked a grenade and tossed it around the corner into the tunnel.

There was a sharp curse in response and the echo of footsteps. A heartbeat later, the grenade exploded. As dust and debris swirled, Kaiden and Loretta slipped past the stone fingers and opened fire.

"Clear," came Kaiden's comment, sharp in my ear. "Let's move."

Harrod and I entered the tunnel; the dust in the air was so thick I couldn't see anything more than a small, pale dot. It took me a moment to realize it was a follow-me beacon attached to the back of Kaiden's pack.

The darkness and the rubble initially restricted our speed, but then the tunnel curved around to the right and pools of yellow light beckoned. They guided our way and allowed us to run.

There was no sign of the Mareritt defenders, but I doubted they'd gone into full retreat. That was not their way.

The siren finally cut out, and the ensuing silence again felt threatening. The Mareritt remained out of sight, and that only increased the tension thrumming through me. What were they doing? Securing the chamber that held the ice weapons? Or something else?

I suspected the answer was *both* and had to clench my fingers against the heat that surged in response.

The tunnel's slow curve finally straightened; in the

distance was a large archway and, beyond it, a well-lit chamber that at first glance seemed empty.

And yet foreboding pulsed. Whatever the Mareritt planned waited for us in that chamber.

Kaiden signaled a halt. "Harrod?"

"Five ahead," came the soft response.

"Only five?"

"In the chamber, yes."

"Meaning there *is* another force?"

"There's some sort of staircase at the back of the chamber. There're at least a dozen men there."

"If that's the greeting party," Loretta said, "what are the five doing in the chamber?"

"I dare say we'll find out soon enough." Kaiden's voice was grim. "And the weapons? Has the earth any sense of them, Harrod?"

"There are three heavier weights sitting to the right of the arch; it could be them."

"Or it could be something else entirely," Loretta said. "This is a trap."

"Probably." Kaiden glanced at me. "Want to rain a little fire hell all over them?"

"Gladly."

I raised a hand and unleashed. My flames roared through the darkness, hit the archway..., and stopped dead. There was some sort of barrier in front of it.

Kaiden raised his rifle and fired several shots. There was a slight shimmer as the barrier we couldn't see caught each bullet and then dropped them harmlessly to the ground.

"Well, that leaves us with—" Kaiden cut the rest of his words off and tilted his head slightly. "Is that singing?"

Even as he spoke, energy surged, a sensation that both

prickled and chilled. The warmth leached from the air and each breath became visible. My gut clenched. "It's not singing—it's *invoking*. There are ice mages in that chamber."

"Harrod, get us in there."

"Trying to," came the sharp response. "But the earth is being restrained by magic."

"Can you break it?"

"If I can find a chink in the net they've cast, maybe. Keep moving. I can multitask."

We ran on. But the closer we got, the more powerful those waves of energy became.

Then, without warning, the ground in front of Kaiden dropped away. He would have fallen had not Harrod lunged forward, grabbed his pack, and hauled him back. The air that drifted up from the chasm smelled dank and wet, and from far below came the distant sound of tumbling water. It was the sort of drop that could kill—and had almost done exactly that.

The earth shuddered, and a stone platform formed across the chasm, a thin line of solidity over deeper darkness.

Harrod took the lead, running over the slender bridge and then moving across to the right of the tunnel. He pressed his fingers against the wall, communing with the earth as he led the race toward the arch.

But the air was so cold now that breathing hurt. My fires surged, keeping me warm, but the others didn't have that option. Loretta's hair was icing over, and Kaiden was clenching and unclenching his free hand in an obvious attempt to keep the blood circulating to his fingertips.

Ice also formed on the walls, and every step was accompanied by a soft crunch—both underfoot and from our stiffening clothing.

The waves of power shifted, changed. The earth shook, and this time, it wasn't Harrod. Thick shards of stone punched up from the ground behind us, a deadly forest that chased us toward the archway. The walls began to shake, and a network of cracks formed on the ceiling and quickly spread. As cracks joined, chunks of stone fell. We dodged and weaved through the dust and debris, avoiding most but not all. Many of the rocks were now as sharp as any knife and just as deadly. Blood flowed from a dozen different wounds, but there was nothing I could do. Nothing except run and hope that somehow Harrod broke through the magic and got us inside that chamber.

We were close to the arch now. Close enough to smell the stink of the Mareritt. Close enough to see the soft shimmer of the magic protecting the gateway.

If Harrod couldn't break through it, Randal's death and our race through this darkness were all for nothing.

"Harrod?" Kaiden barked.

"Close." His reply was absent and his skin ashy. Sweat ran down his face despite the ever-increasing bite in the air. "I've punched a small opening into the chamber, but I can't break the magic that stopped Nara's fire."

The earth shook again. Harrod spun around, a look of sheer horror on his face. I half turned, caught a very brief glimpse of a brown wave, then it washed over me. I lost my footing but somehow rolled into a ball, keeping my head tucked in as much as possible as stone and earth and ice tumbled all around me.

Then the roaring fell silent and I came to a sudden stop; for several seconds, there was nothing but an eerie creaking that ran through the dark and dangerous earth all around me.

It was a sound swiftly overrun by footsteps.

The Mareritt were coming.

A hand reached through the muck cocooning me and pulled me out. Harrod, not Kaiden. My breath caught as fear surged, but then I spotted him, rising from a mound of dirt on the other side of the tunnel. He was as battered and bloody as me, but that didn't matter. Nothing did right now except survival.

I couldn't see Loretta and prayed to the wind that she'd survived, that she was, at worst, just knocked out.

The singsong chant of the mages reached toward a crescendo, and power once again flooded the tunnel, crashing over me as hard as the dirt wave had only seconds before. I staggered back and would have fallen if Harrod hadn't grabbed me again. Alarm churned through my gut, and my fires surged in response, but the heat pressing against my fingertips found no release. The mages were once again restricting my fires.

May the wind help us all...

Movement caught my attention, and my gaze shot past Harrod. The shimmering wall spanning the arch fell, and Mareritt flooded into the tunnel, their weapons up and firing.

I knocked Harrod out of the way, and the bullet that would have punctured his chest hit my shoulder instead. It spun me around and filled my world with a very different kind of fire. With a strangled cry, I dropped to the ground, one hand pressed against my shoulder and warmth pulsing over fingers. Harrod grabbed me and pulled me behind the cover of a rock.

I sucked in air, fighting the looming darkness and the thick urge to be sick, and reached for the inner fires. The mages might be able to stop my external use of them, but they couldn't stop internal use. I directed flame to my shoulder, melting the bullet and forcing it from my flesh before sealing the wound to stop the flow of blood. It hurt—the wind only knew how much it hurt—but if I gave in to unconsciousness now, it might well be the end of me.

"Here, take this and keep them off me as long as possible." Harrod shoved his rifle at me. "I've punched a small hole into their web—I just need to widen it and then create the breach on this side."

I braced the rifle against a nearby rock, pressed the stock against my good shoulder, and began firing. Across the other side, Kaiden was doing the same. Loretta still hadn't appeared, and while I remained hopeful she wasn't dead, that was growing more and more unlikely.

One Mareritt fell, then two, then three. The rest scrambled for shelter behind the many rocks that separated us.

But these soldiers were little more than a distraction. The mages intended to freeze us and then simply walk in and shatter us, as they had my kin and all those in old Esan. It was already beginning—the air was so cold it was practically visible. Harrod's sweat had frozen onto his face, and his fingers and ears were gaining a bluish-gray hue.

We had to do something about the magic. Had to stop the mages to have any sort of chance.

And I knew, deep in my gut, that neither Harrod nor the earth magic was going to do that in time to save our lives.

"Harrod?"

"What." His reply was terse, distracted.

"That hole you've punched into their magic—"

"Isn't yet big enough for any of us to get through."

"But *is* it big enough to shove a rifle into?"

His gaze shot to mine and he smiled. It was a rather fierce thing to behold. "Hell, yes, it is."

"Then punch through the wall on *this* side so I can get to it."

His gaze narrowed. At the junction point between the arch's wall and the tunnel, dirt and stone sprayed outward. As the dust cleared, a fist-sized hole was revealed.

Harrod handed me a couple of clips. "I'll tell Kaiden what's happening, and we'll keep them off you the best we can. Good luck."

I took a deep breath, gathering courage and strength, and then thrust up and ran. A tide of earth and stone rose and raced beside me, shielding me from the barrage of bullets instantly aimed my way. Metal thudded into the earth and drew sparks from stone inches above my head, but none hit me, thanks to that wall. I shoved a new clip into the rifle, leaped over some rubble, and spotted movement to my right. A soldier appeared, his face masked against the cold but his eyes gleaming with fury. I raised the rifle, but before I could shoot, he went down, the back of his head disintegrating in a spray of blood and bone. I leaped over his body, my eyes on the hole in the wall. I was close, so close.

Another two Mareritt appeared. The chest of one exploded outward, and he went down hard, a shocked gurgle on his dying lips. I shot the other, but his momentum was enough that he stumbled into me and slammed my bad shoulder into the wall. A scream tore up my throat, and pain became a red tide that threatened to overwhelm. I sucked in air, pushed him off, and stumbled on.

More soldiers appeared. The liquid wall took care of them, hitting them, forcing them down, smothering them.

I reached the cavern wall and slid to a halt, shoving the rifle into the hole before looking through the sight. Three mages stood directly in front of me not twenty feet away. Another two were slightly to my left. Each group had their hands linked and their eyes closed. The rhythmic sound of their voices sharped dramatically, and ice sheeted the wall in front of me and ran over the rifle's stock.

Time had just about run out.

I aimed and fired, taking out the set of two before the other three even registered something was wrong. As the dead dropped to the ground, I took out a third mage. The thick waves of energy fell away, and fire surged across my flesh, melting the ice from my clothes and the nearby walls. One of the remaining mages barked an order and then the two of them retreated. Soldiers appeared from the rear of the chamber and raced toward the archway. I took several more shots, saw one of the mages stumble and fall. Heard a metallic groan and knew the archway gates had just been activated.

"Harrod!" Kaiden said.

My protective wall melted away as Harrod moved his focus to the archway gates. I pulled the rifle out of the gap and flung fire, setting the nearest soldiers alight even as I speared flames at the retreating mages.

"Nara, watch out!"

Kaiden's cry had me spinning around. Five soldiers charged me. I dropped low, bullets smashing all around me, and again unleashed my fire—it was a wall of furious heat that cindered the soldiers in an instant and then raced on, through the doors, into the chamber. There were few screams; they simply didn't have the chance.

Blood dripped over my lashes. I brushed it away with the heel of my hand and then thrust up and raced toward the metal doors. Harrod had to be nearing the end of his strength, because the earth was struggling to hold them apart. I raced into the room, quickly looked around for some kind of control panel, and spotted it to the left. After scanning the multitude of switches, I found what looked to be the right one and hit it. The doors ground to a halt and then began to reverse.

The earth fell silent. I swung around and studied the chamber, looking for the three ice weapons. They weren't exactly hard to find, given they dominated the right side of the room. But there were also two more under development, and that was more than enough firepower to destroy a good portion of Esan's wall.

Kaiden appeared. "No matter what happens from this point on, we've at least achieved what we set out to do. Keep watch. I'll set the explosives."

"What about Loretta?"

"Harrod's digging her out."

"She's alive?"

"Yes."

Relief swept through me, even though her life—and ours—was still very much on the line. I reloaded the rifle and moved across to check the dead were indeed dead. "Two of the mages escaped. I daresay we'll have more company soon."

"And sooner than you might think." Harrod appeared in the doorway, Loretta slung over his shoulder. She wasn't conscious and had a deep cut across the back of her head. Despite the blood matting her hair and soaking her coat, the wound no longer bled. Harrod had obviously sealed it before he'd picked her up.

"There's at least two dozen Mareritt in the tunnel," he continued, "and they're bringing in heavy machinery. We've probably got ten minutes, if that, before they punch a hole through the rockslide."

"Head up the stairs," Kaiden said. "I'll follow once I've set all the explosives."

His gaze briefly met mine, his blue eyes bright. We might be trapped between mages and soldiers, we might be bloody and nigh on broken, but he was very determined that we'd damn well survive.

We *had* to. There was still too much we needed to do and far too much we needed to explore.

I ran across to the stairwell. The stone steps were deep, built for feet far bigger than mine. Another remnant of that old civilization, I suspected. No sound drifted down from above, but I had no doubt the mages were up there somewhere. I just had to hope they were the ice mages rather than the ones who could restrict my fires.

I climbed, keeping my back to the outer wall and my rifle pointed upward. Far above, light flickered, though I wasn't sure if it was artificial or not.

Harrod followed me, his expression grim and skin ashen. "You need to go faster than that, lass. They're almost through the slide."

Fear leapt past wariness and pain, but this time, there was no accompanying surge of energy. I nevertheless pushed on up the steps to the next landing, raced around it, and continued on. Harrod was five steps behind, his breathing harsh and the scent of his sweat stinging the cool air. Loretta remained limp and unconscious over his shoulder.

From lower down the stairwell came the sound of echoing footsteps. Kaiden, I knew without looking back.

The light high above us grew closer, brighter. Moonlight, I realized. This stairwell led back outside.

And once we were there, the drakkons could help us.

Even as hope surged, the guttural sound of a Mareritt shouting orders rolled up the stairwell. They were now in pursuit.

But what about the explosives? Had they found and deactivated them? Was that why they hadn't yet gone off?

Even as I thought that, the explosives detonated, one after another. Dust and debris funneled up the stairs as the screams began. Then, over the top of all that, came a rumble —a deep, ominous sound that echoed through the walls and the floor, growing in intensity even as thick cracks speared across the ceiling.

"The chamber and stairs are collapsing," Harrod shouted. "Move it!"

I dredged up strength from who knew where and pounded up the stairs as fast as my aching legs would allow. Up and up we went, but the moonlight and the freedom it offered were getting no closer. But the surviving Mareritt and that ominous rumbling certainly were.

Gunshots rang out, and I instinctively ducked. Bullets burned past the top of my head and thudded into the nearby wall. I swore and spun around, pushing back to allow Harrod past and then flinging fire over the top of Kaiden, directing it down the stairwell. The screaming began and the stretch of burning flesh rolled back up.

"Move, move." Kaiden pressed his hand against my back and pushed me upward.

We sprinted after Harrod and the distant promise of freedom. The rumbling grew louder; dust and stones fell all around us, cutting visibility and making every step treacherous.

We hit a landing that was longer than the others. I raced toward the next set of stairs. Heard Kaiden swear, slide to a stop, and fire his weapon. Saw, out of the corner of my eye, movement to my right. Even as I called to my fire, something hit me side-on and sent me tumbling. I had a brief glimpse of icy skin and blue-white hair before the soldier's weight hit me again, pinning me, his hands around my neck and his body like ice. Ice that poured from his fingers into my skin.

Mage, not soldier.

Fire surged in response, erupting across my entire body, burning my clothes as they burned into him. As his ash fell around me, I rolled to one side and pushed onto my hands and knees—where I remained, sucking in air in an attempt to find the strength to rise. I *had* to rise. The stairwell's shuddering was now so violent the ground buckled, and the roar of imminent collapse was too damn close. But blood poured from my eye, and my head felt as if it was caught in a vise.

Then a hand grabbed my good arm and hauled me upright. Kaiden. Still alive. Still fighting to survive.

I could do no less.

But my legs were like jelly, and every step brought me closer to collapse. I was running on empty—but at least I was still running.

The exit had to be close—I could smell the night and the musk of drakkons—but the roar of disintegration was even closer.

We weren't going to make it...

Harrod appeared above us, his face as pale as the moon behind him. He bent and pressed his hands against the ground. For a second, nothing happened; then the stairs stopped moving, the walls stopped shaking, and a path appeared through the thick sea of debris covering the steps. Kaiden grabbed my hand, hauling me up the remaining steps and then out onto a long, wide ledge. To our left was another set of stairs that ran down the side of the dome to the ground. We were free of the mountain but still deep in the heart of the White Zone and a long way from help...

And then I heard it—a deep bugling cry that rang across the night. I looked up and saw the drakkons sweep in, their scales gleaming like bloody fire in the coldness of the moon's light.

I closed my eyes and felt tension leave me.

Our transport out of here had arrived.

We were finally safe.

EPILOGUE

I crossed my arms and leaned against the parapet. The vast old wall that guarded the entrance into Zephrine had once again survived the destruction that had befallen the rest of the city during the brutal six months that had followed our desperate attack on the ice weapons and our subsequent flight to safety.

The Mareritt had not given up easily. They destroyed what they couldn't hold, be it this fortress or cities such as Husk and Renton. They poisoned the fish farms and burned vast tracts of forests, even as their remaining mages attacked our forces with magic and ice.

All that changed the night we took the fight to their doorstep. Not with fire and fury but with the earth itself. Four earth mages—strapped into specially designed harnesses, each one slung between two drakkons—were carried deep into enemy territory with me and Oma in the lead and Kiva on rear guard. We flew high, out of their sight, on a moonless night, until we reached the Laseeta Fault, an eight-hundred-mile crack that ran through Mareritten from north to south and took in a number of cities, including Orkadden and Frio—their main living hubs.

Four mages weren't enough to spark a major catastrophe along the fault, but they were still able to get a damn good shake happening. Buildings fell, and thousands were killed.

It was a warning, and one the Mareritt heeded.

A truce was called. Negotiations began. If Esan's leaders had learned anything during the bitter years since the destruction of my Zephrine, it was the fact that occupation was never a guarantee of peace.

A trade deal might not be either, but it was at least a start.

And anything was better than war. There'd been too much destruction, and too many people had died, both in this time and in mine. There *had* to be a better way.

A gentle breeze rifled through my hair—hair that was once again blue-white rather than stained black. But bits of ice remained in my brain, as did the mottling on my body. I'd accepted both now—not only because there was little point worrying about what I couldn't change, but also because my mottling had gone a long way to changing entrenched opinions and given true half-breeds some hope that eventually they would be truly accepted.

The thick scent of drakkon teased my nostrils, and I looked up. Oma swooped in, her wings gleaming gold and her scales fiery red against the bright blue skies. She flew over the top of me, then dropped low and landed on the wall. Once she'd tucked her wings in, she sidled closer and snaked her head toward me. I smiled and rubbed her eye ridge.

I'd never forget Emri and all she'd meant to me, but Oma and Kiva were now lodged deep in my psyche. They'd healed me—made me closer to whole than I ever thought possible. We were three rather than two, and forever connected via that indefinable and yet indestructible link that bound kin to drakkon.

Mareritt come, she said after a few minutes.

"Yes." My gaze returned to the far end of the pass. Dust rose as five open-top vehicles approached—the Mareritt officials who'd sign off on the trade agreement and hopefully start a new era of Arleeon and Mareritten cooperation.

Should burn, Kiva grumbled. *No like this not attack business.*

I glanced up again. She was sitting on a ledge halfway up the mountain, her tail flicking from side to side. Every part of her body exuded discontent.

We lost three drakkons in the war, remember. Peace is better.

Peace is boring.

I grinned. *You can hunt—there's plenty of capras in the mountains.*

Capras not as much fun to chase as Mareritt.

There *was* that.

Below me, the gates opened and five Arleeon vehicles pulled out to meet the Mareritt party. While truce and trade terms might have been agreed, Esan's leaders were taking no chances. All negotiations had happened in the no-man's-land of this pass. Esan remained out of bounds, both Break Point and Black Water passes were under Arleeon control, and Zephrine, once it was rebuilt, would become the main trading center. I had mixed feelings about that. While it did make sense, my entire family—everyone I'd known and everyone I hadn't—had lost their lives defending this place in an effort to keep the Mareritt out. And now, thanks to the impending agreement, we were flinging the gates open and inviting them in.

A new nursery had been established deep in the Red Ochre Mountains, in an area high in the peaks that had been renamed Sorrel's Point in honor of my sister and all those who'd followed her into the trap—a trap I may or may not have sprung.

The location was so remote—and so deep within Arleeon's heart—that no future warmongering Mareritt intent on wreaking havoc would ever get near it. And that was just as well—the Mareritt might have handed over their remaining stock in the last couple of weeks, but overall, drakkon numbers remained dangerously low.

Some of the drakkons we'd released had found their bond mates—in fact, one of Kaiden's sisters had been chosen by Ineke. Others remained bondless, but I had no doubt that would change as the drakkons grew used to being free once more. It was my job to reestablish training facilities and teach both kin and drakkon the ins and outs of flying and fighting as one.

Esan's leaders had also reached out to those in charge of Gallion—a distant land we'd once held strong trade ties with—and offered land and subsidies to any air or earth mages who'd settle here and help us rebuild. The response had been overwhelming, and I rather suspected the drakkons had a lot to do with that. Gallion's drakkons had died out so long ago that they were little more than a myth to most of the population there.

The two sets of vehicles came to a halt on either side of the open tent that had been set up for treaty purposes. Dignitaries from both sides climbed out of their vehicles and moved into the shelter. My gaze swept the soldiers accompanying Esan's councilors. I spotted Loretta and Harrod, but Kaiden was nowhere to be seen.

A heartbeat later, I realized why. He was here, on the wall, walking toward me. Joy danced through my heart, and I couldn't help my silly smile. But that was all right. We had the time for silliness—and a whole lot more—now.

He stopped beside me, his shoulder resting lightly against mine as he leaned on his forearms and studied the meeting below.

"Aren't you supposed to be down there?" I asked, amused.

His grimace made the scar that ran from above his eye to the base of his chin—a souvenir from a Mareritt knife that had come far too close—stand out starkly. It would fade in time, as the one on his neck had, but for now, it remained a vivid reminder of just how close I'd come to losing him. "Yes, but I'd still rather shoot the bastards than talk pretty with them, so it's better if I remain out of the way."

I chuckled softly. "Kiva said something very similar."

"Kiva is a very sensible drakkon."

And Kaiden is wise, she said.

As far as males go, Oma added.

I laughed, a sound that echoed through the expectant hush holding the pass captive. Drakkons rose on their hind legs, their wings outstretched and gleaming as they bugled in response, filling the air with their happiness.

It might have been a hard-fought victory, with a high cost to both human and drakkon, but that sound made everything worthwhile.

I blinked back the prickling tears. "Do you honestly think the Mareritt will hold to the agreement?"

"In the short term, yes. Long term, maybe." He shrugged,

the movement momentarily increasing the depth of contact between us. Desire shimmered through me. This man's body —and the delight it could offer—might now be as familiar to me as my own, but a simple touch still had the power to stir. And always would. "They are by nature a warrior race, but they've traded peacefully with other countries for centuries. There's every chance that they'll now do the same with us."

"And if they don't, we rattle their cities again."

"Indeed." He was silent for a moment. "I've accepted the appointment as fortress commander."

My gaze shot to his. "I thought you were planning to buy a farm somewhere and live out your life growing vegetables and raising fat swine?"

"In my more insane moments, I certainly *did* contemplate that." He turned to face me, a smile on his lips and his heart in his eyes. "But can you honestly imagine me tending fields? I'm just as likely to kill the crops as raise them."

I laughed again, even as my heart skipped into overdrive. "And given the earth mages have a long road ahead repairing all the damage the Mareritt caused, we certainly can't afford to waste the production capabilities of what viable farmlands we do have left."

"My thoughts exactly. And as I said to my father, my heart is here in this goddamn fortress, so I might as well be, too."

He cupped my cheek with his palm. I briefly closed my eyes and pressed into his touch, enjoying the warmth and the emotion that flowed through it. The link that had been evident almost from our first meeting was now one of heart and soul. He was as much a part of me as Oma and Kiva. I couldn't imagine my life without any of them in it.

Even if my life was far different—in both place and time —from the one I'd imagined as a child.

He lowered his hand, though the heat of his touch lingered on my skin. "I do have a new plan when it comes to raising things, however."

The sudden seriousness in his expression was somewhat spoiled by the bright mix of joy and love in his eyes. I raised an eyebrow, my heart lodged somewhere in my throat. "You're going to raise fat buildings instead?"

"No. I was actually thinking along the lines of children. Lots of happy, chubby little children."

He reached into his pocket, pulled out a small wooden box, and opened it. Inside, sitting on a cushion of silk, were two rings of red stone. Etched into the surface of each was the golden image of two drakkons entwined in a mating flight. Commitment rings. *Kin* commitment rings.

My gaze jumped to his, but I didn't know what to say. Didn't know how to express all the love tumbling through me.

"Marry me, Nara, and make me the happiest man in Arleeon." He plucked one of the rings from the silk, then caught my hand and slipped it onto my finger. The tears prickling my eyes tumbled past my lashes and raced down my cheek. "Let's raise an entire grace of children together even as we once again raise this city from the ashes. Let's create a lifetime of joyous memories and erase the shadows of the past that still linger in this place and in your heart."

I took a deep, shuddering breath and then plucked the second ring from the silk. "I accept your proposal, warrior, and offer you one of my own."

I slipped the ring over his finger. As simply as that, we were committed.

His fingers wrapped around mine and tugged me closer.

"And what might that be?" he said, his breath so warm against my lips.

"That we start the whole making babies thing straight away."

He laughed and kissed me fiercely. Then, as the drakkons bugled their agreement to our joining, he swept me up into his arms and carried me down to our chamber in the unbroken heart of the old city deep in the mountain. Where we did indeed, over the long course of that afternoon, conceive the first of many children.

I might have lost everything I'd ever known, but I'd also gained everything I'd ever wanted.

Life really couldn't get much better than that.

ABOUT THE AUTHOR

Keri Arthur, author of the New York Times bestselling Riley Jenson Guardian series, has now written more than forty-five novels. She's received several nominations in the Best Contemporary Paranormal category of the Romantic Times Reviewers Choice Awards and has won RT's Career Achievement Award for urban fantasy. She lives with her daughter in Melbourne, Australia.

for more information:
www.keriarthur.com
kez@keriarthur.com

ALSO BY KERI ARTHUR

Kingdoms of Earth & Air

Unlit (May 2018)

Cursed (Nov 2018)

Lizzie Grace series

Blood Kissed (May 2017)

Hell's Bell (Feb 2018)

Hunter Hunted (Aug 2018)

Demon's Dance (Feb 2019)

Wicked Wings (Oct 2019)

The Outcast series

City of Light (Jan 2016)

Winter Halo (Nov 2016)

The Black Tide (Dec 2017)

Souls of Fire series

Fireborn (July 2014)

Wicked Embers (July 2015)

Flameout (July 2016)

Ashes Reborn (Sept 2017)

Dark Angels series

Darkness Unbound (Sept 27th 2011)

Darkness Rising (Oct 26th 2011)

Darkness Devours (July 5th 2012)

Darkness Hunts (Nov 6th 2012)

Darkness Unmasked (June 4 2013)

Darkness Splintered (Nov 2013)

Darkness Falls (Dec 2014)

Riley Jenson Guardian Series

Full Moon Rising (Dec 2006)

Kissing Sin (Jan 2007)

Tempting Evil (Feb 2007)

Dangerous Games (March 2007)

Embraced by Darkness (July 2007)

The Darkest Kiss (April 2008)

Deadly Desire (March 2009)

Bound to Shadows (Oct 2009)

Moon Sworn (May 2010)

Myth and Magic series

Destiny Kills (Oct 2008)

Mercy Burns (March 2011)

Nikki & Micheal series

Dancing with the Devil (March 2001 / Aug 2013)

Hearts in Darkness Dec (2001/ Sept 2013)

Chasing the Shadows Nov (2002/Oct 2013)

Kiss the Night Goodbye (March 2004/Nov 2013)

Damask Circle series

Circle of Fire (Aug 2010 / Feb 2014)

Circle of Death (July 2002/March 2014)

Circle of Desire (July 2003/April 2014)

Ripple Creek series

Beneath a Rising Moon (June 2003/July 2012)

Beneath a Darkening Moon (Dec 2004/Oct 2012)

Spook Squad series

Memory Zero (June 2004/26 Aug 2014)

Generation 18 (Sept 2004/30 Sept 2014)

Penumbra (Nov 2005/29 Oct 2014)

Stand Alone Novels

Who Needs Enemies (E-book only, Sept 1 2013)

Novella

Lifemate Connections (March 2007)

Anthology Short Stories

The Mammoth Book of Vampire Romance (2008)

Wolfbane and Mistletoe--2008

Hotter than Hell--2008